SCATTERED
SEED

OTHER TITLES BY
FRANCINE THOMAS HOWARD

Page from a Tennessee Journal
Paris Noire
A Waltz in Tennessee
The Daughter of Union County

SCATTERED SEED

A NOVEL

Francine Thomas Howard

LAKE UNION
PUBLISHING

Text copyright © 2022 by Francine K. Howard

Published by Lake Union Publishing, Seattle
www.apub.com

Amazon, the Amazon logo, and Lake Union Publishing are trademarks of Amazon.com, Inc., or its affiliates.

ISBN-13: 9781542032797 (hardcover)
ISBN-10: 1542032792 (hardcover)

ISBN-13: 9781542031097 (paperback)
ISBN-10: 1542031095 (paperback)

Full cover design by Faceout Studio
Cover illustrated by Holly Ovenden

Printed in the United States of America

First edition

SCATTERED SEED

Chapter 1

جسد المرأة العفيفة "That's got to be it!" *The Body of the Virtuous Woman.*
Folashade clamped a hand over her mouth as the thought whispered out
of her throat. She looked at the black lettering scrolling down the length
of the red leather spine of the book. جسد المرأة العفيفة Yes, no mistake.
Those were the words written right there in Arabic. She'd almost missed
the thin volume squeezed between the two bigger and thicker books,
one called *The Female Succession in Property* and the other, *The Property
Rights of the Concubine.* Especially since all three had been stacked on a
low shelf in the back corner of Papa's library. The perspiration that had
threatened her this past quarter hour finally won out. The beat of her
heart moved the fabric of her under dress. She swiped a hand across her
forehead, but not because of the heat in this men's wing of Papa's house.
Her father had ordered the workmen to double and triple the thickness
of the mud walls because, he explained to all three of his daughters,
his study housed some of the more important manuscripts in all of
Timbuktu. The room had to be kept as cool as possible.

Folashade glanced over at the heavy acacia-wood table with its
carved legs crisscrossing into arabesque shapes that had been pushed
flush against the shelves. Rows of books rose up to the ceiling of all
four walls, almost as though the works were reserved only for those who
cared to make the extra effort. But that was silly. Wouldn't all of her
father's students be interested in this aspect of Qur'anic law?

She remembered one of Papa's lessons just last month on how to date the age of a book. *Look for cracks and peelings in the leather or the bindings. Check for cover warping.* But all she could see on this volume was the spine. *The Body of the Virtuous Woman* could be two, three, hundred years old. Maybe even written during the reign of the great Songhai in the nine hundreds. But, she'd also have to remember—as Papa had taught her—a number of volumes in the masjid library came from the north. A place where the people did not use the Hijri, the calendar of the Holy Prophet. Those dates would be different. Something about Gregorian. This year, her year, 1118 AH would be . . . would be . . . 1706 to them, the foreigners. Her birth year, fourteen years ago, would be . . . would . . . She'd really have to ask Papa for another lesson. That was, if she didn't get caught this morning. She should move back to the other side of the little library and onto the mat where Papa had left her. There, the light for reading was best, and the air cooler and less dusty for breathing. But she couldn't get her mind and her body to agree.

A quick wave of panic enveloped Folashade. She'd better decide, and in a hurry. Take the book or not? Father had always been generous with his children's education, even though the three of them were girls. And he was more lenient than the fathers of other females of the nobility. All noblewomen were expected to master the written and spoken word in multiple languages. Behind the scenes, wives often acted as their husband's secret negotiators with foreign visitors. But Papa made sure his daughters also understood mathematics, astronomy, history, and philosophy.

Since they were very young, Papa had permitted his girls access to the back room of his office, even though females were not allowed to attend the University of Sankore. To amuse his offspring, Papa had supplied Folashade; the prissy Adaeze; and her best friend and middle sister, Bibi, with books on poetry, literature, and the family histories of the grand families of old Timbuktu. Of course, he'd not allowed any of them to touch books of the Holy Qur'an. His loving nature had not stretched that far.

Folashade freed herself from the narrow opening and scrambled to her feet. She slipped both hands underneath the table edge. Much too heavy to lift, and too noisy even to scoot across the carpeted floor. In the adjacent room, separated only by a thin archway and a partially closed door, she heard Father rise from his chair. A fresh wave of panic swept over her. She dropped back to her knees, chose the largest of the curlicued openings, and squeezed her slender body through the space supporting the marble-topped table. Praise be to Allah, her governess hadn't yet succeeded in fattening her up despite the woman's ever-increasing efforts.

Governess Nago clucked that her charge was much too skinny to become a royal bride. And, with only three months till the beginning of the rainy season, every day had become an eating battle. *Look at you,* Nago had despaired, *fourteen years old and still with the body of a tall, skinny boy except for those two growths rounding up high on your chest.* Folashade's breasts were already of a big enough size to nurse a year-old baby, Nago clucked as she pushed yet another huge bowl of rice spiked with the meat of goat into Folashade's resisting hands.

Folashade shook her shoulders in disgust now, just as she had then. Babies. Husbands. Ugh. What sensible girl would want such aggravation? She had to get her hands on that book. *The Body of the Virtuous Woman.* She had to know. Maybe there was a way to save herself after all. What did the Holy Qur'an say about it? Was she really required to submit the most intimate part of herself to the knife—she didn't care if the blade was of pure gold—just to marry some fool of a boy who was only third in line to the throne anyway? She laid her hands over her breasts. Maybe these, she thought, looking down her body, but that other? Never.

Bibi had declared the experience so awful that, had she really understood what the slicing meant, she would have set fire to herself like the widows of the Indian maharajahs and rolled her scorched carcass into the Niger River. Adaeze, on the other hand, behaving like her usual sanctimonious self, had decreed the atrocity was the least a virtuous woman should allow in honor of her husband. Folashade flashed on the image of her eldest sister's twenty-year-old nincompoop of a spouse. What kind of an honor was that, and to do so for a boy terrified to go into battle even against the gazelles? But Adaeze hadn't finished her lecture. She had blabbed on about virtue and modesty. Without such a procedure, her sister had declared with her newly acquired queenly airs, a woman could be considered wanton. Wanton? Folashade hadn't given Adaeze the pleasure of realizing she had no idea what "wanton" meant.

Folashade's outstretched fingertips jiggled the book free from its resting place, a thin layer of sand dropping to the carpet. She heard Father resettle himself in his chair. She backed her way through the opening, scraped the right side of her hip, turned around, and on her hands and knees, crawled to the mat on the opposite side of the room where Papa had left her.

Chapter 2

The solid tap on the outside door startled Folashade from the page she was reading. Not one of Papa's students for sure. The door thrust open in her father's outer office before she heard her father push back from the table.

"Toure." The lead scholar of the University of Sankore's foreign language division burst into the room. "How goes the translation?"

Folashade heard Papa rush to his feet as his superior entered. "It goes well, Professor D'bime, though the document is not as old as it first seemed."

"Oh? That is parchment, is it not?" Professor D'bime sounded doubtful. "Though I had not had time to do more than a quick examination before I handed the document off to you."

Folashade shifted on her mat and stretched her body just enough to get a skinny glimpse of Papa's back through the barely opened door leading from his private library to his outer office.

"And, I am grateful for the opportunity, Honored D'bime." Papa gave the man his usual respectful honorific.

Professor D'bime was brilliant with the Hebrew, Latin, and European languages, Papa often praised, but his rank in the nobility was lower than Papa's own. Folashade scooted herself closer to the mat's edge to catch a glimpse of the Yoruba tribesman. Papa had taught his girls to offer great respect to men of scholarship even when they came from common stock. Knowledge was more powerful than great warriors in battle.

"The writing, I believe, is not of the Indies." D'bime's deep voice carried its usual authority. Folashade shifted her body closer to the door, her book in her hands. She hoped the scrunching of the mat underneath her had not carried into the other room.

"Ah." Father gave out that sound that always prefaced, *I've discovered something new.* "It is what the document is not written on that forced me to look beyond the Indies. To the East." Papa squared his shoulders.

"The East? Surely, not as far as that."

"Cathay." Father sounded triumphant as he turned in profile and pointed to the object on his desk. "This document is not written on parchment but rather a different material."

D'bime's face came into view as he bent down to Father's worktable. Folashade slipped off the mat, the book clutched to her stomach. Father had translated a book from Cathay? She knew where that was. On Father's cartograph, there had been a large landmass to the right of the Indies. The word written across the area was "Cathay." She had to learn more about this faraway place.

"This document is written on paper made with rice." Papa laid a hand on the table next to the manuscript. "Not the skin of animals."

"I see," the professor interrupted. "These are the markings of the people of Cathay. Do they tell of the time of Marco Polo?" His voice carried excitement.

"No." Father's voice was softer than Professor D'bime's, but adamant. "I believe this work was not written by those native to Cathay but by the people of Europe. Look at how the lines of the pictures are formed. I have seen other works from Cathay, and those calligraphers show a great deal more skill than this rather amateur attempt at writing the Cathay language. And, see here"—Father laid a forefinger on the manuscript—"these words are not Cathay at all. They are all written in the Portuguese, are they not?"

"Ah yes." Professor D'bime squinted as he leaned closer to the document.

"And they tell us of the founding of a Christian church in a place called . . . Macau," Father added before the professor could finish his own translation. "This, I submit, is the work of followers of the Christian religion." Father tapped his finger on the manuscript. "I believe this word—'J-e-s-u-i-t'—is written in both the Portuguese and the script of those of Cathay. See."

Folashade wanted to see. She kicked the mat aside, used her hands to push off the floor, and jumped to her feet. *The Body of the Virtuous Woman* dropped to the carpet with a soft thump.

"What . . . who do you have in there, Toure?" D'bime bolted upright, pushed Papa aside, swept open the mahogany door, and stared straight at Folashade, the tie of her gold-bordered caftan slightly askew, revealing her thin cotton under dress.

Father whirled around, a scowl of disapproval on his face.

"A woman!" D'bime raised a fleshy hand at Folashade as he turned to Papa. "I have spoken to you before about not allowing women into the masjid. It is an affront to Allah."

Papa shot another glare at his daughter. Folashade quickly stepped out of view and tucked tight the loose edges of her caftan.

"Folashade is my daughter, and not yet a woman, as you well know." Papa put authority into his voice.

"Hmm." The professor didn't sound convinced.

Folashade heard the man make his way toward the archway. Before she could kick the book under the mat, Professor D'bime filled the entire doorway with his looming frame, the smell of his morning's breakfast of boiled rice and corn steaming out of his open mouth.

The features of the dark-skinned Yoruba were silhouetted against the light flowing from the two good-sized windows in the front room of Papa's office. Folashade shivered at the man's condemning glare. D'bime shifted his eyes from her before finally settling on an object lying on the floor. *The Body of the Virtuous Woman.*

"What is that?" The professor addressed her father, who stood just behind his superior in the archway. He kept his eyes on Folashade.

Folashade, perspiration prickling her underarms and threatening to slide down her chest, watched her father's gaze follow D'bime's pointing finger. Papa looked quizzical as he squinted to read the title of the book. She sucked in her tummy and stepped between the archway and the mat. She fanned out the bottom of her now-secured robe in her best hope of drawing the professor's eyes from the floor and up to her contrite figure. She lowered her eyes.

"Good morning, Honored D'bime." She put on her most meek voice, the same simpering tone Nago had Adaeze practice for months before her wedding. "Father has allowed me to come to his library to search out books on the responsibilities of a good wife." She stared at the carpet Papa said came straight from Arabia. Still, she could feel her father's wrath rake her body for the lie. Oh, Allah, protect. What would the punishment be tonight?

The professor stormed into the room, almost touching Folashade, and scooped up the book. He stared at the cover. But before he could open the volume, Papa held out a hand.

"Thank you, Honored D'bime. That is the book I was about to reshelve." Papa slipped the volume from the professor's grasp and turned it facedown on the table without even a glance.

"Toure." The professor harrumphed. "That book carries the title, *The Body of the Virtuous Woman.*" He turned an angry face back to Folashade. "Suppose this girl got a look at the inside?" The red henna covering his man scent—she suspected the Yoruba didn't bathe as often as the nobles—overpowered the room. "You didn't, did you?"

Folashade gasped as she willed her hands not to touch the tribal mark scarred horizontally across her forehead. Professor D'bime had just committed a sin against Allah. He had berated her directly—a noblewoman of the tribe of the Bambara.

"D'bime." Papa's voice was soft, but Folashade could feel the crackle of lightning in the small space separating the three. Papa had not used the honorific he always bestowed upon the Yoruba scholar. "Though my daughter is not yet a woman . . ." Papa let the threat hang in the air.

Had she been a woman and that dreadful cutting already done as it should have been when she turned ten, then Papa would have been obliged to report D'bime to the court, demanding satisfaction for the affront committed against his family's honor. Speaking directly to any unrelated woman was an offense, but to speak unbidden to a woman of the nobility could bring dire consequences to the offender. The loss of his job would be the least of D'bime's worries.

"If the eyes of my daughter"—Papa looked as if he'd grown fifteen centimeters and now towered over the taller D'bime—"have accidentally fallen across the title of this book, I shall discipline her." He walked to his outer door and guarded it while D'bime, his head lowered, timidly left the room.

"Thank you, Papa. I accidentally knocked the manuscript to the floor."

Father reached her in one great stride. He grabbed her arm and squeezed. Her eyes stung from the quick arc of pain. Her eyelashes flickered as she stared into Papa's face. Her father never, ever inflicted pain upon his girls. Discipline, oh yes, but pain? Not ever.

"Do not compound your sin"—Papa's brown skin, the color of the coconut, turned as black as Niger mud—"by offering up a lie. D'bime had every right to be offended." He jerked hard on her arm and pulled her into his outer office. His lips set in a line as hard as the marble top on his desk-table as he scanned her face.

The heat in Papa's usually cooler outer office sapped Folashade's breath.

Her father's chest looked like it might explode through his blue-and-gold embroidered tunic. "What loss of your senses prompted you to touch this"—he stared at the volume as though the table held a viper—"this book?"

"Papa." Folashade knew she would be deprived of something big if she raised her voice to her father, but some impulse other than her own forced the words out of her mouth. "I thought that if I could see the words for myself, then I would know if the thing had to be done. If the Holy Prophet demanded, expected, wanted me, or any female, to undergo the full procedure . . ." The words fractured in her throat. "And, you, Papa, you promised Mama." Her heart thumped, and Father's rug-covered walls seemed to take on a dance all their own. What had she almost said? Oh, Allah, please forgive.

Papa's hand dug harder into the fleshy part of her upper arm.

"Ooh." The cry whispered out of her mouth. Papa jerked his hand away as though her arm were as hot as one of the mud bricks drying in the Sahara sun. "My daughter, I know what you think you believe." He snapped both hands behind his back. "But even that does not allow you, a female, to lay hands on the Holy Book. The Great Prophet is clear in his wisdom."

He lifted his head but stared across to the far wall. "The act is something that must be done, but just how much is not the affair of any woman."

The Body of the Virtuous Woman. "I really didn't. But what words I did see said some of the cutting was required of a good wife. Yes, that part I read. But, Papa"—she squeezed both hands in front of her—"not everything. The book said that for the sake of the husband, not all pleasure should be removed. I don't know what pleasure the book is talking about, but whatever it is, Papa, I don't want it removed."

"Folashade!" Father's shout rattled her ears, and her left knee buckled. "How dare you speak to me of such things." His spittle sprayed the air. "How dare you read such things, such subjects, such topics, that can only be properly discussed during the ceremony, and then only with the *furasi*, the woman who answers those questions." Papa pressed his tunic hard into his chest. "You have not only touched a volume not meant for your eyes but you have also presumed to understand something written in the Holy Book." Father's teeth clicked over every second word. "This is quite impossible and a great affront to Allah."

"But, that book"—Folashade nodded her plaited and beaded head toward the volume—"it is not the Holy Qur'an." The words spun out of her before the vision of Nago's face flashed her warning. Folashade could hear the woman's words pounce: *Your mouth will lose you stature in your husband's household. Because your mother's family is royal, you may be your husband's only wife, but he'll make a concubine his favorite if you're not careful, and believe me, that woman will find a way to make your life miserable.* Folashade tapped at her ears to make the voice go away.

"That book . . ." Papa's voice sounded as if it came out of the end of a hollow reed. He shifted his eyes from the offending volume. "That book you dismiss with such little regard pertains to the law, Folashade. No, it is not the Holy Qur'an, per se, but its words carry the weight of the Great Prophet. This is a topic I may not discuss with you." He leveled his how-could-you-be-so-hurtful face to her. "As for the other. Your mother. I recall my promise."

Folashade examined the carpet and the series of woven camels patterned into it with great care. The rug was brought to Timbuktu by traders from the Indies, Papa had declared as he first unrolled it over his mud-brick floor. Papa was the only parent she'd known since she was three years old. Disappointing him was worse than being denied her dearest wish: a chance to travel to faraway places, maybe even Madagascar. "I'm sorry, Papa," she spoke to one of the woven dromedaries.

Her father turned his back and walked to the window closest to his front door. "Folashade . . ." He cleared his throat. "If it were possible, I would spare you from . . . I would honor the promise to . . ." The muscles in his back flexed. "But the situation does not allow . . . It cannot be."

"Papa, I don't really need to marry Amiri. Can't I just be the daughter who cares for you now that you're in your old age?"

The rumblings of a hollow laugh reached her ears before her father fully turned around. "Old age? Ah yes. In two months' time, I will see my fortieth rainy season. Since my own father saw more than sixty, I had hoped for at least one or two more decades for myself." The smile flickering across Papa's face faded. "No, my stubborn daughter, you may not choose to avoid marriage."

"But, Papa—" Nago popped into her head. Folashade refused to allow her distant cousin to stay. "If I must marry, why does it have to be to a royal? Please choose somebody who doesn't care about such things. Like the cutting. Maybe one of those from the far north, or even to the east."

"The north or the east, you say?" One corner of his upper lip twitched upward. "Better still, not marry at all. I had no idea you admired the life of your kinswoman Nago so much."

Nago? She opened her mouth, but no new argument formed in her head. She'd forgotten the circumstances of her mother's second cousin.

"Hmm. Without words, are you? Do you forget that Nago's mother refused her father's choice of a husband and married a salt merchant who was not only terrible in business but died before a suitable husband could be found for his daughter?"

"I know, I know, Papa. Nago's mother had no money for a proper dowry for Nago, and the two had to move from relative to relative, acting as servants. If only Nago had been a boy." Her eyes searched the carpet for a camel matching the first. "You took Nago into our household after Mama died."

"Of course. It would be a dishonor upon the nobility of your mother's family if I allowed her kinswoman to languish in a hovel in Bamako stringing cowrie beads to support herself." He worked his mouth. "But still, my most rambunctious girl, you are willing to marry a foreigner, are you?" A tiny smile played across his lips. "Maybe one of the ones from Cathay? Or maybe one of those Jes-u-its? Oh no, I hear their priests do not marry. A very odd thing." He laughed aloud as he drew her to his chest. "No, my daughter, I cannot have you living in the rough dwellings of those of the north. Why, I hear the houses of most of those of Europe are not even as fine as the poorest Tuareg tent. Many without windows, and even with uncovered floors of dirt." He crinkled his nose. "And the sanitation. They bathe no more than once a year."

Folashade lifted her chin from her father's chest and searched out his eyes. "Granada, Papa, I could live there in fine palaces."

He pushed her away from him. "Hush, girl. You know as well as I the Moors are no longer welcome in Spain. You will marry Amiri. That's that." He gave his head that final shake meant to close all discussion.

But she had always been the one to wheedle her way around Papa. "Can you, at least, delay my marriage until I'm fifteen?"

"You are already a scandal. D'bime hinted as much. Both of your sisters were married at fourteen. Even with them, I delayed the ceremony four long years in honor of your mother." His shoulders stooped and he returned to the window. He was thinking about her again—his only wife.

"On her dying mattress"—Papa's voice barely carried across the room—"I promised her I would spare at least one of her girls from the . . . the knife." The word was almost swallowed in his throat. "She suffered so from the procedure." His voice rose. "It killed her, and the death took eight years in the coming." He whirled around. "Folashade,

I will delay your marriage until the beginning of the next dry season, but you cannot remain here in Timbuktu. You must spend the time in service to your sister in Djenné."

"Djenné. Serving Adaeze? But, Father, she's impossible. Why, she . . ." Folashade read the look of *no more* in Papa's face. This time, even she, his favorite child, could not change his mind.

Chapter 3

The first fly settled on her bare arm while the second landed on her cheek as the Songhai sewn boat oared its way around the last bend of the Niger River before reaching Djenné. Folashade looked around the boat, this one constructed from the doum-palm tree, for Nago. What was the woman doing now? It was her job to ward off flies in the heat of this blue-sky day. Nago no longer had the excuse that her efforts had to be divided between both of Papa's girls. Bibi was a married woman now—even a mother—as hard as that was to believe. Her sister had her own servant for the fly-whisking task. In fact, Bibi had more servants than Adaeze, and they weren't just destitute relatives, either.

Folashade swatted away two flies as she turned to Nago, who pretended busyness with the strap on the woven crate carrying Folashade's caftans for her months-long stay in the clutches of the grand-only-in-her-own-mind Adaeze. She leaned forward on one elbow. Nago couldn't miss her on this cloudless afternoon, yet her cousin still occupied herself with the latch.

How could one salt trader, Nago's father, lose everything in business, while another, Bibi's old man of a husband, be so successful? Of course, Doudou was a merchant in more than the salt trade. He transported rugs from Persia, gold from the West, spices from Madagascar, and the books Papa so cherished from everywhere. A fly almost the size of a river rock made itself at home on Folashade's sandaled foot.

"Nago!" she shouted as she shook herself free of the insect, who hummed in the air once before aiming straight back at its target. "These flies refuse to leave me alone." The clear waters of the Niger kicked up little in the way of waves as the six crewmen furled the sail, pulled in their oars, and glided the craft the last fifty meters to shore.

"Flies leave no one alone." Nago tightened the strap but kept her eyes on the carrying case, not on Folashade. "Stop swatting at them as only a child would, and the flies will soon tire of you." She sucked in her lower lip. "Every proper woman knows this."

"Nago"—Bibi, sitting on the bench in front of Nago, turned in the boat, pivoting sideways to Folashade while she addressed the cousin-servant—"have you prepared my sister's jewelry? Adaeze will welcome us with dinner as usual, but tonight, the women of the king's family will be in attendance. You will, of course, present Folashade at her usual best."

Allah's blessing on Bibi. She was only sixteen, but since she'd gotten married two years ago, Nago treated her better than Adaeze. Could her respect have something to do with the wealth of Bibi's husband, because Nago sure used to berate both of Papa's younger girls without mercy? Bibi's words clicked in Folashade's head.

"What women?" Folashade stared at Bibi, who wore her most serious look. "Not Adaeze's mother-in-law? I've heard the queen never dares to leave the king's side." Folashade leaned across Nago to get closer to Bibi. "I heard the king favors one of his concubines over the queen, and if the queen leaves the two of them alone, I heard she wonders if she might be displaced."

Nago's slap across the back of Folashade's head, sending a streak of pain down her neck, felt all too familiar. She jerked upright and glared at her governess. At least getting married would free her from the older woman's abuse.

"It is not appropriate for a girl"—Nago lifted her chin and stared out at the almost silt-free waters of the Niger before she leveled her death-spear look at Folashade—"who is not yet a woman to hear such things."

"I heard them from you," Folashade hissed at her nanny. "I heard you tell one of the other servants."

"Humph." Nago turned her back to Folashade.

"Bibi"—Folashade rubbed the sore spot on her head as she leaned forward again—"please say I needn't stand for some sort of inspection before these women? I'm not doing that."

"Of course, you must." Bibi held up a hand, shielding her face from Nago. She softened her look and her voice. "The queen is Amiri's mother, too." Bibi reached out a hand and pulled Folashade almost off her perch as she whispered, "The king has a son by the concubine, not yet sixteen, and his mother is maneuvering to have him marry you, and not the queen's boy, Amiri."

"Bibi," Folashade grumped, "I don't want to marry either one of those idiots!"

"There is Djenné," Nago announced as the boat rounded the final bend and the buff-colored houses on the hill stood in welcome. She turned to Folashade and narrowed her eyes. "Of course, you will stand for inspection." She gave a respectful nod to Bibi, who kept her eyes on the servant. "Fear not, I will have the roughness of your sister polished with the henna. And I will have her perfumed with the scent of satsuma from Arabia you've given her." She turned back to her charge. "If your sister keeps her mouth closed, she will be passable."

The doum-palm canoe stopped some twenty meters from shore, and six of the local youth waded out to carry the noblewomen and their belongings to the marshy beach. Nago handed the crate to one of the young men, hitched up her own tunic, and made her way, knee deep in the waters of the Niger, to the waiting Princess Adaeze and the cluster of tents flying the royal standard some forty meters from the riverbank.

Adaeze waved a hand in Bambara greeting, a bejeweled gold bracelet reflecting the afternoon sun sliding from wrist to midforearm.

Folashade groaned. The way her eldest sister paraded about, anyone would think the woman's dunderhead of a husband held her in higher esteem than the favorite wife of the great Mansa Musa!

"Adaeze"—Folashade glowered at her sister as her bearers set her feet on solid ground next to Bibi—"we come to Djenné every dry season. To escape the heat of Timbuktu. Remember?"

Adaeze twisted the bracelet on her arm; the sparkle of the coin-sized ruby flashed into Folashade's eyes. Her sister obviously wanted all of Mali to know the gem had come from Siam. The princess kept her smile in place as Bibi made the expected half bow.

"When will you do something with her?" Adaeze spoke through pulled-back lips and clenched teeth.

Bibi shrugged her shoulders as she turned to the nurse holding her boy, Balaboa. The one-year-old giggled and held out his arms to his mother.

Adaeze swept her caftan around her as she flicked a wrist at her staff to lead the way to the tents. She called over her shoulder to Bibi, "Do let the nanny take care of Balaboa. You're not supposed to carry him."

"You forget"—Bibi lifted the tot from the nanny's arms—"I'm not the royal one."

Folashade followed her sisters in procession to the largest of the two royal tents. "Adaeze," she called out as Nago rushed to catch up to her, "why are you leading us to tents?" The thought of the scrutinizing queen scanning Folashade as though she were a casaba melon being judged for the royal table sent a chill across Folashade's shoulders. "Aren't we going to your house? Uh, the royal enclosure?"

Nago grabbed the collar of Folashade's caftan. The girl almost twisted an ankle as the governess brought her up short. "Do not question a princess in front of her servants," Nago spewed as she jerked the collar again. "I despair that you shall ever learn to behave as a respectable royal. If only your father had allowed the procedure when you were of the proper age, then there might have been time for sufficient training."

Folashade reached for the front of her under dress. Nago had yanked hard, and Folashade felt the fabric cut into her neck. How was she possibly going to last through an entire dry season living with the likes of Nago and the wretched Adaeze, who had yet to acknowledge the presence of her youngest sister?

Adaeze waited as two female servants parted the door flap of the largest tent, its top adorned with a black-and-white zebra skin. Two spear-carrying males, their tribal markings reflecting their Bambara royal servant status, stood on either side of the flap. "Bibi"—Adaeze lifted her voice into the air as she addressed her middle sister—"we're spending the night here because my home is being readied for tomorrow's arrival of the queen and her entourage. Besides, it's much cooler by the river." For less than the time it took a fly to retarget its victim, Adaeze's face softened into the protective big sister Folashade remembered. Pretty, even, though she'd never be a match for Bibi. "We'll have fun." Then changed back again.

Folashade, still held in tow by Nago, waited while her older sisters entered the tent. As the governess gave her a rough push through the opening, Folashade conjured up Nago's fate if she were forced to marry either Amiri or the concubine's fool of a son. When she became royal—even half a royal—she'd make Nago serve her on her knees, speak only when spoken to, and bow to her seven times an hour. That was, unless Folashade decided to banish the woman to some distant Tuareg relative who lived smack against the hottest sand dune in all the Sahara.

Folashade's tormentor led her to one of the overstuffed cushions in the deep recesses of the tent. She tried to bend her knees to sit, but Nago held her upright until Adaeze, surrounded by a flutter of servants, ensconced herself on a pile of silk cushions. Bibi sat next, and with a whole lot less fuss. Nago finally released her grip on Folashade and pushed her forward into the cushion. Folashade pulled up her most damning look for Nago as she scrambled in a most unroyal fashion to right herself. Her caftan tangled about her ankles while her under dress pushed up to her knees. Nago looked toward the top of the tent, no doubt beseeching Allah to free her from the awful fate of tending Folashade. The servant positioned herself within arm's reach as Folashade rearranged her attire. A second servant opened decanters of perfume. A sweetness highlighted with night-blooming jasmine floated through the tent.

Bibi adjusted her bright-green caftan as she scooted her son onto her lap. The boy fussed.

"Hush, Balaboa." Adaeze waggled an arm at one of the servants. Even in the dimness of the tent, lit only by the sun filtering through the still-open flap, and two rectangular slits positioned on either side of the canvas, the brilliance of her sister's ruby and the smaller emerald next to it sparkled. "After you greet your cousins, you three children can play by the water."

"Auntie Bibi! Auntie Fawa!" Amadou, Adaeze's three-year-old son, broke free of his nanny's arms as soon as the child's feet touched the ground. He flung himself onto the cushion holding Bibi and Balaboa.

"Bring him here," Bibi called out between laughs as she tried to separate the hugging cousins.

Even Adaeze grinned as her servant approached Bibi and the children. Adaeze sat up from her cushioned elegance. "Take them all outside for a splash in the river." She turned to Bibi. "After the journey you've had from Timbuktu, Balaboa will love playing in the Niger instead of being stuck in a canoe sailing on it." She looked at Nago. "My servants will show you where to prepare my sister's articles for tomorrow." She waved an imperial hand. "In fact, all of you can leave us."

Nago frowned like she wanted to dispute Adaeze's quick dismissal, reconsidered, and quietly followed the children and the other servants through the flap opening. Folashade lifted her own eyes to Allah. A

Nago-free evening? Maybe this visit with her pretentious sister wasn't going to be that bad after all.

"Father should replace that woman." Any hint of humanness that might have come from Adaeze in the last few moments evaporated as she scrunched around to face Folashade. "If that woman were worth a cup of cow's milk, she'd have taught you something by now." Adaeze's face, despite its appealing oval shape, took on the scolding look of a woman old enough to be thirty.

"Nago?" Folashade burrowed deeper into her own cushions, her arms folded across her still-budding chest. "I'll not argue with you. She should be dismissed. For your information, Adaeze, I have been taught a thing or two. In fact, just two days ago, I read what the scholars really think the Great Prophet said about . . ." More than the shocked expression of Adaeze's face caused Folashade to pause.

A wide-eyed Bibi turned to her younger sister with something akin to fear spreading across her face. "Folashade"—that Bibi darted her eyes and crinkled up her forehead stalling for time was plain to see—"this journey has tired us all. Why don't you go into the other tent and take a nap?" Bibi worked overtime to save Folashade, but from what?

"Bibi," Adaeze shouted, "have you taken leave of your senses?" She pointed a damning finger at Folashade. "We—you and I—have less than twenty-four hours to get *your* sister ready."

"Would you two please stop talking about me like both my ears are plugged with sand. I am here, and"—she turned to Bibi—"I am not tired. I know what I read in that book. And you"—this time, it was Folashade who aimed the withering hand of condemnation at Adaeze—"will not put me on display before a woman who hates me before she's even met me!"

Adaeze slammed a fist into the red silk of her cushion. "For the goodness of Allah! You are fourteen years old. How can you still be such a child? Of course, the queen doesn't hate you. She merely wants to see that you are worthy of her son."

Bibi shifted upright. "Adaeze, not so hard on her. Please. She still has her dreams."

"Folashade"—Adaeze's voice dropped two levels on the anger scale—"I care about you. You are my sister. I know you have your dreams. We all had our dreams. That is the best part of Papa. He allowed us our dreams, even though we are mere females. He encouraged us to learn everything. Even things all the scholars say will only confuse the heads of women." She swallowed as she twirled the bracelet around her wrist. "But even Papa has to answer to someone." She lowered her voice, though no one other than the two male sentries standing guard outside the tent could possibly have overheard. "He's done all he can. Papa knows it's my turn. And Bibi's."

Folashade looked to her middle sister. Bibi almost always stood up for her against Adaeze, especially since the royal wedding four years ago when Adaeze had moved from big sister to this most obnoxious queen-in-waiting. Now even Bibi's eyes shone caution.

"Sister. Folashade. Dear"—Bibi dropped her voice—"Papa gave each of us the most precious thing. Time. He let us fill our heads with all the knowledge we could stuff inside. He gave us the time to do that. But now you're fourteen. Four years past the age when . . ."

Folashade pushed herself to the edge of her cushion and planted her feet firmly on the floor. "That's what I'm trying to tell you two. I did just what Papa wanted." She bit down on her lip. "Well, maybe not exactly *how* Papa wanted it." She didn't have to share that part of her forbidden-book story with her sisters. "But he wanted me to use my mind to learn things." She lowered her voice so much, Bibi waved a hand to pantomime *louder*. "I found out, discovered, that the"— Folashade cleared her throat and spoke just loud enough to hear her own voice—"that cutting business, it doesn't have to be everything. It can just be a little bit. Maybe even a pretend thing." She threw in the last bit, lie that it was, knowing neither sister had ever touched the Holy Book, and could not contradict her.

"And where did you hear that?" Was Adaeze about to swoon? The way her dark eyes widened, and the manner in which that gray pallor snaked underneath her sister's cocoa-brown skin, made Folashade wonder.

"The same place I did." Bibi settled back into her cushion as she turned toward Folashade. "Papa's library. Only, I didn't get caught."

"You read *The Body of the Virtuous Woman*?" Folashade asked. A bird sounded its presence outside. She finally remembered to snap shut her open mouth.

Bibi nodded.

"What are you two talking about?" Adaeze's skin tone still hadn't returned to its usual shade when she swiveled her head between Folashade and Bibi. "*The Body of the Virtuous Woman*? That doesn't sound like a volume Papa would allow any of his daughters to read. How? When?"

Folashade fixed her eyes on Bibi. Her sister had read the book? That same book? Learned that the cutting didn't have to be so severe. Something called "pleasure" could be spared? But wait. She jabbed the air with an open palm toward Bibi. "You did marry. You married Doudou. Before that, you had the ceremony. The woman used that awful thing on you. Ugh." The thought stormed into Folashade's head. "For all your complaining to me about how awful the ceremony was, you had the other one! The knife wielder didn't cut away everything!"

Folashade jumped to her feet and danced her way over to Bibi in her best Bambara victory style. Before she could throw herself onto the cushion like Adaeze's daughter, Fanta, Bibi held up a hand, frowned, and shook her head.

"It's not that easy. That's what Adaeze and I are trying to tell you."

Folashade stood flat-footed in front of her middle sister. "Tell me?" she mouthed. "You two are trying to tell me what?"

"Why do you think I asked Papa to accept Doudou's marriage proposal?"

What made Bibi ask such a silly question? Doudou's wealth, of course. Why else marry a man already possessed of three wives, a bunch of nondescript concubines, and only Allah knew how many children? Folashade harbored her doubts but remembered her middle sister as the twelve-year-old she'd been when Nago first made the outrageous claim.

What was there about Bibi that wasn't also true of her two sisters? Yes, Bibi was the tallest of the three, and she alone possessed those amazing eyes—amber, speckled with gold—so much like the mightiest lion. But all of Papa's girls had those twin cone-shaped things sprouting from their chests that Nago said men admired. Still, was it really necessary for the nanny to order the seamstress to make all of Bibi's under dresses so tight that her sister's chest pointed through the thin cloth? Worse, Nago demanded the sewers stretch the fabric almost to the breaking point over Bibi's backside. Her sister's behind looked like an overripe melon. Disgusting.

According to the gossiping governess, Toure's middle daughter had been deemed too poor for marriage to a nobleman despite looks that made grown-up men drool. While the drooling part sounded ridiculous, the never-satisfied Nago hinted that more than the family's teetering financial state had doomed Bibi's chances of a suitable marriage. Something about the cutting, Nago crowed, but Folashade was never quite sure what. Bibi settled on the dreadful, crude, and ignorant Doudou because he was wealthy. If that was the truth of it, why now was Bibi trying to say more?

Adaeze adjusted herself on her silks as she pulled the mango basket closer. "I know what you're thinking." She selected a ripe fruit, blemish free, and tossed it to the still-standing Folashade. "Both of you. I always have." She pitched a second mango to Bibi. "I advocated for Bibi to marry Prince Amiri, but there were . . . complications. Papa didn't have the dowry for a second daughter to marry into the royal family. I'm afraid he almost bankrupted himself because of me." She picked up a fan and batted the air. Perspiration beaded on her forehead. "But

Doudou would accept a smaller dowry as long as . . ." She looked down at the carpeted floor.

Could that witch of a governess have been half-right?

Bibi rolled the mango between her palms. "As long as he could marry into the nobility." She lifted her chin and studied the patterned lion painted across the topmost part of the tent. "One of Mama's rings was all he wanted." Were those tears forming in Bibi's eyes? "Just a few garnets from Mozambique. Two or three diamonds from the land of the Mandinka." She shrugged her shoulders. "And as long as I perform my duties to his satisfaction, he will care for me in great style, and he will continue to provide for Papa. All in exchange for becoming a member of the nobility."

Folashade looked from sister to sister, struggling to blank out an I-told-you-so image of Nago grinning at her. "You sold yourself for Papa?" Her eyes settled on Bibi. "For the price of a small ring? One of little value? He would never ask that of you. Of any of us." How unlike Bibi to say such dreadful things about Papa. She squeezed the mango so hard, the skin broke and a trickle of juice oozed onto her fingers.

"No, Folashade." Bibi played with her fruit. "You don't know my every thought, and neither do you, Adaeze. Yes, I understood that I had to marry a man of means, and, no, Folashade, Papa never asked me to marry Doudou. He wanted better for me. He wanted a man I could respect. Admire. A man who valued knowledge as much as we do." She stroked the mango. "My husband sells books by the hundreds, but he rarely reads one. Doudou says he has no time to waste." She looked up. "Papa hoped, wished, marriage for me. Perhaps to one of the other professors at Sankore. But I understood our father couldn't afford that luxury for me. I chose Doudou. Not Papa."

Folashade lifted the mango to her mouth and let the juice drip onto her tongue. She spoke between swallows as she shifted from foot to foot. "I've never really cared for Doudou. The man smells of the dung of camel."

"Folashade!" Adaeze shouted. "Doudou has been most generous to this family. Every time he's invited to this household, he brings the most magnificent jewels." Her hand clamped over the bracelet.

Adaeze's father-in-law might have inherited kingship, but he possessed neither the skills nor the wealth of a warrior to obtain such an insignia of royalty all on his own.

Bibi let the mango drop from her hand and into the folds of the cushion. "My husband's well aware that he receives an invitation to the king's household only because he can bestow gifts. Folashade, what you say of Doudou is true. He does smell of camel and salt and mud brick, but also of vanilla, cardamom, and the perfumes of Egypt, Greece, and Persia—all the things he buys and sells." She spoke to a stitch in the silk cushion. "But his smells are not the worst part of marriage to him."

"Oh?" Folashade barely noticed as she dribbled mango juice over Adaeze's cushions. "What could be worse than being married to a man who cares nothing of books other than to buy and sell them for huge profits?"

Adaeze shook her head so hard, the gold ornaments adorning her braids clanged together. "I'm not sure she should know everything, Bibi," she whispered to her middle sister. "She hasn't had the ceremony yet, and the knife wielder hasn't explained the responsibilities of a woman."

"I most certainly do understand." Folashade jutted her chin out. "I read in the book that the ceremony need not be full."

"You read nothing." Anger flashed from Bibi's voice. "Adaeze and I are trying to save you from our mistakes."

"I made no mistake." Adaeze bristled.

"Perhaps not. But you married a boy who is neither brave nor bright, and the king is not much better."

"Bibi!" Adaeze sparked. "I am a loyal wife to my husband, and I protect the people of Mali."

Bibi shot Adaeze her are-you-sure-about-that look. "Again, perhaps. But all Mali offers up prayers five times a day that we are not attacked because, if we are, we have no warrior king to save us." Bibi turned to face Folashade and ran her tongue over her upper lip. "The ceremony, the one you think you know so much about, and the one I fought so hard to have, has put me in poor standing in my own home." Bibi's eyes, shaped so much like the nut of the almond tree, and ringed with lashes that curled almost to her eyebrows, filled with tears. "Everyone knows that Doudou already had three wives when he married me."

Folashade stared at her sister. Of Toure's daughters, Bibi had always been the strongest, but now . . .

"Of course, we're of the nobility"—Bibi blinked—"and you know what that means. I was given the honorary rank of number-one wife when I married Doudou, even though I was his fourth bride." She brushed a hand over one eye. "But my husband prefers another."

Folashade frowned. Was that disbelief in Bibi's eyes or resignation?

"His third wife." Bibi's long lashes swept her cheeks. "A woman older even than Nago. She is his favorite—a woman who has seen thirty-five wet seasons. Folashade, if you think Nago treats you like a stubborn camel, you have no idea how hateful Kadi is to me. And with Doudou's permission."

Folashade dropped to her knees on the carpet beside Bibi. "Your own husband allows such treatment?" She tried to pull her sister's head to her shoulder. "I'm so sorry."

Bibi laid an arm across Folashade's shoulder. "I do not tell you my secret to make you sorry for me. I share my story so you don't make the same mistake." She swallowed. "The excision ceremony is a horror no girl should go through. Yes, I convinced Papa to allow me the lighter procedure." Bibi's eyelashes fluttered. Her hand tightened. "I know you've never looked at . . . at the results. No unmarried girl is allowed such intimacy, but you're right. Everything was not cut away. But don't you see? That is the exact problem."

Folashade shook her head. She didn't see at all. "I do not want anything cut. But if I must, and Papa says I must, then I will have the same procedure you had."

Adaeze sighed as she dropped her uneaten mango to the carpet. "Folashade, you really must grow up. You will have the ceremony. The full ceremony. Everything must be cut. The way it was done for me." She winced and swiped a quick hand across her lap. "It is the only way to protect you. And, for sure, that's the only way you'll be allowed to marry into the royal family. Don't you realize that you've only been asked to marry Prince Amiri because Doudou will pay the dowry for you?"

Something clogged Folashade's throat. The space between her eyes hurt.

Adaeze leaned forward. "I know Amiri and his preferences. But that is where the light will shine bright for you. If you can persuade him to give you a son and a daughter right away, then I can guarantee he will trouble you no more."

Persuade? Now she had two of them talking to her in riddles. Bibi and Adaeze. Doudou was paying her dowry? Why? And, more importantly, why would she want to undergo such a painful, awful procedure just to "persuade" a boy only a shade smarter than an ostrich to give her children she didn't particularly want?

"No, she doesn't see." Bibi laid a hand against Folashade's cheek. "You are the last innocent of Papa's girls. He has done so much for us, but now we must make the best of what he's given us." She turned to Adaeze. "Let me speak plain to her."

Adaeze nodded.

"Folashade, without the full procedure, with everything cut away, you can only marry a man who thinks less of you"—Bibi's grab for air landed full in Folashade's ears—"as a woman."

"Less of me?" Both sisters looked distressed. Was that why they were still speaking gibberish?

Bibi frowned. "Your husband will believe that you've had or are capable of inviting other men onto your mattress."

"Other men? My mattress?" The pain between Folashade's eyes shot to the back of her head. "I don't even want a husband on my mattress, why would I want other men?"

Bibi turned to Adaeze and shook her head. "It's about the pleasure."

"Bibi!" Adaeze almost scooted off her cushion. "Not now! I've changed my mind. She's not ready."

Bibi looked from Folashade to Adaeze and back again. She parted her lips. "It's what some men believe of a woman who has not had the full procedure." She sucked in a breath almost loud enough to alert the guards. "I know what *The Body of the Virtuous Woman* says. The full cutting is not required by the Prophet. Just enough to ensure a woman's chastity to her husband."

Chastity? Pleasure? This being married thing must be something awful. Clearly Bibi was miserable, and Adaeze acted the good wife only because, someday, she would be queen of Mali.

"That's the procedure I had. The one that allows the possibility of some pleasure." Bibi cut through Folashade's thoughts. "But my husband condemns my choice, every day. He thinks the procedure left me with the ability to enjoy certain activities." Her eyelashes fluttered as she turned to Adaeze. "Not that I ever have, mind you."

The queen-in-waiting's cheeks sank into deep hollows.

"To enjoy what?" Folashade tapped Bibi's arm to prompt her into finishing her words.

Her sister stared at her sandaled toes, as pretty as the rest of her. "Neither Adaeze nor I want that for you." She looked up at Folashade. "Have the full procedure and marry Amiri. I will ask the *furasi* if I can sit with you during the . . . the procedure."

Nago stepped through the flap, leading Fanta, who was dripping river water from her tunic. "Sorry to interrupt, but I'm told the meal is ready to be served. Guinea fowl with plantains. And I have sorted out the selection of caftans Horon Bibi brought for her sister. I would like Musomanin Horon Folashade to come to the other tent for a trial fitting." Nago paused but not long enough for Adaeze to countermand her suggestion.

Folashade looked at her servant. The woman had just used the honorific, noble young girl, to describe Folashade—a startling first. Why?

"And we must remember Musomanin Horon Folashade needs to be polished to perfection. That will take more than the few hours I've been allotted." Nago folded her arms across her own skinny bosom.

"Go, Folashade." Adaeze sighed. "I think you know what you must do."

Chapter 4

The breeze from the Niger brushed Folashade's cheek as she watched the savanna grass dip the top of its green stalk into the river. She blinked at the sun as it grew rounder and rounder. A red streak zigzagged across the glowing disk from left to right, fracturing the sun into a thousand stars. "Oh no," Folashade, standing on the bank, breathed. She ran toward the water's edge as the tiny sparkles arced downward toward the Niger. Her heart pounding, she waded into the water, cupped her hands, and reached to scoop up fragments no bigger than her thumb. Her caftan, the color of the sky at purple twilight, floated in the river behind her. She bent low to gather the pinpoints of sun. There were too many. But capture them she must. What would the world do without its sun? She knew: take off her caftan and pile as many slivers of the Allah-giving light into the garment as possible. But Nago had sewn the caftan to her under dress. The more she tugged to loosen the garment, the tighter it clung to her body. She yanked at the cloth one more time, but now, the stitches from the sewing needle pricked her skin. *Ow.* The rivulets of the Niger grew tongues and licked at the sun sparkles. Folashade turned her face toward the sky. The world, her world, was growing darker.

Boom!

Folashade's arm jerked from her sleep mattress and struck her cheek just below the right eye. The Mandinka diamond in the fancy Doudou-given bracelet Nago had forced over her arm last night scraped her cheek. She winced but the noise deafened her pain. What was that sound that pulled her out of her dream?

Boom! "Move it. You, over here! Get that one!" Words bombarded Folashade's ears. But these words, these sounds, were not of the tongue of the Bambara. "Move it. Get the one running toward the town! Come here, wench." Wolof! Strident, commanding shouts in growling voices that ran from somewhere along the riverbank came from mouths who spoke in the language of those to the far west. Wolof speakers were in Djenné.

The sleep had gone from Folashade's eyes, but not her mind.

"What? Who?" Bibi's head popped up from the mattress her servant had stretched kitty-corner to Folashade's last night. As Bibi bolted upright, her linen sleeping cover slipped to her waist, revealing her bare chest.

Folashade grabbed her own linen sheet and held it tight to her chest as she sat up. Adaeze lay straight-legged on the royal mattress across from Bibi, linen pulled to her chin, her eyes almost as round as her gold-loop earrings.

"Over here. Over here, you Bambara bastards," the downriver Wolof shouts blasted more insistently.

Nago, closer to the center of the royal tent, scuffed a knee as she clambered over the sleeping mattress holding Fanta and her nanny. Amadou, tucked between the two, began to wail. Nago grabbed around the child's chest, jerked him to her, and slapped a hand over his mouth, all before his governess could make a move.

Bibi's eyes swept past Nago and on to Adaeze. "It's Wolof." Her voice rode waves of ups and downs. The rhythms of disbelief. "Whoever it is, they're speaking Wolof." She moved to her knees, completely dislodging the linen shift as she scrambled toward Balaboa and his nanny.

Folashade clutched at her linens. Why was Wolof being spoken so early in the morning? Trading was done in the center of Djenné. In the souk. And after first meal. Not here on the banks of the Niger. Wolof was one of the trade languages from the West. "Nago, get my under dress." She turned to Adaeze, who lay unmoving on her cot. "Sister, why are Wolof here on the beach and shouting so?" Heartbeats pounded in Folashade's head.

"Not Wolof. It cannot be." The queen-in-waiting, still flat on her back, shook her head with the uncontrolled movement of a palsied elder. Adaeze's strained voice told Folashade her sister didn't believe her own words. "The Wolof, the Mandinka, they're from the coast. The waters of the ocean. Yes, they come to Djenné in trade, but not like this." Adaeze's eyes fixed on the top of the tent. "They can't be Wolof."

"Who's in those tents? Bastards, tell me!" The sound of Wolof ram-rodded the tent.

Nago sat frozen like one of those green statues from Cathay that decorated Bibi's house. Jade. The cousin-servant tightened her hand over the struggling Amadou's mouth. Folashade rummaged in the clothes hamper for her under dress. Bibi's personal servant jumped from her sleeping spot on the carpet and met her naked mistress in the center of the tent. She pushed the under dress over Bibi's head while the girl fumbled to pull out the sleeves of her green-and-gold embroidered caftan.

"Adaeze!" Folashade yelled at her sister, who still lay supine as her servants sat on their haunches, their terrified faces staring at the princess. Folashade yanked her under dress from the hamper and slipped it over her head. She leapt to her feet, marched over to Nago, and pulled the woman's hand from Amadou's mouth. "Let the child breathe, in the name of Allah."

Nago worked her mouth once, twice, but only a gurgling sound emerged.

"Well, well. What have we here?" The Wolof, his skin colored the shade of deeply burned charcoal, stooped as he forced his tall frame through the tent flap.

The stench of the man rolled in Folashade's throat. She held her breath. It had to be done. Folashade squared herself in front of the intruder. Her belly roiled as she glimpsed outside the open flap. Four more Wolof slipped thick, knotted ropes around the necks of the Bambara guards. Blood streamed down the royal servants' faces. Folashade saw the cause. Big, bloody, gouged-out spots on the sides of their heads told her: the royal guards had been bludgeoned.

"And what are you?" The Wolof intruder waved a spear at Folashade, but the way the man tilted the weapon told her the business end wasn't intended for her. Not just yet.

Folashade, her heart thumping to her throat, stared past the spear. She willed her eyes to travel to the greater danger—the screams, the cries of terror down the beach. She craned her neck around the massive figure of the Wolof and struggled to peer through the tent flap. Her eyes searched down the marshes and out to the Niger. Chaos. Everywhere. Feet struggling to gain a faster perch on the sand, arms grasping for some invisible rope to pull them to safety, faces paralyzed with fear. Bambara, Fulani, men, women, and children chased by taller, more muscular Wolof, their intruder faces streaked in battle markings. Blood. Screams. Cries. Shrieks. Curses. And the smell. What was that odor? Smoke, yes. Gray smoke surrounded the smell, but the emerging scents were not like the tangy fragrance of roasting gazelle or goat. No, this smell stung the eyes and hurt the throat. This was the smell of bitter. Gunpowder.

Something from behind yanked Folashade's arm. Hard. Bibi. Her sister moved Folashade behind her. Bibi planted herself in front of the intruder. The man took a step forward, his eyes opened wide. Musk and blood and danger roiled last evening's dinner of guinea fowl and plantain from Folashade's stomach to her throat. As Bibi stared down the stranger, Folashade understood what must be done even without her sister uttering a word. Adaeze. Her sister was queen-in-waiting, the highest-ranking royal in the enclosure. She could not be seen naked by a vile male intruder. Folashade blocked her sister's body from view while Adaeze's servants dressed the next queen of Mali.

"How dare you enter this tent without invitation." Bibi's voice rode between the high pitch of the hyena and the threatening growl of the mother gorilla as she addressed the Wolof in his native tongue.

From behind, Folashade watched the little trembles racking her sister's body, but from the front, Folashade was sure the Wolof saw only a woman who seemed to grow taller with every turn of the sun's shadow.

"You are clearly a Wolof. You have not been invited to come to Djenné. The best trading of slaves is done in Timbuktu. Go there." Bibi's voice dropped deeper just as it grew louder with every syllable she uttered.

"Mandrake. Sherizem. Inside. Get these women out in the sunlight. I believe we've got something here." The grin on the Wolof's face spread lopsided.

"You've got nothing here." Bibi jerked her chin higher.

The Wolof advanced one more step and stooped to take a closer look at Bibi. "You speak Wolof? How did that come to be? You have the clear look of the Bambara. Beautiful. And your language is Bambara."

"I speak the language that tells you to leave this tent. Now."

"It is I who tells you to quit Djenné this very instant." Adaeze, in her pale-blue under dress, topped with a red-print caftan, swept past Folashade. She laid a hand on Bibi's shoulders and moved her sister aside with a gentle but steady push. The royal planted herself in front of the invader. "I am Princess Adaeze, first daughter-in-law of the king of Mali. I suggest you leave now before you have raised any more ire in the eyes of the king."

Folashade bit down on her lower lip so hard she felt a bead of blood. What had happened to the sister who lay so terrified just five minutes ago? Adaeze's servant had managed to slip on even more bracelets next to the magnificent one given her by Doudou. Now Adaeze looked the part of a royal. Folashade's eyes swept down to her sister's feet. Bare. Even multiple servants apparently could not locate her shoes.

"Take them all to the beach." The Wolof reached Adaeze in two strides and grabbed her braceleted arm. "I've captured one of the king's women."

Folashade couldn't tell which sister reached Adaeze first. She glimpsed Bibi grabbing Adaeze's free arm while Bibi's right knee kicked at the manhood-covering scabbard the Wolof wore. What would Papa say of such behavior? But now was not the time to ponder Papa. That spear. She had to wrest it away. Folashade wrapped both hands around the shaft as she angled her body to twist the weapon from the Wolof's hand. *Uh.* She almost had it. The Wolof, clutching Adaeze with one hand, and struggling to block Bibi's kicks and thrusts with his feet and body, loosened his grip on his spear under Folashade's constant tugging. *Ooh.* A grip as tight as an elephant's trunk squeezed her middle. Arms with muscles that felt as strong as iron crushed her stomach. Air sucked inside her with no place to go. She couldn't get a breath in or out. Folashade's head lolled to the side. Her eyes bulged as she stared out through the flap window. The sky was gray, almost black. The screams and cries drifted away into soft mews. As for the sun, it was all but gone from the earth.

Chapter 5

Brightness, mingled with deep shadow, flickered across Folashade's closed eyelids. But it was the stink of the man, much more pungent than that of the tent-invading Wolof, that forced open both eyes. Arms jerked her to her feet. Her knees wobbled in the softness of the marshy riverbank. Folashade clenched her eyes tight against the brightness. What was it? Had the sun survived? No, not likely, because that smell, that smell of bitter, still lingered in the air.

"Qu'est-ce qu'il y a vous l'homme noir dit me spécial." Another voice. Another sound meant to be words. But the words were neither Wolof nor Bambara. The voice, more annoyed than angry, floated through the mellow vocal range used by the best griot reciters.

Fear shook Folashade. She had to find out the meaning of the new sounds. Memories of an ancient drumbeat played in her head. Danger. She turned to the sound of the voice, but her eyes and nose took in the sights and smells on the beach before her mind could sort out the strange words assaulting her ears. She struggled to take a step toward the carnage, but her ankles twisted in the soft ground of the riverbank. Bits of sand stuck between her bare toes. A rough Wolof hand shoved her shoulder to shoulder against one of Adaeze's maidservants. Adaeze? Bibi? Her sisters. Where were they? Folashade craned her neck over the moaning women pushing against her, searching for a glimpse of the royal tent some forty meters behind. In the space between the royal enclosure and the women and children now herded almost into the waters of the Niger, she counted only two bodies. Both of them dead. The royal guards. The smell of death strangled in her throat.

Boom! Folashade's head snapped back. Oh, merciful Allah, what was that noise louder by tenfold than thunder?

Fresh screams shredded the air. Another servant, Bibi's this time, dropped to her knees in front of Folashade, her eyes looking up, pleading to the noble to make it all stop. Bibi, standing ten meters up the beach, turned wide, searching eyes toward the tents. The trembling shook Bibi's body as her stare finally sorted out Folashade from among the wailing women. The noise ringing in Folashade's own ears collided with that look of panic on Bibi's sweat-streaked face and disappeared into the smell of bitter. *Oh, Allah, spare us.*

Folashade felt a trickle of urine oozing down her leg. Hordes of women and children shrieked as brawny Wolof men punched, pushed, and shoved them into a space between the riverbank and the cliffs of Djenné. Folashade opened her mouth like a fish gulping in air as she looked upon thirty or more marauding, cursing, shouting Wolof men clutching strange-looking iron bars, mahogany clubs, and metal-tipped spears. Whack. War clubs slammed into Bambara men, spears jabbed at the sides and stomachs of women. With shouts and curses loud enough to startle the birds into flight, the Wolof intruders separated mother from child, herded old from young, and shepherded the few local men away from the dozens of women. Wolof shoved some of the trapped here, others there. *Oh, Allah, do not forsake us! Where are the king's guards?* A great whoosh of air entered Folashade's mouth and overflowed her tongue with bitter. Then she saw it.

Down the beach, the gray smoke lifted in a slow puff off the Bambara's chest as the guard lay still on the ground. Even some fifty meters distant, Folashade knew the man was dead, his chest torn away, the white of rib bone poking through the dark red oozing over the man's frame.

Then he appeared. Him. Walking down the beach. A ghost. The form of a man had something brown growing from his head where hair should have been. He walked and uttered sounds like a man. The figure's headdress hung to his shoulders with a slight curl at the end, like the tail of a chimpanzee. The ape hair swung in the air with every step the thing took. But it was the skin of the ghost—that was what that pale-pink covering could be called—that kept Folashade's eyes fixed on the apparition.

It, the thing, walked like a man but not as tall as most Wolof, nor even Papa, who stood almost two meters high. The thing spewed sounds out of its mouth like a human, but was it a living creature of this time and place? Look at the clothing. No person of Mali would ever wear such attire. Pants, for sure, and brown, but they were tight and outlined the creature's form in a most disgusting way. They stopped at the knee where the garment was fastened with some sort of cheap trade buckle. But the greatest affront to Allah: the creature wore no tunic to offer modesty. And modesty was most needed. The man's tight upper leg, clefted backside, and that bulging front could be seen even by women. Whatever it was the male creature concealed between his legs, Folashade was certain that sight was not meant for uncircumcised female eyes. She fought to look away, but the vision held her transfixed. Instead of the respectability-required tunic, the man-ghost wore a thick leather skin over his chest and back, but his arms, covered in a dirty white full-blown sleeve, were free. And this thing walked toward her group.

He kicked up sand and bits of grasses as he strode closer. He planted himself in front of her group of women and children from the two royal tents. He stood close enough for her to see the color of his evil eyes. Even with Bibi and servants blocking some of her view, Folashade had her answer. She'd seen the eyes of the creature. Blue, but a blue doused with a thin layer of cow's milk. No ghost stood before her. Nor was this an apparition conjured up by an Imam to scare children into proper behavior. Not even Nago could have invented this form of fright. This thing standing before her was a European.

Folashade squeezed her behind muscles tight. She refused to let one of the ones Papa called barbarians without manners or learning see her wet herself.

"*Où sont les damnable femmes vous dit moi son.*" A voice growled out sounds that resembled words. Folashade chanced sneak peeks at the thing's lips. The barbarian had a language, a meaning for the strangeness pouring from his mouth. Fear doused with danger shivered over Folashade, but her ears alerted her. To save herself, her sisters, and all the Bambara, the faster she ordered those sounds, the less frightful the outcome of this attack.

"Look at this one, Monsieur Charbonneau." A Wolof, the first man to enter the tent, pushed the flat of his spear against Bibi's side.

The sounds struggled to rumble themselves in order. The spear-carrying Wolof had uttered a name. *Monsieur Charbonneau.* Folashade let the breath she had been holding ease out between her lips.

Her sister jumped, brushing into the arms of the nanny holding a shrieking Balaboa.

"*Silence le enfant.*" More words from the barbarian, but this time, the albino aimed his noise at Balaboa.

Le enfant. Balaboa. Baby. Folashade took in a gulp of air, praying to Allah her guess was right. The barbarian scowled as his voice graveled at the Wolof by his side. The white man scanned the group before him. His eyes settled on Bibi.

"You, Bambara bitch. Quiet that brat or he is dead." The Wolof man's accent was atrocious as he addressed Bibi, but he spoke passable Bambara.

Bibi glared at the intruder. She didn't favor the tall Wolof with even a look of disdain. Bibi had always been the brave one. Folashade watched her sister set her jaw in the way that told the world she would show no fear. She slipped Balaboa from his nanny and buried the child's face into her shoulder. She patted the baby's back and cooed soothing sounds to him. All the while, her eyes stayed on the barbarian. Bibi must have sorted him out, too.

"Be careful how you speak to my sister." Adaeze, the bright of the resurrected sun sparkling off the Siamese ruby in her bracelet, pushed the crowd of crying and shaking women apart as she stepped beside Bibi. "One might mistake you for a barbarian." Her flawless Wolof almost matched her nerve. "What do you call yourself?" Adaeze's chin tipped up as she pulled out her most haughty voice.

Folashade felt her jaw go slack. Adaeze? Her pretentious sister daring to defy such a nasty intruder?

"I am called Malick by those who are worthy. You are not." The Wolof's snort landed hard on Folashade's ears.

Monsieur Charbonneau swiveled his head between Bibi, Adaeze, and the Wolof standing beside him. For Folashade, the man's face was an easy read. Confusion. The barbarian finally settled his eyes on his associate, Malick. He spoke to the Wolof in the strange tongue. What was that language? The river rock that rested over Folashade's chest pressed down even harder. She had watched Father decipher the letters of the European writings, though he was not as expert as D'bime. Still, Papa could make sense of the letters. But those were on paper for the eyes to see, not the ears to hear, though sometimes he and D'bime tried to speak the letters out loud. What could this European's language be? Portuguese? Perhaps. Spanish? Maybe. Something called English? The people of that far northern land had just written their own Holy Book; though, of course, it was not the real thing. Papa said they called theirs the Saint James Bible and it glorified the Prophet Jesus.

The barbarian worked his mouth to speak and narrowed his eyes toward Adaeze. He stopped. His eyes rested on the bracelet adorning her sister's arm. *"Comment une femme noire,"* the man began, but he ended with the word *"bijou"* as he stared at the adornment on Adaeze's arm.

Folashade calmed her trembling enough to repeat the sound in her head. *Bijou* could mean bracelet.

The barbarian suddenly raised the iron stick he held into the air, accompanied by more of the outlandish sounds.

Ten or twelve Wolof stopped their prodding and sorting of the groups they'd trapped on the beach. Most of the women and children had been forced to the ground. The marsh waters soaked their bodies from where they sat, their damp clothes clinging to them. The raiders stomped among the captured women and children, shoving their heads down into a bow. Clubs across hapless backs and fists pummeled into innocent necks slammed heads downward for those slow to react.

Dinner invaded Folashade's mouth from the wrong direction. She clamped her teeth shut and tried to close her throat against the insistency of last night's plantains. As her throat spasmed, she followed the full shine of the sun as it crossed the face of the barbarian. The man sported something covering the lower half of his face. Hair? But much lighter than that growing out of the headdress on his head. The bottom end of the facepiece narrowed at the point where a man's chin was supposed to be. What was this? Men didn't grow hair from their faces other than curly stubble—not hair that looked like that of the gorilla.

Folashade's eyes stung, and her nose dribbled. *Oh no.* There was something much more awful and ominous about this man who sported the countenance of an albino gorilla. The war stick in his hand, the one he'd held aloft to summon more guards, was no ordinary piece of metal. She sniffed, and the intake stung away the bile threatening to overflow into her mouth. From that long thing made of iron had come the gray smoke and the bitter. A gun.

"Vous! Ici!" The barbarian lowered the iron stick as the Wolof invaders ran up and stood in line formation behind him. Was he their leader? He bobbed his head at Adaeze as he continued his nonsense words. The man trotted out a crooked smile as he poked the stick at Adaeze's under dress. He lifted the front of the garment to her knees.

What, oh, Great Allah, is this barbarian doing?

Her sister couldn't have understood the interloper's language. Adaeze, nor anyone else in Timbuktu, had ever heard the European language spoken, at least not spoken by a real European. Oh wait. What had Papa said? There had been another white-skinned one, years ago. But none after that first one came to Timbuktu in the 1241st year of the Hijri. That one spoke the European languages, but he had not been allowed to return alive. Adaeze crossed her hands in front of her chest as though protecting herself. Whatever the intruder had just said meant particular danger for Adaeze.

"What are you doing here with this barbarian?" Adaeze slowly lowered her hands as she lifted her chin. She singled out the Wolof who had first entered the tent. "Tell this fool with the ungodly color to his skin that he must leave the royal enclosure immediately." She turned her face to the European. "My father-in-law is king of all Mali, and I am Princess Adaeze. You and"—she lifted her Doudou-braceleted arm with all the regalness Nago had instilled in her and pointed a finger at the European—"and those Wolof do not belong here."

A deep, throaty laugh escaped from the European's mouth at the translation, though it was difficult to see the curve of his lips through his gorilla mask.

What was that sneer on the man's hair-covered face? Folashade shifted to Bibi. Her sister's arms wrapped tighter around Balaboa. Bibi's cheeks drew into her mouth. Whatever the barbarian had said in that dreadful language, Bibi had somehow understood.

The Wolof called Malick blinked and turned a surprised face to the European. The man aimed words at the barbarian that reminded Folashade of the honorific Papa bestowed on D'bime. *Monsieur Charbonneau.* Without chancing a stare, Folashade added the Charbonneau sound to her list of alien words. That must be a name.

Something more than the sun's reflection glinted in Adaeze's eyes. "Of course, I am fluent in your Wolof." The tiny wobble in her voice would be noticeable only to her sisters, not these strangers. *"What is the gibberish this thing speaks?"*

The European moved with the speed of a charging lion to grab Adaeze's arm.

"Ah. No!" Adaeze's voice rode the notes of the djembe drum from low to high as the white man yanked her beside him and whirled her around to face the captured women and children from the royal tents.

The man tightened his grip on Adaeze's forearm and wrenched it behind her back.

"Allah"—Adaeze's cry was quick, low, and guttural as her shoulder jutted forward—"spare me this pain."

The invader ignored her cries. He forced her to him, her arm wedged between his chest and her back. He clamped his left arm just under her breasts. Adaeze's gasps for air mingled with the labored breathing of the terrified Bambara. The girl's braceleted free arm scratched and tugged at the cloth shirt covering the barbarian's encircling arm. His lips pulled back in a tight grimace, the infidel drove his leg into Adaeze's right hip, lifting her leg millimeters off the ground. She grunted. Her arm dangled at her side, the bracelets sliding down her wrists. The creature jammed the side of his face into Adaeze's neck, twisting it into a peculiar angle.

"Oh. Allah, help!" This time, Adaeze's cry was high pitched like a captured night bird in its death throes.

The White One grabbed at the bracelet with his free hand. He twisted the ornament from Doudou around Adaeze's wrist.

The Charbonneau person jabbed his left arm upward into Adaeze's breasts.

The princess whimpered. Folashade wasn't sure how she managed, but she pushed the servants aside, slipped around Bibi, and lunged straight for this fool of a man. But her feet shuffled in place, then kicked backward. A hand grabbed her caftan and under dress. Nago. The governess tightened the cloth at Folashade's neck. The sound she wanted to make from her throat strangled in her mouth as Nago threatened to garrote her, for real this time.

The European shouted the word "*prostituée*" with disdain.

Folashade's arms twitched, the muscles in her legs pumped, but her eyes could only stare as the barbarian's right hand reached for the top of Adaeze's pale-blue shift. With one quick move, the heathen gathered the soft linen in his hand. For a long, dreadful second, he fingered the top of the dress.

The sound of cloth separating against itself pained Folashade's ears more awfully than thunder. Tiny bits of pale-blue thread, so light they floated in the air, grew to the size of carrion birds. The barbarian shredded Adaeze's garment from neck to navel.

"Ah!" The shriek rising from the captured princess filled the riverbank.

Folashade's world went silent. The river birds refused to flap their wings into flight. Even the pleas, screams, and cries of those entrapped against the cliff quieted. All eyes turned to the barbarian and his royal prey. Adaeze lifted her free arm as though it carried the weight of a cartload of mud bricks. Trembling fingers fumbled for the jagged edges of her under dress. Her hand struggled to gather in one torn edge. She stretched her fingers to collect the other side of the garment only to lose the first edge in her frantic search to gather both ends together. Her neck wrenched against the infidel's cheek, her face contorted in pain. She struggled to bend over to cover herself, but the White One, his sleeve-covered arm just under her now-exposed breast, held her fast. Adaeze squirmed against the man to free herself. The barbarian circled his right hand to the front of his captive, found her breast, and squeezed it.

The sun beamed overhead, so why were shadows covering Folashade's eyes? The picture playing out before her had to be a lie. But that awful whoosh of air Adaeze took in as the man tweaked her nipple sounded more real, more terrifying, than the worst of the wet-season downpours. It couldn't be true that the breezes off the Niger suddenly dried up and took all the air in the world with them. Folashade watched her sister's head snap back into the White One's shoulder as he finally moved his chin from her neck. Adaeze jerked upright. The dark center of her eyes widened and blocked out all other color. The stranger's hand, covered with sprigs of that strange yellow fur, slid down Adaeze's naked belly, stopping at the end of the slitted under dress, just below her navel.

An insect landed on Folashade's upper lip as her stomach flip-flopped. What she watched had to be some terror dream brought up by Nago. The intruder's hand seemed to separate from its sleeve-covered arm to take on a life of its own. The hand gathered the still-intact remnants of Adaeze's under dress.

That sound of cloth ripped apart again. More awful than a lion shredding a cheetah between its teeth. The light linen separated under the man's rough tug. In front of Adaeze's sisters, her children, her servants, and the Wolof invaders, the barbarian tore apart the under dress of the next queen of Mali from her navel to her triangle of hair—and beyond. Niger River insects buzzed from Folashade's upper lip to her ear. She wanted to blink away the nightmare. Her eyes refused. Bat away the awful quiet of shock. Her ears refused. She wanted to turn her head. Her head refused. As the sun made its threat to leave the sky ahead of time, the barbarian jammed his hand between Adaeze's legs. Why didn't that round thing in the sky just go away, and take its brightness with it? Leave her and Adaeze in total darkness.

Adaeze's head slumped to the side. The barbarian stroked a place where no hand other than the woman's own should touch. The sand from the riverbank squished between Folashade's toes, sucking her feet deeper into the marsh. The water, feeling like the steam off a boiling pot, threatened her knees. She took in one, two, four, breaths as quick as she could. Her head felt light, but she had to endure. The man, his devil blue eyes wide like the lowest of scavenger birds, moved his hands over Adaeze's personal spot. Folashade took in a breath that held her lungs captive for long seconds. She spotted her first glimpse at the horror-filling work of the knife wielder. That burst of last night's plantains finally filled her mouth and spilled past her lips and down the front of her under dress. The infidel, staring at where his hand touched, grunted a noise that carried surprise. He jerked away and began a slow caress up Adaeze's body. That hand, his hand, touched the breast of the captive princess and encircled it.

"Ah, ah, ah . . ." The sound, that mind-numbing sound Folashade had never before heard, erupted from her sister's throat in a nonending moan of misery.

The fur-covered hands blurred before Folashade's eyes as they jerked to Adaeze's shoulders. The barbarian whirled her around to face him, finally freeing her arm. Too late. Adaeze's knees turned to nothing. She slumped to the ground, the silk of her new red caftan fluttering after her. *Merciful Allah.* The cloth cascaded down over one breast, the other hidden by the reeds of the riverbank.

Allah poured strength that freed her mind into her. Folashade broke loose of Nago's death grip, only to be pushed back into her nanny's chest as Bibi thrust Balaboa into Folashade's arms. The middle sister rushed at the White One, but even the tigress that was Bibi could not move beyond the phalanx of Wolof guards that pinned her arms to her sides as they lifted her aloft, her kicking feet half a meter off the ground.

The barbarian stared at Adaeze as she lay crumpled on the marshy beach, her eyes closed, her body unmoving. With his booted foot, covered in more leather skins, he eased the caftan off Adaeze's body. One of Adaeze's legs had fallen across the other in her faint, offering her a small measure of propriety. The barbarian spread her legs apart with the toe of his boot. Adaeze didn't move. He stared at her naked body. Folashade saw flashes of brown-stained teeth emerge from the gorilla hair on the man's face. He squatted before the fallen Adaeze and touched her personal spot again. More of his language spouted through his lips. The barbarian eased himself to his feet and walked to Bibi.

Bibi's foot made contact with the man section of the barbarian's pants. He jumped back and escaped the full impact. He laughed as he laid a barrage of sounds upon her.

"So, that is the way of it, is it? And are you another princess?" The barbarian looked at the bracelets adorning Bibi's arms as he waited for Malick to begin his translation.

Among the five or six ornaments Bibi always wore, the one ringed in nine creamy-white pearls that Doudou said came straight from Cathay, and at a dear price, had always been Folashade's favorite. Malick finished his words.

Bibi bumped a hip into the stomach of her captor. "If I am a princess or not is of no consequence to you. I demand you cover my sister." She aimed her venom at the invader, though she spoke in Wolof. "For what you have done, you will die. You will both be buried in the sands of the Sahara to your waists, and you will be stoned to death. Allah promises it." She slammed the back of her head into the chest of the Wolof translator, who held Bibi fast.

"I will insist upon no easy death for you. I will have the king draw out your stoning. You will be buried to your neck. Like a woman," Bibi hissed as she raked her fingernails down the tunic-clad thighs of the Wolof.

The man grunted as a trickle of blood stained his trouser leg. He looked at the barbarian. Malick did nothing to retaliate against Bibi.

"Then I will have you stoned just to the point of unconsciousness, revived, and stoned again. All through the night." Bibi spit on her captor's encircling arm.

After Malick growled out the translation, the barbarian let out a laugh that carried down the beach. "You are an arrogant enough bitch to be a princess, all right." He touched a hand to his forehead and bent over at the waist in front of Bibi. "I'll taste your royal-ness soon enough."

Adaeze's eyes fluttered open. She squinted against the sun. The princess groaned as she moved. She lifted her head. A look Folashade had never before seen on her sister's face flooded Adaeze. The princess tried to roll to her side and away from the group of gawking men. She snatched for the edges of her caftan. One of the Wolof guards jerked Adaeze to her feet at the command of the barbarian. She had no time to cover herself. Her caftan flapped open again, and Adaeze threatened a fresh faint.

"Let me get a closer look at this one from the front." The barbarian ordered two men to hold Adaeze between them, her arms spread-eagled.

Each man shifted the remnants of the caftan from her shoulders. One of them pulled away the tattered scraps of her under dress. In the bright sun of a Djenné dry-season day, the next queen of Mali stood naked before three dozen strange men. Folashade watched as her sister's body, her curves like one of those Greek statues in Papa's books, moved from a slump to standing straight and tall. Folashade stared at her sister. Adaeze's back straightened, and the queen-in-waiting seemed to grow as tall, taller still, than Bibi. She poked out her chest, even aiming her breasts at the barbarian. She assumed a wide stance.

"You have seen what no man who is not my husband is allowed to see. For this, you will die." Adaeze's voice boomed along the beach. "But first, you must promise me one thing." Her eyes locked on to each of the Wolof men staring at her nakedness. "If Allah is to permit you to enter Paradise, then you must convince this barbarian to kill me. Now."

"No!" Folashade screamed as she shouldered her way past the open-mouthed women, now stunned into silence. She planted herself in front of the barbarian. Even Balaboa, his head dug deep into her shoulder, had quieted his whimpers.

"You will not lay a hand on my sister, you unthinkable creature who grows fur on his body like a baboon." Folashade had no time to wait for the Wolof to translate her perfect rendition of his language.

The barbarian took his puzzled eyes off Bibi and turned them to his new inquisitor. The sharp angles of the words floated up from the page on one of Papa's books. Folashade had heard her father make those same sounds. If only she could remember them now.

"*No da-ñar . . . a mi . . . hermana.*" Had she said it right? No harm to my sister. It was the Spanish Papa had read. "*Ne ferait pas de mal de mi . . .*" What was the word the people of France used for "sister"? *Think, Folashade.*

Her wait was short-lived. The barbarian arched an eyebrow; the blue of his eye felt like the zig of lightning coming out of the stormy wet-season sky. He'd understood. This Charbonneau, this European, spoke French.

"This young girl speaks French?" The smile blazed through the hairy face enough to expose the stained teeth for an instant, then it turned to a frown. "How does a Black know to speak my language? And one not much more than a child." He turned to Malick, still struggling with Bibi, to translate. "Tell this one the other two have one hour to decide which of them will give herself to me first. If they refuse, I will kill all the children. The young ones are of no use to me." He looked at Balaboa as he nodded toward Folashade. He stared at the infant as though he'd seen the boy for the first time. The barbarian's eyes drifted to the still-naked Adaeze. His gaze resettled on Folashade, Charbonneau jabbed the iron stick at Balaboa and Folashade. "This one, this not quite a woman, I will turn her over to my bearers. She is not to my taste. Some may enjoy the bodies of half women, but not I." He scanned Folashade's face and body once more, the outline of her curves, which were covered by Balaboa's legs wrapped tight around his aunt's waist, concealing most of her form. "One hour. Bring me a willing woman, one who will give me her best, because only her best will keep that child

50

alive." Charbonneau waded into the circle of captured tent women and discovered Amadou wrapped in the robe of his nanny and Fanta hiding behind her governess. The barbarian tapped both children on the head before he turned to the naked Adaeze, whose eyes seemed fixed on someplace not of this world. "I want a woman who will please me so much I will spare these children. Otherwise, they, all three, are dead. One hour."

Chapter 6

What a strange thing was the thinking part of a person. Sometimes thoughts and feelings that should be in a person's mind put themselves to sleep. Adaeze pressed the fresh under dress to her body so hard, her nails dug into her own tender skin. Why was she hurting herself? She searched her brain. Something like an answer wanted to awaken, she was certain, call out its truth to her, but it slumbered on. She didn't want pain. Instead, she wanted to smile, but the workings of her face would not allow her such a luxury. But a smile was warranted, wasn't it? She was inside the royal tent and dressed in a fresh yellow under dress. But wait. Hadn't this morning's under dress been blue? For a flash, her head hurt, but then settled back into its rest.

Adaeze burrowed deeper into her cushion, but her body quivered. She looked up at Bibi and Folashade. They were inside the tent, too, standing over her. She could see them as they stared down, wide-eyed, at her. How curious the expressions on their faces. What possibly could be fretting them? Bibi, brave, brave Bibi, and even Folashade, her dear naïve little sister, were inside. With her. Safe. But, of course, they were safe.

"No. No. Never! Do not touch me!" That sound, those women-words, filtered into the royal tent from down the riverbank. But they were so soft, as though they hid themselves through layers of the finest

Egyptian cotton. What could they mean? Wails rose and fell outside the tent like a song of mourning. The song of sorrow from women.

Oh, mighty Allah. Adaeze's nails, the ones her servant had filed to pointed tips and doused with henna to please the queen, dug deeper into her side. Something thumped inside Adaeze's head. Deep inside. Had she heard that sound screamed aloud before? The sound of women facing something so dreadful, the mind could not right itself. Her ears hurt, but not where the holes for her earrings had been pierced. No, her ears hurt deep inside, even beyond where the cotton lay packed. Her ears had heard that sound before—women undergoing some sort of torment. Being violated. That sound. She'd heard it not long ago. *Oh, mighty Allah.* That sound that ground into her soul made her trembling unstoppable. That sound that made her stomach cramp to rid itself of something vile. That scream, she had made it herself.

"Adaeze!" Bibi's voice fought its way through a rumble inside her head louder than a pride of lions attacking their prey.

She felt Bibi lay a strong hand on her shoulder. Her sister shook. A nightmare. The cotton fell away. Adaeze felt her chest unlock. It had all been a terrible nightmare, and Bibi was determined to rouse her.

"We must think of a plan." Bibi's voice sounded reasonable, but only as reason sounds in a nightmare.

Adaeze stared at her middle sister, who looked back at her as though she expected Adaeze, the queen-in-waiting, to answer.

"But I do have a plan." Adaeze's voice sounded like someone else's in her own ears. Nago? No. Maybe her mother in her last sickness. Adaeze captured Bibi's eyes, and all the noise folded down into itself. "You must protect Amadou and Fanta." The tent blazed with light from a sun somewhere in the heavens, even though the heavy tent canvas had always before kept the rays at bay.

"Amadou? Fanta? Protect your children?" Bibi looked at Adaeze as though her older sister's mind had floated away. "Adaeze"—she bent down and clamped both hands tight over Adaeze's shoulders, her voice oozing patience and pity—"of course, I'll protect the children. Yours and mine." She jerked her head toward the closed tent flap. "We're all going to protect the children. You, me, and Folashade."

Adaeze fluttered her eyes. Good. Maybe the thinking part of her could go back to rest. "It is settled, then."

Bibi's beautiful face, colored so much like Adaeze's favorite drink from the cacao bean, scowled puzzlement back at her. "What's settled?" Bibi leaned in closer, the sign of worry etching her forehead. "Nothing's settled." She spoke in a half voice. "That's what we must do. The two of us. Come up with a plan to stall"—her fingers massaged the muscles in Adaeze's shoulders—"these invaders until the queen and her entourage arrive. But we'll need more than an hour."

"I've just told you"—Adaeze raised herself on her elbows, her body felt as heavy as a cartload of mud bricks, her cheek brushing the side of Bibi's face—"I already have a plan. Now that I know the children will be safe, I can fly to Paradise and into the arms of Allah without a care. Then you will all be safe."

"Paradise? Allah?" Bibi landed both knees hard on the cushion, her hands fluttering on her thighs. "Stop such nonsense talk. You will not fly anywhere. Not today." Her fists pounded the tattoo of urgency. "We must sort out a way to buy time."

Folashade, still clutching Balaboa, crept beside her sisters, the child's toes scudding across the carpet. "Adaeze, I know it must be a struggle after what you've gone through, but you must help us, me and Bibi, come up with a plan," the girl's animated voice sputtered. "I think I know about the White One. He's of France, I'm almost certain. What did Papa tell us about the ways of the barbarians of France? I don't know why he's here, but if we could sort that out, then we can make a plan to get rid of him."

"Folashade!" Bibi managed her most commanding voice. "Stop your chattering! These men are slave catchers. Malick and the other Wolof are being driven by the Frenchman. He is called Charbonneau."

"Don't be silly." Folashade shot back her usual know-it-all little-girl answer. "Slaves are bought and sold in Timbuktu. They have been since the beginning. I know some are passed through Djenné, but slave catchers do not descend on people like us. We are nobles."

The sounds of her sisters' squabble floated in and out of Adaeze's ears. *Slave catchers. Djenné. Timbuktu.* There was no reason she should care who and why these men were here. Only one thing, the important thing, mattered. Adaeze, daughter of Toure, Sankore's most illustrious language scholar, whose wife descended from the greatest Malian king of them all—Mansa Musa—had been dishonored. Worse. She had dishonored her husband. She had dishonored her king. She could never be queen of Mali.

Yet, the answer was simple. So simple. Why couldn't her sisters see it? She, Adaeze, would give herself to the White One called Charbonneau. Delay him for more than the hour Bibi fretted about, though Adaeze hadn't quite planned out the how of those details just yet, then make him drag out her execution. That would surely allow the queen and her entourage enough time to rescue the others.

Bibi sucked in her lower lip. Her trembling spread to her shoulders. "Me." The word came out in a whisper as the girl's eyes drifted to the mango juice stain left from yesterday. "Me. I will be the one"—her voice strengthened as she lifted her head and stared into Adaeze's eyes—"the one to attend the barbarian."

What was Bibi talking about? The smile that had refused to come before curled Adaeze's lips. Of course, it would. The answer was plain to see. Bibi was just being her usual stubborn middle-sister self.

Folashade squatted on the floor, Balaboa between her knees, her eyes reflecting the non-understanding of the uncircumcised. "We'll pay them." That little smile on her sister's lips glistened almost the way it did when Papa presented his youngest with a special book.

Bibi snapped her head around to Folashade. "Pay them? Pay them what?"

"Those bracelets on your arm, Bibi." Folashade scooted onto the cushion, dumping Balaboa on the carpet. "And that." She pointed at Doudou's bracelet on Adaeze's arm. "I saw him, the barbarian, look at it like he wanted it for himself."

Folashade's words faded in Adaeze's ears. Her sister was rambling on about bracelets. Some remembrance of herself standing on a riverbank in front of the Charbonneau person entered Adaeze's head but refused to linger. Yes, she understood that, somehow, she had dishonored her husband and her king. But the how was too hazy to clutter her brain. Adaeze shifted her eyes to Balaboa sitting squarely on his bottom where his aunt had left him. Drool dribbled from the baby's lips and tears glistened on his cheeks, but he uttered not a sound. Nago, cowering seven meters away, crawled over to comfort the toddler.

"A ransom?" Bibi's back straightened as she fingered her bracelet. She glanced at her son and signaled Nago. "Folashade, creatures like the barbarian are so uncultured. What's to stop him from"—the words gurgled in her sister's throat—"from stealing our jewels off our arms and still dishonoring us?"

Folashade looked back at Balaboa, who stared, wide-eyed, from aunt to mother and back again. "Of course, the barbarian can take the jewels he sees. I'm sure he's a thief as well as a slave catcher, but that foul-smelling man doesn't know where the other jewels are hidden—the really big pieces." Her eyes brightened. "Your necklace, Bibi, the one with the giant emerald, should pay the ransom for every one of us here. Besides, he doesn't want us as slaves. All of us would be a horror at the job." She scrunched her nose.

Adaeze watched as Bibi and Folashade called out in unison, "Nago! You have hidden the jewel basket well, have you not? You always do."

"Uhh." The voice in the corner sounded nothing like the governess who had once been so commanding over all Toure's daughters. "I never really hide the jewels," she said, her voice reeking fear. "I believe"—the cousin-servant's eyes darted from sister to sister as her voice faded into her throat—"Folashade's new gems are safe enough in their basket." A weak upturn of her lips fleeted across Nago's face.

"And I know where my necklace is hidden." Bibi touched her throat. "That emerald is a quarter the size of an ostrich egg. Doudou gave it to me when Papa consented to the marriage—sort of a compensation for him already having three wives."

"I'll make the offer." Folashade bobbed her head as though she'd solved the problem all by herself.

"You'll do no such thing!" Bibi turned to Folashade.

Adaeze struggled to blink understanding into her head. What was this talk of emeralds and ostriches? Not needed. Her own sacrifice would be enough to appease the infidel.

Chapter 7

"Which royal wench will be my first?" The barbarian stood as the sun, just at midmorning, glowed at his back. The smell of the river carrying silt from the north meshed with the sweet scent of the walnut-sized fruit of the black-and-yellow tree on the opposite shore. Grinning through his hairy face, the intruder scanned the royal women he'd ordered lined up before him on the riverbank.

Adaeze, standing apart from her sisters and in the front of the group of captives, looked down at her body. She had to make sure. Yes, the gold-embroidered red caftan covering her fresh yellow under dress would make a perfect, and beautiful, burial shroud. But how would that happen? How would he kill her? He could use the war club. No. Blood would gush over her under dress and drench the delicate yellow in deep red. She couldn't permit that. Perhaps the infidel would use his gun that discharged awful gray smoke. No, that would never do. Her rib bones would be exposed. Worse, the under dress would be shredded as well and soaked in spurts of blood. Perhaps she could ask to be strangled. Yes, that was it. Then both caftan and under dress would remain intact and unstained. Better still, after it was all over, and as a way for Adaeze to regain a small part of her honor, the garments could be made part of Folashade's trousseau. Folashade. The brightness of the thought pleased her despite her uncircumcised sister's incredible naïveté. Folashade, Toure's youngest, and soon-to-be bride, would be the next queen of Mali.

Adaeze tightened her stomach muscles. *Allah, allow the strength to do what must be done.* She had to step out of the safety of this crowd of cowering women and children. Step out and face the barbarian. All by herself. She swallowed once, twice. "If I may request," she put one foot forward. No, that wouldn't do. Her voice rang much too soft as she struggled to face the devil. If she could just look into those pale eyes as empty of color as the man's soul. "If I may request to die by a method of my choice." The last words shrank back into her throat as she glimpsed Malick. The well-muscled Wolof stood equal distance between her and the barbarian. The intruder's eye caught hers. The meaning behind his twitching lips was clear. *I know your truth.*

"Ahh." The human gorilla pulled back his lips even before Malick, his second-in-command, could begin his translation. "So, Princess, you are anxious to be first? Don't fret. I shan't disappoint. Let's hope you don't, either." He grabbed Adaeze's arm.

His touch felt like an ironsmith's bending tool, heated to a glowing red.

"No!" Bibi's shout rang out across the waters of the Niger. "Me!" She slushed through the soft marsh toward the barbarian, sinking in almost to her ankles. "Me. You must take me. I am the one you want. The one to do your bidding." Bibi's head jerked over her left shoulder to give a quick, reassuring glance toward her son. "The one to give you pleasure." She dropped her voice so low, Adaeze almost missed her words. "My sister isn't capable of delivering the delights I suspect you fancy." The barbarian narrowed his eyes in confusion as Malick slithered his way through the translation. Scores of Wolof intruders played triumph across their faces as their barbarian leader pulled Adaeze closer to him. Bibi had spoken in Bambara, no doubt to keep the Wolof invaders unaware of her plan for as long as possible. Good. Malick busied himself untangling tufts of rope in a clear pretense of ignoring Bibi. Adaeze fought down the shudder that grabbed her body. Where her duty lay was clear. As the eldest sister, the idea of Bibi's sacrifice was unthinkable. Of course, Bibi couldn't be the one to disfavor herself for this horror of a man. There was no need for two of Toure's girls to be dishonored. But what was in her sister's head when she declared Adaeze incapable of delivering "delights"?

"She is unworthy of you." The strength of Adaeze's words surprised even herself. Allah must have awakened the thinking part of her. "You are clearly a leader among your people. A man of honor." Her throat hurt.

Malick, who spent little time in concealing his disdain for the disgraced Bambara, tossed an armload of looped rope to another of the intruders encircling the cowering Bambara as he puffed out Adaeze's words, but not Bibi's.

"A man of honor who should be served by no one less than a princess." Adaeze's knees buckled, but the barbarian's tight grip kept her upright.

The White One swiveled his head between Bibi and Adaeze. She watched the pink lips curl into a leer, clashing against the yellow-stained teeth.

"Am I to believe that the royal ladies are fighting over me?" He let his gaze linger over Bibi as he called over his shoulder to Malick.

Adaeze shut her eyes against the stares of both Wolof and Bambara. She inched her free hand toward the man's sleeve-covered arm. She bit down hard on her tongue to keep the bile inside. She loathed the feel of the creature. The barbarian's muscular arm felt like the coldness of a wound-tight exhibition cobra.

"She"—Adaeze struggled to flicker open her eyes as she stroked his arm—"my sister is but one woman among four of her husband's. She has had little practice in the ways of a proper wife." The sun danced around the sky, and Adaeze's body felt light enough to float to the heavens to catch it. She willed her mind not to see the sixty or so pairs of eyes scouring her every move. She knew nothing of being a proper wife. Though she had nothing with which to compare him, Adaeze was certain her own princeling of a spouse acted very much the child in the tasks of husbandhood.

Through flickered lashes, Adaeze watched Bibi, surrounded by loathsome Wolof, shift her feet in the muck as she confronted the invaders as though she had no fear. Adaeze knew that trick. Only she and Folashade understood that the way Bibi jutted her chin signaled a false bravado in a mind filled with fear. With one quick move, Bibi yanked Adaeze's hand from the barbarian's arm. The girl sucked in her lips, then poked them out. Adaeze watched Bibi struggle to bring forth words. No sound emerged.

Charbonneau pushed Bibi aside. "You're the prettiest all right, and a spitfire. I like that. But I'll save you for later."

Rump! Boom! Bum! The sound came in patterns from across the river beyond the black-and-yellow tree. The Djenné drum. The drum was delivering a message. Rump. Boom. Bum. Bibi turned a wide-eyed stare at Adaeze. There could be no doubt. The beat of her heart picked up in time to the talking drum. The queen's entourage was on the way. But the drumbeats didn't tell Adaeze how close they were. How many warriors accompanied Her Highness? Never mind. No matter how few warriors, the Bambara elite guard would make quick work of these ruffian infidels.

"Monsieur Charbonneau." Malick, a rare frown on his face, cocked an ear toward the sound of the drums as he addressed his barbarian leader. "Our scouts have spotted pirogues heading this way. Three boats, about a dozen warriors. Five or six women. And an old one bedecked like a queen."

With a lightning-quick move, Charbonneau's arms wrapped around Adaeze's middle, crumpling her linen shift. The beast shoved her hard into the arms of his second-in-command. Malick pinned her backward against his chest. The scream that demanded to be heard caught in her throat as she watched the barbarian lay his fur-covered hands on Bibi.

"Gather up these wenches," the infidel shouted as he waded into a crowd of trembling Bambara, dragging Bibi with him, his iron stick held in the crook of his arm. "As many young ones as you can cram into the boats. Especially this one." He shoved Bibi into the arms of another warrior a few centimeters shorter than most of his comrades.

Malick, smelling even more of camel dung and sweat, wrestled Adaeze toward a lineup of boats, their construction unfamiliar, floating out from the cliffs of Djenné. River rock, silt, and clumps of grass picked at her feet as she fought back. She swallowed her pain as she rammed the back of her head into the man's chest that felt more solid than the hide of the rhino. She dug her elbows into the hardness of Malick's stomach. She kicked at the fiend's shins. He tightened his grip around her waist. Breaths huffed out of her as he half carried, half dragged her past the first of the enemy boats tethered at the foot of the cliff.

Adaeze caught glimpses of the craft as the man booted her closer. The vessel, almost two and a half times as large as the elegant ones that floated down from Timbuktu, looked unfit for transporting anything other than chickens and goats. And the smell. Bile clogged her throat. *Oh, Allah.* The stench of fear-filled human bowel remains wafted from the very boards of the vessel. Adaeze gagged, but the bile refused to leave her throat. Malick wrenched her farther up the beach. She spotted three more vessels, their dark sails furled, their sides undecorated, the stink of misery and fear just as strong.

She raked her captor's forearm with her fingernails. The Wolof's grunt carried the sound of pain, and he loosened his grip. Adaeze squirmed from his suffocating grasp, but before she could fill her lungs with air and take a good step, the monster snatched her back. Spittle from Malick's mouth ran down her neck as he lifted her off her feet and carried her the six meters to the first of the lined-up boats. With grunts from a breath that smelled of uncleaned teeth and un-scaled tongue, the man lifted her off the ground as though she were a meter of Cathay silk, and hoisted her toward the boat's edge.

"No!" Her flailing feet gouged for a grip against the boat. She used all the strength left in her to push against the slatted wooden sides. "No. Never!" Her Wolof speaking voice quavered. No matter. She would not allow the beast to put her aboard this stinking wreck of a craft. She swung her head right, left, right, left. The sound erupted out of her in a howling bellow as the monster suddenly lifted her to his shoulders and slammed her hard into the larger boat. The scream coming out of her mouth rose from low to a piercing wail as both knees landed on the floor. She slid between two slatted benches, her shoulder and one hip scraping against an oarsmen's bench seat. A splinter that felt as long as Nago's sewing needle lanced through her under dress and lodged into her thigh.

"Ow." She grabbed at her leg and felt for the offending sliver as she struggled to right herself. Shrieks, screams, arms, and legs that seemed disjointed from their torsos pounded her ears and her body as the Wolof pitched other captives into the boat. A servant's bare foot clipped Adaeze's ear. She let out another yelp of pain. Her face, her head, her shoulders, all absorbed the unintentional blows. Another woman's elbow punched into her neck just as Adaeze managed to lift her chest to the side of the enemy vessel. She dragged each breath out of her lungs. If she could have managed tears, they would have stung her eyes at the pain. Then she caught sight of the horror on the beach.

While the inside of the boat was chaos, the struggle on the river-bank was madness. Adaeze's neck and shoulders ached as another errant leg bumped into her. She held on to the wooden side. Her fingertips numbed. No matter. She had to find them. Her children, her sisters. There, almost at one of the royal crafts, Adaeze caught view of a struggling Bibi fighting off another of the invaders. Her sister kicked, spit, butted, and scratched at her captor. But the Wolof, his sweat-soaked body clear even among all the chaos, held her tight as he dragged her away from the royal doum-palm canoe and down toward the cliffs of Djenné where the barbarian boats awaited.

"Run!" Adaeze's scream melted into the cacophony on the beach. "Get away, Bibi! Get away!"

A hand swept across Adaeze's face, blocking her view of her sister. She managed to stretch her neck around the flying bodies of two women just as Bibi freed her pinned arms and reached both hands behind her and upward. Bibi jammed her thumbs into the invader's nose. The man's shriek rattled across the riverbank. A flicker of pleasure soaked through Adaeze. But it was too late. The warrior laid an arm against Bibi's throat and pitched the girl into the invader boat directly behind the craft holding Adaeze prisoner.

"Bibi!" The sound squawked out of Adaeze's raw throat.

Bibi's face and trunk rose and fell among a clutch of arms and legs at the front of her own captive vessel. A sturdy Wolof, almost as tall as the second-in-command, picked up one of the few Bambara males and dropped the youth directly on top of Bibi. The boy, one of her own royal guards-in-training, had just turned twelve. Still, his slim body drove Bibi from Adaeze's sight.

Adaeze dodged more people as they plunged inside her craft. She tightened her grip on the boat edge. She held on with all her strength as she struggled to hoist herself over the scramble of bodies. She laid both forearms across the narrow edge. If she leaned forward enough, she could catch glimpses of the riverbank. A cramp seized Adaeze's gut. Bibi was captured, too. But, please, Allah, what of her other sister, Folashade? Amadou. Fanta, little Balaboa, all nowhere to be seen. Then, he appeared.

Out of a sea of Black bodies, the albino barbarian raced up and down the riverbank like a devil possessed. He shouted in his language and waved that iron stick. He barked at his Wolof henchmen. "Young ones! You bastards! Take only the young, healthy ones. Those built with good muscles. Not many of them on this damnable piece of river. Bloody bad luck!"

Adaeze heard the anger in the man's voice. A fresh shudder wracked her body.

"And only those strong enough to make the march to the coast." The barbarian jerked the gun toward one of the four waiting invader boats as he continued his gibberish tirade. "Leave the old ones. And the young children. They'll never make the goddamn journey. Women. Grab as many young ones as you can. But only those with good-sized tits. Once we get them to Gorée, they'll make your efforts worth the while."

If only Adaeze could understand the barbarian's language. She had made out the word "Gorée." Something beat into her mind from one of Papa's lessons on geography. Gorée was a place, maybe one to the west where Papa said lay a large body of water. If only she'd paid more attention. A place, but which place? Where were these men, these dreadful men, taking the Bambara? Folashade, with all her youthful ignorance, could not have been correct. Were the royals being kidnapped for ransom and being taken to a place called Gorée? Adaeze shifted her weight and dangled the bracelet in the air. If this was a kidnap, then the promise of a substantial ransom would free them all. She wrenched her shoulder as high as she could, hoping Charbonneau's eye would be caught by the glimpse of gold and he would come to her. With the clashing of bodies on the beach, and the struggling bodies inside the boat, she could not see the man. When she did capture his attention, this imbecile of an infidel had to understand that jewels even greater than the ones she wore lay hidden in the royal enclosure. Someone's heel dug itself into Adaeze's chest. She gasped as she prayed to Allah. *Please allow this barbarian to know the art of the bargain. Accept a trade.* The jewels and her body in exchange for the freedom of the other royals. A fresh slash of pain pelted Adaeze's shoulder as she struggled against the writhing arms and legs punching, pushing, and pulling at her. She wiggled her right arm aloft, waving it frantically. But Doudou's bracelet, smudged with blood, mud, and grass stains, still sparkled. A woman, Adaeze couldn't tell which servant, lurched her back into Adaeze, jostling her away from the side of the boat. Adaeze's arm flung out to regain her handhold. Too late. An errant knee punched her in the stomach. She doubled over and dropped between the slatted benches, opening a fresh bloody gouge on her back.

Oh, Allah. Pain, more cutting than binding ropes on a camel, raged through her body. She fumbled to press her torn dress into the spot just under her shoulder blade. She couldn't reach it. "Allah, have mercy." There had to be a way to save them all. There had to be a way to alert the creature about the magnificent jewels that remained, blessedly, onshore. Saving her people would be her last act as a royal, but where was he, this barbarian? She had to locate him, get him to understand greater riches could be his in exchange for Bambara freedom. But, trapped as she was, she still had to sort out how this was all going to happen.

If only she could push aside the bodies holding her tight, blocking her view of the riverbank. *Merciful Allah, deliver.* One of Bibi's servants suddenly rolled to her knees, thrusting aside the elbow of a third woman pinning Adaeze prisoner. Free! Adaeze scrambled to her knees and scratched for a fresh handhold on the side of the boat. She leaned her weight on her elbows. Each breath pained her chest, but there he was again.

But, oh, Allah, the fiend had sighted a fleeing Folashade. Her sister, carrying Balaboa, ran toward the center of town, stirring up great clumps of grass and wet soil as her legs churned in the marsh. But the barbarian, dodging between groups of club-wielding Wolof and screaming women, was faster. He caught up with the girl just as she pounded past the royal tent, her blue caftan flying behind her. Charbonneau spun Folashade around and yanked her arms wide, spilling a now-howling Balaboa to the ground.

Adaeze struggled, grunting, to free herself of the boat. Climb over the side and run to her sister. Rescue the girl. Nothing. She could only watch as Folashade threw herself at Charbonneau. The girl pulled at the hair on the creature's face with the ferocity of a mother jaguar. Adaeze watched as tufts of yellow-colored fur appeared in her sister's hands. The barbarian's howl traveled to the craft carrying her. He grabbed the back of Folashade's neck, doubled his fist as she tugged at the pointed thing on his chin, and punched her in the stomach until she went limp. With one fluid move, he flung the girl's now-still body over one shoulder and weaved his way past one of the royal servants as she pulled at the arm of a three-year-old while a Wolof invader pulled on the child's other arm. Charbonneau made his way to another vessel, third in the lineup, and dumped the hapless Folashade headfirst into the craft. A woman slumped next to Adaeze raised her bloodied head. Her mouth formed the shriek of the terror she must have felt, though her voice was silent. Nago. The barbarian suddenly appeared on the shore next to Adaeze's boat, his shirtsleeves and chest covered with flecks of blood. He pushed the governess down with the long barrel of his gun and climbed into the boat, his feet using Nago's chest as a boarding platform.

"Get the damnable sails up and those bloody oars in motion." He shaded his eyes with one hand as he looked upriver. "You tell me the drums say we have a half hour head start," he called out to Malick, who scrambled aboard the lead boat carrying a familiar-looking woven basket in his hand.

A woman flung an arm around Adaeze's shoulder and dragged her from her viewing perch. Adaeze used her right palm to push herself upright. Through one eye, she watched the second-in-command inch closer to the barbarian.

Malick's guttural voice spoke in a mixture of Wolof and the French Folashade insisted the barbarian spoke. "The drums tell me twenty to thirty minutes, but these are not war canoes, and they are going at a leisurely pace. Like to a party. We can easily outrun them." He lifted the lid from the green-and-blue-chevron woven basket. "And the payoff could make us all rich men when we return to Rufisque."

Rufisque. The sound from the Wolof's mouth jarred Adaeze into a lesson taught by Papa. Rufisque was a moderately large village near Dakar. The place was located to the west where the big waters lay. *Allah, spare us if that is the destination.*

Charbonneau shifted his feet to regain his balance as the form of a young boy bumped into his leg. "You're already headman in your village. If I do need your services again, I trust you will not desert me." The barbarian lurched forward as the weight in the boat shifted.

Adaeze, one knee sliding on and off the head of one of her countrymen, watched Malick give the barbarian a nod of the head that almost looked like a bow. The man's eyes were hooded. She'd understood almost nothing of the exchange between the two, but she had grasped the mangled phrase, "rich men." Malick had mingled the Wolof words with the foreign tongue Charbonneau spoke. Adaeze managed to turn her head toward Nago, now curled up at her feet. The basket Malick switched between hands tipped to one side. The drawstring closure looked tightly closed. Whatever was in that basket, Nago would know for certain.

"Nago!" Adaeze hissed at the fallen figure. The woman lay still, her eyes staring upward. "The basket, the basket with Bibi's emerald necklace. Where is it?"

A trickle of blood eased out of the governess's mouth and down into the fold of her chin. Nago's eyes fluttered once, twice, then closed. *Please, Allah, let it not be true.*

"Nago. No," Adaeze pleaded. Not Bibi's magnificent necklace. That jewel, that treasure, Bibi's emerald necklace was Adaeze's best bargaining tool. It must be kept away from this monster of a barbarian until it was time to pull it out. The sun chose the top of Adaeze's head to direct its most fierce rays. The lapping waves of the Niger decided this was the perfect time to suck all the moisture from her throat. That basket that gave Malick cause to call himself a rich man could not be lost. Please, Allah, do not allow that woven vessel to contain the ransoms for her children, her sisters, her people. Adaeze eased her knee into Nago's side. She nudged the woman. The maid-relative answered by drawing her legs to her chest. A low moan eased out of the woman's mouth.

"Keep your head down, Princess, I'll get to you later." The barbarian laid his boot across Adaeze's shoulder and forced her to bend over as he struggled with the Wolof tongue. "Princess, I've left your children onshore." He dug in the boot. "I've found something much, much better—jewels fit for a queen." The grin she glanced up to catch scattered more pain through her body than his boot.

She heard the creature's laugh, though she could no longer see his face. He slammed her head against the rounded boards of the boat, the mahogany floorboards smelling of reeds, the fish of river water, and the stench of human waste. She held her breath and closed her eyes. Blessed blackness. Her ears decided to join her eyes and nose in solitude. Even if she could understand Charbonneau's gibberish, her ears decided on a rest. Other than the swish of the oars and the wisp of the little breeze bellowing the sails, all had gone quiet. Good. Now while she awaited the queen's rescue of her sisters and children, her thinking could go back to sleep.

Chapter 8

The growl in Bibi's stomach had grown softer now, weak, even, as though her body accepted the futility of longing for food. How many days had it been since that five-hour paddle ride of horror down the Niger? She remembered yesterday and the day before with no more than captured flasks of river water and a few berries to ease the cramps in her belly. Her forehead throbbed right above her eyes. No, the days numbered three. She looked up at a red sky signaling sunset. Red, the color of blood. Her arms, legs, head, her entire body, ached. She had walked, hobbled as she was with her legs linked by a tight rope knotted around her. The two ends attached to two servant women, one in front, the other behind. Walking through the brambles and brush each and every day without stopping. After yesterday, or had it been the day before, she'd stopped trying to estimate the time. Her body must have trudged five or six hours with no rest.

When the enemy vessel first made landfall near a beach that felt more solid ground than marsh, she'd been relieved to be free of the suffocating boat ride down the Niger. She was still alive and prayed for the mercy of Allah that her sisters and the children had been left behind.

The growl in her belly and the thumping in her head eased, and the memory of that first evening zigzagged into her head. Night had fallen, and the barbarian had ordered his four boats stopped along the riverbank under a canopy of trees. *Ugh.* The thought of the man brought on a fresh wave of dry heaving. That first night, her ribs pained, her arms throbbed, her legs covered with scratches and gouges, she and the other captives had been ordered from the enemy craft. Oh, Allah, there they stand, both of her sisters. Adaeze. Folashade. A wave of fear buckled Bibi's knees. Oh no, Allah. Not all of Toure's daughters. Even Nago, her eyes as vacant as a dead hyena, sat slumped on the ground as she lifted her head toward the other two nobles. And before all the captured Bambara paraded the albino barbarian.

That night, that first night, Bibi clutched the sides of her torn and bloodied shift. Courage. Surely, Allah would not deny her every tool in her arsenal. She had to face the infidel. Bibi had expected the fool to come to his senses. As uneducated as Europeans may be, according to Papa and D'bime, even these with skins the color of ghosts must realize the danger of kidnapping the future queen of Mali. But instead of releasing them all with a deep plea for forgiveness, this Charbonneau had allowed the women, and the few youths in his clutches, no more than two hours sleep before he force-marched them beyond the moonlit riverbank. Yet, Allah had shown his power.

Her sisters were among the captured women. Almost all of them young, except Nago. But Allah the Mighty had spared the children. Balaboa, Fanta, Amadou—they were not among the taken. The other women whispered that the children, all of them, had been left in Djenné. Alive. Since that first night, the prisoners had been marched two more days into ever-increasing vegetation. Neither sight nor sound of the river, the blessed, beautiful Niger, could be sensed.

"Ow." Folashade, tethered four women ahead of Bibi, cried out as she stumbled over a tree root. "I can't take another step with this dreadful rope around my ankles!" she railed in Wolof. "Take this thing off me and my sisters. We are nobles!"

Folashade stopped in her tracks, bringing the line of ten women to a halt in a place surrounded by much more greenery than even in Djenné. There were no sand dunes here. They were definitely moving west.

"Keep walking, Bambara bitch, or I will lay this into you." One of the Wolof warriors waved a long stick with four leather thongs attached, each end wrapped tightly around a small rock.

"Wolof"—Folashade's body shook—"Wolof vulture!" the girl retorted with her strongest invectives. "How dare you speak to me that way. Take this thing off my ankles, you—you bastard!"

"Folashade." Bibi's voice rose with her shock as she shouted at her sister. Papa had never permitted such language from his girls. "If you want to be alive when the queen's troops reach us, don't antagonize any of these infidels until we can come up with a plan." Bibi chose Greek to speak to her sister, a language she prayed that ignorant fool of a Wolof guard would not understand.

The warrior turned a blank stare on her as he paused in front of Folashade. Surely, the youth, who couldn't have seen more than eighteen dry seasons, would not stand there waiting for the girl to issue an apology. Stubborn Folashade dropped her head and limped along. After a parting glare, the young guard, his tribal marking striping his face, moved over to the line of young men, where he cracked the four-tailed stick in the air.

"Night will fall soon, Folashade. We'll work on our plan then." Bibi spoke to Folashade with her lips barely moving while she searched out her elder sister. "Before full moonrise, these insults to Allah's name will surely allow us more of a rest. We've moved three days steady. Women are dropping all around us. None of us can keep up this pace much longer."

Adaeze, in her torn yellow under dress, had been shorn of her red caftan. Worse. The princess, who had spoken no more than five words in these three days, didn't seem to care.

"Plan? It's futile to talk of a plan when we're forbidden to speak to one another," Folashade called out softly. "In any language." She looked over her shoulder after first checking that the Wolof guard busied himself with other hapless captives. "Bibi, I'm worried about Adaeze. She looks so"—Folashade hushed as another Wolof guard stalked the line, this one older, a look of cruelty upon his face—"unlike herself. Almost like she doesn't know herself. I'm frightened."

"I'll not tell you again, you Bambara noble bitch. Shut up or I will lay this into your backside." The Wolof's flaring nostrils mixed with the deepening frown lining the man's face made his look even more ominous. He stood over Folashade, snapping the four-tailed stick at his side. "Then we'll see how a haughty noble bleeds."

"Set them down here." The barbarian swept aside a tree branch as he shouted to his second-in-command. He approached the group from the front of the line. "Take care not to damage the merchandise."

These past days, Bibi had seen precious little of the albino except from afar. Now she had to force him into a bargain. The queen's troops had yet to reach them as the interlopers trekked them through ever-thicker foliage, taking them farther from the river. Bibi's stomach fluttered. Would the queen's troops find them? Surely, the king would know of their circumstances by now. Yet, His Royalness was not known for his boldness. Bibi shook her head so hard, one of her beaded braids slapped at her cheek. She must push aside such ridiculous thoughts. Of course, the king of Mali would rouse himself and from somewhere pull up the strength to rescue his daughter-in-law, despite his well-founded reputation as a weakling and a coward. Bibi bit down on her tongue. Such thoughts were unworthy of Allah.

The barbarian. He had to be her only focus. Had Folashade said the thing spoke French? Papa had taught his girls the languages of the ancient world—Greek, Persian, Latin—but she had seen but a few of the European words and heard even fewer. Bibi scrunched her forehead, struggling to remember the words on the page, and trying to recall the sounds Papa and D'bime put to those symbols.

"Monsieur. S'il vous plaît." She could think of no more French. "Permission to speak to your exalted self," she filled in with Wolof,

though she was loath to include the odious second-in-command in what she wanted to be a private conversation with the barbarian.

The Frenchman turned a startled face toward the group of women tethered with Bibi. Her group knelt and squatted on the underbrush, some taking the opportunity to relieve themselves. Folashade turned her back to Charbonneau. Bibi sat with her knees bent, her ankles secured to women on either side of her.

"Monsieur. S'il vous plaît?" A look of puzzlement crossed the barbarian's face as he started a slow walk toward Bibi's group, muttering the sounds that had come from Bibi's mouth. "That sounded almost like French. I believe the wench tried to speak the word 'please.'" He passed Folashade without a shred of recognition, stopped, and turned a questioning face to Malick stationed with Adaeze's group of captives.

"Not possible, Monsieur Charbonneau," the muscular Wolof called out. "Few Europeans travel as far inland as Djenné. These wenches would know nothing of the languages spoken on the coast."

Bibi's chest hurt from holding her breath, but she had to try. "Oh please, Allah." *Ecrire.* Let that be the French word Papa had taught for writings. Even her familiar Wolof was tiring her. "And, I, Monsieur . . ." Her mind pulled up Malick's sounds. His tongue had just twisted itself into words that must be the name of this European. "Monsieur Charbonneau," she worked her tongue. *"Moi* Timbuktu." Bibi held her eyes steady into those of the barbarian as her mind ran through the mixture of Wolof and French she'd just uttered. That garbled combination of French and Wolof had to be enough to intrigue the barbarian.

The man's blue eyes widened in surprise as he scanned the line of kneeling and squatting women. He inched himself down the group, staring into each female face, and Folashade's back, his head shaking no until he reached Bibi.

"Ah." The barbarian's voice sounded familiar as his booted foot stopped at Bibi's folded knees. "One of the princesses. The beautiful one." He knelt down in front of her, his breath smelling of dried goat meat. "You are of Timbuktu?"

While the prisoners had been given nothing but river water and a few berries, their captors had been fed, even if the food was suitable only for those who traveled the Sahara. The barbarian dropped to his knees, and one furry hand swept to Bibi's chin. She shuddered. The man lifted her chin while Bibi set her jaw to stop her trembling. Eyes the color of a rain-washed sky stared at her, setting off a fresh round of turmoil in her belly. Those eyes reminded her of a tale Nago had related to her in the long ago. Some dreadful demon must have taken Charbonneau's soul and replaced it with such unnatural eyes.

"So, it is French you are struggling to speak." The lips pulled back into a grin that looked lopsided on the man's face. "What other surprises do you have for me?" His sleeve-covered arm wiped away blood caked on her cheek.

A poorly disguised grunt meant to fool no one erupted from Malick as he shifted his feet and moved his glare from Bibi to the four shorter Wolof standing between Charbonneau and his second-in-command.

Bibi turned her eyes back to lock into those of the devil. She'd understood not one word of his language, and Malick hadn't bothered to translate. She could not allow the barbarian to grasp any of that. She raised her braceleted right arm and turned it slowly in the fading sunlight. If only she recalled the French word for "jewel."

"Djenné." She tried another tactic. She willed her face muscles to form a half smile. Bibi fought down the bile rushing from her stomach and leaned in closer to her sister's torturer. Her cheeks sucked in as she stared at the devil himself.

"Djenné." The word stumbled between his lips. His hand swept from her chin toward the bracelet. "The beach we just left. Where we found you and your sisters." The barbarian reached a hand toward the bauble.

Bibi jerked her arm behind her before this Charbonneau could fondle the ornament. "Emerald. More." She held her stare, though her heart thumped. She had spoken in Wolof.

Malick took a half step forward, his eyes fixing on the bracelet.

"Em-a-rald." Charbonneau's eyes returned to the bracelet. "Ah yes. 'Emerald' in my tongue." The barbarian turned toward Malick but asked nothing. "You have other jewels in Djenné. That is what you are telling me." His lips pulled back in a broad grin. "Oh, you are a pretty one, all right, but I already have your emerald." His fingers traced a V on her neck.

The bile erupted onto his hand. His touch, his smell, and, oh, Allah, he had spoken of the necklace—her best bargaining chip.

The barbarian rocked back on his haunches, pulling up tufts of the long-bladed grass to wipe the vomit off his hand. "I see you add touchiness to your list of annoyances. I'll soon get that out of you." His laugh carried the sound of grating sand.

What had the monster barbarian said? That smirk on his face felt like an iron bolt thrust into her chest. Please, no, Allah. Do not allow this man to have discovered the emerald necklace.

"Diamond." Bibi's mind reeled. She had to think of another answer. "Rubies of Siam. Silk from Cathay." Allah, let at least some of the words be French. "Timbuktu."

"Monsieur." Malick broke away from a growing group of invaders who failed to disguise their glances at the ornament on Bibi's wrist, and her mixture of French and Wolof words about exotic jewelry. "This one will speak any words to you to save herself. The wealth of Timbuktu is of the past." The man stood no farther than a meter from his commander.

No matter how loathsome was Malick, Bibi had to center her focus on the barbarian. By the way his eyelids flickered, she knew she had landed a hook into the barbarian's hide.

"Diamonds." Charbonneau scanned her body. "Cathay, Siam, and Timbuktu. Pretty one, tell me all you know of Timbuktu." He glanced up at Malick for the French-to-Wolof translation.

Bibi parceled out her words. Malick might bring more harm to her and her sisters if he understood too much. "Riches in Timbuktu. Djenné." If only she had command of the French word for "ransom." "King"—she suppressed a sigh of relief when the French word popped into her head—"wants daughter back." She kept her eyes away from Malick's face.

Bibi aimed her index finger at her chest, then waved her arm to include all the other captives. "Bambara"—she spread her arms wide— "all for riches." Allah, let this barbarian understand.

Those soulless blue eyes blinked the glimmer of understanding at her. "I believe I hear you speak of riches." With a move so quick, Bibi almost missed it, Charbonneau raised his head and scanned the squatting women, their dirt-caked bodies stood over by Wolof warriors. The barbarian scrambled to his feet, looked over at Malick, then down to Bibi. "I believe this one is trying to bargain with me. If I free all the women, her so-called king will pay a large ransom."

"She lies. My men took everything of value on that beach." Malick allowed his eyes to lock for an instant too long with Bibi's.

Papa had always told his girls to learn about a person by more than a casual glance at the face. To really understand, you had to sense what hid behind that face. Malick definitely harbored plans for his tribesmen that far exceeded any action the barbarian might have plotted.

"In the name of Christ Most Holy, the world knows Timbuktu once had more gold than all the world." Charbonneau turned a glare on Malick. "You tell me no, but you talk of Djenné, not Timbuktu." He walked five meters away, stopped, and twisted around to stare at Bibi as he stroked the yellow fur on his chin. He turned his back to her once more as he called out to his second-in-command.

"Timbuktu. That's what this wench is talking about. Could there still be hidden wealth in that place?" Charbonneau stalked over to the head Wolof, who towered over him by almost four centimeters. "Tell me now, or our agreement may not be renewed for my next venture. Do not forget, Malick, I have made a very good money division for you once we reach Dakar."

Bibi watched as Malick composed his face into what she presumed was supposed to be humility.

"You ask of Timbuktu. I shall tell you all I know." The man spoke in Charbonneau's tongue. "I can assure you it is a place of the long ago, in my father's father's father's time. No one travels there anymore. I heard the entire city has been taken by the sands. The travel there cannot be done."

"Yet, this wench speaks of gold and diamonds. You tell me she is lying. How can I be certain it is all gone?" The barbarian shot a quick look at Bibi. "Rather than taken by the sands, perhaps it is those very sands that conceal whatever wealth is left."

"All is possible, Monsieur." Malick's words landed in Bibi's ears as just the opposite.

Bibi watched Charbonneau's hand quit his fumbling with the growth on his chin as he turned to Malick. "Three days since we last heard the drums. Three days walk with no one following." The man pivoted toward her.

She steeled herself against the shudder threatening to make her fear obvious. Charbonneau stared at her as though he were trying to decide if she was worth the price of silk from Cathay or a threadbare scrap of cotton cloth from far south of the Sahara.

The blue eyes bored into her as the man placed one booted foot in front of the other. The barbarian measured his pace back to Bibi, his eyes darting between her and the sparse, hacked-out trail they'd just left. When he reached her, Charbonneau lowered himself to the ground, the stench of his unwashed body threatening a new overflow of bile. "I understand what you're offering me. Gold and gems from Timbuktu in exchange for the freedom of all your Bambara." He stumbled out his words in Wolof.

Bibi felt the man's eyes execute a second roam over her body. Never mind. *But, please, Allah, let one of the beast's sounds mean yes.*

The barbarian jammed his face only centimeters from her own. "You speak a good deal of bravado, Princess. I give you that." His hand swiped across her breast. "But I believe you wish to outwit me. I number those who've accomplished that trick to be very few. And never a woman." He scrambled to his feet. The man carried the look of a triumphant giant as he towered over Bibi. "You call yourself a princess. You certainly behave as one." A smile worthy of Nago's worst nighttime scary tale laid itself over the man's face. "You may be too smart for your own good. You, after all, are only a woman."

Bibi lost the battle with the threatening shudder. Her shoulders shook more than the time the fever laid her low for five days. Oh, Allah. She had angered the barbarian!

Charbonneau called out to Malick. "There is no Timbuktu. By my reckoning, we can afford a good night's sleep." He looked down at Bibi. "Give the prisoners a full measure of rations." He strode up the line and stopped before Folashade.

The girl had turned half around.

"That one." He nodded toward Bibi. "I'll have her in my tent tonight."

Chapter 9

What was that pressed against her lips? Adaeze felt the distinct taste of food. Whatever the substance, berry or dried goat, it caked on her dry lips. More than the hint of food assaulting her mouth, a strange man shouted at her in Wolof.

"Eat, damnable Bambara bitch." Sometimes Adaeze's dreams seemed so real. Even her nightmares. For certain, she was caught in the throes of her worst nightmare right now. Her tongue flicked away an unwanted berry.

"I will entertain you in great fashion." Bibi's voice. But her sister was speaking Wolof. "If you will free all the others."

Entertain? There must be a royal reception in the offing. A party perhaps for Adaeze's mother-in-law, the queen. Odd, though. Bibi had not shared that information with Adaeze. So unlike her middle sister to speak in such a put-upon haughty manner. Crack! A streak of lightning zigzagged through Adaeze's head, pushing aside the fog of these last three days. The barbarian walked ten paces ahead of Bibi, who was being carried like a load of mud bricks against the chest of a burly Wolof. Her sister's feet dangled centimeters off the grass. These Wolof, the strangers who had invaded Djenné, were now holding the royal court for ransom.

Adaeze grunted, her feet under her as she started to rise, only to be wrenched back to the ground by the tether shackling her to a woman on her left. Ugh. Adaeze's knee protested. She sat on the ground and untangled enough of the rope to allow more movement. She sucked in a gasp and stood just as the despicable white-skinned barbarian approached her.

"No." She pulled up the French word. "Where do you take my sister?" Adaeze smoothed a hand over the shredded remnants of her yellow under dress. She could feel gouges and blotches paining her body, and what this man had done to her. Never mind. She would allow no harm to come to Bibi. If she still breathed, she would fulfill her duty.

The barbarian's eyes shifted to Adaeze and the Doudou bracelet. "Ah, Princess, we meet again. I think I'll have a taste of you, too."

Adaeze snapped her arms to her side. "Me." That had to be the foreign word for "me." She continued in her flawless Wolof. "Not my sister. Only me. Whatever plans you intend, I demand the respect of my rank. I will be the one instead of her."

"Malick, tell me this one's meaning," the barbarian called out to the second-in-command.

The Wolof's eyes darted from sister to sister as he translated.

The barbarian stared at Adaeze. "So you say. You want to be the only one to please me." A lopsided smile twisted through the fur on his face. "Well, I must declare, you do look a fright, but I can include you, too, since you're so insistent." He chuckled as he turned to Malick. "Cut this one loose from the others, and for the love of God, clean them up." He nodded toward Adaeze. "I'll take that one first." He looked at Bibi. "I'll save the best for last." The barbarian smirked at Bibi as he strode farther up the line. He stopped, called once more to Malick. "Oh, here's one more of them. Get her, too." He pointed to Folashade. "Might as well make a party of it."

◆ ◆ ◆

Adaeze gritted her teeth as one of the Wolof guards trickled a few drops of water over a handful of grass and shoved it at her.

"You. Bambara, make yourself look like something." The guard, reaching only the shoulders of Malick in height, looked as though he hated the job assigned him.

"I realize, Wolof fool"—Adaeze watched the young man's face register surprise at her condescending Wolof—"you are completely unaware of what you've done. You are not allowed to address me or my sisters in that manner. Nor are you permitted to lay a hand on a noble personage." Adaeze lifted her chin, sucked in her cheeks, and sniffed the air in the manner Nago had drilled her so hard to master, a mannerism expected of a princess of the royal house of Mali. "It is an affront to Allah. Hold that cloth in front of me so I may finish my toilette without prying eyes." She sniffed again and let her shoulders show a shiver. Now to wait and see if her royal disdain had made an impact on this imbecile of a Wolof.

The man—a boy, really, and not much older than her own husband—called out to a fellow guard. The two scrambled to hold up a sheet of mud cloth in front of the royals. If she and her sisters huddled together with their backs to the guards, they could look the part of women seeking modesty amid trying circumstances. Now it was up to Adaeze to control the expressions and movements of her sisters well enough to disguise their real motives. Adaeze had to use this precious secret time to convince Bibi to abandon her foolish plan.

"Bibi, come closer." Adaeze chose Persian. "We have little time to finalize what must be done." She took the dampened grass and rubbed it over her face. Even the wetness stung her cuts and bruises. "I will give myself to"—the word stuck in her throat—"to the barbarian."

"No!" Bibi's head shook so hard, Adaeze was afraid the sound of her braids slapping against her face would be heard by the guard. "I can't allow you to give yourself to him. Not again. Besides, I've already engaged this man called Charbonneau in a discussion. With a little more time, and if I try a few of the bed tricks I've been forced to watch, I hope to gain freedom for some of us." Bibi looked determined to ruin herself.

"You've had a discussion with the barbarian?" Adaeze scanned her sister. "I find it difficult to believe, since your French is little better than mine." Despite the scratches, blood, and dirt covering the girl's face, Bibi's beauty could not be denied. Adaeze grunted against the shiver running down her back. She would not, could not, permit her middle sister to be defiled by this barbarian.

Bibi swept a hand toward the tuft of grass Adaeze held and yanked it away. The girl lifted her own ripped under dress and scrubbed at her body. Bibi turned to Folashade. "Cover your ears." Bibi's voice was low but commanding as she pushed the back of Folashade's head toward the ground. Bibi grabbed her youngest sister's wrists and clamped both of the girl's hands over her ears. Folashade grimaced as Bibi squeezed her own hands atop. But at least Folashade did not cry out. Bibi kept her hands firmly in place as she peered over Folashade's head to Adaeze. She mouthed, "I watched my husband with his favorite wife, and, oh, the bed tricks she used. You've never seen such arms and legs flailing about. One up here, the other down there. Nothing like Nago ever instructed us. If I must, and I know I can, I will use each and every one of those despicable ways on Charbonneau if that will free even one of us." Bibi's voice swallowed in a shiver that brought her shoulders almost to her ears.

"You'll do no such thing!" Adaeze's dry mouth spit out the words. "Are you blind? It is plain to see I can never be queen." Her fingers clutched at the jagged edges of her ruined under dress. "Not after what happened." She pulled back the cleaning grass and swiped it down her own belly. "Can't you see? It must be me, not you. Think of Papa." Her eyes roamed Bibi's face. She had to make her sister understand. "You know it would bring on Papa's death if he learned two of his daughters had been ruined."

"Are you three ready?" Malick called out. "Monsieur will become impatient." He pulled down one end of the mud-cloth sheet the boy-guards held.

"How dare you." Adaeze pulled the remnants of her yellow under dress around her as she half turned in her squat toward the man. Her mind whirled. Three. Wolof had said three. Herself. Bibi. Folashade. There was no reason why her youngest sister need be ready for anybody. The girl was yet to be circumcised. Unfit to grace the bed of any man. Adaeze moved to her feet and faced Malick. At least she'd been freed from those dreadful shackles. "I am the one he wants. I am ready for him."

Bibi started to rise.

Adaeze pushed her sister down with a foot. "I will be the one to entertain the barbarian." She swallowed hard. "But as I do, Bibi, I beg of you, attend Folashade. I think, perhaps, the barbarian may have unsavory plans for her as well." Something akin to the feel of a goat-butchering knife stabbed its way into the center of her belly. "Oh, Bibi, while I do what I must, you must devise a plan to spare our little sister."

Malick, his face marked by exasperation, grabbed Adaeze by the arm, squeezing hard. "What did you say, wench? Speak only Wolof, not whatever tongue you just used." The man pulled her away and hurried her deeper into the vegetation.

"Bibi, please. Protect Folashade. She cannot be the next queen of Mali if she is unpure," Adaeze called out in Persian as the guard yanked her arm so hard she felt it separating from her shoulder.

The tent stunk of unclean barbarian. Musty. Stale. Pungent. Stomach churning. But his was not the only source. Adaeze clutched the mud-cloth wrap Malick had thrown at her after she'd shed the scraps of her under dress. Bits of grass, oil from the cooking, the smell of feet, and unwashed bottom clung to the mud cloth. Adaeze bit down on her tongue as she kept her chin lifted. One hand played at the loose knot she'd tied over her left shoulder. She had draped the stiff cloth as best she could to both conceal and offer up the look of allure. When she took a step, one bare leg pushed through the front opening—the way Nago had taught her to entice her reluctant boy-husband into making Adaeze the mother of the second in line to the throne.

At first, Adaeze had been confused by Nago's sudden change of tactics. Her cousin-servant trained Toure's daughters for months before their weddings to show no response in the marriage bed. To do so would suggest non-chastity. But after two months with no nuptial bed in the offing, Nago mapped out her war plan. Adaeze, as principal wife, must be the woman to deliver an heir to the Malian throne or be denied her queenly title. But Adaeze feared she was an even less adept pupil than before.

The mud cloth she wore tonight was not the fine silk of Cathay Nago had layered over her nakedness to stir a prince. The roughness of tonight's soiled mud cloth pricked at her body like a dozen of Nago's sewing needles. But no matter. Whatever had been thrown over her had to be carried as though it were the softest of silks, especially designed to stir the nature of a man. If only she had a drop of sandalwood perfume to smear behind her knees. That, too, had been one of Nago's tricks. How difficult was it going to be to lure the infidel to her body, and away from Bibi? Adaeze suspected all men weren't quite as reticent in these matters as her prince. Bibi hinted at bed tricks. What bed tricks? Other than those Nago had taught both of Toure's married daughters, how to dress, when to move and when not to, and how to adorn her assets,

Adaeze felt a void of knowledge. She clutched the edge of the mud cloth tighter to control a fresh shudder.

"Take it off." The barbarian, sitting cross-legged on a piece of soiled rug, looked up at her as he muttered in his strange language. "I want to see if those tits are as firm as I remember."

Adaeze's eyes fluttered, and she felt her knees buckle. Oh, no, Allah. She mustn't faint now. This Charbonneau person, illuminated only by a lantern, sat naked, his chest covered with a light sprinkling of the yellow fur. Praise to Allah, the stained brown garment Papa said the Europeans called pantaloons lay across his manhood, sparing Adaeze that awful sight.

The barbarian scowled, then brightened as his hand dipped underneath the pantaloons. "You looked good enough the other day for me to want a second look. Off!"

Adaeze jerked. The fool was shouting. She stared into his wide eyes and looked at his moistened lips. The man's face, the part not covered by that ghastly yellow fur, had turned the color of a pink sunrise. And more. Her boy-husband had never shown that look. Oh yes, once. But it was not for Adaeze. Never for her.

While the men were still at evening prayers in the first months of her marriage, and before success came to the conjugal bed, she'd slipped into the war room to retrieve a book on the geography of Mali when she spotted one of the king's generals. Adaeze remembered the shock that held her transfixed. The general sat in the teakwood chair reserved for important royal visitors. Stark naked. With his manhood on full display. The remembrance of that engorged member brought a fresh shake to Adaeze's shoulders. That member had been only centimeters from her kneeling husband's mouth. Instead of the limp stub of manhood the prince usually presented to her, this time, Adaeze saw the full length and girth of the princeling's claim to the throne. Adaeze's breath struggled between her chest and her throat to release itself as she stared at her husband. The boy's eyes were wide, his smile askew. Wetness leaked from a corner of his mouth as his lips formed a wide circle. He leaned in. *Oh, Allah, that is the look on the face of the barbarian this night!*

"What damnable thing is this? The wench is on the floor." The barbarian's booted foot stood only centimeters from her head. "The woman has fainted."

Her knees had failed her. Adaeze felt the roughness of the rug against her face. Its stench roiled her stomach and brought up a dry heave.

"Roll over, wench. You wanted this." The man slammed her to her back. "Begged for it."

Adaeze clamped her teeth shut, but the rest of her body worked on its own. Her eyes glued themselves closed. Hot air flamed her throat, and she could utter no sound. She needed to speak to this man. At least set her eyes upon him. Disarm him with a smile. More. She had to find a way to slip her arms around his neck, play her fingers around his ears just as Nago had instructed. Pull him close while she spread her legs. Nago's lessons paraded through her mind. Adaeze understood what to do, but her body responded with nothing. She struggled to ease a tiny breath between her lips. Good. Her fingers began to twitch. Now if she could order her eyes to open.

Snap. Something, someone, jerked open her makeshift mud-cloth gown and shoved the folds to the rug beside Adaeze. She felt hot breath. The barbarian fanning her breasts. She must open her eyes. They refused. Form her mouth into a smile. Trick him into mistaking her misery for pleasure. Her body denied her prayers. She felt hands, rough from outside work, squeeze her breasts, then race down her belly to grab at her knees. Barbarian hands jammed her legs to her hips, forcing air out of her belly. Adaeze prayed the moan that escaped had been heard by Charbonneau as ecstasy, not agony. One eyelid flickered, then returned to its job of shielding her eyes. A load, heavy as a half cart of bricks, crashed itself between her legs. Oh, Allah, the inside of her thighs hurt from the stretch. The twitching in her fingers moved to trembling in her hands. Something wet, the barbarian's tongue, licked at her belly and moved toward the nipples she had used to nurse her children. Fingers. His. One, two, maybe three, kneaded her breasts, then stroked across her body to grab at the hair on her private place. The fingers, his, slid lower, probing her scars of honor.

"What in the name of Christ Most Holy is this?" Charbonneau's fingers suddenly withdrew their unwanted attention. "Now I remember what I felt that first day. Woman, you've been cut!" The barbarian suddenly raised himself on his elbows.

Adaeze's eyes flashed open. Even through the furry hair on his face, she read the confusion.

"What damnable act did you do to deserve such a torture?" He rocked back on his haunches, splaying open Adaeze's legs farther than thighs were designed to go. One hand dropped in slow motion and traced over her scars a second time. "My God!" The man's shoulders shuddered.

Adaeze strained to decipher the French. She was certain the man had called upon his god. It could not be so. Infidels had no god. That look of revulsion upon the man's face was apparent. The words he'd strung together were lost to her, but one thing was evident. This barbarian—was backing away from her and moving closer to Bibi. A bolt almost as strong as wet-season lightning rammed through her body. The smile that had refused to work itself to her face now beamed. The eyes, once barely open, now glinted fake desire. Her arms, which had felt like iron, reached out to encircle the man above her and, with a strength she didn't know she possessed, pull him to her body. And with the one last trick Nago had instructed, Adaeze's hand searched for the barbarian's quickly deflating member, stroked it with a passion she did not feel, and guided the growing object inside herself. Charbonneau sprung to life.

A red-hot rod like that straight from the blacksmith's anvil jammed into Adaeze, reaching beyond her stomach, almost to her chest. The stink in her nose, his stink, the pounding in her ears, the pain in her private regions, the agony in her heart. No matter. She had performed her last royal duty. Bibi was saved, and now Adaeze could rest. Allah, the most merciful, shrouded her in blessed, beautiful darkness.

Chapter 10

Folashade's shoulders shook as she darted glances between the knee-high grass where Bibi hovered over a curled-up Adaeze and the Wolof guards ten meters distant who barked orders at their bewildered prisoners. She looked up at the sky. The sun was not yet in sight, but streaks of rose brushed away more of the lingering moonlight. Early mornings had always filled Folashade with a sense of renewal. A fresh day to conquer. Not this morning. Even the shackles now missing from her ankles brought her no reprise. Fear covered everything. What was happening to her, to her sisters, to all of them? Mercifully, the guards paid scant attention to the patch of grass where she stood as Bibi struggled to rouse a strangely vacant-eyed Adaeze.

"Bibi, hurry up." Folashade let the Persian words ease out of her mouth with the tiniest amount of lip movement. "Get Adaeze on her feet before the guards turn to us." A shiver wracked Folashade's body although this day threatened to be as hot as the last. "They're using the lash to move the women to their feet. Even on Nago." She flinched as she watched a Wolof snap the stone whip across her cousin-servant's left hip.

Folashade fixed on the horizon as Nago's shriek filled the air. The first curve of brightness that was the sun peeked back at her. The long night of horror was almost over, but what would this fresh morning bring as Nago whimpered? Those first three nights after Djenné had been ones of light sleep despite Folashade's weariness. Sleep, even in two-hour spurts, was a luxury she could no longer afford. Then came the first of those three dawns when her eyelids blinked open to the sound of spoken Wolof. Her heart clung to the fringes of hopeful promise. Surely, the king, frantic over the kidnapping of the royal court and his daughter-in-law, would have long since dispatched a war party. But as darkness gave way to light at each new awakening, Folashade heard no sounds of approaching warriors. No war drums threatening attack. No thunder echoing through the ground reflecting marching feet. Nothing. Folashade's hands grabbed the flesh of her thighs and pinched hard. If only she could cry. Allow the tears to flow. Anything that would remind her of the normal. But tears stuck in her fear. While her heart prayed for deliverance, her head knew better. Even though her sister pretended otherwise, Adaeze's father-in-law was no warrior, and the thought of the husband, the heir, leading a warrior troop forced the flicker of a grin onto Folashade's face. But if not the king or his weakling son, then who would lead the rescue on this the third sunrise of her captivity?

Folashade's hands dug into her legs as she squeezed her thighs to stop their trembling. She chanced another glance at her sisters. When Malick first carried a limp Adaeze from the barbarian's tent, the sun had been almost two hours from rising. As soon as the Wolof dumped Adaeze's naked body next to Bibi, who feigned sleep, Folashade felt the first full impact of that thing she'd read about in Papa's books on war. That thing the writers of military histories say soldiers feel on the eve of battle. Terror. Some horror had overtaken Adaeze, but what kind, she was not certain. Adaeze lay on the ground as motionless as a gazelle caught in the mouth of a lion.

The kidnap of a royal court was nothing new. But an outrage like this, the ruination of a future queen, had never been among the lessons of history Papa or D'bime imparted. Folashade stroked her hands, thigh to knee, to calm the roiling in her stomach. As somber as things were, the tumult in her belly told her it was worse than even her wildest imaginings. Folashade gazed at Bibi, still struggling with Adaeze. Bibi knew more than she was telling. Something so awful that only Papa's most secret books could describe the magnitude of the horror. Books that Folashade, even in her most thorough search, had yet to uncover. Adaeze must have found out that truth last night. This morning, Folashade's sister acted as though she were not of this world.

A rustle in the grass jolted Folashade toward her sisters. She stared down at Bibi in a half squat, one arm around Adaeze's waist, the other flailing to pull the princess to her feet. Bibi turned to Folashade, her face patchworked with panic as Adaeze's naked body eluded her grasp and slumped to the ground. Bibi's eyes read terror. Folashade had never seen such a look on her sister's face. Folashade turned to the sound of unshod feet crackling through the dry grass. Three of the young Wolof guards headed straight for her and the spot of earth concealing her sisters. "They're almost here!" Folashade shrieked her Persian just as the first youngster, surely no older by two than her own fourteen years, stormed toward her. She caught sight of the stone lash as the youth swung it in her direction, the boy-guard's face pinched in anger. She grunted as the whip grazed her right leg.

"Princesses, you're not in such favor this morning, now are you?" The second Wolof youth, more stout than his companions, swatted Folashade's cheek with the back of his hand.

With blood trickling from her scratched leg, Folashade stumbled sideways into a tangle of weeds. Her right foot caught in the mass, and she tumbled atop Bibi, who had sprawled herself over Adaeze. Crack! Crack! Crack! The whip landed all around the trio, snapping the grass to ground level. Now the entire encampment could see the disgrace of the nobles.

"Bambara bitches, on your feet or I will give you a proper taste of this lash."

The whip zinged past Folashade's head just as Bibi righted herself, planting her knees across Folashade's neck and hips. Folashade, her nose and mouth buried into Adaeze's left side just above the rise of her buttocks, gasped for breath. She squirmed against the weight of Bibi's body to free half her face. Folashade managed to squint open one eye. She caught a glimpse of Bibi's hands as they snatched at the hem of Folashade's own garment. Her sister's breath came in hot spurts as she began tearing off strips of cloth.

"Bibi," Folashade croaked from her still-trapped lips. The dress had been ripped to her knees. Bibi's hands moved out of Folashade's sight. She could only hear the sounds of cloth tearing, but this time, it was not her own garment. Suddenly, Bibi's hands moved back into view. Her sister's deft fingers laid a skinny strip of cotton against the cleft in Adaeze's buttocks, just centimeters from Folashade's trapped face.

Bibi's weight shifted and Folashade took in a half breath. "My sister cannot stand, you of low intelligence, until she has been properly covered." The wavering ups and downs in Bibi's voice studded the air. "What your master may or may not look upon is not for your lowly eyes."

"Master?" Disdain colored the words of the thinner guard. "Malick is my master, not that albino Frenchman."

Bibi slid her knee off Folashade's neck to her shoulder blade. Air flooded her lungs. Folashade twisted her head. Now both eyes were free. The stout youth stared down at the entangled bodies of the sisters. A third adolescent Wolof looked on and frowned. The trio's leader jerked his head toward Nago's line of prisoners, and the chubby young man scampered away as Malick stalked toward the group. As Folashade strained to free herself of Bibi, Malick took three quick steps, reached over, and shoved Bibi to the shorn grass, her legs lifting in the air. He reached down, grabbed Folashade's arm, and yanked her to her feet. Pain shot from her fingertips to shoulder.

"How dare you." Folashade's words faltered in the dust of her throat.

"You are playing a dangerous game." Bibi, covered in bits of grass and dust, scrambled to her knees. "There is more than one royal here who enchants your master." She righted herself to her hands and knees. Her chest heaved as she planted one foot on the ground and half kneeled near Adaeze.

"What is this hellacious commotion?" The infidel stamped his way through the grass, his fire stick pointed toward the ground. "Oh, that one." His eyes sifted through the carnage on the grass and bored into the curled-up Adaeze, her knees to her chest, the few scraps of cloth sheltering her body. The man's eyes hardened as his glare drifted from Adaeze to Bibi.

Bibi moved to stand, using as much of her slim body as she could to conceal Adaeze. "My sister is not for you. You will find much more pleasure in me." She took two faltering steps and positioned herself in front of the barbarian, standing no more than one meter away. Bibi swayed as her fingers fidgeted at a rip in the bodice of her under dress. With deliberate slowness, as though she'd practiced the move under Nago's tutelage of how to entice a man, Bibi spread the opening wide enough to expose a part of her left breast.

Folashade's eyes stared at the brown mound. "Bibi!" she shouted before she could take back the sound.

"All three of you." Charbonneau jerked his head from Bibi to Folashade. "Have you all been damaged down there? I am believing this indecency must be some sort of royal punishment." His lips screwed together. "Though I can't imagine any husband wishing such a horror on a wife."

That was a look of disgust on the white face.

Bibi sucked in a breath as her right hand moved back to the tear in the cloth. She began a steady tug at the opening. The sound of ripping cotton rattled into Folashade's ears like the keen piercing tone of a young goat feeling the first of the killing blade across its belly. Folashade threatened to repeat the goat's lament as she watched Bibi's full breast burst through the tear. Folashade bit her lip to keep the voice of shock within her throat. That Bibi was trying to exchange herself for Adaeze was plain. But Adaeze had failed in whatever she'd attempted with the yellow-haired man. Folashade wasn't sure if she wished Bibi better luck or not.

The barbarian stared at Bibi's naked breast, lifted a hand toward the nipple, stopped, and shook his head so hard the stringy fur on his head attacked the air. "I've had enough of all of you." The infidel turned his back on Bibi and headed toward Nago's group.

"Monsieur," Folashade called out as she fought to remember every French word she'd ever seen from Papa's books or heard from his lips. Her Wolof captor jabbed a fist into the small of her back. Never mind. She had to speak. "Clothes." Now, what was the word for "sister"? The Wolof lifted his knee to her buttocks and pushed. Folashade stumbled but kept her eyes on the barbarian. When the word refused to obtain a reaction, Folashade pointed to the still-silent Adaeze now being yanked to her feet by a fresh pair of young Wolof.

Adaeze's bare breasts bounced, and her head jerked right, left, right. Her left leg caught behind her right ankle as her knees spread open, revealing all the hair on her woman's place. Adaeze's eyes reflected nothing. Folashade jabbed her elbow into the belly of her guard. She had to get to Adaeze. Protect her. The guard grunted, tightened his grasp on Folashade's wrist, and wrenched her arm behind her back.

"Aah." Folashade's cry was low but deep.

The barbarian stopped, turned, stared, and scowled. "Clothes?" He'd understood. The man nodded toward Adaeze, who now slumped in the grasp of the two young Wolof, the side of her face lying against her left shoulder, her eyes staring but not seeing.

Folashade looked on as one of the young Wolof's gaze roamed Adaeze's form from breasts to the area between her legs. A crooked grin crossed his face as his hand slid toward her woman's place.

"You two, there!" the barbarian shouted, his forehead reddened. "What in the name of God Most Holy are you doing?" Spittle wet the fur on the man's chin. "Get a wrap on that wench. Cover her!" He raised the metal fire stick to his shoulders and swept it in the direction of the two Wolof.

The duo stood unmoving as though carved of ebony.

The sounds coming from Charbonneau's mouth were measured. "If you don't keep your hands to yourselves, and off my property, I'll have you stripped naked, lashed until your skin hangs in shreds, and then leave what's left of you here for whatever and whoever wants the carcass!" With a hard nod, the barbarian turned and stalked past the shackled line of women prisoners.

Whatever the man had said caused the two youths holding Adaeze to push her toward Folashade as though she were a venomous snake. Folashade ran to catch her sister before the girl hit the ground. She grabbed at her shoulder while Bibi reached for Adaeze's waist.

"Adaeze." Folashade resorted to Bambara. "Help us. If we're to get through, then you've got to be able to walk."

One of the young Wolof returned, ran up to Folashade, aimed his eyes at a shrub almost as tall as a tree, and dangled a mud-cloth wrap in Adaeze's direction. Folashade grabbed the heavy cotton and pushed Adaeze against Bibi while she quickly draped her sister in modesty. Even her sister's head was covered.

"Adaeze!" Bibi's voice commanded in Bambara. "Move your feet." Bibi stomped her own sandaled foot over Adaeze's bare toes. "Where are your shoes?"

Folashade tightened her grip on Adaeze, whose limp body felt as heavy as a hundred mud bricks. Never mind that Bibi had spoken the forbidden Bambara. Getting Adaeze moving was the only worry right now.

"Mmm," Adaeze murmured as she shifted her feet under her. She lifted her injured right foot. "Shoe?" she struggled.

"Yes! Yes!" A quick smile played across Bibi's face as she caught Folashade's eye. "Your shoes, but they're not important now. You're speaking! I'll give you my shoes if they'll help you walk."

Adaeze moved her eyes between her sisters and settled on Bibi. "Shoes?" She looked down at her feet. "I don't seem to have on any." Adaeze shook her head, the heavy mud cloth slipping to her neck. "Nago. I must speak to Nago. She is really derelict in her duties. If she weren't our mother's cousin, I'd have her whipped."

Folashade's hand dropped from Adaeze's body a second before Bibi released their sister. Adaeze's knees buckled but she remained upright. "Nago? Adaeze, she's over there and she's already felt the lash." Folashade shook her head.

"Nago?" Adaeze swiveled her neck in all directions, but her eyes never landed upon the hapless relative. "Yes, when I find her, I will instruct her to have ten pairs of shoes made for my wedding trousseau. And this dress she's made for me is much too rough for my skin." She stroked the mud cloth. "Cousin or not, she really must be punished for such an affront. And then there is her tardiness. Has she forgotten that she's to prepare a wedding trousseau for a future queen? We only have another two weeks before the first of my wedding ceremonies begin."

"Wedding trousseau. Punish Nago." Folashade stared at Adaeze, who turned to her, a smile on her face.

"You are still so very young." Adaeze laid that simpering face on Folashade again. "When you are to be married, as I will be within the fortnight, then you will understand the importance of a proper trousseau."

Folashade reached an arm to Adaeze's neck and pulled her head against her shoulder. Folashade stared at Bibi. Her middle sister stood with her shoes in her hand, her mouth agape.

"What does our sister speak?" Folashade mouthed. "Bibi, there is something amiss with her."

Bibi dropped to her knees and slipped the sandals over Adaeze's feet. "I'm not sure." She spoke to the trampled grass. "Her mind. I've heard that sometimes when there are great horrors, then the woman might have troubles with her memory." Bibi's eyes looked up at Folashade. "Whatever it is, you and I will deal with it later. Right now, we've got to get her moving. Those guards are leaving us alone for now, but they know we're speaking Bambara, and soon, they'll make sure we regret it." She jumped to her feet, grabbed Adaeze by the arm, and marched her forward.

"Are we off to another party before my wedding?" Adaeze took a step, then two. Her right knee trembled, straightened. With her feet under her, Adaeze staggered after Bibi. "I do love parties."

Folashade followed close behind.

Chapter 11

The squeal of the spotted hyena flicking through the canopy of overhead trees had long ago lost its impact to frighten Bibi. Yesterday, or was it the day before, one of the women from Adaeze's court died. Malick left her body for the leopards, the hyenas, and the lappet-faced vultures. Charbonneau hadn't shown a care. Bibi hadn't known the woman. Not really. She was one of the lesser servants barred from the royal tent in Djenné because of her insufficient rank. But she was young. When the thirst in Bibi's body relented for a moment or two during these last twenty-four hours, the thought of how the girl died filtered into her brain. The woman couldn't have been more than Bibi's own sixteen years, and unmarried. Oh yes, she had been one of the two not-so-pretty girls assigned to entertain the Wolof men.

"We'll bed down here for the night." The stout Wolof tormentor.

Keeping calculations in her head along with anything else from her other life was getting harder and harder for Bibi. But there had to be at least thirty Wolof for the forty or so captured Bambara. Thirty men and two Bambara girls. Though her stomach was empty of all but a few berries snapped up from a red-stemmed roselle, and a small hunk of bread, Bibi lost even that content as she doubled over.

"Now what ails you, Bambara?" the guard grumbled. "You've been given extra food."

Bibi swiped a hand across her lips. Days, or was it hours, ago, she'd given up answering back to the Wolof. The act drained too much energy. She and Folashade needed every ounce to keep up with Adaeze. Bibi looked over at her sister marching along in her borrowed sandals. Ever since the futile night Adaeze spent with the barbarian, and that disastrous next morning, Adaeze seemed a woman cleaved into two. She walked a steady line with growing strength despite the limited diet. She moved as imperious to her surroundings as the old queen. When Adaeze's mud-cloth garment gaped open, revealing a breast, or more, she ignored her shame and strode on as though she were fully garbed in court finery. But far worse than her ignored immodesty was her conversation, if the words coming from her mouth could be called that. It was as though Adaeze had never been kidnapped from Djenné.

"Set them down here. We'll spend the night by this watering hole." The barbarian, sweaty, strode into view, the almost-set sun behind him, some unfamiliar plant scenting the air.

Blessedly, Bibi had seen precious little of the man.

"You fools have already killed one of the merchandise. I'll be damned if I allow you to lose another." He looked over the prisoners as though inspecting for spoilage in a bin of overripe melons. The last rays of the setting sun glinted off something attached to a thick string suspended from his reddened neck.

Oh, Allah, Adaeze's bracelet! In the tumult of that night and its morning aftermath, Bibi had forgotten that Adaeze had been shorn of her jewelry as well as her clothes.

"Give that back!" The sounds gurgled out of Bibi's dry mouth. "You have no right to lay your hands on a royal ornament. No less wear it. It's a sign of rank." Her finger shook as she pointed at the infidel's chest.

Charbonneau swiveled in Bibi's direction. He looked over at Folashade, who was settling Adaeze on the ground, covered with soft vegetation. He turned his gaze to the still-standing Bibi and cocked his head. He frowned his non-understanding.

Bracelet. Jewel. Bibi had no idea of the French words. She turned a face to Folashade, praying to Allah that her sister could decipher her plea. Barely perceptible shakes of Folashade's braids dampened Bibi's scant hope.

"*Perle.* Jewwl." Folashade's face brightened as she barked out the French word.

Bibi scrunched the pieces of her torn dress together as she stepped closer to the barbarian. She laid her free hand across her forehead. She'd lost count of the number of days of dirt, sweat, and grime that caked her body. No matter how unruly her looks, she had to face down this scandalous man who dared dishonor everything royal. "That jewel belongs to my sister. You have no right to it." She jabbed a finger toward Adaeze.

The barbarian's laugh started out as a low rumble, gained momentum, and shook his belly and shoulders. He walked toward Bibi, bent close to her face, and dangled the Doudou ornament in front of her. His blue eyes sparkled.

"How dare you." If only she knew a few choice words of French. "May Allah send you to damnation and keep you forever from Paradise." Let him hear the forbidden Bambara. To be kidnapped was one thing, even shamed, but to bear witness to the desecration of a royal object was intolerable. Bibi grabbed for the bracelet.

The barbarian jumped back, holding the jewel just beyond Bibi's reach. "Oh, you are a fiery one, all right. So you believe this little pretty belongs to your sister." He stuffed the bracelet underneath his short tunic as he eyed the two bracelets on Bibi's own arm. "Let's see what you will do to earn this one back."

Bibi jerked up her chin. She deciphered none of his words, but she understood his meaning. Her protests were not being dismissed. He did not strike her down for speaking her native tongue. A sprinkle of hope. But this was a man who knew no honor. She watched Malick approach the two of them, that iron stick, his gun, slung over one shoulder. As she watched the man's shoulder swag as he neared, Bibi dismissed the Wolof as one not worth her best bargaining efforts.

"Monsieur, the ground is soft. Water is nearby. No signs we're being followed. I offer you apologies. My men were careless with that last wench. We do seek your permission to try another. I will guarantee greater care."

Charbonneau's face flashed annoyance. "Can't you see I'm busy with this one." He jerked his head toward Bibi. "Speak to me later." He wobbled his jaw in impatience as Malick backed away, nodding his head.

The barbarian turned back to Bibi, his words coming slow. "I'll say this for you princesses. Down there is an ungodly mess, but you all have tight-looking tits and beautiful faces." With a quick move, he slapped Bibi's protective arm from her ripped bodice.

Bibi sucked in small bits of air as her chest throbbed. Her eyelids flickered as the barbarian slipped his hand through the tear in her under dress. She held her breath as his finger stroked her. She grunted her knees to hold steady as barbarian fingers spread around her breast, squeezed, and moved it in a slow circle. A smile that reminded her of Doudou at his most lustful pasted onto Charbonneau's face.

Oh, Allah. Bibi's legs threatened to fail her, and her eyes clamped shut. She willed her eyes to seek his and ordered her knees to lock. With all of Allah's help, she had the chance to make right what Adaeze had failed. Through this last day, her mind had paid scant attention to pondering the whys of Adaeze's nonsuccess. But no matter how slim, here was a second chance. And more than a royal bracelet was at stake.

"I'll take you now," the barbarian growled in his indecipherable tongue. "Clean you up myself." His hand slipped off her breast to her arm. He pulled her through the tall grasses, past Nago's line of vacant-eyed women, beyond the shorter group of shackled and chained men who wore the look of those forsaken by Allah, and into the heart of the Wolof encampment.

The beginnings of night had fallen upon the group. The Wolof cooking fires blazed. Cooking fires intended for themselves and their ghost-skinned leader. Bibi's stomach had long ago lost its expectation of hot food, but her nose still remembered the pungent smell of roast wildebeest, and her mind recalled the successful Wolof hunt and kill of yesterday. The group's first fresh meat. Charbonneau paraded her past the firepits and headed her toward the watering hole. Her mouth too dry to salivate, she fixed her eyes on the back of his leather tunic. She would never allow these interlopers the pleasure of seeing her hunger for food they would never allow.

"Uhh." Bibi's ankle twisted as she stumbled over a piece of dried boar dung. The monster was leading her to the watering hole where the night-drinking animals might attack a stray human being. Her.

He tightened his already firm grip on her forearm as a bramble caught the jagged edge of her under dress. She'd feel his finger marks for days.

"Get some water and cleaning cloths in here right away!" The barbarian stopped cold, and Bibi plowed into his back. Praise be to Allah, Malick was not the Wolof in calling distance.

Her face was enveloped in his smelly shirt. She freed herself enough to watch the man pull back a flap attached to a long, wide strip of mud cloth strung between two trees, three hundred meters distant from the water. The meerkats were already dipping their faces into the watering hole. Antelope couldn't be far behind. As he yanked her inside the strung-together tent, she noticed weathered brown and beige patterning on a second piece of mud cloth attached to a higher branch, serving as a sagging, makeshift roof. Though he left the flap ajar, the interior of the structure remained in gloom. Bibi's eyes struggled to adjust. The barbarian, his fingers replaying their assault on her arm, marched her six paces forward. She tripped over something solid and box shaped. Her naked feet felt mud cloth underneath. A makeshift floor? He dropped her arm. Bibi rubbed at the soreness as she watched the man walk deeper into the recesses of his night shelter. She took in a breath now that Charbonneau had his back to her. She had to gather her wits. Bibi's eyes traveled the room. Behind her, and close to the flap opening, she made out the outlines of a box big enough to hold both herself and Folashade. She strained to look. The black-and-white striping of zebra hide covered the lid. She remembered that box. On the few days when she and her sisters had been marched close to the head of the line, Bibi watched two, sometimes three, Wolof men in their thirties carry the cumbersome-looking thing on their shoulders. Perhaps whatever was inside held the key to Bambara freedom. She took a small step to get a closer peek just as the barbarian struck a match. He applied it to the lantern in his hand. As some of the gloom faded, the man set the light at Bibi's feet.

With the flickering flame, she took in the measure of the room. Perhaps nine meters by ten. A cot lay behind her, just to her right and within touching distance of the zebra trunk. Charbonneau had stationed her in the center of the room.

"Here." Charbonneau spoke to a Wolof approaching the doorway, his muscular body blocking out the brightness of the cooking fires.

The warrior invader held a large, scarred gourd with both hands. Strips of cotton cloth lay doubled over his bare left arm.

The barbarian grabbed at the objects. "Close the flap after yourself. Keep your distance."

In the renewed dimness, Bibi stared after the shadowy figure of the barbarian as he made his way toward her. Her ears registered the man's heavily accented but passable Wolof. She'd remind Folashade to stick to Persian.

"Sit." He squatted near the gourd, his matted sun-colored hair brushing his shoulders. Charbonneau dipped a scrap of cloth into the wooden basin. Water dripped from the cotton and down the man's sleeve-covered arm as he held the scrap aloft.

Bibi, directly across from him, held her face stiff as she eased herself to her knees. While he still squatted, she could meet his eyes with her own. Dare to demand the respect due a noblewoman. She laid her braceleted left arm in the scanty folds of her under dress while she reached for the washcloth with her right.

He jerked the rag away. "Oh no. This is a job I'll do myself." Lantern shadows played across his face. He wet his lips with his tongue as his eyes widened. "Now, where to start? Oh yes, at the top, as the bottom is as damaged as your sister's. An unfit sight for any man to see." More French than Wolof.

Bibi ran the French sounds through her head. She'd understood too little, but she couldn't allow this man to know that truth. Time. That's what she needed most. Time to sort out the ways of this uncivilized creature. What he wanted. What he was thinking. Some Europeans were educated and could reason. Papa had said so, though he suspected their ways were inferior to those of the people of Timbuktu. Could this barbarian possibly be one of the educated ones? She had only minutes to uncover the truth of him. Adaeze, Folashade, all of them, depended upon her to outwit this man. She stared into his eyes.

With a move so quick, Bibi almost toppled to the mud-cloth floor, Charbonneau grabbed the neck of her dress and, with both hands, ripped it open to her waist.

"Allah." She swallowed back her prayer. She punched her fisted hands into her sides and inched her knees apart. He stared at her nakedness. The Doudou look planted itself on his face again.

Charbonneau's smile was crooked as he raised himself to his knees. Now he towered over her by a good eight centimeters. Bibi's breath rattled in her throat as she waited. The man drizzled water from the cloth over her forehead, around her cheeks, down her nose, and finally across her lips. She blinked water from her eyes as he dropped the cotton back into the gourd. He sucked in his lips as his fingers fumbled with the strings on the front of his short leather tunic. He dropped the garment to the floor and slipped his undershirt over his head. Bibi's knees failed her. First the left trembled, then the right buckled. She sank to her haunches, her hands moving to cover her breasts, her mouth opened to catch every gasp of air. She felt light-headed. She closed her eyes and her body swayed. Her forehead brushed against rough cloth. The feel of radiating heat saturated her face. Her eyes flickered open, and she stared directly at the growing bulge in the barbarian's trousers. She clamped her teeth over her tongue as she jerked herself upright. If pain would keep her alert, and away from this, she would bite her tongue until it bled.

"Not yet. We'll get to that later." The barbarian's hand slipped to his man place. He reached for her shoulders and pulled her back to her knees.

Charbonneau turned to the gourd and rewet the rag. Bibi steadied herself, the shreds of her dress in her hands. Oh, Allah. Doudou's musty smell stormed her nostrils, and the picture of her husband entwined with his favorite concubine jumped out of its hiding place. Doudou had made Bibi watch the two in their lovemaking. Surely an affront to Allah. "Look and learn so you are not totally useless to me in the night," her husband had growled. If she could be spared that thing Doudou demanded of his favorite. Her mouth over his man place and those slurping sounds.

Bibi fought down the dry heave before it shook her body. Charbonneau, now running the cleaning cloth over her breasts and belly, hadn't noticed her shaking. Her eyes fluttered for an instant just as he ripped open her dress from waist to bottom edge.

Oh, Allah, preserve. Let the lantern light hide her woman's place from this man's eyes as long as possible.

Charbonneau kept his eyes on her breasts as he pushed off his pantaloons. She fixed her gaze on his chin. Her arms ached as though they had minds of their own as she battled her muscles to comply with his demands. He pulled her to his fur-streaked chest. Water ran in rivulets down her back from the cloth in his hand. He pressed her breasts hard into his chest.

Merciful Allah! She could not do this thing. Allow her death. Her throat seized as Folashade's face burned through her eyes and into her brain. No. She could not die. She was unworthy of Allah's mercy. Her obligation was to sacrifice herself. She had but one prayer for Allah. Give her the strength to do what she must.

Chapter 12

The palest color of mango sneaked around the flap openings. Dawn was about to put in an appearance at last. Bibi lay as still as she could in Charbonneau's arms, his man place spooned against her bare bottom, quiet—for now. She'd lain awake all this night, struggling to hold her body together as the barbarian drifted off after each of his four attacks on her. This morning, she feared any movement would stir a fifth. All her tears had dried inside her. Now she understood the why of Adaeze. No woman could remain in a body that no longer belonged to her. Not when a man had commandeered it in the most foul manner. Adaeze had no choice. Bibi understood. Adaeze's mind had to save itself. It fled to another place, a place that wrapped its arms around her, keeping her safe and warm. Last night, Bibi had gone to the same spot. Allah ordered them both to return to the world of duty. Bibi battled the wildebeest and made her way back. Adaeze could not.

"Twelve? You say you've killed a dozen Egyptian plover." Malick. He must have stood just outside the closed tent flap. "If that gun was in my hands, I would have brought down four dozen more." His voice was low as though he spoke more to himself than one of his underlings. "As it is, these twelve will be enough to feed fewer than half of us." Malick raised his voice. "I see you've bagged an antelope. With our other kill, and now antelope, we may have enough meat to keep us halfway through this trek."

"Halfway?" A young but rough Wolof voice. "You didn't tell us we'd go hungry."

"Tell you? There is no reason I must tell you anything." Annoyance burst out of Malick's voice.

"You, and the elders, explained they had a plan like no other. And when we succeeded in this venture, our clan, indeed all of Rufisque, would receive great bounty," the less cultured voice groused. "Everyone, not just our village, would concede that Rufisque harbored the most clever, the most daring, the most ambitious of all the Wolof."

Bibi's ears, the ones that had gone deaf in the pain of last night, picked up every word of the young warrior who dared challenge Malick.

"Timbuktu was the great secret prize. Not scrounging nearby villages for stragglers. Small groups of Fula, Serer, or Mandingo. Timbuktu was where the real treasure lay." The young voice lifted in a quick laugh. "The people of Timbuktu would not know we were on the way. We'd snatch them before they could raise a decent alarm. Bring them back to Dakar. Sell them to the infidels for a great price. Our village would be the pride of all."

Charbonneau's breathing became less regular. Bibi tightened her belly muscles. Please, Allah, allow this man to stay asleep long enough for her to sort out the rift among her Wolof capturers. Any weakness in the barbarian would help her push the man into a bargain.

"And so it will." Malick's voice rolled through the tent flap, but this time carried a calm reassurance. "But we shall not reverse our course and head back to Timbuktu."

"But the elders spoke of the simplicity of the plan. Enter a contract with the barbarian. Steal a hundred Bambara men and boys. You recall our great excitement, Honored Malick," the younger voice poked at his leader.

"Karem, your youth forces you to dream of old. As with all things, it is the dreams supported by wisdom that come true. That you do not yet possess." The uptick in Malick's words announced he expected more argument.

Bibi held her breath as Charbonneau moved his arm.

"The stories the elders told of Timbuktu." Karem did not disappoint. "The men were reputed to be straight of limb, facile of mind, and draped in cloth of gold. They lost their power, but to this day, no one knows the whereabouts of their wealth."

Malick poured more feigned reassurance into his voice. "Those tales told by our elders are all true. The great Mansa Musa did make Timbuktu the wealthiest place on Allah's earth. That great emperor brought down the economy of mighty Egypt with all the gold he possessed." Malick paused just enough for Bibi to take in three soft breaths. "But, Karem, in your youthful ignorance, you allowed your mind to dwell on only the glories of Timbuktu's past, not what happened later."

Bibi keened her ears, but she heard no response from Karem.

"Many, many tribes, Tuareg, Moroccan, the Songhai. So many. And each took the gold, the gems, the wealth of that city. Karem, I do not ask you to doubt that bits and pieces of gold may still exist, but those items are well hidden under the sands. The Timbuktu of your mind is long gone, and I will hear no more about it." Malick's voice swept back to one of authority. "Go and bother me not about your dangerous proposal. Our village has a contract with this man, and as honorable men, we shall fulfill it."

She heard the man's footfalls walking away from the makeshift tent.

The bile rushing to Bibi's throat from her nearly empty stomach doubled its taste of sourness. Charbonneau may not hold all the power in freeing the Bambara from capture. She, Adaeze, Folashade, all her tribeswomen, were in uncertain hands. One misstep could prolong this disaster. The barbarian's breath brushed her neck. She lay as still as she could, fighting down her own breathing. Charbonneau shifted his body. She had little time to think, but think she must. The kidnapped Bambara were being taken to the land of the Wolof, far to the west. To Dakar. Little of this kidnap plan made sense. They were to be held for ransom or bounty on the coast but far from the treasury of Mali. That would complicate the delivery of the ransom. Adaeze's dull father-in-law, the king, would never find his way to the coast. Too many questions. Things she needed to sort out. Bibi shuddered.

The barbarian grunted, and Bibi grabbed at her stomach. The dead servant and the horror the girl must have gone through before she mercifully died eased into her mind. Bibi stared at the mud-cloth floor, its splashes of brown and black conjuring up the loose garment worn by the hapless servant girl. Bibi gnawed at her upper lip.

"Uh." He was awake.

Please, Allah, let there be no more. "Ahh." Bibi bit down on her tongue too late. She could not retrieve her frivolous prayer.

The barbarian's fingers spread wide in a stretch, using her hip to ease himself to his elbows. "Mm. Is that morning I see?" He bolted upright. "It's damnably late. What hellacious reason kept Malick from alerting me?"

She lay still and brought up her sleep breathing. Bibi tried to imitate the snore of Nago. She felt the barbarian's eyes upon her.

"But maybe not too late for one more, Princess." His voice softened as he pulled her back from the edge of the cot, turning her on her back. "Princess, and that you are, but I must call you something else. What is your name?" His words purred.

Bibi held her eyes closed tight. He was speaking to her, but all in his own tongue. He hovered over her, his hand on her belly, his face only centimeters from her own. Now could be the time to start the bargaining. She fluttered her eyes open.

"What is your name?" All French from the man.

She repeated the sounds in her head. One could be the French word for "name." She had to be clever. She answered in Wolof. "You wish to know my name."

He nodded. "Yes. Your name." His eyes searched her face, a hint of satisfaction on his lips.

Her mouth twitched a tiny smile in return. "Bibi. My name is Bibi."

"Bibi." He pointed to her. "So, you are called Bibi." He stroked his forefinger down her chest. "I've heard African names have meanings. Tell me, Bibi, the meaning of your name."

French again, and she'd only understood two words other than "Bibi." She forced her lips into a smile. He still hovered over her, pinning her to the cot. She touched his chest and, with a gentle push, gained enough room to lift to bent elbows.

"How are you called?" She fretted she hadn't gotten enough of the sounds right.

A look of pleasure spread to Charbonneau's eyes as he rolled away from her and sat up on the cot. He reached for a stuffed cushion and propped it behind his back. "You want my name. Thundering damnation. You are a Black wench who can speak French." His laugh rumbled into her ears as he rubbed her thigh. "Bibi, you are quite the woman. As for me, I am Charbonneau." All French.

Bibi kept her eyes on the man as he reached over, retrieved his pantaloons, leather tunic, and shirt from last night; rolled them together; and pushed them behind her shoulders. Monsieur Charbonneau. She'd gotten his name. He didn't seem angry this morning. She thanked Allah for showing her how to leave her body. Now she was back and had to remain. Yet, it could be too soon to start her plan, rudimentary though it was. As a first step, he had to be willing to trade Adaeze's bracelet for Bibi's pretended eagerness in bed.

Charbonneau kissed her nose as his hand moved down to her woman's place. "Thanks be to God Most Holy, you do not bear all the scars of your sister."

She turned her face away from his kisses and wriggled her left arm against his shoulder. "I am hungry." Food popped into her mind to give her time to think. Adaeze's bracelet was crucial for this first step of her plan for freedom. Charbonneau nodded. "Of course, you're hungry, Princess. Bibi. Me, too." He laughed. "I think we forgot all about dinner last night. At least I did." He searched her face. "Praise be to Holy Jesus, you did not recoil from me as did your sister." He stroked her woman's place. A scowl cascaded down his face. "Tell me, Bibi, why do you and your sister have such awful markings?" His French was unintelligible.

"Monsieur Charbonneau." Malick. "Forgive the interruption, but I have readied the captives to march before the sun rises much more beyond the horizon."

Charbonneau eased off Bibi just as her stomach set up its last death rattle of hunger. "I will alert you when I'm prepared to travel. Now bring food and drink to the tent."

Bibi deciphered every third word of her tormentor's mélange of French and Wolof. The barbarian had asked for food. But she knew not if he'd included her in his morning meal. Her hunger kept getting in the way of good thinking. And all the Bambara depended upon her. She grabbed Charbonneau's hand and laid it across her belly. With her own hand atop his, she moved the two in little circles. She turned her eyes to him and pasted her best expectant look upon her face. She uttered the Wolof word for "food," but before he could react, she chanced French. "Sisters." The grumble from her stomach filled the tent. Thoughts struggled to get into her head. She moved his hand to her woman's place. She fought her smile muscles into a flicker of movement.

He cocked his head toward her as his lips twitched. His hand jerked lower on her woman's place. She felt him fingering her scars of honor. His forehead crinkled into a frown, the line between his brows lay deep.

"What did you do to deserve this?" His hands probed her honor scars again.

The muscles in Bibi's stomach tightened into a knot. Something bothered this man. Something so awful, it quieted his man want. That would never do. Making Charbonneau believe she could please him was key to her forming a plan. She pondered the only word she'd understood in his barrage of French. He was curious about her sister's badge of honor. "Adaeze."

He pulled his hand from her and sat up against the cushion, his arms folded across his chest. He stared between her naked legs. "Yes. Your sister." He spoke slowly in Wolof. He shook his head as though he were searching for the correct Wolof word. "Cut. Knife. Hurt. Your sister." His hand moved back to her scars. "Why?"

Bibi fought to keep her stare at him modest. Oh, Allah. Looking at his fur-pocked face, Bibi understood. Nago had been right! This barbarian objected to her woman's place because she had not had the full ceremony. The one Nago insisted all of Toure's daughters undergo. Every outside part of Adaeze had been cut away, along with a few inside jabs, as was appropriate for a future queen. But Bibi had ignored Nago's pleadings and begged Papa to remember her mother's last wish for her girls. No ceremony. Papa had agreed, but only partially. Most of Bibi's woman's place remained intact. Only the pleasure part had been slashed away. And now her only hope to save herself, Folashade, Adaeze, Nago, that poor servant girl, and the other Bambara all evaporated because Bibi had insisted upon her own impurity! As he did with Adaeze, Charbonneau was rejecting her, and the freedom of them all. Long-unused tears flooded her eyes as something squeezed her lungs free of almost all air.

The barbarian startled. "My beauty, don't cry." He kissed her fore-head. "Did your husband do this? With a woman like you, how dare the bastard."

His French words tumbled in her head. His words, along with what felt like a kiss of distress, added confusion in her head. More loud rumbles from her belly.

"Malick," Charbonneau shouted, "get some food in here."

Bibi took a breath of relief. The man would share his food with her. That was a good thing, was it not? If only she could focus.

Footfalls outside the tent signaled Malick's arrival. At last. "Monsieur Charbonneau. I have brought food."

"Enough for two, I trust. Slip the platter underneath the flap." Charbonneau climbed his naked body over Bibi. "And make ready for departure in thirty minutes." He retrieved the platter and moved toward her. "Here. Try a bit of this."

Even though it was roasted two nights ago, scented wildebeest flavored with roselle shook Bibi's dormant stomach. Toasted maize mounded next to the haunch of meat and sprinkled with the green tips of the roselle lay beside a drinking gourd made of the same dark wood as the platter. Charbonneau took care not to dislodge the teetering gourd as he knelt beside her. Though the drinking vessel was empty, Bibi's stomach roared to life. She dipped two fingers into the maize.

He held up the palm of his hand. "First"—he reached over the food platter to the zebra chest—"let me retrieve one little article." His hands fumbled with the lock and creaked open the lid. He reached inside.

Bibi inched her fingers toward her lips as she peered over his shoulder. Fire sticks. As Charbonneau turned his back to her, she sucked in the maize. Allah, at his finest, could not have granted her a grander gift. As her eyes flickered gratitude, she watched the barbarian plunge his arm deeper into the zebra trunk. Bibi counted four, five, six, eight, guns. Except for the carnage on the beach at Djenné, and the few of her captors allowed to forage for meat, she could not recall anyone other than the barbarian carrying a gun. So, this was where he kept those killing rods. All to himself. He did not trust his Wolof henchmen.

"Ugh." Charbonneau's smile faded as he tugged at something deep in the interior. "There you are." The barbarian slowly extricated his hand.

Bibi licked her fingers once more as she watched Charbonneau. He lifted something aloft. In the gloom of the shelter, she made out the form of a bottle. Still on his knees, the barbarian rotated a dark-colored container in his hands. Perhaps water. That would help wash down the gazelle she longed to taste. The inside of Bibi's mouth felt as gritty as the Sahara.

He wrapped his fingers through short, protruding wires and pulled a cork from the bottle. He grabbed the gourd and poured a liquid into it.

Odd. Water suitable for drinking was not this color. Bibi flinched as the man grabbed the back of her head and pressed the container to her mouth. Her throat tightened but could not escape the torrent of liquid Charbonneau forced through her lips. A trail of fire leapt across her tongue, plunged down her gagging throat, flashing flames from chest to belly. Cough after cough wracked her body. *Oh, Allah. The barbarian has used me and now poisoned me.*

Charbonneau's laugh worsened the inferno. "Libations in a woman always improves her performance."

His French made little sense. Her tongue flickered in and out all on its own. Poison, for sure, but if she could convince the barbarian to find the antidote, then, maybe, she would live. Bibi pulled her hand from her throat and waved the Doudou bracelet toward Charbonneau.

The barbarian, now on his feet, jerked around, his face showing curiosity, then awareness. The corners of his mouth turned up, then flared into a broad smile.

"Ah yes, Princess, I can grasp your intentions. You wish to bargain with me. Your bracelet for your freedom." He peered down at her face. "You see, I do understand you, but there is just one small thing." The barbarian's rough chuckle landed in her ear as he turned back to the zebra trunk. "I already have the emerald you are using to entice me."

Bibi closed her eyes to suck in the first breath of cleansing air as it made its way past her lips and into her throat. The rapid heartbeats slowed in her chest. She eased her eyes open. "Oh, Allah. No." Her lids felt heavy. She couldn't force her lips closed as she stared at what Charbonneau held aloft in his right hand. Jumbled stones, some almost the size of Niger River rocks, gleamed even in the half darkness of the tent.

"I retrieved this little trinket from its hiding place in one of the beach tents. I must say, your precious jewel was not well hidden."

Nago! How careless the woman had been.

A chain cobbling together stones that shot sparks of brilliant green across the top half of the barbarian's face swung from his fingers. *The Doudou necklace! Oh, Allah!* Her best bargaining chip was in the hands of this infidel. Bibi's breathing rattled her own ears as Charbonneau grinned at her. He eased his body next to her.

"I'll wager this belonged to you and not your sister. The man who gifted this was thanking his woman for extraordinary service." His eyes glinted as he aimed his French words at her. The man took both hands and spread the necklace wide over his bare leg. "Not that you've reached those exalted heights. But, in you, Princess, I do see potential."

Bibi shook her head. His words beat into her ears, but even if he had spoken flawless Wolof, she would have understood nothing. Her stomach felt as though it carried ten mud bricks. She couldn't save all the Bambara. She understood that now. But, please, Allah, allow her to gain the freedom of a few. Adaeze. She had to save at least the uncircumcised Folashade. If the barbarian discovered her youngest sister's disgrace, he might throw her to Malick.

"Let's give this another try." The barbarian brushed the necklace aside as he reached for the gourd.

Bibi turned her head from the offending stench. Water for drinking held no odor. Her tongue yearned for the coolness of trickling water, her body ached for its refreshing powers. But the water smelled of rotten grapes. He pressed the half-full gourd to her lips and rust-colored drops trickled into her mouth.

Ugh. Bibi jerked. Not water. Instead, the taste of fermented fruit assaulted her tongue. This time, she made out distinct flavors. Like melon, but not a melon she'd ever before tasted. Far worse than the taste of berries once chewed by goats, a running river of fire erupted over her tongue, licked its way to the back of her mouth, and sent its inferno rampaging down her throat. She turned to spit.

Laughter rolled through the barbarian's body. "No, no, Bibi. That would be a waste of a good Burgundy I brought all the way from Dijon. Try again." He grabbed the back of her head and forced more of the liquid into her mouth.

Bibi squirmed to free herself. Why was the European offering her a drink of spoiled fruit that burned? Perhaps . . . She pulled away her fists planted against his chest. Poison! The barbarian intended to drown her in poison or at least pour enough of some potent drug into her to render her helpless. Immobilize the women to tame them for the transport to the west. She grabbed the man's wrist with both hands and pulled down hard. The more she struggled, the stronger his hold on her head. He forced open her mouth and rushed more poison down her throat.

Bibi sputtered, fought for breath, swallowed, and sputtered again. The liquid flamed her tongue, throat, and belly. His drug had laid Adaeze mindless, but he had allowed the girl to live. Adaeze's virtue was there for him to see and touch, and in his eyes, verify her worthy of life and a hefty ransom. Bibi was different. This barbarian intended to kill her because her natural woman's state was a direct affront to his god, or more. She could never bring him the bounty he sought.

Charbonneau's eyes danced in delight at her misery as he lowered the half-empty gourd. "Now we're ready for business." French.

Bibi's hands stroked upward on her throat. Her tongue struggled to cleanse the poison from her teeth. She cared little about the man's words. It was too late.

"For you." He reached for the necklace that had slid half off his leg. "You wear one last time. You be good to me. You wear thirty minutes."

Bibi clutched at her neck as the poison strangled her breath. She sought his eyes. The barbarian stared at her, waiting. Yes, she understood his Wolof, but she cared little.

He pointed to her woman's place, then suspended the necklace between his two forefingers. He jiggled the ornament at her. "You do special things for me when you wear the necklace for one half hour."

He taunted her. Offering her the jewel in exchange for some Allah-forbidden game he wanted to play, a game probably more despicable than any of the onerous demands that even Doudou made. No, this was a barbarian trick. After she'd satisfied his unholy desires, with the poison ravaging her belly, she'd be dead long before the necklace ever adorned her neck. There would be no salvation for her sisters.

Change. A new plan. One last prayer to Allah. Grant her the wisdom to turn the infidel's murderous attack into a successful rescue of Adaeze and Folashade. "No. I don't want to wear the necklace." She slowed her Wolof to toddler speed as she stroked Doudou's bracelet. "This, I want to keep."

"Oh?" Charbonneau's face turned into confused frowns. His eyes gleamed understanding, then confusion. "You like bracelet more than necklace." He frowned. "Why?"

The burning in her body quieted. Papa had never discussed the intricacies of dying with his daughters. But a calmness before taking the last breath might well be the first sign of imminent death. But calm she felt even as the lie flashed fully formed in her head. "The necklace was intended for my sister." She swept her hand around the jewel. Bibi waited for Charbonneau to decipher her Wolof. "For Adaeze. Not me." Allah would forgive a lie if the cause were just. "The bracelet was to be mine. It was to be a trade." She held her palm under the bracelet. Her fingers tickled against the fur on his chest. Her heart raced, but she forced herself to look into those unholy blue eyes.

The barbarian squinted and pursed his lips, the workings of his mind almost visible in the changing expressions on his face. He laid the necklace back across his knee. "You don't want the necklace because it belonged to your sister." All French. "You want bracelet because it was intended for you. Odd." All Wolof.

She chanced a nod of her head while the churning in her belly fought the burn now simmering to warmth. The poison no longer rumbled through her as all-consuming. What was required of her next would bring death as an Allah-blessed relief. Far better to lie in Allah's Paradise than walk the earth mindless. Adaeze. Bibi eased air into her nose before she sought Charbonneau's eyes. When his stare matched hers, she pointed first to the bracelet, then down to her woman's place. "Allow." Her Wolof threatened a strangle in her throat. She parted her lips to suck in a stream of air. "Allow me to wear the bracelet the rest of the trek, and I will show you all the wonders of a Timbuktu woman." She transformed her despair into the breathiness Nago had instructed was an essential wifely duty. "Marvels you've never before known." She ran her tongue over her dry upper lip. She would be dead soon after he discovered the lie of her words.

The left side of the barbarian's mouth lifted into a smile. "Timbuktu woman. I've heard wonders once lived in Timbuktu. In the long ago." His lips twitched as he whispered his Wolof. "I hold you to your promise." He slid the bracelet up her arm. "Is your name story a part of your special powers?"

Bibi's fingers went to the bracelet, her thumb caressing the center ruby. "Bibi. My name means"—she captured his eyes—"daughter of a king. Bibi means virtuous noblewoman"—Allah will understand and forgive the lie—"trained in special arts designed to give her ruler husband more pleasure than even in his wildest imaginings." *Now, Allah, grant the miracle of life for Folashade, and the joy of death for Bibi.*

Chapter 13

Pulled shreds of antelope sauced with boiled peanuts decorated Adaeze's eating gourd. Antelope, always Adaeze's favorite, now threatened to disrupt her stomach before she'd taken even the first bite. She clamped a hand to her mouth and turned her head. She caught the last of the fading sunset just as the battle between stomach and mouth turned violent. Adaeze, sitting on the soiled eating mat, rolled to her knees, her face aimed at the grass on the plot of earth where the group made camp. Despite her best efforts to keep the morning's meal of groundnut inside her, the entire content flew to the ground, through the air, and over the bare feet of one of her royal guards.

"Wench, I'll not lose you now. Not when we're this close to getting something worthwhile for all the trouble you've cost us these last two months." The man's Bambara sounded strangely like Wolof.

If Adaeze hadn't known better, she would have sworn the rather rude guard was addressing a fellow servant in the tongue of the Wolof. She'd really have to speak to her husband about replacing this uncouth fellow.

"Now, eat, Bambara wench. Malick says you must look particularly good to the buyers in Dakar." The man lowered himself to a squat in front of Adaeze and reached for her shoulders. He pulled her to her knees. The guard grabbed a handful of antelope from Adaeze's eating platter and aimed it at her mouth.

Adaeze blinked at the youth's audacity. Putting his hand on a royal, unforgivable. There was something to be done about such an affront. She'd sort out his punishment when her stomach settled.

"Your mind has no doubt fled, you ridiculous ignoramus." Bibi's voice came from somewhere above and behind Adaeze. "That my sister is ill must have escaped your blind eyes. Stuffing more food into her will only make her worse. You may then bid farewell to your precious ransom."

Adaeze shook her head. Something about her middle sister seemed off. Bibi, dear Bibi. That girl had often stressed Papa and Nago with her failure to guard her tongue. But in the last few weeks, though it might have been months, Bibi hadn't been herself. Of course, Adaeze's sister was a devout follower of Islam, but Adaeze had often watched her sister rocking to and fro on her haunches praying to Allah to allow her to die. How odd. But all these thoughts, along with the frenzy in her stomach, alerted Adaeze. Best to push all these annoying thinking fragments out of her mind.

The guard scooped up another handful of something that smelled of camel dung. A fresh retch wracked her body from shoulder to knee. This incompetent could not be halted from forcing food into her. Adaeze sighed. This Wolof had to be a minion of Nago. The man must have mistaken Adaeze for the too-skinny-for-a-royal bride, Folashade. Adaeze pushed the guard's hand away just as her stomach let loose another round of the morning's breakfast.

"Folashade," Adaeze managed between gasps, "get Nago. This idiot of a man has confused the two of us. I'm not the one who needs to be fattened for my wedding." A sharp pain, but one cushioned by fog, harbored in Adaeze's head. Folashade wasn't moving.

"Yes, I'll fetch Nago in a moment." But Folashade's feet made no movement, and her Wolof words sounded hollow. More, she cast strange looks over Adaeze's shoulder toward the nearby Bibi.

Bibi stepped in front of Adaeze and next to the unruly guard, who grunted to his feet. "You. Get us water. We will tend to my sister."

The man used his dusty bare foot to slide the plate of antelope along the ground, dislodging bits of food onto the eating mat. "Water, you will have." He glared at Bibi. "But if you do not clean her well, and we do not get our price, then the price you will pay will be beyond your imaginings." His dull, flat eyes narrowed. "I've not survived these two months through sand, crocodiles, savanna, and jungle to lose our big prize now. I am under orders to make certain you three Bambara wenches glisten and gleam when we reach Dakar tomorrow."

Price. This untrained guard did talk foolishness. His understanding must be so poor he had mistaken price for ransom. Adaeze tapped at her ears. She kept the worry to herself, of course, but in these past few weeks or so, sometimes sounds did not reach her ears. She only caught bits and pieces of conversation. But today, the guard's mention of Dakar had landed strongly in her ear. More strangeness. The man spoke of Dakar. Everyone knew that city lay far to the west of Djenné, in the land where the Mandinka ruled for a thousand years. Papa had been there a time or two. Europeans were swarming to the place, Papa disclosed. He had set eyes upon a few himself, and also on one or two of their enormous ocean craft. But Dakar was far away from this camping ground where the king had sent her to summer.

"What a surly man. I am sorry, but he must be replaced," Adaeze called after the guard's retreating back. Her stomach quieted for a moment. She eased herself cross-legged on the mat, her hand over her belly.

Adaeze turned to Bibi, who lowered herself to sitting. "I really don't care for this vacation spot one bit. Bibi, tell Nago to order the bearers to return us to Djenné. I feel I really must rest before my lying-in."

"Lying-in?" Folashade's whispered words were loud enough to be heard five feet in all directions. The girl dropped to her knees on

Adaeze's other side. She grabbed her sister's hand and held it against her cheek. "But, sister dear, you cannot have a lying-in."

Sister dear. It was unlike Folashade to ever address Adaeze in that manner. Nor was it her habit to lay a hand against her cheek. That was the mark of a tender, refined lady. Nago's lessons hadn't reached that far into Folashade's training. "Of course, there will be a lying-in." Adaeze caught the look of puzzlement, mingled with fear, on Folashade's face. Adaeze leaned over to Bibi, cupped her hand, and whispered in her middle sister's ear.

"I misspoke. Of course, Folashade does not understand the whys of a woman's lying-in, but that's what I will be doing in about seven months, I'd say." She giggled.

Adaeze eased away from Bibi. But instead of the relief she expected to see on the girl's face after Adaeze issued her apology, Bibi looked more like the king had lost all of Mali in one minor war battle. Perhaps she should rephrase her apology. Never speak of such topics in the presence of an uncircumcised female.

"Are you ill?" Adaeze stared at Bibi. "Both you and Folashade have been struck by some strange malady at the vacation spot. We really must return to Djenné. I do not like this place." Bibi, her face lined in sorrow, slowly shook her head as her eyes looked over Adaeze's right shoulder straight at Folashade.

"Look, you two. I can understand your reluctance to share your true feelings with me. You loathe this vacation spot where the king has sent us. And now this has happened." Adaeze didn't bother to fight back her smile as she whirled to face Folashade. "I know this is not a proper topic of discussion in front of you, but you will soon be married to Prince Amiri." Adaeze turned back to Bibi. "And, yes, I believe it appropriate to speak openly in front of our baby sister. The time has come for her to understand the duties of a wife. Folashade's been shielded much too long as it is, and Nago is responsible." Nago kept invading her head. That pain between her eyes stabbed at Adaeze again.

Her cousin-servant hadn't been around much lately. Adaeze patted her stomach to clear her head. "I've known for some weeks now. But I've been waiting for Nago to attend me." Adaeze squinted. There was something about Nago, something about this new vacation place, and the rude guards that gnawed at Adaeze. "Never mind. Once the queen arrives, all will work out."

Bibi scooted in front of her sister. She grabbed Adaeze's hands and squeezed.

"Ow." Adaeze tried to pull free. Bibi held tight.

"I want you to listen to me." Bibi spoke in Bambara, not in the Persian she'd been using. "Your husband has been away. He's not in Djenné. He has been away with his friend in Bamako. He left two months before everything happened in Djenné."

Adaeze stared at Bibi. Her sister spoke of Djenné and something happening. Bibi was babbling. Her middle sister looked so earnest, so thoughtful, as though she were trying to impart some critical message to Adaeze. "I'm well aware that my husband has been in Bamako these past months. Training with the king's elite troops. In fact, Toumani traveled there with the king's best general. My husband is eager to learn all the general can teach." Bibi's earnest look alerted Adaeze her sister had a different message. Bibi looked as though a plague had wiped away half the student population of the University of Sankore.

Folashade rubbed gentle circles across her shoulder blade. The girl's eyes were wide with something akin to fear.

This simply wouldn't do. "Both of you look as though you are in mourning." Adaeze enjoyed speaking in Persian. "I do not like this vacation location any more than you two. I do not enjoy living the life of a Tuareg or a Bedouin. Moving every other night, all my possessions on my back. I have no idea why the king ordered us here, but as soon as the queen joins us, I am sure she will sort this all out and we'll be on our way back to Djenné before too many more nightfalls."

"Adaeze"—Bibi drew out her name on one long, slow sigh—"I do not believe you will have a lying-in. There has been no man in your bed." Except. The top half of Bibi's face froze while her jaw wobbled. Sweat popped out on Bibi's brow as she rocked to her knees, her hands digging into Adaeze's wrists. "Tell me you and the prince acted as a husband and wife before he traveled to Bamako." Her voice ended in a plea.

Shock coated Adaeze's tongue. "Bibi," she whispered, "these are personal matters." Bibi grabbed Adaeze around the shoulders and shook her until her teeth rattled.

"Tell me! Tell me! Did you perform your marital duties with your husband any time after little Amadou was born?"

Two guards turned toward the sisters. "No Bambara talk, you wenches. Eat. Fatten yourselves up. Tomorrow we reach Dakar." Both men laughed. "Pity the buyer who gets any one of these three. Princesses or not."

Bibi sucked in a deep breath and lowered her voice. For some reason, she spoke in Wolof. "Tell me, sister dear, did you have the honor of entertaining your husband after the birth of your son?"

Adaeze jerked away from Bibi and batted at Folashade's reaching arms. Even sisters could go too far. "My husband is a busy man. One day, he will carry all the responsibility of Mali on his shoulders. He has already done his royal duty and produced an heir to the throne. There is no need for another." She followed Bibi's direction and spoke Wolof. "You both are terribly rude to bring up such a topic."

Folashade scowled. "I do not know much, it is true, but I do know a woman must have a husband at her side nine months before there can be a lying-in."

"What?" A quick pain arced inside Adaeze's ears, blocking out all sound. It was all this language switching back and forth. Papa encouraged his girls to speak many tongues, and he often laughed when his daughters started a sentence in one language, threw in a few words of a second, and completed the whole thing in a third language. But such a game could be confusing, especially if one were tired, and Adaeze felt quite fatigued. Her ignorant youngest sister was talking such silliness. Of course, there would be a lying-in. Adaeze had all the signs. The same as for Amadou. Folashade could have no idea of what she spoke.

A pain ran right to left across the front of Adaeze's head. It was true. But, somehow, the words of both Folashade and Bibi were true. The prince hadn't invited her to his cot. Oh, if she could only remember. She counted the months. Twelve, sixteen. No. Two years. That had to be wrong. Adaeze shook her head. Bits of memory floated around her brain. There had been that night when something, or had it been someone, heavy and warm pressed down on her body. If only the rain clouds in her head would part, she would remember the body of her husband atop her. That night that squirmed in her memory, she recalled an unfamiliar, musky smell wafting off her husband. New body oil from India, no doubt. The recall of it roiled her stomach again and forced a gag. Then there had been that sensation of something quite unfamiliar—something hard probing, circling inside her. So unlike her husband.

But wait. One of Nago's lessons blasted into her brain. Adaeze plowed her mind to retrieve Nago's words. Ah, there they were. *A dutiful wife had no reason to dwell on the aftermath of her successful enticement of her husband. Once the man had succumbed to his wife's efforts, she was free to contemplate other tasks or even allow herself to go mindless for those few minutes,* Nago explained. *Enjoyment, pleasure, excitement, were all the province of the man. For a woman to even think of such things for herself was sacrilege. Enticement had escaped the woman's lips.*

But wait! Had Adaeze enticed her spouse? More flickers of memory lashed her mind, but they kept drowning in river fog before she could plant them firmly in her head. She must have drawn her husband into her body, because a man had definitely come to her and dropped his seed.

"Adaeze?" Worry so strong it could almost be touched marched across Bibi's face.

"I remember now," Adaeze whispered in Persian, "though it is very personal." She stared at a bare spot on the ground just beyond the eating mat. Her cheeks felt as flamed as though she sat right next to the iron-maker's fire. "He came to me in the night. My husband. Right after this trip began." Her voice barely crept out of her throat. "But I will admit to Allah, I must have been awfully tired, because Toumani did not feel like himself. I mean, he came to me unbidden. And it was as though I wanted to reject his attentions." The pain between her eyes stabbed through her brain to the back of her head. "Bibi, how could that be?"

Bibi stared back at her, the girl's head shining almost like the palsy.

Adaeze leaned into her middle sister and cupped a hand over the side of her face. "You know Toumani was still a boy when I married him. A child, really." She stared at a particularly odious stain on the eating mat. "It is understandable that in the past year he never came to me unless the king ordered him to act as a husband." Adaeze felt the hot breath of a blacksmith's fire consume her from head to chest. "We have been married four years. Six times, he has come to my cot. Just six. And, always, I had to be the one to use what Nago taught us." Something clogged Adaeze's throat. She swallowed, looked up, pushed away such odd recollections, and forced a smile on her face. "Now will you two stop questioning me and pray to Allah I am safely delivered of my husband's second son." When her stomach settled, and her head cleared, she would put these random thoughts in proper order.

Chapter 14

Bibi shivered. But it was not the sight of the endless blue lake where white-tipped waves rose in great mounds to break on the shore that caused her shoulders to shake and her legs to tremble. This mid-morning day already felt warm, the humid air scented of salt. No, it was not the temperature that sent the trembling throughout her much-too-skinny frame. Noise, screams, curses in a dozen languages, moans, grunts, cries, Wolof shouts of insult pounding into Bibi's ears. Noise was the cause of her shock. She squeezed her shoulder blades tight to stop the shaking, but to no avail. All around her, to her left, to her right, the front, the back, sat stockades just like the one where she stood. But instead of goats and ostriches corralled for the killing, dozens of men, most of them young enough to be warriors, a few disheveled women, and a scattering of girls just past the woman ceremony sat, stood, and slouched, herded together like piles of mud bricks. Fences made of stout tree branches half a meter higher than a man's head surrounded the kidnapped. Each face carrying the misery of loss. Strong-backed men brandishing clubs, spears, whips, and even fire sticks guarded every stockade. Like most of Charbonneau's captives, those enclosed were bound by shackles and chains. Whatever garments that once covered their fit bodies now hung in shreds and tatters. Guards, some carrying the face of Wolof, others not, but a hundred strong or more, patrolled the soft earth that stretched a thousand meters along a craggy beach. An island loomed in the distance. What was this place? And what were those faces? More than Wolof patrolled the compounds. Bibi was sure she spotted Yoruba and Mandinka sauntering in the manner of victors. Nor did all those imprisoned carry the look of the comely Bambara. Some resembled Fulani, while others were definitely Serer. Why were they here, and where was "here"? Bibi bit down on her lip. No more questions. She suspected the where of her location, if not the why. This spot of ground looked, felt, and smelled like one of the places depicted in Papa's books about the European religion. That place the Christians called hell. Bibi, still free of her own shackles, peered through openings in the narrow-spaced logs. The barbarian had taken them to a place so far from Allah. People held for ransom would not survive long in these environs. And so many! Now the why of Malick became clear. The Wolof made a business of kidnapping people for money.

Bibi sneaked a glance at one of her Wolof guards. She needed a closer look, not at the man, but at this Christian hell. The barbarian's Wolof guards busied themselves with the still-shackled Bambara, ignoring the nobles. Now was her opportunity. Bibi sidled three meters closer to the fence, careful not to bring unwanted attention, but near enough to gain a better look at this prison camp. One of the wooden boards had worn away, leaving a jagged quarter-meter opening.

She cast a quick look around her. The guards still harangued the other Bambara. She took four steps closer where a coil of rope lay over a plain wooden box. With one hurried step, she mounted the mass. There, through the fence opening, with not fifteen meters separating them, stood the holding pens. Bibi stretched to count the number. Seven, eight, ten, more, and each containing two dozen or more victims. Behind the enclosures, and trapping them against that vast body of water, Bibi spotted a number of squat square-shaped buildings. She stretched on her tiptoes and, for a few brief seconds, glimpsed the tops of substantial buildings, all more than a kilometer beyond the beach, and the outlines of a city. She remembered. Folashade had seen a map and sketches of similar structures. She stepped off the coiled rope, almost twisting her ankle as her mind turned the pages of Papa's book. The ancient capital city of the Wolof, Yoruba, and the Mandinka. This place had a name. Dakar. That big lake lying just west of the beach where the Bambara were held captive was no lake at all. Instead, the frothy water lapping so close to the groans and pleas of hundreds of the kidnapped was an ocean, one the Europeans called the Atlantic. Bibi frowned as she wrapped her arms around her chest. Papa had never described Dakar as a prison camp for kidnapped nobles held for ransom.

"There!" Malick's sudden shout sent a fresh tremble through Bibi. The monster's screams sounded more ferocious than usual.

She turned to see which of the unfortunate Bambara had captured the man's ire this time. The Wolof jabbed his whip repeatedly toward Adaeze.

"That one! The jewelry goes on her. One of the high-and-mighty princesses." He spit on the ground, his spittle spraying the arm of one of the squatting female prisoners. "But wait until the women properly prepare her."

He stalked through the group of seated, still-shackled women he'd ordered stripped of all clothing. The stomp of his shod feet and his girth toppled them aside as he passed. The women's eyes reflected dullness, but no shame. Bibi shivered her understanding. Oh, Allah, had she, like these servant women, moved beyond caring? She shook her head. No. There was still much to do. With Adaeze unable to function and Folashade impossibly young, the responsibility of all the Bambara fell on Bibi's shoulders. She watched as the Wolof captors ladled out even more indignities over the prisoners. Men began uncapping large jars and spilling the contents over their victims. Women cringed as a thick goo spread over them. The guards barked orders and snapped whips over hapless heads.

"Aiee, Allah, they're going to cook us!" one of the servant women screamed out in Bambara. "They're basting us with oil!"

"Rub it in deep. These wenches have to shine and glisten. Get the dust of travel off them! Like this, you imbecile." Charbonneau's second-in-command grabbed one of the jars from a young Wolof, dribbled some of the contents over his hands, and attacked a Bambara servingwoman. Bibi watched Malick's gruff hands smear the girl's emaciated body with the thick goo. When he reached her tiny breasts, he squeezed both hard. The girl, no more than Folashade's own years, whimpered. "Be sure and get the grease between their legs. Buyers will look there."

No! Bibi's feet moved forward, though her head said, *Stand still.* She took a step toward the girl. Though she couldn't recall the child's name, Bibi recognized her as one of the females who cared for Adaeze's hair. Bibi stretched out a hand toward the offending jar.

"Bibi, stop!" Folashade gripped Bibi's arm. "They will turn on us next. These idiots will lather oil over everyone. Not even fresh-pressed oil. The stuff smells of the renderings from three-week-dead hyenas." Folashade whispered her Persian without moving her lips. A deep-purple caftan and brown under dress lay over her left arm. The unmatched garments looked familiar.

Bibi shook her head. "Of course, you are right, Folashade." Something caught her eye. A single stone attached to the bodice of the purple caftan gleamed in the sun. "Where did you get those clothes, and for what use?" Bibi inclined her head, her eyes darting from guard to guard.

Folashade put on her most annoyed look. "That fool of a Wolof ordered me to carry these. I believe they are something Nago packed. I mean, she brought them from Timbuktu. Down the Niger."

"Nago?" Bibi had seen precious little of the woman these past two months. On the day marches, Nago and the others had been forced to walk, while she and her sisters had been allowed to rotate in a palanquin

133

carried by grumbling Wolof. Though Bibi and Folashade had wanted to defer most of their time to the still-befuddled Adaeze, Charbonneau would have none of it. Nago's group had usually brought up the rear and had never been allowed to ride, not even for a passage of fifteen minutes.

Folashade nudged Bibi aside as she stepped in front and walked through the path parted by Malick. She jerked her head and Bibi followed. Nago, her under dress barely attached at the waist, and both of her full breasts bare, emerged from behind another of the Wolof. Her eyes rested on Bibi, her mouth moving in little starts and stops, but only soft grunts emerged.

"Nago," Bibi whispered as she reached for her cousin-servant's shoulder. "Your chains are off, praise Allah."

"You!" Malick called out before Bibi could touch Nago. "Help your sister, then you are to report to Monsieur."

"Help her?" Bibi stared at this resentful idiot of a man who had been forced by Charbonneau to show a semblance of civility to her.

"Make her presentable. This afternoon, important buyers will want to see what they are being asked to pay a mound of cowries for." The lopsided smirk on the oaf's face made Bibi grind her back teeth. "Here." Malick thrust a jar into Nago's hand. "You are a servant to this passel of royals. Oil your mistress. Plait her hair. Put fresh clothes on her"—he jerked a thumb toward Folashade—"and, at last, put on her jewels."

Jewels? The second-in-command held three of Adaeze's lesser bracelets, those once kept in some jewelry box tended by one of her women servants. There was no sign of the necklace. Adaeze was being bedecked for a mound of cowries. A rush of air flooded Bibi's lungs. The ransom! Release was imminent. Bibi fought back a burgeoning smile as she turned to Malick, just as Charbonneau called out from the suddenly open stockade gate.

"Come with me," the Frenchman ordered.

Her spark of elation flickered as she frowned against the sun.

Charbonneau quickened his pace. He beckoned her and took a step inside the stockade. His bearded face bore the mark of impatience.

"Take care of our sister," Bibi ordered a slack-mouthed Folashade as she walked toward Charbonneau.

"I've located a house." Charbonneau managed a smile.

The nights she spent with the man, now almost six out of every seven, Bibi had paid diligent attention to his French words. Bambara freedom depended upon her ability to decipher what Charbonneau wanted with her family. Just now, she'd understood what he'd said. Something about a house. She tried to emulate his sounds.

Charbonneau laughed as he grabbed her arm. "Locate, ma belle. All you need to know is that I've found a proper house to await the sales."

The man hadn't bothered to sprinkle any Wolof into his speech. She'd deciphered the word "locate." Now all she had to do was learn the meanings of "sales." Both words made the barbarian smile, and that couldn't be good for the Bambara.

He turned his back to the ocean, headed up the rocky beach and away from the shore. "Ten minutes' walk, and we're there." He tightened his grip on her hand as he headed toward the buildings that marked the beginning of the city.

Charbonneau stopped his long strides outside a round structure with a proper thatched roof just like the ones in Papa's books of the dwellings of those to the west. Bibi had broken into a half trot to keep up. A man who carried the look of a Mandinka, and a head taller than Charbonneau and dressed in a fine tan tunic and trousers, stood outside the door, his head decorated with the cap of a Wolof dignitary, his brow furrowed into a scowl.

"Is this one of the wenches?" He looked over Charbonneau's shoulder and directly at her. "She's too skinny to do any sort of work." The Mandinka laid a hand on Charbonneau's shoulder and moved him aside. He scanned Bibi as though he were searching for flaws in a goat promised to be perfect. How dare the man!

"You, sir, are impudent." Bibi caught the look of censure on the face of Charbonneau as she snapped out her Wolof. Charbonneau glared at Bibi. With a ransom over, her captor's disapproval was to no avail. She squared her body toward the Mandinka. "I am a daughter of the house of Toure of Timbuktu, and sister to the next queen of Mali."

Fury wracked her body. No. She took in a breath. She was too close to her goal now. Free her sisters at the least. Then allow herself to die. She must remain calm. Every move she made, every word she spoke to each of these Allah-forsaken men, held the key to Bambara freedom. Focus on what little fortune had fallen her way in these disastrous eight weeks, and not on the insults of an ill-bred foreigner. Bibi kept her eyes on the Mandinka. Something in the way he stared at her made her wonder. Could this man just be pretending his disdain? Could he have been secreted into Charbonneau's world to affect her release? After all, Adaeze was certainly being adorned for something. She shook her head. Hope and questions were not in order today. Better to focus on this delicate time in the ransom bargaining, and the few positive things Charbonneau had granted her sisters.

He kept her and her sisters covered. Except for the debacle on the beach that first day, no man other than Charbonneau had seen the sisters naked. With her cajoling, he had allowed them to spend one or two of their evening hours rearranging the plaits in one another's hair. He had even given them triple portions of the food fed to the others, so they had known only a little hunger. He had insisted that they immerse themselves in whatever river water they passed. Plainly, it was to Charbonneau's benefit to keep his prized hostages healthy. A pang of regret welled in her chest. If only she had the bed skills to include her Bambara tribeswomen in better treatment. Her hand tugged at the bodice of her under dress. She had given all she could to the barbarian, Charbonneau. All the nights. She forced her mind back to the now.

If Allah smiled on her, this could be the day she and all the Bambara were ransomed. And if that day had finally come, she should offer praises to the Prophet rather than complain against the Mandinka's arrogant rudeness. The man may well have been sent by Adaeze's father-in-law as the go-between emissary in secret dealings. That the king of Mali had managed to put in place ransom negotiation at all was reason enough to offer up profuse prayers of thanksgiving.

The well-dressed man's lips drooped. "She's a royal, all right. Haughty enough to be turned away from Allah's favor." His fingers stroked his naked chin as he continued his head-to-toe inspection of her. "Take off that scrap of a rag she's wearing. I want a proper look at her ornaments."

Ornaments. Words in all of her languages garbled in the throat. If this man were a secret emissary of the king, he had to feign harshness to gain a bargaining upper hand with Charbonneau, but the Mandinka's fresh insults staggered Bibi. Her teeth clamped over her tongue. Maybe pain would remind her to be still while this negotiator schemed for Bambara freedom.

Bibi looked up at Charbonneau, his battle to decipher the visitor's words clear on his face. She captured his eye, swept a hand across her covered breasts. "Ornaments." She executed a quick glance downward to her belly.

Charbonneau's lips parted and his face reddened as he turned to the king's negotiator. "Not her, you fool." He sputtered his Wolof mixed with French to the negotiator, who poked out his lower lip. "At least, not yet. She has sisters. Two of them, and each comes with something special."

The Mandinka straightened his back. "I have no idea of what foreign gibberish you are speaking. I've been told you have special merchandise to unload. Well, let me see this special cargo." He jabbed a thumb at Bibi. "Don't waste my time."

Charbonneau turned to her, a questioning look on his face.

"My body. Man wants to see." Thoughts whirled in Bibi's head as she parceled out her newly learned French. She could not allow this stranger to see her unclothed body, emissary or no. His demand for a look must be based upon the king, or more likely the queen, to determine if the noblewoman had been harmed during the kidnap. Surely, the king of Mali would not be silly enough to withhold ransom if he believed any of the royal women had been sullied. Air caught in Bibi's throat. "I need a woman to look. Not a man." She faced Charbonneau as she pronounced her words in Wolof.

The Mandinka stamped impatience. "I have no more time for foolishness. I will not pay even a thousand cowries for a woman I have not personally examined." He turned his back on Charbonneau.

"I understand why I must be examined." Bibi tamped down her panic at this unknown bargaining tactic. "I bear no visible marks of injury." She turned sideways from Charbonneau and lowered her voice to this emissary. "I have not been harmed, but you must grant me the modesty of a woman examiner." She paused. "A woman will know the truth of my statement." Bibi kept her eyes on the emissary and away from Charbonneau.

The Frenchman reached Bibi in two strides, grabbed her shoulders, and shoved her behind him. He raised his voice in Wolof. "Emeralds. Diamonds. Rubies. And royal women."

Now ten meters distant, the emissary stopped and turned to face the pair. He cocked his head. "You speak to me of gems. What gems?" He took two cautious steps toward the squat house where Bibi and Charbonneau stood in the doorframe.

Charbonneau nodded as he pushed Bibi into the interior and stepped inside without turning his back. Light from two square-cut openings lifted the inside gloom. Bibi glanced around. Through an arched doorway of the pink stucco two-room structure, she spotted the corner of Charbonneau's zebra-topped trunk. She turned back to the doorway just as the emissary entered.

"Well?" The Mandinka folded his arms.

Bibi clamped her jaw shut to keep down her trembling. Her father had trained her to be a negotiator for whatever husband she might one day have. Toure had trained all his girls in this basic requirement of a noble wife, but Bibi had never witnessed negotiations quite like these. Charbonneau spoke of gems he'd secreted. Bibi had worn the Doudou bracelet until last evening when the prisoners were herded into the stockades. Now, they, too, were to be bargaining chips. Bibi felt a quick flash of lightness to her soul. With the jewels thrown in, maybe this barbarian was prepared to release all the Bambara. Bibi shut her eyes for the briefest of time. This horror was about to come to an end.

"Three women for sale." Charbonneau's Wolof sounded strong if abbreviated. He kept his back to Bibi as he faced the Mandinka emissary. "One hundred seventy-five thousand cowries." He held up three fingers. "Each. Three sisters."

"One hundred seventy-five thousand cowries per woman." The emissary's voice boomed. "I think not, you French bastard. The English are paying twenty-four pounds sterling for the hardiest of men. And you demand twenty of me for a woman. In the best of shape and possessing the best bed skills of a woman of the Orient, I will pay no more than twelve pounds. One hundred thousand cowries for all." He looked over Charbonneau's shoulder. "And only if I can see this one naked and the others look like her."

Charbonneau grunted, though Bibi couldn't tell if the cause was non-understanding of the spoken Wolof or refusal of the price. She held herself still, almost denying breath. Papa had been diligent in ensuring his daughters became skilled negotiators, but this was a technique he'd never shared with Bibi. Charbonneau swung his head in a slow arc.

"Woman to see this one. No man. Woman, only." His Wolof carried the note of certainty. "For this one"—he gestured over his shoulder at Bibi—"fifty thousand cowries. Six pounds sterling." He sucked in his lips. "Good woman skills. Special. Jewel special. Together. Six pounds sterling."

The emissary's laugh was low. "Show me these gems, and I will consider a woman examiner."

Bibi watched Charbonneau stand, unmoving. She kept her place behind him, but she peered around his back to address the emissary.

"You will give me a woman examiner?" She kept her voice soft and simpering in her best Nago-instructed manner. "After you see the jewels, you will guarantee I get a woman examiner." Bibi clipped in her last words. She could not be too obvious about her suspicions that this Mandinka was really in the pay of Adaeze's father-in-law.

Odd. The emissary looked at her as though her mind had snapped, but Charbonneau's shoulders lifted.

"Come back in one hour with the woman. Then I will show you the jewels." He spoke in his odd mixture of Wolof and French.

The Mandinka emissary narrowed his eyes, took one more look at Bibi, and nodded. "I'll return right after evening prayers." He swept out of the stucco cabin.

Chapter 15

"There." Charbonneau slipped the toggle through the gold fastener of the Doudou bracelet he'd just placed on Bibi's left arm.

Bibi, seated on a heavy-cotton floor pillow, stared at the man's hands as he took the polishing cloth to the gemstones for the fourth time since the muezzin sounded evening prayers. The Siamese ruby glowed especially bright in the lantern light. The smell of the jasmine-scented perfume he had rubbed over her before she donned the gray under dress and topped it with the embroidered red silk caftan filled the little stucco house. Charbonneau rocked back on his haunches and smiled.

"You are perfect, my beauty. Thanks to Christ Almighty, I brought that trunk of silks I found in one of the tents on the beach. Fine silks, they are, and with you wearing one of them, our Mandinka will be most pliable." His smug smile showed his angled lower teeth. "If you and this bracelet don't bring me at least two hundred livres, two hundred thousand cowries in your money, I'll give up the slave-trading business."

Bibi slid her hand down the length of the caftan. She remembered it being stitched, one of the garments intended for Folashade's meeting with the queen. Now stolen by Charbonneau. As she stroked the silk, one of the man's French words pounded at her. Slave. He had uttered the word "slave."

"Slave." She fought to keep the question out of her voice.

Charbonneau stood, looked down at her, and shook his head. "You have been a real pleasure to me. A beauty for certain. But a man cannot be a fool." He chuckled as he stepped into the cabin's second room.

She watched as he secured the lock on the zebra-topped trunk, the necklace still inside. Her stomach twitched. Something was off-kilter. She'd been perfumed and gowned and for no other reason than to ensure the ransom payer she was healthy, unharmed, and regal. Adaeze, too, had been prepared. Something gnawed at Bibi. Folashade. In any ransom release, her youngest sister had to be included. Bibi's midday meal roiled her stomach. "Monsieur, all the sister of me," she called out in her French, "they examined, too?"

Charbonneau stepped back into the main room and plopped himself on a rough-carved ebony wood bench. "Your sisters? You are the key to this deal, my sweet. If I can arrange a high price for you, then you will all go as one lot." More French than Wolof. He reached over and straightened a fold in her caftan.

Why hadn't she studied harder when Papa showed her books in French? Charbonneau mentioned a key. A key to Bambara shackles perhaps. She rummaged her mind for the words to the next question as Charbonneau stood to trim the lantern wick.

The emissary's shadow preceded his call. "I trust you have the gems to show me." His arrogant voice flooded into the cabin. "I've brought a woman to examine your wench, but she'll not touch her until I've had my look at the jewels." He pushed open the cabin door. Charbonneau backed up to Bibi, reached down, and pulled her to her feet. He held out her left arm. The two side emeralds twinkled in the twilight, illuminating the open door.

The emissary stepped inside, his hand batting at the gloom. He took five paces toward Bibi, reached a hand toward her wrist.

Charbonneau straightened her elbow and rotated her forearm before he slipped her to his side. "You had the look."

"You call that a look?" The emissary shook his head. "I'll need a proper inspection of the stones. I see emerald and ruby. Might the other four be garnets?"

Charbonneau's hands slid from Bibi's shoulders to her waist. She noticed the little shakes of his head. Had he missed most or all of the emissary's question? She tilted her head toward Charbonneau, kept her eyes on the sandaled foot of the Mandinka, and spoke low to her captor in his French. "Ruby of Siam. Two emeralds of Ghana. Four garnets of Mozambique."

"Hurry it up!" The emissary folded his arms.

Charbonneau propelled Bibi closer to the lantern sitting atop a low table in the center of the room. He took her hand and slid the bracelet up and down her arm. "Siam. Ghana. Mozambique. The best quality."

"Remove it from her arm. I need to examine the stones more carefully."

"No." How much Charbonneau had understood, Bibi couldn't gauge, but his response was emphatic. "Woman and jewel, together." He beckoned the emissary closer and slowly draped Bibi's arm over the emissary's hand. He lifted the lantern. She flinched as the man's thick fingers grabbed at the bracelet, one fingernail scraping her arm. She kept her body still. The man breathed in as he bent over to stare at the Doudou bracelet. The smell of this day's cardamom-spiced goat meat permeated his breath.

The man finally stood straight. "What will you expect for the bracelet alone?" He turned to Charbonneau and raised his voice when Bibi's captor hesitated. "Bracelet. Cowries. Livres. What offer do you expect?" The emissary tapped his right foot as though he were waiting for a backward child to figure the answer to a simple problem.

"The jewel and the woman." The cockiness in Charbonneau's voice landed on Bibi's ears.

She took in the breath she'd been holding for many long seconds. The ransom was about to be settled.

"You require both in the same sale. We shall see." The emissary strode to the cabin door and called out, "Manuela."

A woman colored like a Tuareg but without their more angular features, green eyes, or curly hair, walked slowly into the room. Bibi stared at the visitor's clothing. What sort of garments were these? Manuela, covered from neck to ankle in a cotton fabric, cinched at the waist, wore the blousy sleeves that resembled the shirts of Charbonneau. A vest, though of heavy cotton, not leather, topped a bodice that sported buttons like the Europeans. The first three of which were unfastened. Bibi struggled against laying a hand to her mouth. The rise of the woman's bosom was clear for any man to see. Was this Manuela the woman to whom Bibi must submit for an examination? This was the woman Bibi hoped to coax into being her ally. Her stomach flip-flopped.

Charbonneau grunted. "This is one of the women from Gorée." He switched to Wolof from his French. "Gorée woman." He shook his head, his doubt transferring to Bibi.

The Mandinka shot a look of disdain toward Charbonneau. "Of course, you demanded a woman examiner. I've brought you an expert. A woman skilled in dealing with the women prisoners on Gorée. She is a second-generation guard. Born on the island."

Oh, Allah. Something was wrong. Very wrong. Talk of guards on a place called Gorée. Bibi brought up every one of the maps of Dakar she remembered from Papa's books. If even one carried the place name of Gorée, she could not recall. Her trembling caused Charbonneau to cast her a curious look.

"Get on with it, then." Charbonneau laid a hand on the emissary's shoulder and guided him toward the door. "You and I will step outside." He gestured to a spot ten paces beyond the cabin door.

"Where do you propose to take me? I agreed to a woman examiner, but I insist upon being present."

Charbonneau pushed the man with force, turned, and closed the door. Bibi could see the shadow of his feet standing guard over the

entrance as the two men argued in their disparate tongues. She turned
to Manuela.

"You will find I'm healthy." Bibi had planned to say so much more
to this woman to affect her release, but Manuela's attire confused her.
Did this woman, who bore little resemblance to any of the West African
tribes, even speak Wolof? She stared at Manuela's face. Her nose was
not as broad, nor her lips as full, as a proper Wolof, nor was there any
of the Hausa about her, nor the Mandinka.

"Oh, you do speak Wolof. I was told you do." Manuela chuckled. "One thing I do not doubt is your cleverness. Now off with your
clothes. I will see if you are as healthy as you claim." The woman's Wolof
bore a strange accent.

"You are aware, are you not, that I am the daughter of Toure of
Timbuktu, and sister to the future queen of Mali." Bibi ended her dec-
laration not at all certain if she had disclosed too much too soon. The
turmoil in her stomach continued unabated.

"I did hear you were being passed off as a royal. That bracelet on
your arm suggests some wealth in your background, but I suspect it was
your woman's trickery that gained you such a prize. In any case, lift your
under dress so I may examine your circumcision."

What an outrage. Bibi sucked in her cheeks. She needed this
woman to affect Bambara release, but some requests insulted propriety.
Bibi turned her back to this strange woman, shrugged out of her caftan,
and lifted her under dress to just under her breast. She held the folds
tight across her back. "As you can clearly see, my back is unscarred. A
whip has never touched me." She dropped the under dress and turned
back to the alien woman. "By the way, I am Bambara. What is your
tribe?"

The woman's low laugh and flat brown eyes that reflected no mirth
sent a fresh chill through Bibi. "Tribe? You have much to learn, royal
or not." The woman snatched the hem of Bibi's under dress and lifted
it to her waist, exposing her woman's place.

Bibi reached for Manuela's arm. She did not see but felt the blow to her stomach as the woman made contact. Bibi gasped as she lay panting on the floor of the cabin, the back of her head throbbing where she had struck the hard floorboards. "Ugh." She grunted as the woman laid one knee on her belly and pressed the other across her neck.

"Monsieur. Help!" Her words strangled in her throat as she fought to find escape from the offending knee. As she writhed on the floor, the woman's fingers probed her woman's place, pinching and squeezing. Bibi tried to buck the woman off her body, only to feel Manuela's knees press down harder. Bibi's tongue protruded.

"I've never seen a royal cut like you before." Her knees digging in deeper, Manuela shifted her body and shoved Bibi's under dress to her shoulders. The woman's heavy hands grabbed and bounced both of Bibi's breasts. "Well, you conniving, little bitch. You've come up lucky." With the same quickness with which she mounted Bibi, she slid off.

Bibi's eyes opened and closed spasmodically as she lay gasping. Before her lungs could gather in enough air, the woman grabbed her arms and yanked her to standing.

Manuela nodded toward the discarded red caftan. "Get that thing on." She dug her fingers into Bibi's shoulder as she spun her closer. "Now, if you get your hands on more jewels just for me, I'll watch out for you." Her low-grunted words hacked into Bibi's ears.

Bibi clutched her stomach and panted. She ordered her knees to bend. She stooped to retrieve the caftan and rubbed at her neck before she slipped her arms through the garment. Pictures from Papa's books, the face of her long-dead mother, emeralds, even the queen, all flashed pain in Bibi's head. But an anvil deep inside her head pounded, pulverized, and reformed all the fragments in her brain into one certainty. Whatever was transpiring between Charbonneau, the Mandinka, and this woman was no ransom negotiation. Some unseen hand pushed her to her side. She took in great gulps of air. Negotiate. Whatever horror she, her sisters, and all the Bambara were now in, Bibi's duty remained the same. Her voice finally made a comeback, though fog stormed into her brain.

"Jewel," she managed. "I do have jewels." Whatever this Manuela wanted, Bibi had to make the woman believe it was forthcoming. "More bracelets. Not as fancy as this one, but you must give me time to get them." She moved to her knees as her voice struggled to erupt.

"I have no doubt you'll use your cunning to get them out of this Frenchman. Give them to me, and not the Mandinka, and I will see that you have a degree of comfort when you get to Gorée. Bring me enough, and I will get one of the Europeans to impregnate you. Dutch or Portuguese. Which do you prefer?"

Impregnate. European men. Bibi's mouth opened and closed. She preferred neither. Her mind rushed to the one memory she had struggled hard to put out of her mind. Balaboa. Her baby. She'd clung to the dream her son was safe in Djenné. And now, Manuela spoke of another child. By a European. The bile came up quick and fast. Bibi doubled over as she cupped her hands to her mouth. Vomit oozed between her fingers.

"Oh, you silly girl. If you only knew what awaits you if you do not please me."

The door flung open, and the emissary walked in, the barbarian close behind.

"Well?" The taller man looked impatient.

Bibi wiped her mouth with the back of her hand. The false emissary's body swayed in the doorway as she tried to keep him in focus.

Manuela parsed her Wolof. "She has no royal facial markings"—the woman paused as she shot a warning glance—"but that might not disqualify her. I'll need a better look. Tomorrow. In the daylight. I can say"—she looked Bibi up and down—"this one has the ability to please the European men of the West Indies." She shot a glance at Charbonneau. "She has not been too badly used."

More words collided in Bibi's head. Manuela spoke of the Indies? The land of tigers, elephants, and wealth almost as fabulous as the Timbuktu of old. No. Manuela had spoken of the Indies to the west. Some of Papa's visitors talked of recent European exploration. White-skinned adventurers like Marco Polo had gone off searching for the Silk Road. Papa's guests declared these sailors had located a landmass in a place they called the New World. The West Indies. A place where sugar was grown and the need for laborers was high. If only she'd paid more attention to Papa's visitors.

The Wolof grunted as he flashed a quick look of satisfaction. "Perhaps we can do a bit of business tomorrow if Manuela approves your woman." He stared at Bibi as he addressed Charbonneau. "If she's not truly a royal, I cannot be expected to pay more than fifty thousand cowries."

Charbonneau smiled. "Tomorrow, we deal." He waved his hand toward the door.

With head nods, the false emissary and the strangely attired woman left. Charbonneau closed the door, crossed the floor, and gathered Bibi into his arms. He kissed her.

"I shall miss you, ma belle, but you are going to make me wealthy." He danced her around the little floor as he called out his French.

Bibi leaned into his body, her knees threatening to fail. She had to clear her head. "My sister Adaeze. I want to see her tomorrow." Folashade and Adaeze had to be alerted. If Adaeze, with her mind now enveloped in a thick shroud, had emerged even for a second, she might reach the same conclusion as Bibi. The ransom that seemed so imminent was a false promise. The bile threatened to return. Something far more sinister than the two-month march from Djenné awaited them all. Even pleasing Charbonneau these many nights might prove a tame game compared to the unknown Manuela threatened. Bibi had to secure the bracelets from Adaeze and devise a bargaining plan to present to the witch from Gorée. Bargaining for what, she was uncertain.

But one thing was clear. Every move Bibi made from now on had to be the right one.

"Come. Lie with me. This could be one of the last times." Charbonneau pushed her to the small carpeted space on the floor, ignoring the narrow cot where he usually slept after he finished with her. He lifted her dress, stroked a hand down her left thigh, and covered her with kisses.

Chapter 16

Folashade sat still on the covered verandah of the long one-story bluff-colored building, Nago behind her. She rested on her heels while Nago wrapped a length of stiff cloth around Folashade's head, catching three or four of her beads in the fold.

"Ow." She grunted her pain, but instead of the swat on the back of the head usually delivered by Nago for such an infraction, the cousin-servant kept struggling to intertwine the cotton cloth.

Nearby Wolof men sniggered. Folashade shot a quick glare at the men. How could Nago be expected to know how to wrap two meters of stiff fabric into any semblance of a head covering? Women of Timbuktu did not wear such a thing. Folashade tucked this fresh affront into that mind-place where she determined to make things right once she and the others were released. Nago grunted as the fabric came undone for the fifth time and slid down Folashade's face. Folashade slipped her hand to Nago's bare knee and gave her a tiny pat. The guards smirked even more. Folashade fixed her eye on a verandah pillar as her hand played with the green leaf-print under dress the Malick person instructed Nago to lay over her. She wanted to bring it to her nose. The fabric had the feel and scent of the sand of Timbuktu. Home. A fresh tremble wracked Folashade's body. This was one of the dresses Nago had stitched to impress Folashade's future mother-in-law. Folashade strained to picture the queen's face, but the image in her head floated in and out of focus.

Even the countenance of her stupid about-to-be betrothed blurred in her mind's eye.

She plunged both hands into the folds of the fine linen under dress. Where was the matching green brocade caftan? That silk fabric had come straight from Cathay, courtesy of Bibi's ever-eager-to-impress husband. Folashade sucked in her lips. No more complaining. She was clothed, while Nago continued to endure the indignity of bare breasts. Pitifully, the servant-cousin displayed no concern over the disgrace as she followed Malick's orders. Nago smeared the stinky grease all over Folashade's body, even between her legs. When the Wolof busied himself elsewhere, Folashade inched her finger to the soiled and ripped under dress she'd just removed and wiped off as much of the stink as possible. Still, Nago's only response was her tired breathing.

"Folashade." Adaeze's voice broke through the barrage of thoughts roaming Folashade's mind. "These beads are not right." Her sister's tone was almost as bright and chipper as back in Djenné. Adaeze tapped her head where row after row of red and green beads decorated her plaits. "They clash with my dress." Adaeze stared down at her brown under dress as she shifted the purple caftan out of her way. "I really need more jewels embroidered on this gown." Adaeze sighed. "Nago really must do better than this."

"Of course, Adaeze." Folashade turned to Nago, who had given up her effort at tying the turban-style covering. The piled-up cloth sat lopsided on Folashade's head, one end of fabric dangling over her right eye. The dress Adaeze wore had been intended for Nago, never for a formal member of the royal court. The servant looked uncaring and acted as though she'd heard none of Adaeze's litany of complaints. "I'll ask her, my sister."

Folashade tucked in the loose end of her makeshift turban as she watched Adaeze. Her sister lay semi-reclined on a wooden bench supplied by Malick. The man had even posed Adaeze on the cotton-covered pillow and dared her to move. There was something to be said about the loss of a mind. Adaeze, in her less-than-stellar dress and adorned in a trio of everyday bracelets, still looked regal. The man bent one of her knees while the other lay straight. He had pushed one arm behind Adaeze's head and stretched the under dress tight across her chest. Folashade stared at her sister. Adaeze, in her mismatched clothes, looked ridiculous, though Nago, in her proper mind, would have preened proud approval.

"Give me a look at the wenches." Charbonneau, puffing, almost always began his orders in French. "I see he is yet to arrive." He walked onto the verandah as he addressed one of his Wolof minions. "Good."

"Ah, but we are right behind you," Malick called out from the stockade gate. An even taller, cap-wearing man in a smart-looking embroidered tunic and pants strode just at his heels.

Folashade squinted. The burnished decorations on the new arrival's head covering suggested a dignitary of some sort, but not of the Wolof clan. Perhaps this man had been assigned by Charbonneau to affect her release. She hadn't dared stir up the hope of freedom with Bibi, not after her sister's sacrifices, but all this greasing up and re-dressing made her wonder. Freedom negotiations had to be underway.

Charbonneau stalked to a halt in front of Folashade. He pointed a finger at Malick. "You've mixed up the clothes. I wanted that one on Adaeze." He whirled around to face his second-in-command, who halted right behind the Frenchman. "And where is the matching coat?"

"Are these the two you want me to see?" The taller, more elegantly dressed man elbowed his way ahead of the dreadful Malick. He sneered his disapproval.

Folashade glanced between the three obviously angry men as she grabbed at the turban that threatened to topple from her head. Too late. The entire thing unraveled in her hands. She sucked in a breath as she faced Charbonneau, and his forehead sunk into an even deeper scowl.

"This, you call a royal?" The new fellow, taller by a centimeter than even Malick, looked down at Folashade as though she were a dung gatherer.

Charbonneau, his face as red as henna, turned and walked over to Adaeze. Malick slipped beside Nago as soon as the tunic-wearing dignitary turned his back. The Wolof grabbed the servant's ear and shoved her at Folashade. He pantomimed retying the turban cloth. Nago sucked in her pain, rubbed her ear, nodded, and retrieved the cloth from Folashade's lap.

The stranger stared down at Adaeze, who jerked her shoulders but held her pose.

"What royal favor have you come to ask?" Adaeze stared up at her visitor, her eyes struggling to focus.

Folashade detected a quick but passing flash of unease in her sister's expression as though a few seconds of lucidity had crept into the girl's mind and Adaeze finally sensed the reality of danger. The look faded too soon. Now Adaeze wore a face of regal disdain.

Folashade rummaged through her mind of tribal markings. She scoured the face of this stranger. *That's it. He is Mandinka.*

"Bambara." The well-dressed Mandinka startled as he sought out Charbonneau. "This one speaks Bambara."

Charbonneau looked back at the visitor, the redness in his face fading. "Bambara." He nodded.

"Yes. Bambara," the dignitary grumbled. "Where is an interpreter? Dealing with ignorant foreigners is too trying."

"I can assist you." Folashade tried to infuse each Wolof word with what she believed would be a Mandinka inflection. Praise be to Allah, Bibi wasn't present to hear Folashade's bold offer. Her sister would have suffered apoplexy at Folashade's audacity, but something had to be done. And this may be the sisters' best opportunity to set the stage for their own rescues. "Of course, my sister speaks Bambara. We are of

Timbuktu and the house of Toure." She watched the fellow's face. There was something about this man's hard eyes that boded no good.

The Mandinka glared at Folashade, scanning her up and down, but this time with much more care. He strode over to her still-kneeling form. "You claim to be from Timbuktu." His laugh was more of a grunt. "I doubt that. No slaves have come to Dakar from Timbuktu. The distance is too great."

Folashade clambered to her feet, pushing Nago aside, and destroying the servant's latest efforts at turban tying. Though he topped her height by a good third of a meter, this latest Wolof tormentor had to see she was no slave. "And you are correct. Aside from our wars, no person of Timbuktu has ever been enslaved."

The man turned to Charbonneau, who held his ground beside Adaeze. He watched as Adaeze's face moved from a grimace to serenity and back again. "You've trained your wenches well. They certainly carry the haughtiness of royals, as well as the look." He shook his head and turned back to Folashade. "It is certainly unfortunate you speak only rudimentary Wolof. If you are who you say you are, and I'm not at all convinced, then do your best to make this fool understand my words."

The thump of Folashade's heart moved down to her feet, up to her ears, back to her chest, and repeated the cycle all over again. Her French vocabulary consisted of only a few words and phrases. "I am not one used to having my word disputed." Except for Nago, Papa, and her sisters.

"My, my. You certainly know how to act the role of the haughty. Tell him"—the Mandinka jerked his head without looking at the Frenchman—"that I will examine you both. If you are in decent-enough shape, I will offer him six pounds sterling." He paused. "Let me see. In his money, that would be some fifty French livres. To you, fifty thousand cowries. And that is for the pair of you."

Folashade had always been Papa's quickest child at math, but it wasn't Archimedes's theories that consumed her now. This Mandinka was offering no sort of ransom. His cocky arrogance was unmistakable. He was speaking of buying. She and Adaeze were being appraised like the fattest goats in the square at Timbuktu. And like the goats, this horrible man had mentioned an examination. Oh, Allah, they were to be sold as common slaves. Folashade turned to Charbonneau. Convincing this Mandinka she could communicate with Bibi's tormentor was now her biggest challenge and almost the key to her release.

"Monsieur." She was sure of her French pronunciation for the man's title, but the rest all depended upon what she could dredge from Papa's books. "Me, Adaeze. All for . . ." What was the French word for "fifty"? She slipped her hand slightly behind her, angled her body, and flashed five fingers ten times at Charbonneau. "Livre." She held her breath as Charbonneau stared back at her, his face pinched.

The Frenchman slowly shook his head. Folashade felt her knees tremble. Charbonneau turned to the dignitary.

"Not possible." He jerked his chin in the air as he pronounced his Wolof mixed with French. "No fifty livres." He pulled Adaeze's arm, her trio of bracelets jangling as she winced. "I have more gems." The Frenchman bent down to Adaeze and laid one hand against her back. He pushed her out of her silly pose.

"More?" The Mandinka turned from Folashade to Charbonneau. "Are you offering more jewels, presumably for the same price?"

Folashade glanced from Charbonneau to Adaeze. As the barbarian shook her wrist, Adaeze stiffened, her jaw set like hardened mud. She jerked her hand away. Charbonneau, startled, locked her arm in a firm grip. Adaeze's eyes fluttered, and her head lolled to one side for a second. Folashade watched the muscles in her sister's face wobble. Adaeze opened her eyes. No sign of today remained in them. The rank of royalty unfurled from forehead to chin.

"What give you for this one? Jewels with her." Charbonneau twisted one of the bracelets as he struggled through his childlike Wolof. "This is of nothing. More come. Emerald, ruby."

An impatient look crossed Malick's face as he waited for Folashade. Her eyes darted between the cap-wearer and the Wolof, who cocked his head as he awaited the answer. The man grunted and shot an impatient look toward the stockade gate. There was no more time.

"This man is of France," Folashade began, willing as much strength into her words as she could muster. "He assures you he has more jewels."

"Simpleton of a girl!" the Mandinka boomed. "I know what the Frenchman is saying. The problem is, he does not understand what I'm speaking. If you actually speak this man's addled tongue, then tell him to show me this 'more.'"

Folashade turned to Charbonneau, who cast her a confused look. "More bracelet of Adaeze." She got out the phrase without pantomiming. "Man see."

Charbonneau gave Folashade a quick but curious nod before he spoke. "I will show this man my wares, but only after we close the gap on the price." The man of France must have caught the intent stare in Folashade's eyes as she struggled to take in his French. He mixed in Wolof. "For her"—he inclined his head toward Adaeze—"I take offer of four hundred livres."

Folashade moved toward the Mandinka before the barbarian could call out the cowrie conversion. She pursed her lips and nodded in her best imitation of transferring the words inside her head. Now all she had to do was weave a plausible-enough tale from the few bits and pieces of the man's French she did understand.

"Monsieur insists you first make a reasonable offer." Folashade prayed to Allah that was the meaning of some of the white-skinned one's words. "Then he will show you jewels so magnificent your eyes will dazzle." Folashade clamped down on her tongue. Better to let the tall man digest this piece of news first. Folashade focused on Adaeze's bracelet gifted by Doudou. Surely, that trinket had to be part of the bargaining, and she was right to hint at it. She chanced a quick peek at the barbarian, whose face still carried a quizzical expression.

"And the amount this fellow mentioned?" The well-dressed man looked at her and parsed his words as though he were laying a trap.

"Four hundred livres for Adaeze and myself." She made a slow turn toward the barbarian. "Four hundred thousand cowries." She held her breath as she struggled with the pound sterling conversions.

The Mandinka worked a wad of spittle in his mouth as he turned back to Adaeze. "Four hundred thousand cowries? This one's wearing the clothes of a serving wench"—he pointed to Adaeze's mismatched outfit—"and those bracelets, decent enough but of a simple design. The gems are quite ordinary and small. Altogether, they can be worth no more than two pounds sterling. Seventeen thousand cowries. Nowhere near four hundred thousand." He turned to Folashade, more of a smirk than a smile upon his face.

Praise Allah. This hyena of a man had just given Folashade the key. Now how fast could she do the conversion? She turned to Charbonneau. "No four hundred livres," she repeated, this time with more conviction.

Charbonneau slammed his fists on Adaeze's shoulders. The girl let out a little cry as the barbarian planted himself inches from the Mandinka's face. Spittle sprayed the air as the Frenchman's face reddened. "Tell this pompous ass I showed him one of the jewels last night. That bracelet alone is worth two pounds sterling. Without a woman attached to it. Now he must make me a real offer, or I go elsewhere." Charbonneau spewed his venom in his usual mixture of French and Wolof. He jerked Adaeze from the bench. He clasped his hands tight around her shoulders and held her in front of him. "This one is not the prize, though she is a royal." He shook her shoulders, and Adaeze's entire body wobbled. "With this one comes a magnificent necklace. One worth four hundred livres all by itself. All I ask is that you give me four hundred livres for the two women, and I will allow you the purchase of the necklace at a discounted price." He tilted Adaeze toward Folashade.

Folashade caught a quick glimpse of her sister's eyes as she was being shoved about. They reflected back nothing.

The Mandinka dignitary stepped back, bumping into Malick. "What is the fool saying?" A flash of discomfort shrouded the official.

Folashade took in a breath as she rummaged the numbers swirling through her head. "And the necklace." She dug her fingernails into her palms. Surely, Charbonneau had included the word for "necklace" in the spate of words he'd spit out.

The Mandinka shoved Malick aside as he busied himself straightening his tunic. "What of the bracelet I saw last night?"

Folashade opened her mouth, but the French words inside her head refused to disentangle themselves.

"I've had enough of this. Bring both wenches with me," Charbonneau growled at Malick. "I'll deal with you later for the clothing mix-up." With one quick move, Charbonneau pushed Adaeze toward Folashade and waved his arms toward the Wolof commander.

"Adaeze!" Folashade leapt forward as her sister's crumpled body slumped toward the ground. She gathered Adaeze in her arms just centimeters before the girl's right knee slammed into the marshy ground. Folashade tried to drag Adaeze to her feet, but her sister's legs twisted into the soft earth.

"Wenches. My house," Charbonneau barked his Wolof as he turned and headed for the stockade gate.

Malick, his own tunic stained with perspiration, glared at Nago as he jabbed his forefinger at several of the Wolof guards. "You! Take that one. You and you, grab the other bitch!" He stormed toward Nago. "As for you, I see you are incapable of acting as a lady's maid. I'm going to see to it that you service my men until the ship arrives. All my men." He slapped the side of her head. "You are so old and dried up, Monsieur will not sustain any lost income over you. You are not worth even twenty thousand cowries to us. My men can have as much of you as they can stomach."

The Mandinka official's eyes darted in multiple directions as Malick brushed past him. Folashade sank to her knees, her arms wrapped around the limp Adaeze's waist, whispering Nago's name. Three, four, or more, young Wolof descended upon the two. Folashade felt Adaeze being yanked from her arms just as another warrior slipped an arm under Folashade's hips. He swooped her into his arms. She closed her eyes and let her head fall into the man's sweaty chest. Her body and soul felt drained of all feeling. She twitched her eyes open just enough to see the group troop out of the stockade, following an angry-striding Charbonneau up the path and away from the encampment. Folashade struggled to blink back the darkness threatening her. Not now.

Chapter 17

Bibi laid the dampened cloth across Adaeze's forehead as she and Folashade shifted their sister's back against the stack of pillows on Charbonneau's cot. Bibi placed the empty goblet the barbarian had thrust into her hands on the floor. In his French, he had ordered her to pour some of the liquid down Adaeze's throat, the same burning, foul-tasting dark-amber wetness that he often sampled himself and sometimes forced down her own throat.

"Adaeze! Adaeze!" Bibi's voice was insistent but soft as she rubbed the wet cloth across her sister's forehead.

Adaeze's eyes flickered open. She stared at the closed cabin door. The voices of the trio of men standing just outside rose in an ever-increasing crescendo of anger. Charbonneau and the Mandinka dignitary dominated the shouting match. Malick interjected only an occasional clarifying word. Each time Charbonneau's voice spit out his French and his doggerel Wolof, Adaeze's eyes clamped shut and her head tucked into one of the cushions.

"Well? I've shown you the bracelet," Charbonneau blurted out in his French. "Last night. If you believe you can take any of these women to Gorée without giving me a fair price, then you are in for a sad truth."

"Uhh," Adaeze gurgled.

In her haste to retrace Charbonneau's words, Bibi had clamped the cloth over Adaeze's nose and mouth.

"Sorry," she muttered. Another reference to Gorée.

"Adaeze. You must open your eyes." Bibi looked down at her sister, dropping the cloth over the girl's chest as Bibi's hands moved to Adaeze's wrist, and the bracelets. She ran her fingers across all three. As plain as they were, fine gold, for sure, but made up of only simple swirls and curves, and with garnets no wider than a fly's wings, Manuela had still coveted them. If only Bibi could rouse her sister into a moment of lucidity. Instead, she put a light hand over the girl's wrist. "I think we're going to need these, though I'm not quite sure why." Her bare foot kicked the goblet under the cot and out of Charbonneau's view when he stepped back into the cabin.

Adaeze's eyes remained closed, her lashes resting on her cheeks, her body still.

The Mandinka banged the already-open door against the cabin wall as he brushed past Charbonneau. He stomped toward the center of the room and planted himself next to the mahogany-wood table. Bibi sucked in a breath and tightened her grip over Adaeze's forearm, concealing the bracelets in as casual a pose as she could manage.

"My arm!" Adaeze startled alert.

Bibi kept her eyes from her sister as she eased her hand away, praying the Mandinka negotiator had been too busy preparing a fresh assault against Charbonneau to pay her more than scant attention.

Charbonneau's glowering stance as he squared off against the Mandinka brought Bibi's attention back to the Frenchman. He moved toward the man, stopping just centimeters away. The negotiator, ignoring the Frenchman, scowled as he scanned the room. His eyes settled on the cot and the three sisters.

"She is the one." The Mandinka took a step closer to Folashade, brushing Charbonneau's shoulder. "She is the wench who can tell me, in the name of all that is holy, the meaning of your gibberish." The negotiator hooked his forefinger at Folashade. "Speak!"

The girl darted her apologies to Bibi. "What is it you wish of my sister?" Folashade had clearly gotten herself into a new brand of trouble. Bibi looked to Charbonneau. Neither of these men wished her or her sisters well, but one might be more evil than the other.

"If your sister is inadequate at the task of making sense of the words of this Frenchman, then let us see how well you can do the task. Though, I suspect you are nothing more than a barely educated concubine of the nobility." The Mandinka sneered at Bibi. "Tell your master I have come to see the bracelet of last night." The brown-skinned man leaned forward and peeked at Adaeze's forearm. "A well-worked piece of gold, for certain, but not good enough for this sort of dealing." He dismissed the bracelets with a wave of a hand as he finally looked toward Charbonneau. "Show me this necklace you continue to babble about."

Bibi's mind whirled. Out of the corner of her eye, she read the panic on Folashade's face. What had the girl done?

"Monsieur see jewels for arm and neck," Bibi translated to Charbonneau, her fingers digging into her thighs. Images of Manuela and this unknown Gorée marched into her head, her stomach sending out waves of increasing unease. She shook her head. One thing was clear. She couldn't piece together the reason, but those bracelets held the secret to safety for the three Bambara sisters. "Gorée. We go?" The words escaped before she had time to caution herself.

Charbonneau stared at her. A chill ran down Bibi's back. She watched the man's mouth open and close. No sound emerged. His eyes widened for the passing of a second. Bibi shivered. Her words had made him uncomfortable.

He turned his back and headed toward the second room. "Tell him not to follow me," Charbonneau ordered as he pulled shut the mudcloth curtain dividing the two rooms.

The Mandinka moved after Charbonneau, but Bibi held up a hand. The man halted half a meter from the heavy cloth divider. The sound of a key inserted into a lock floated through the mud cloth. The lid of the zebra-topped trunk cranked open. Her captor emerged a moment later carrying a pouch. He beckoned toward the cabin door. Charbonneau and the Mandinka stepped outside, closing the door behind.

Malick took three steps toward the arguing duo as their voices drifted into the room. His eyes shifted to the cloth separating the two rooms. The Frenchman's aide turned and glided toward the opening. He ran his fingers across the dividing curtain.

"What does the foreigner hide in there?" Malick whispered to Bibi as he clutched the cloth in one hand.

She straightened her back as she eased her arm to Adaeze's elbow. Her sister's eyes opened, and she grabbed at her stomach. Folashade placed a hurried hand over Adaeze's under dress and rubbed gentle circles over her pregnant belly.

"Hide. He hides nothing," Bibi answered the lieutenant. "Your master stores the supplies for the journey in that room. All things you have seen before." She paused. "Supplies he might need on Gorée?" She hadn't wanted her voice to end in an uptilt.

Malick's subdued laugh filled the air as he shook his head. "You question Gorée. You name the foreigner as my master." He chuckled. "You have much to learn about me and who stores what on Gorée Island."

Island. The man had just named Gorée not only as a place but as an island. Bibi turned to question the Wolof further when Charbonneau and the negotiator stepped back into the cabin, their faces unreadable.

The Mandinka negotiator walked over to the cot, angling past the barbarian and his lieutenant.

Bibi took her arm from Adaeze as the Mandinka stared at her. She lowered her eyes.

"This one"—the dignitary pointed to Bibi—"the wench you showed me last night, and the one you are clearly enjoying, allow me to see the size and shape of her tits, and we may have a deal. In fact, I shall require a close look."

Bibi jerked her head up to meet the Mandinka's eyes. The chill running down her spine deepened. She turned to him as he grabbed her right arm and pulled her to her feet. A grunt threatened to escape, but before she could utter a sound, Charbonneau shoved her behind him. He guarded her as he turned and reached for Adaeze's arm. Bibi peered over his lowered head as he yanked off the three bracelets from her sister. He spun around and slapped them into Bibi's hands.

Questions flooded her mind. No matter. Her prize now lay in her hands, and she would use every prayer ever uttered to Allah to keep it there. The corners of her lips threatened to twist into a long-forgotten-how smile. No matter the cost, she must devise a plan to keep these jewels, jewels so coveted by Manuela, even if Adaeze could offer no help. Bibi fondled the bracelets. She sensed the swish of air an instant before she glimpsed Charbonneau's open hand lashing out toward her. The force of his push against her chest plunged her deeper into the cabin's gloom. Off-kilter, she almost stumbled to the floor. Her chest pained. She didn't care. One. Two. Three. All three bracelets still lay in her hands! Charbonneau turned back to resume his ongoing argument with the Mandinka. Bibi lowered her arms to her side while she kept her eyes straight ahead. As quietly as she could, she slipped the bracelets over her left wrist just as Charbonneau grabbed Adaeze's feet. He pulled her sister to the edge of the cot, her feet scuffing the hidden goblet into view. Her captor leaned over and laid the Doudou bracelet, unfastened, across Adaeze's left wrist. The stones sparkled even in the half-light of the cabin. A smile threatened to erupt across the Mandinka's lips.

"Let me make myself clear." Charbonneau straightened and faced the dignitary, offering the man only a half view of Adaeze and the bracelet. "Four hundred twenty livres, forty-eight pounds sterling, you may have both this woman"—he tapped Adaeze on the thigh—"and this bracelet." He turned to Folashade, who had scooted to the foot of the cot. "That one is only a child, but one I suspect has never been touched. I know the going rate for healthy female imports in the Americas. For the young one, you may give me one hundred fifty livres or seventeen pounds sterling."

The Mandinka's smile turned into a protruding lower lip. "I gather this fool's meaning. His mind is as crazed as this woman he is trying to pass off as a princess if he believes I will take her, even with the bracelet. Now, what I will pay . . ." The Mandinka stretched out an arm toward Bibi as he let his words fade in his throat.

Charbonneau took two steps backward and bumped Bibi further from the man's grasp, this time sending her thudding against the cabin wall. She stifled a fresh grunt of pain when a loose nail in the wallboard gouged into her shoulder.

"If this is the woman you want, I will tell you what you will pay." Charbonneau squared his shoulders as he faced the dignitary. "Four hundred livres for her alone." He reached inside his blousy shirt and withdrew something.

Bibi heard Folashade and Adaeze gasp in unison. She rubbed at her shoulder and stretched on tiptoe to look around Charbonneau. The man held something close to his chest. She chanced a step forward just as he turned and moved toward her. She closed her eyes and stiffened against another blow. She sensed the speed of him moving behind her when Charbonneau clamped his hand hard into her shoulder. She felt the blood ooze through her under dress. Before she could mount a protest, the man who held her prisoner propelled her toward the cot. Bibi pressed her hand over the bracelets. She could not lose them now. Charbonneau stood behind her as though she were a shield. He pushed something heavy and cool against her neck.

"Oh, Allah," she cried out before she could calm her alarm. Both hands went to her neck, the bracelets softly clanging together. Her fingers fumbled for the encircling stones—the center one as large as she remembered—the size of her thumb and a third. Her emerald necklace!

Charbonneau tugged her to his chest. She felt the outline of his man place—quiet for now. His scarred hand jammed the necklace against her neck.

"Another six hundred livres, sixty-eight pounds sterling, for this little beauty." Charbonneau's breath brushed Bibi's ear as he lifted the jewel and jangled it in front of the Mandinka.

Bibi turned to the well-groomed man. She stared at the insignia on his cap. The Mandinka's eyebrows lifted in pleasure. The chill in her back spread through her entire body. Her mind allowed her the truth, but in her heart flickered the tiniest of flames she could be wrong. The look glinting out of the man's eyes squeezed the life out of that hope just as the last coals on a long-eaten goat died. None of the Bambara would be released. They, along with Adaeze, Folashade, and herself, all faced some sort of auction block on this place called Gorée Island. The pain of a question slashed across Bibi's forehead. She knew little of the price of slaves, though she knew they were bartered back home in Timbuktu. Charbonneau and the Mandinka had argued with great fury these past two days. The gap between their price points was vast. Why?

"You have taken leave of all your senses," the Mandinka official's voice sang out in anger. "My traders tell me only the most beautiful women fetch even twenty pounds sterling in the New World. While you may have captured three females of an admittedly appealing above-average prettiness, even a modicum of beauty, only one can truly make a man weak with want." His eyes made a second journey over Bibi's body.

She shivered but willed her hands away from her breasts.

The Mandinka lowered his eyes and focused on her hips. "She looks well suited for her future tasks." The muscles in his cheeks spasmed. "For her, I can get two hundred livres in the West Indies, but you must realize I can purchase her for no more than ten pounds sterling. Eighty-five livres. Mind you, she may be seasoned, but she must not be pregnant." He cocked his head at Charbonneau. "By the looks of it, you have enjoyed yourself quite enough."

Bibi felt her feet slide from under her. Pregnant. No, not her, but Adaeze, yes. And Charbonneau did not yet know he'd fathered a child. Bibi tried to straighten her knees, but they refused to hold. She slumped back into the barbarian's arms. Her eyes shut and refused to open. She felt him lower her to the cot. She heard the man mumble something about Adaeze as her sister's body shifted from the bed. Spare them. Spare Adaeze, who could not even acknowledge the true father of her child. She, Folashade, and Adaeze were all to be sold as slaves and shipped to someplace called the New World.

"Oh, Bibi. Not you, too. I can't lose you both." Folashade's voice, with its rising wail, roused Bibi. "One of you must keep her mind about her, or what will become of us? Bibi, I can't, I won't, become a woman whose only use is to make sure men are pleased. And what of Adaeze?"

Bibi turned to look at Folashade. Despair that did not belong on the face of one so young blemished her baby sister's budding beauty. Bibi bolted upright, her feet brushing Adaeze's shoulder.

Her eldest sister sat on the floor, her back against the cot, her knees drawn to her chest, the pewter goblet inches from her hip. She hummed a song that Nago had once used as their nursery lullaby.

"I heard." Folashade's lip trembled, and her eyes widened as she mumbled her Persian. "Bibi, I understood him. Them. I mean, I made out as many words as I could from the barbarian. He said sell. Us. Oh, Bibi," she wailed. Folashade's voice strangled in her throat. Tears trickled down her cheek as she threw herself into Bibi's arms. "We are to go to the West Indies."

Bibi clutched her sister and rocked her close just as Nago had done when both girls were babies. Bibi blinked but no tears flowed. "Folashade," she soothed. "No more talk of such things, but tell me, what else did the barbarian say about the sale?"

Sounds mixed through the gurgle of salty tears buried Folashade's words into Bibi's chest as the girl wrapped her arms tight around Bibi's back. "So many figures, my head hurt."

Bibi felt the worry lines that only old women carried deepen her forehead. All the money conversions tossed between Charbonneau and the Mandinka over jewelry, and that other. None of them—Folashade, Adaeze, or herself, even with the barbarian's tutelage, possessed the bed skills to command such a high price.

Folashade's sobs rose but garbled the words in her throat.

Charbonneau pushed open the cabin door. He pointed a finger at Bibi. "Hush up that girl." He slammed the door behind him.

How dare the French monster threaten her sister, an uncircumcised girl-child who believed she'd just been condemned to the role of concubine.

"As for that one"—the barbarian reached down for Adaeze, still curled up on the floor—"if you cannot get her to act lively toward a man, I will have a dozen men show her how."

"No." Adaeze's cry was loud and keen as she burst awake. "No." She scooted to the center of the room, her legs churning against the floorboards, her arms flailing the air as her bottom bounced toward the center table.

Charbonneau stared after Adaeze, his mouth open. Adaeze, her eyes narrowed, blazed an unflinching glare back at the Frenchman. Her right hand reached toward the table, her eyes never leaving her torturer. Her fingers searched the tabletop until they fumbled against the lantern.

"No!" she keened again, her body rocking as she gathered the lantern into her hands. She juggled the hot glass until she got a firm grip on its handle.

With the speed Adaeze exhibited as a child when she outraced all the other children of the nobility, she planted one foot on the floor, steadied herself, and with one lightning-bolt quick move, hurled the flame-lit lantern at Charbonneau. The glass holding the oil and the burning wick shattered as it struck his chest. Smoke and shards of glass sprayed the room and stuck into the man's clothing. Flames escaped and licked at the cloth on the front and sleeves of his loose-fitting blouse. He batted the flames with both hands.

"Kill him! Kill him! Kill him!" Adaeze's voice pierced the air as she leapt to her feet.

She looked so much like the picture of the women warriors in one of Papa's ancient books, that Bibi, coughing through the smoke and stench of burning cloth, could not mouth a sound of caution. Bibi watched Adaeze twist around and reach for the low table. With one hand, she grabbed one leg and lifted the sturdy furniture to her shoulders as though it were no heavier than a meter of linen. Her feet pounded across the floor toward her tormentor, her hands gripping the table. Charbonneau looked up from his smoldering clothing just as Adaeze pushed the heavy mahogany into him with the force of the mightiest of the Timbuktu warriors of old. One table leg caught the barbarian in his man place. Adaeze jerked the piece of furniture upward with both hands, her jaw set.

"Ah, God! You damnable bitch!" Charbonneau gasped as both hands went to his pantaloons. He doubled over and sank to the floor.

Adaeze pounced on him, straddling his head between her knees, squeezing hard. Her fists pelted his back as he grabbed at her legs.

"What in the name of Allah is all this ungodly noise?" Malick stormed into the room, stopped in an instant, and stared at the melee before he stalked toward Adaeze. He reached behind her and grabbed her around the neck.

"Take your hands off my sister!" Bibi struggled to free herself from Folashade. "Let her go!"

The large Wolof jerked Adaeze from Charbonneau, spun her around, doubled his fist, and punched her in the belly. Adaeze, air easing out of her in one long gasp, slid limp to the floor. Charbonneau staggered to his knees, a hand still holding his man place. He inched toward Adaeze, swinging his free arm back, his fist clenched. Bibi pushed Folashade to the cot and scrambled, off-balance, to her feet. Oh, Allah, give her the strength to reach the barbarian before he killed Adaeze. Bibi's ankle turned as she jumped toward the Frenchman, both hands groping for his arm. She spotted a scorched place on the sleeve of his shirt and ripped it open. Bibi looked down at his reddening skin. She dug her fingernails into his forearm and lowered her head. She opened her mouth and bared her teeth just like the attacking lions in one of Papa's picture books. Before she could bite into the forming blister, Charbonneau jammed the palm of his hand under her chin. With the force of a blacksmith breaking cold iron, he snapped her head back. Her neck arced sharp pains down to her fingertips. She lost her grip as her head slammed into the wooden floorboards, one foot twisted under her hip.

"Oh." Bibi's fingers grasped at the floor as she struggled to right herself. The pain in her neck cranked up, and her numbing fingers felt as though they were reaching for cotton. "No." The word was so softly uttered, it barely reached her own ears. Bibi managed to get her feet under her. She spotted Charbonneau, his face as red as the back end of a hyena, just as he lunged after her. She lifted a hand to ward off his blow. Too late. He caught her by the throat and pulled her to her feet. Her eyes felt too big for their sockets. Her tongue took on a life of its own and lolled outside her mouth. In her misery, Bibi sought out the form of Adaeze. She shut her eyes and imagined Papa's most elaborate Qur'an, the one she and no other women were allowed to touch. When the barbarian finally succeeded in murdering her, please, Allah, make him spare Adaeze. Charbonneau shook Bibi as though she were a straw doll in the hands of an angry Tuareg child. He held her only inches from his face, a face as dark as the blackest day of the rainy season. The barbarian pushed and kicked her to the cot. The walls of the cabin wavered around her. Bibi's knees gave way. She clamped on to Charbonneau's wrists with both hands. He batted her away as though she were a fly settling on his bare arm. With one move, he jerked around to face the cot.

"No. Not you." Charbonneau's voice growled his anger.

Bibi turned her head just as the Frenchman kicked out a booted foot and tripped Folashade, who'd started toward the fallen Adaeze. Folashade tumbled to the floor next to her elder sister.

"Monsieur"—Malick, his face looking smug, planted his sandaled foot across the side of Folashade's face—"these wenches must be kept quiet."

Folashade's cry of pain was lost in the groan of protest in Bibi's own throat.

Malick slid his foot from Folashade's cheek to her mouth. "That Mandinka cannot be more than thirty meters away. If he has heard anything or believes these wenches are nothing but trouble, even the deal you have just made will be lost to us."

Bibi tried to locate her sisters. Her neck and throat throbbed. She felt Charbonneau grab at the collar of her silk brocade caftan as her knees buckled again, threatening to throw her facedown on the cot. She winced as the barbarian wrestled the silk overdress off her.

Bibi clutched at the folds of her under dress. If Charbonneau was determined to make her defilement complete by disrobing her naked in front of his Wolof henchman, she was determined to bring honor to her final moment of life. She wrapped her arms tight around her waist, awaiting his hands tearing at the fabric. Instead, Charbonneau's knee rammed against the back of her thighs. She collapsed to the floor, both of her legs jarring pain into her hips. Her under dress, intact, caught under her knees.

"Allah, mercy!" The scream that had waited so long to erupt filled the cabin.

The barbarian, his breath steaming her neck, wrenched her arms behind her back.

"Ahh," she yelped as Charbonneau slipped the knotted sleeves of the caftan around her arms. He yanked them tight. Bibi bit down on her lower lip.

"I've cut as good a deal as I can for your crazy sister." He leaned the side of his face into the pain in her neck and pushed her head into the thin mattress.

Tears flooded her eyes as she struggled to turn her head.

"The next time you touch me unbidden, wench, I'll see to it that you find yourself on your back in a Santo Domingo cane field buck naked, your legs spread so far apart, you fear they will break. I swear by the blood of Jesus Christ, I will have at least ten of the lowliest slaves take turns on top of you." Charbonneau, bursting out his angry French, pressed something hard, cold, and metallic against the back of her neck. The goblet! The stench of the drying contents brought bile to her throat and spewing out her mouth.

He bore down on the drinking gourd, pressing her face even deeper into the skinny mattress and her own vomit. Her nose clogged with the debris. Each gulp of fouled breath came too soon and too short.

"If you don't calm your sisters once they get to Gorée, I'm afraid not even the necklace will save any of you."

The bones in her neck cracked.

"Do you understand me?" Charbonneau slid his knee up to the soreness already in her shoulder. He bore down.

A scream mounted in her throat, but skewered between Charbonneau and the mattress, no sound emerged. The darkness threatened to envelop her. Bibi fought to bring in a breath, though it might be her last. Now her toes slid into numbness. The sounds in the room muted and threatened to disappear. From somewhere, perhaps above, perhaps to her right, or maybe below—a wave of air as cooling as the wind off the Niger swept the blackness aside. Sound suddenly flooded back into her ears. Her toes wriggled their relief. Air bathed her lungs. Charbonneau grabbed the front of her plaits and yanked her head off the cot. She heard the goblet thud to the mattress next to her head.

She was alive—for now. She prayed she could believe the same of Adaeze and Folashade. Bibi's eyes watered as she struggled to locate her tormentor. She tried to lift her head, but the agony was too great.

"Secure all three of these damnable wenches." Charbonneau's sound came from the middle of the room. "As for that daughter of Satan, she's as crazy as one of those laughing hyenas."

"So I have believed for some time," the loathsome second-in-command responded.

Allah, strike the man dead and keep him forever from Paradise.

"'Tis nothing but the truth." Charbonneau. "But if we can bring back her mind even for a little while, she still looks decent enough to sell for a few pounds sterling. We will be long away from this place before a Western man discovers how little pleasure she can give."

Adaeze. The hated barbarian spoke of her sister. Bibi sucked in her lips and eased her neck a centimeter to the right. Though her eyes were glazed with pain, there stood Charbonneau. She watched as the mud-cloth curtain fluttered open and he limped into the other room. She shut her eyes. The struggle to keep them open pained her neck all the more. The cabin was silent except for the sounds of Charbonneau rummaging through something. Adaeze, and even Folashade, uttered neither a grunt nor a groan.

"Here," Charbonneau, his voice stronger, barked, "use these to tie the wenches."

Bibi grunted. She shifted her head another centimeter. There stood Charbonneau holding three lengths of coiled rope. He tossed them to Malick. Bibi's head dropped to the mattress, her cheek bathed in her own sick. She shut her eyes. There was no need to see any more of the barbarian or sort out his angry words. His meaning was clear. Four sounds of this last hour stood out in her head. "Gorée," "necklace," and "New World." She, Adaeze, and Folashade had been sold as slaves. They were all on their way to Gorée. And Manuela.

Chapter 18

The boat rocked across the waves with ten times the ferocity of any canoe Folashade had ever sailed. Travel along the Niger had never been like this. She planted her shackled feet on the bottom of the craft, praying for balance. Even so, with each lurch over an oncoming wave, she fell against Adaeze. Her sister, who had mouthed not a word since that terrible scene in the cabin yesterday, stared straight ahead through blackened, half-shut eyes at the back of Bibi's head. Charbonneau, on the forward bench next to the middle sister, sat sideways, keeping an eye on all three of his prisoners. Folashade felt the all-too-familiar lump forming in her throat. But, no, she was not going to cry, even though the shackles that held her hands cut into her wrists. She would not give the monster who planned to sell all three of them into whoredom the pleasure of seeing her misery.

Charbonneau glared at her as the wind off this lake picked up. No, this was no lake. Instead, the body of water that splashed into eternity had a name. The Atlantic Ocean. She had read of this great body of water in several of Papa's books, and Bibi had confirmed the truth of it. Folashade's nose began to run. She lifted a hand to wipe it, her chains weighing down her wrists. Charbonneau gave a sly little smile just as a breeze lifted his hair into his eyes. Good. May Allah strike him blind. Folashade turned away from his warning glare and looked at the fast-approaching island in the distance. Already, she could spot the outlines of buildings on the rocky prominence, and the wharf where skiffs carrying other victims were docked. Bibi had told her, but she already knew. This place was called Gorée. Gorée Island, and it was the place where captives were shuttled to be turned into slaves. This midmorning was hot, but nothing like the heat of her beloved Timbuktu. Fresh tears threatened just as the boat dipped low and to the left. This time, Folashade toppled into Adaeze's lap. Strangely, her sister, bound wrist and ankles with shackles just as she and Bibi but suffering the added indignity of an iron collar around her neck, sat as regal as the queen she might have been, her balance undisturbed, her hands still.

Folashade righted herself as the boat slowed. Better to stare at the island, now just meters away, than dwell on the unknown that awaited them all. As the boat neared the dock, a number of locals waded into the water, coils of heavy rope and metal chains over their shoulders. She watched the men toss lengths of the confining restraints toward the deckhands, who secured them to iron pillars on the craft.

"You." Charbonneau jabbed a finger at Malick sitting behind Folashade and Adaeze. "Jump. Make people ready to go."

She squinted as the Wolof used Adaeze's shoulder to hoist himself forward in the craft. The sailors still maneuvered the boat to anchor in tight quarters between two already docked skiffs. Folashade sniffed the air. Did she and her fellow kidnapped victims all carry the stench of caked human waste about them? She stared at the craft to her far right, a third filled with vacant-eyed and chained women, but few men. She held her breath against the putrid smell as she took in the look of her new surroundings. She assessed the milling crowd at the end of the dock. Twenty, thirty, almost fifty, prisoners stood in segregated clumps along the beach, surrounded by stacked crates. Guards stood by each group. Men here, women there.

Curses and shouts from the boat to her left brought her attention to Charbonneau's men. A trio she recognized from the overland trek poked and prodded five women trying to exit the skiff. Folashade blinked against the morning sun slanting into her eyes. There was Nago standing fourth in the pitiful lineup. Folashade started to call out to her cousin-servant, who stood stooped, her ankles tangled in chains as she tried to lift a leg over the edge of the craft. No. Seeing her kinswomen in the same helpless condition as her would only deepen Nago's despair. Folashade bit down on her lower lip as a Wolof guard flayed a stick across Nago's naked backside. Her cousin, silent, dropped to her hands and knees and crawled out of the boat, her pendulous breasts swaying with each labored move.

"You!" The barbarian barked at another of his Wolof guards. "Get the two off." He rose to his feet, pulling Bibi along with him. He guided her off the boat and onto the dock.

Large Wolof hands Folashade did not recognize grabbed Adaeze under one arm and yanked her to her feet.

"Careful of my sister, you dunderhead." A lifetime as playmates to fools more stupid even than Adaeze's husband might await her and her sisters, but Folashade would never play the meek, compliant woman, not as long as Allah allowed her breath.

Her Wolof guard responded by dragging Folashade by the wrist chain over the next row of seats. Her ankle shackles, too short to clear the distance, caught under one foot, and she went to her knees.

"Up, you troublesome bitch," one of the more unpleasant guards from the overland trek barked.

"I'll not tell you again," Charbonneau called from shore in his French. His reproving tone unmistakable. "Be on guard with those two but take care not to injure them."

The Wolof grunted, but stooped and swept Folashade into his arms. He carried her over the boat ledge, holding her body tight against his sweat-drenched chest. She turned her head to keep from inhaling the sour, overpowering stench of musk about the man. He traveled along the entire length of the dock before he set her feet on the sandy beach next to Charbonneau and Bibi. The wind died down, and the full impact of the sun beamed on her bare head as sand and pebbles swept over and into her sandals.

"Walk them this way." Malick, waiting some twenty meters closer to town than the dock, beckoned Charbonneau and the Wolof guarding the three sisters to follow.

With pronounced grunts, Folashade's guard laid his hand into her back as Charbonneau's second-in-command turned and headed up a hill lined with squat stucco buildings resembling stores and family housing. She glanced around to see who else made up this little parade. She and her two sisters, along with their captors, were alone in this procession. As she moved from the beach, she looked behind her. She tried to catch Nago's eye, but the woman stood encircled by a crowd of the kidnapped, at least fifteen, from Charbonneau's group. Men looking like Serer, Yoruba, Fula, as well as Wolof, surrounded the captives. But wait. Other men paraded the cobbled streets of this Gorée—men with skin the color of Charbonneau. What snatches of Wolof Folashade heard from their mouths was as ragged as that spoken by the barbarian, yet many talked with an accent that differed from his. With the guard's prodding, Folashade pushed one tired foot ahead of the other up the steep hill as the ghost-skinned men strolled past her. Curious, only a few of these Europeans carried the same string-straight hair as the infidel. One man, with eyes as brown as a clump of soil and skin only a shade lighter than a Tuareg, caught her looking at him. The initial scowl on his face turned to surprise as he appraised her from her once-polished head to her now-ashy feet. He took a step toward her just as Folashade's guard jabbed his fist deeper into her back.

She kept her groan silent. If only she could rid herself of these dreadful chains, or if they were lengthened enough to allow her a full stride, she would outwalk this disgusting Wolof. Up ahead near the top of the hill, Charbonneau pulled Bibi by the hand as they passed another series of houses standing almost wall to wall. Masses of people who looked like Wolof locals paid scant attention to the chained group marching past them. Women, with baskets of fruit, clothing, and cooking utensils balanced on their heads, threaded themselves along narrow streets. Men in loose-flowing tunics gestured with one another as they sidestepped animals and jostled aside women too old or too slow to veer away from their betters. Up ahead, Folashade could see little other than the fleeting back of the hated Malick as he made yet another turn in the crooked uphill road.

A boy, no older than twelve and waving a stick at two goats under his care, paused in his downhill trek to stare first at Bibi, then at Folashade. "You poor devils. You must have sorely displeased Allah." The boy's singsong voice filled the air. "You're going to the Americas!" The youth laughed as he laid his staff against the hindquarters of one of the animals and skipped down the street.

Displeased Allah? The child had taken leave of his senses. Was there a war with which she was unfamiliar, one that rendered her and all the other Bambara prisoners of some conquering army? Folashade squinted her eyes more in confusion than against the sun. There could be precious few other explanations for why this child, too young to be a warrior, jeered at hapless females who had never been combatants. If the child possessed a modicum of Allah-given decency, he should be offering help instead of derision. Her head throbbed, and the muscles of her right eye twitched, even though she wanted them quiet. Folashade stopped and turned her head toward the boy's receding back, hoping answers might materialize from somewhere.

"Keep moving, bitch!" This most disagreeable guard raised his voice.

She tripped under his fresh shove but regained her footing. Without taking another step, she glared at the fool of a guard. "If you utter that word one more time against me or my sisters, I promise such displeasure you will beg for Allah's mercy to end your life as quickly as possible. The French are harsh in their treatment of men who disobey their orders." She adjusted her chains and folded her arms. "And if you think you can appeal to Malick, from what I've seen and heard, he will turn on you and sell you into slavery if you cause harm to me."

The guard's eyes blinked, stared, and blinked again. Folashade looked at the twenty-year-old. His mouth made little smacking sounds. He jerked his head, the hint of fright on his face, and pointed to the uphill path. He waited until Folashade took her own time to resume her steps. He walked beside her, silent.

"This is the place," Charbonneau called out as he herded the group through a makeshift but sturdy wrought-iron gate. "Let her know we're here."

Folashade sorted through the French. Charbonneau's little entourage had stopped at parts and bits of a building made of rock. The place looked old, and nothing like the structures of Timbuktu. She caught scraps of possible new building. Her guard gestured her through the gate. On one of the outer walls, Folashade noticed two large cylindrical chunks of metal projecting two meters from the exterior walls surrounding the entry. The round openings at the front of the smooth iron objects carried the diameter of half her arm—shoulder to elbow. She sucked in a breath. The metal pair's similarity to the iron fire sticks Charbonneau used to kill and injure sent a tremor through her body. These were the same thing. Guns. But where Charbonneau's fire sticks could hurt only one man or woman with each blast, these objects looked of a size enormous enough to mow down ten or twenty with each firing.

Now fully inside the enclosure, Folashade looked over at the barbarian and Malick. The two conferred near the center of the dust- and sand-filled inner courtyard, Bibi next to him. Charbonneau held on tight to the chain at the girl's wrists. Bibi, battered and bruised from yesterday's melee, paid the barbarian scant attention as she took inventory of the building surrounding them. Folashade followed her sister's gaze. Bibi, too, was struggling to sort out the nature of this place. She read in Bibi's face the same apprehension that she had. Only Adaeze, staring at some distant spot, remained unreadable.

The smell of salt-scented air drifted on the wind into the enclosure. A slapdash second story surrounded by walls on three sides had been set atop one of the original stone buildings. Despite its age, each wall stood as thick as a man's arm reach. Folashade counted more of the great guns that pockmarked the area. She tried to discern the original color of the paint covering the decaying edifice. Scraps of a one-time salmon pink caught her eye, but she couldn't be sure. She turned back to the entry. The compound was completely separated from the rest of the rocky settlement. Anyone attempting escape through that gate would be quickly seen. She turned to Charbonneau still arguing in the central courtyard.

Folashade shivered. Despite the aging construction, this place was a well-protected fort. A rudimentary balcony jutted out from the second floor. There was something odd in the building's configuration. Remnants of two facing staircases, only one of which seemed walkable, reminded Folashade of something. Oh yes. Back in Papa's library when she had been desperate to find out what the Qur'an said about the need for the full premarriage ceremony, she had sneaked a peek at her father's hidden book. Inside the covers of *The Body of the Virtuous Woman*, somewhere between chapters three and four, she had uncovered a drawing of female insides—the place where babies were housed before birth, the shocking words had declared. She'd wanted to read more, but D'bime had caught her just at that moment. Folashade remembered the text. Women, it seemed, had two such curving structures inside their bodies, structures that surrounded something called a womb. She swallowed hard at the memory that belonged to another life.

"So you have made your deal after all." A woman stepped through the remains of a bottom floor arch and called out to the nearby men. "I welcome the care of this particular group."

Was this the woman Bibi told her came to Charbonneau's cabin a few days back? Bibi had called her name. A strange one, for certain, and definitely not Wolof, Bambara, Fula, or any of the dozen or so languages with which Folashade was familiar. Oh yes. The woman was called

Manuela. But more than a strange-sounding name mystified Folashade. The woman was bedecked in an odd assortment of clothing. Certainly nothing a respectable female, nobility or not, in any West African land would ever drape over herself. In some ways, Manuela's costume resembled garments depicted in one of Papa's books on European dress in Spain or Portugal. Manuela, if that was her name, wore a cotton garment that laced up the back with strips of leather. The outfit carried a voluminous skirt that flowed to the ankles and a bodice that covered her front almost to her chin. Instead of a respectable pair of sandals, Manuela sported a woman's version of the boots worn by Charbonneau. A necklace made of iron completed her unflattering costume.

"Where will you house them?" Charbonneau addressed the big-boned woman.

"Follow me. Despite the look of the place, you will see the accommodations are generous." She patted at the big pouf of crinkly hair she wore knotted at the back of her head and tied with a strip of blue cloth that did not match the plain brown of her dress. She walked with the stride of a man rather than the dainty steps of a properly trained woman. Nago reminded Folashade often enough, usually with a slap on the ear.

Folashade looked up as Bibi, being tugged by the barbarian, turned a quick glance to her. She signaled Folashade her questions about this strange creature. Folashade nodded her head. She'd gotten Bibi's message. The sound and cadence of Manuela's words almost matched Charbonneau. She spoke his French. But how could this woman be one of the French ones? Clearly, the blood of some African tribe flowed in her veins.

"Step lively." Malick, holding Adaeze's collar chain, walked up to Folashade before she could further ponder the mystery of Manuela.

Folashade followed the lieutenant and trudged out of the sun, and under the arch. She walked into the shadows of the building's interior and closed her eyes to relish the cooler air. Instead, each fetid breath gagged in her throat. The smell of sickness, decay, despair, and death smothered her. Her chained hands covered her nose and mouth, but the cries and pleas from somewhere assaulted her ears. Up ahead, Manuela suddenly halted. Folashade watched Bibi, twenty meters in front, sway. Only the barbarian's quick grab around her waist saved her sister from falling to the floor. Malick tightened his grip on Adaeze's chain and dragged her along a narrow, almost-airless, dark passageway lit solely by a few scattered candles. With each forward step, the dim outline of humans cramped into tiny cubicles fronted with thick iron bars and heavy metal doors greeted her. She questioned her eyes and ears. What was she seeing? What was she hearing? Twenty to thirty naked male prisoners were crammed into each cage, stooping, squatting, or struggling for a foothold in the tight quarters. Moans and cries ranging from the angry to the pitiful beseeched Allah in eight or more languages. Folashade's ears throbbed with the pain.

"Sisters, throw yourselves into the waters." An Ibo dialect.

"Let the sharks devour you." This time, Benin. "Better dead than to leave Africa."

"Kill yourselves before it's too late and they lock you up in here." The faint wheezing of an Ashanti.

"Oh, Allah." A trickle of bile-infused saliva dripped from Folashade's mouth. The Wolof leader grunted in disgust but not at the spectacle of horror surrounding him. Instead, the man directed his impatience at Folashade's unmoving feet. With a grunt he slipped an arm around her waist and tucked her to his side like a warrior's spear, her feet dangling inches off the stone floor. Vomit splattered the ground.

"The women's accommodations are on the other side." Manuela's voice floated in and out of Folashade's ears as Malick set her feet on the floor in front of a closed rectangular-shaped door. "And are different, of course. Not so many to a space."

Adaeze stared at a buckle on Manuela's black shoes. Bibi leaned into the barbarian's shoulder, her body trembling.

Charbonneau scowled. "These women must not be housed with any others, is that clear?"

"Of course, Monsieur," Manuela answered. "But you must understand the special accommodations you request are difficult to come by. A fee must be paid weekly for special upkeep."

Folashade struggled to sort out the French. She looked over at Bibi, who had recovered enough to push away from Charbonneau. The look on her sister's face alerted Folashade that Bibi, too, was working on the translation. Perhaps, together, once they were left free of their captors for even a moment, the two sisters could sort out this clearly important exchange between the European and the African woman who spoke the barbarian's language. So far, Folashade had made out "fee," "accommodations," and "special."

"I've made arrangements for these women to sail on the *Trouvadore*. Until then, I will pay you eight thousand cowries for each week's stay." Charbonneau didn't look happy.

"Ah, the *Trouvadore*. That one carries the flag of Spain. Let us see. That ship sailed from Gorée just two months ago carrying a cargo of almost four hundred." Manuela's smile reminded Folashade of those who made false promises while grinning in your face. "A two-month voyage to the West Indies, another month or so to off-load the cargo. After a second two-month voyage back to the ship's home port of Barcelona, an additional month in port." Manuela's smirk looked triumphant. "You can see you are asking me to offer my best accommodations for a half year or more. That would be quite an expensive stay, wouldn't you say?"

"All the better." Charbonneau's voice edged annoyance. "You'll have a steady source of income. Ninety thousand cowries until she sails. That should cover all."

"Ninety thousand. Ahh, Monsieur, I could not possibly survive on such a paltry amount."

Charbonneau handed the chain encircling Bibi's wrists to Malick, whose forehead furrowed into even deeper wrinkles. The barbarian passed Folashade as he walked back to the entry. "Take the women to their new accommodations. I will make payment arrangements directly with your commandant." The Frenchman hadn't bothered to face Manuela. He disappeared through the arch.

Manuela's skin tone darkened as she scowled after the man. "We'll see about that. Bring the bitches this way."

Folashade lifted her head as Manuela swished out of the passageway and stalked under the balcony overhang. Stumbling along, Folashade watched Manuela turn right and then left. She mounted the staircase, placing each foot carefully. Up ahead, Bibi, now being shepherded by Malick, had no opportunity to turn to her sister. No need. Folashade grasped the significance of every word of Manuela's accented Wolof.

As usual, Charbonneau's Wolof liaison showed no mercy as he pushed Adaeze and dragged Folashade up the treacherous steps. Noises from ten, twelve, languages on the ground floated up the stairs. At the top, Folashade looked over the chest-high balcony. Another line of chained, dejected-looking kidnapped men and women filtered through the gate, their Wolof guards shouting at them as white-skinned men showing little patience stood in the enclosure to greet them.

"This is the best I can offer." Manuela stopped abruptly and fumbled for something inside the bodice of her dress. She extracted a large key. "And it is too good for the likes of these troublemakers. Why men are so taken by a pretty face, and a big front, I cannot fathom." The sound of the heavy mahogany door, with its malaligned and squeaky hinge cranking open, drowned out her words.

Manuela had stopped three doors beyond the staircase landing. Stacks of round iron balls four times the size of a melon could be seen peeking through the slats of a wooden crate near the south wall. Worse. Mounted through a slit above the crate was the back of another of those oversize fire sticks. Folashade shivered as a burst of ocean-scented wind fluttered the hem of her under dress.

Manuela stepped into the interior. Malick dragged Bibi and Folashade over the threshold. Folashade turned to see Adaeze walk in without the urging of a guard. Filtered sunlight streaming through a rectangle cut near the ceiling of this ten-by-ten-meter space silhouetted Adaeze's face. There was no other natural light in the room and no way to see anything of the outside world. Adaeze, the once queen-in-waiting, showed no recognition that this prison differed in any way from that of riding the smooth waters of the Niger. Folashade looked past her sister across the bare wooden floor to two cots, each covered with leaf-printed mud cloth. Adaeze looked fascinated at the ribbon securing the frizzed bun at the nape of Manuela's neck. Folashade tried to make eye contact with Bibi, but her middle sister scanned the room as Manuela stationed herself in one corner. Two crates cushioned with the same fabric as the bedcoverings opposed one another, and acted as chairs.

"I trust your master understands these accommodations are rarely used for slaves." Manuela gestured to three hooks jutting from the wall as she turned to Malick.

"Bother yourself not about what the Frenchman understands." The Wolof looked as though whatever smidgen of patience he possessed had fled.

Manuela pointed to a length of fabric draped over one of the crates. "These rooms are reserved for our visiting family members."

Malick released one of his more disdainful snorts. "I had no idea you half-breeds had any family members who cared enough to visit. And to clear your mind, if you have one, I am Wolof, and except for a few miscreants, we have no masters."

Folashade and Bibi jerked almost in unison to watch the dueling pair. Manuela straightened her back and poked out her chest as she tried to stretch taller to lessen the head-taller Malick. Folashade turned her head toward Bibi. The man had mentioned half-breed. Bibi would have to explain the term to Folashade. Bibi darted a glance at Folashade. Her sister gave a barely perceptible nod of her head. She'd understood. Now if the sisters could exploit this disagreement between the foreign-looking woman and a man who held her in low regard.

"My family has acted as guards for those of your countrymen"— Manuela let the last word hang in the air—"for two generations. You capture them. We merely care for them. Many times, my grandfather's people came straight from Portugal to visit and aid your grandfather's tribe."

It wasn't the lie that had to be obvious even to Adaeze that befuddled Folashade, it was the references to half-breed and Portugal. Folashade knew perfectly well that Portugal lay next to Spain, and it, too, had been occupied by the Moors. Had Manuela's Moorish grandparents come from Portugal? Or had her Portuguese grandfather traveled to the land of the Wolof and married a woman of Gorée? Folashade had never heard of such a thing. She'd have to ask Bibi, whose face suggested she already had the answer.

Malick grunted as though he, too, understood the lie. "Your tale may or may not be, but safe to say this whole business has paid off handsomely for you half-breeds."

Manuela bristled, but mumbled more to herself than Malick. "If you wish to use these accommodations for these haughty women, I suggest you recall that we descendants of the Portuguese are permanently employed here on Gorée as prisoner guards."

"The deed is done." Charbonneau strode through the open door, looked around the space, and nodded as he turned to Manuela. "Your commandant will make it clear the women are to have two meals a day and are to be allowed outside walks once a day. It is crucial they maintain their looks when they board the *Trouvadore*. Is that clear?"

Though Folashade had only grasped a few words of the barbarian's French, the frown creasing Manuela's forehead and driving the lines between her eyes deep into her brow left little doubt that she'd understood each and every French word.

"What is clear is that I am in charge of the women's wing of this fort." Manuela's voice menaced. "You, as am I, are Christian. In case you have forgotten, the commandant is a Wolof, and a Muslim." Manuela was quite the expert at allowing her words to dangle in the minds of those she clearly intended to intimidate. "Muslim men do not often come uninvited into the women's quarters, and these rooms are reserved for the guards. I, and I alone, control what goes on here."

Malick pursed his lips. "Bastard children of white foreigners take on airs they do not merit."

Manuela's mouth gaped, her earth-colored eyes narrowed, but she kept her quiet.

Charbonneau shrugged in non-understanding as he walked toward Bibi. "I, or my assistant, will check on these women each week. If I find them unfit for travel, then your commandant will seek an answer from you. The one in control."

Manuela switched her glare from Malick to Charbonneau, who looked at her as though she were of too little regard to return the gesture.

"Which two of these wenches will be my guests?" Manuela finally found words as she addressed her question to the cloth hanging on the hook.

"These." The barbarian jabbed a finger at Adaeze and Folashade. He reached for Bibi's hand and started toward the open door. The Frenchman nodded at Malick. "He will see they are settled. Especially that one." Charbonneau looked at Adaeze as he stepped across the threshold, dragging Bibi with him.

Bibi planted her feet on the floor. "But, Monsieur, please. Stop. You forget the chains." She held out her wrists as she turned to Charbonneau and tried her French. "Chains. Arm. Foot. Off, please. You go. Me here." The barbarian's eyes swept the room. He pursed his lips but said nothing. He tugged Bibi's leash.

She pulled against the chain. "Chains no good. Off, please."

Charbonneau, his jaw set, turned his back and shortened his grip. Had he not understood her French?

Bibi turned to Folashade, a quizzical look on her face. She tried to jerk her wrists to her chest. "Chains go away, Monsieur. Me, sisters. Here."

Charbonneau yanked harder as he took a step toward the door. Bibi, her head shaking in confusion, pulled against the barbarian. Manuela slipped from the shadows and rushed toward the pair. The French-speaking woman raised her stout arms and shoved Bibi into the barbarian.

Manuela's outstretched hand held the girl against Charbonneau. "I'd say the downstairs cells are for the likes of you." Manuela smirked at Bibi. "Make yourself of some use to those poor heathen men destined for slavery. One last go at a woman will make their waiting time more tolerable. I am sure you agree."

Charbonneau, his mouth in a grim line, gathered Bibi to him.

Bibi, her face half buried in Charbonneau's chest, called out to Manuela. "You are a female, are you not? Please have mercy for your fellow woman."

Manuela stepped back, lifted her chin, and smiled.

"Monsieur." With Manuela's nonanswer, Bibi tilted her head up to Charbonneau. "Monsieur, I stay. Adaeze. Folashade. You go."

The barbarian looked down at Bibi and, with the slowness of a land turtle, shook his head.

Folashade's heart thumped out of time with the turmoil in her belly. She watched Bibi's eyes widen. Her sister's mouth opened and closed, but no words emerged, only a sound that began as a whisper. Folashade clutched at her own stomach as that voice climbed to the heights of an animal fresh in the jaws of a killing jackal.

"I'm not to remain here with my sisters? Then where do you take me?" Bibi's words rode a wave of wail and moan. "To jail place? Me you make go to men?" Her words slowed to Wolof. "All those men in their filth and misery. That's where you're taking me."

Charbonneau watched Bibi's lips move, but he uttered not a word.

The stain of disbelief stamped across her face. Air pounded into Folashade's lungs. The muscles in her legs twitched. Her sister was to be turned into the lowliest of whores by this fiend of a man to whom Bibi had sacrificed her honor. Never! This monster, this infidel, in his cruelty, had to be stopped. Heat like the sun flooded her. Beneath the scraggly hairs on his chin, the strands in Charbonneau's neck tightened and beckoned to her. Strength pumped into Folashade's feet. She stormed across the floor toward the barbarian, her outstretched fingers splayed. The blue of his eyes glowed, inviting her. Quick breaths propelled her forward. Folashade's fingertips aimed at those eyes. Her legs pumped faster. She smelled the foulness of his unwashed body. Almost there. Two meters more. Now! She lunged. Her feet tangled. Bits of rough-worked metal entwined around her ankles, her instep, her heels. Her neck and shoulders snapped backward. Folashade plummeted to the floor, her face striking less than half a meter from Charbonneau's black boots.

The guard's feet pounded across the distance and stopped next to her head. "Up, bitch, you wench. On your feet!"

Folashade ignored the man's orders. She clawed along the wooden floor. The guard grabbed her ankle chain and tugged backward. She dug her fingernails into the wood as she used her elbows to propel herself toward Charbonneau. Splinters from the rough boards ground into her hands and knees.

Bibi's sandaled feet moved in front of Folashade's eyes as her sister stepped backward, her ankle chain grazing the top of Folashade's head. Bibi, her feet apart and fixed on the bare floor, stood between Folashade and the barbarian. Folashade kicked at the guard as she struggled to right herself. Bibi dropped to her knees.

"Monsieur, please." Bibi stretched her chained arms around Charbonneau's legs, her neck arched as she sought his eyes.

"Bibi?" Adaeze's voice drifted out of her throat as though it were unsure of its surroundings. "Bibi, I order this man to allow you to remain with us." Her voice dove back into her mouth.

"Secure those two now," Charbonneau barked as he bent down to pry Bibi's fingers from his legs.

"No!" Bibi shouted in the infidel's ear.

With each finger Charbonneau snapped back, Bibi screamed the warrior's battle whoop as she bounced her forehead against his leg. The barbarian, his jaw set, his eyes glaring, lifted a knee under Bibi's chin and pushed upward. Her cries died in her throat as she tumbled backward. She crumpled to the floor. The monster of a fiend stooped and pulled Bibi to her unsteady feet. He clamped his hands around her shoulders, and with a rhythmical motion worthy of a master cloth weaver, Charbonneau began shaking her. Folashade was certain she heard a snap in her sister's neck. The beads in Bibi's plaited hair streamed out around her with each violent movement and then slapped back into her cheeks.

"Mm. Mm," Bibi moaned.

"Stop. Stop you man of no God," Folashade screamed. "Or I will have Allah strike you dead!"

Charbonneau, his face scrunched like an overripe melon, continued shaking as though Folashade's words were no more than the pretend threats of a child.

Manuela moved to Folashade's side. The back of the woman's hand stung Folashade's left cheek. "You will learn to keep your mouth closed or you will find yourself with bleeding hands from gathering the sugarcane."

"No. No. No. Monsieur."

Bibi's voice bobbled with each shake. Her knees buckled. Her chained hands clung to Charbonneau's sides. "I go."

The barbarian, spittle spewing from his mouth, winced but continued the violent shaking. "You hellacious woman. You are going where I tell you!"

"Jail. Me. I go. No trouble." Bibi's head waggled on her neck. Her words spurted out on little puffs of air. "I go. No trouble if you help sisters."

The hideous Frenchman, sweat beading his forehead, let one hand drop from Bibi's shoulder. He swept a sleeve over his mouth. "No trouble. You do as I say with no more nonsense."

Bibi drew her clasped hands between them, the chain swaying against both their bodies. "Yes. I obey. Sisters no to jail." Bibi paused and sucked in a breath. "Me, yes. I go quiet to jail. If sisters no go, I work hard make jail men happy. Much cowries for you."

The sound of the barbarian's deep breaths filled the room as he swept up Bibi. Folashade, her cheek still stinging, watched the man. What depth of monster was he? Her sister had turned herself into the worst kind of woman to save Adaeze and Folashade. Bibi had sacrificed everything to this infidel. And this was how she was repaid. All air felt squeezed out of Folashade's chest. She looked at the man as he walked onto the balcony carrying Bibi, limp in his arms. *No, Allah, this cannot be.*

"Bibi!" Folashade crawled to the still-open door.

The guard slammed her shoulder against the frame as Folashade's eyes followed her sister.

Bibi lifted her head from the French fiend's chest as he approached the staircase, her brown eyes threatening to fade into nothingness. "Give these to Manuela." Her voice was weak as she slipped the three bracelets from her arm and tossed them to the corridor floor.

The barbarian, holding Bibi tight, headed down the stairs.

"No. I go together, Bibi. Man happy I make."

Folashade tried to lift her body from the doorframe as this most unholy Frenchman bounded down the stairs. The guard dragged her inside.

"Manuela," Bibi's voice, thin as mountain air, drifted up the staircase, "protect my sisters. Unless you want the truth of your treachery known."

Chapter 19

She really must speak to Nago about the quality of her bedcoverings. How could the future queen of Mali be expected to get any rest lying on such an insult to the nobility? Adaeze, stretching the skin-prickling cotton sheet to her chest, followed the ray of morning sun as it entered this rather tiny sleeping room. Funny. The ray landed exactly across Folashade's nose and lips as she lay in her own bed secured against the adjacent wall. The soft little stops and starts coming from the girl's mouth told Adaeze her baby sister still slept. The lump in Adaeze's belly suddenly jiggled, and she sighed. If Folashade didn't undergo the full procedure, the girl would never know motherhood. Not that this third pregnancy had been enjoyable. But, thanks to Allah, the worst was over. No more sickness in the mornings, though her still-absent husband would have neither noticed nor cared. Adaeze turned her head to look at the clothes-hanging hook on the far wall. She frowned. Nago, again. Yesterday's garments still hung there. Never mind, her pregnancy was progressing. In another few months, she would be brought to term. But for some reason, she could not calculate the number. She really must ask Nago. But, as usual, the woman was missing.

"Folashade." Adaeze raised her voice just enough to awaken her sister without jarring the girl. "Nago is absent again. I need you to help me sort out my time."

"Adaeze?" The girl awakened as though something more important than a dream called her. "Adaeze?" Folashade sat up in bed and stared at her.

Adaeze lifted her head from the cot. Now what addled her sister? Folashade looked at her as though she'd not heard nor seen Adaeze utter a sensible word in months. "Folashade, why do you stare? I am speaking Bambara. Have your ears gone silent?" Adaeze remembered. For the past few days, the girls had been playing language games. Though she couldn't quite recall all the details, perhaps Adaeze had broken some rule Folashade had dreamed up in the night.

"Sorry. I'm pleased you are awake." For no reason Adaeze could fathom, Folashade decided to speak Wolof to her sister.

Perhaps this was one of their play languages. Never mind. The language was of little consequence. The timing quandary was an odd puzzle. "Folashade, I seem to have lost track of the months. I believe the weather has changed. We should now be in the dry season."

Instead of the rational answer she expected, her youngest sister stared, the girl's mouth open and her eyes wider than Adaeze had ever seen.

"Folashade, are you ill?" Adaeze searched her sister for signs of sickness. She raised up on her cot and pulled her knees over the little bump of her stomach. "Have you contracted a fever that has taken away your senses?"

"Senses?" Folashade glanced at the door.

Adaeze sighed. Something was, indeed, amiss with her sister. She'd have to speak to Bibi about it. Bibi. There was something about Bibi she should remember, but the stress and strains of this new pregnancy had wreaked havoc upon her memory. "Now what was I saying?" She turned to Folashade.

"Adaeze . . . you . . . you're speaking."

"What an odd thing to say. Of course, I'm speaking. I've been speaking ever since you came here to Djenné. We must get the doctor to cure whatever ails you before the queen arrives. It will never do for her to believe her son is to marry a woman who cannot put two sentences together. And, why do you look at me so?" A flash of annoyance bathed Adaeze.

Folashade looked at the floor. "Sorry, it's just that you-you've asked for my help."

"Now I find you stammering. Your hearing seems impaired. I just explained. The months. With the rainy season late this year, I've lost track of the months of my pregnancy." Adaeze rubbed her hand in circles over her belly. "I can feel this one is another boy—a second heir to the throne." The smile came easily. "Toumani will be pleased."

"Yes. Of course." Folashade talked to the floor. "Your husband will be pleased." She slowly lifted her head and looked at Adaeze. "The months of your pregnancy. Yes. That would be about four months, Adaeze. We've been here in Gorée for a little over two of those months."

"Two months? Here?" Adaeze laughed. "Of course not. The queen was only a day or two's sail from Djenné when you arrived yesterday. You couldn't possibly have been at my home for two months."

"Adaeze, we are not in Djenné, we are in . . ."

What was wrong with Folashade's mouth? She took an eternity to form each word, and it swallowed in her throat.

"A place called Gorée."

Alarm wracked Adaeze. Gorée? Her sister was imagining things. "Nago! Bibi! Both of you get in here. Now! Something's wrong with Folashade. Very, very wrong." *Oh, what will the queen say?* A wave of fear settled over her.

The key turning in the lock brought Adaeze's attention to the heavy mahogany door. There was something about that door. It refused to open when she tried the latch, not that the ankle bracelets someone had given her allowed for much movement; it must have been her father-in-law. Now, what had she been thinking? The door swung open, and a woman in garb that did not belong on a servant to the queen of Mali stepped through the opening.

"You." The woman, fingering an ornament suspended from her neck, walked to the center of the room. "Yes"—she pointed to Adaeze—"stand!"

Stand? Who was this arrogant foreigner who dared order anything of the king's number-one daughter-in-law? The woman would be stripped to the waist and whipped in the Djenné center square for her impudence.

"Do not look at me as vacant-eyed as a dead gazelle. On your feet. I will get the truth out of you."

Adaeze watched the woman, as tall as herself but a time and a half heavier, stroll over to her cot. Adaeze lifted a hand to push away this rude servant. Too late. The woman grabbed the plaits at the front of Adaeze's head and yanked her to her feet. Adaeze tripped over her ankle ornament. Only the woman's hand planted against Adaeze's chest prevented her from falling. As she regained her footing, the woman reached down and grabbed the hem of the nightdress and lifted the worn garment to Adaeze's shoulders.

"What do you do?" Adaeze shouted as the woman's fingers, as strong as a man's, moved up to Adaeze's naked breasts.

"Ahh." Shame raced down Adaeze's face and stuck in her chest. She tried to form the words, *Do not dare touch me*, but where was the sound to push them out?

That old pain that lurked right behind her eyes burst forward again. No wonder she couldn't find the words. Just as well. Why did she need words? When this misery in her head came forth, words, either speaking or hearing them, only made her head throb all the more. What she needed right now was to think of the important things. Things that would make her a better queen of Mali when her time came. She watched that curious bit of iron bounce against the woman's chest as this foolish servant prodded and squeezed Adaeze's body. Not important.

Only that simple piece of metal, obviously made by a junior apprentice, mattered. The child-worker had merely affixed two intersecting posts, one shorter than the other, in the most basic of styles. The woman grabbed Adaeze's wrists and jerked them over her head. A hand as solid as a skilled brickmason thumped Adaeze's belly.

Allah, I pray you, make it stop. The words whispered in Adaeze's head.

The woman released her, the crossed metal piece grazing Adaeze's wrists. Wait. The object suspended from the servant's neck looked almost like the Christian crucifix she'd seen in Papa's books. She squirmed to gain better focus on the dangling object. Why would a self-respecting woman, especially one in the employ of the royal household, wear such a thing?

"Keep still. You have hidden the truth from me long enough!"

"You are not allowed to touch my sister in that manner." Somewhere through a barrel, Adaeze heard Folashade saying words that were better locked in Adaeze's head.

"This one is pregnant." An accusing voice, not Folashade's, spoke up. "Now, for the question. Is the father Bambara or European?"

Adaeze took in a deep breath. The room smelled of jasmine, jasmine in a cloud so thick, she could no longer make out the mouths of the people as they spoke. She could only hear their tinny little words fade in and out. Had one of the voices said "pregnant"? Who could be pregnant? Surely not Folashade. She was yet to be circumcised. What man would want her?

"Well, well. Your crazed sister has turned up fortunate."

"Fortunate?" Could that be Folashade speaking? Her voice sounded as though it were being blown away in a windstorm.

"You should be as fortunate as your sister." Was that the sound of arrogance from the woman's big voice? "I suppose I could give you some consideration. That other one, the Frenchman's bed whore, did leave me the bracelets. I could, perhaps, persuade some man to take you to his bed. But only if you remember you are not royal in this place."

There were stops and starts in the woman's words. Had Adaeze heard all of them? Bracelets? A man's bed?

"Bed? What makes you think I'd want to go to any man's bed?" Had Folashade dove deeper into the barrel?

"You are not yet a woman. Perhaps that explains how little you know of women's choices in these matters." The big voice again.

Adaeze felt the strong hands of the owner of the voice lay her onto the cot. It felt good to stretch out again. Besides, it was time for her afternoon nap. It was afternoon, wasn't it? She was too tired to open her eyes to check out the movement of the sun. Why didn't this room have a sundial? Instead, she rolled to her side, turned her back from those funny voices, and drew her legs to her chest, her under dress bunched at her knees.

"You do not know, do you?" The voice, that other voice, not Folashade's, sounded surprised.

"I don't know what?" Now Folashade was playing hide-and-seek from the depths of a maize barrel.

"Women prisoners intended for slavery in the Americas are spared the journey if they become pregnant by one of the Europeans."

"Ugh." The sound that gurgled out of the depths might have belonged to Folashade.

Manuela delivered an unmistakable snort. "My own grandmother was one of the fortunate ones. She made the sacrifice and became pregnant by my Portuguese grandfather. The pregnancy was discovered just as the slave ship arrived for loading. My grandfather wanted to see what the product of such a union looked like."

"Allah, spare us the shame." Folashade?

Why did the girl sound as though Nago had fed her the carcass of a decaying rat?

Sleep drifted in and out of Adaeze's mind. Had one of the voices said something about babies? Babies with Ibo, Yoruba, Benin mothers and infidel white fathers who wore crosses? Adaeze's eyelids grew heavy. Impossible. That would be an affront to Allah. Good that sleep was on its way. As queen of Mali, she would never tolerate such an abomination.

Chapter 20

"Monsieur Charbonneau." French drifted into Bibi's sleeping ears. French with a thick Wolof accent.

She opened her eyes. Something heavy lay across her chest. Charbonneau's arm. She lifted it as quietly as she could from the still-sleeping man and laid it on the tiny sliver of cot space between them.

"Monsieur. I need a word with you." The sound of Malick's voice called through the shut cabin door. He switched to his native Wolof. "A ship has come into harbor."

Charbonneau snorted. He slid his hand to Bibi's belly, his breath still signaling sleep.

"Monsieur, I insist you wake." The senior Wolof, whose animosity toward Bibi had only increased since she escaped her jail sentence, lowered his voice and continued in Wolof. "I know that whore next to you is awake. I demand you awaken your master now."

Bibi measured her breaths. Let that dreadful man leave. He only brought more misery.

"Wench! I know you hear me," Malick called out.

Charbonneau jerked. Bibi stiffened and waited. He took in a deep breath, grunted. More asleep than awake, he fumbled his hand to her woman's place. She jerked. Charbonneau startled awake.

"Did I hear a voice? Who is it?" His breath spewed out the remnants of last night's boiled lentils.

"Monsieur! I need you awake." Malick's insistent tone betrayed a hint of annoyance.

Charbonneau rested an arm across his forehead. "What could that fool possibly want?" He turned to Bibi and rubbed her shoulder.

"I have news of importance. A ship has come into port."

"A ship." Charbonneau lifted to one elbow. "This is a damnable port, man. Unless the *Trouvadore* has arrived a month early, do not bother me." He lowered his body next to Bibi.

Bibi's hand reached for her chest, only to land on Charbonneau's back. She struggled to untangle herself from her captor. He pulled her closer and caressed her breast.

She was never ready for this man's assaults. Yes, he had spared her from the horror of the cells on Gorée and all those suffering men, but his had been no act of kindness. Her French tormentor kept her away from other men only to ensure his own solo pleasure. She'd thanked Allah that day, but in truth, which was worse? The bodies of dozens of innocent distraught men, bound for who knew where, on top of her, or the man place of one white barbarian inside her?

The infidel rolled on top of her.

Malick spewed out his French and Wolof at a rapid pace as though there was precious little time to waste. "A ship, one with rather ragged credentials, I admit, has come into harbor. An English ship with a shady-talking captain. But the man says he has British investors who want a quick trip to the Americas with a lucrative cargo."

"An English ship, you say." Charbonneau turned from Bibi. "The English are damnable liars and not to be trusted."

Malick pushed the door slightly ajar. "These men speak of fat purses to those who can produce a lucrative cargo and want a speedy trip to the Americas."

"Hold a minute more." Charbonneau tucked the sheet around Bibi, donned his trousers, and moved to his feet. "Get in here, Malick, and your words had better be certain. Tell me more of the lucrative cargo." He reached for his blouse. "Have you passed words with this captain?"

Bibi pinched the sheet closer to her body. Something in the pause from Malick jabbed at her suspicions. The Wolof had plans that did not fully include Charbonneau. But maneuvering which man would be to her advantage? Malick made it clear he held her and all the Bambara in low esteem.

"Monsieur," Malick began the French-laced-with-Wolof words Bibi sensed would be a lie, "the negotiations belong to you and the captain, though I did hear much talk on the docks."

"I am assured you did hear much talk of English treachery. Tell me more of what they seek in a lucrative cargo." Charbonneau walked to the door and opened it wider.

Malick took one step closer, his body slanted in the doorway. "From the talk on the dock, the English seek something unusual to the men of the West Indies. Something of high value. Perhaps not legal."

"Hmm. As I suspected. But perhaps worthy of an inquiry." Both hope and doubt poured out of Charbonneau's mouth in Bibi's ears. "Thirty minutes, Malick. Arrange a meeting with the so-called English pirate, and I will be there. What say you, his name?"

"Trilby Welles. Captain."

◆ ◆ ◆

The pier on Gorée where Bibi stood lay adjacent to the old fortress where Adaeze and Folashade were imprisoned. Splashes of fading pink from the old stones still visible. A ship that looked of slapdash paint and of no particular size loomed in front of her. The wooden figure of the top half of a woman with wavy hair that streamed down her back decorated the front of the craft. On the side were the letterings of the Europeans. Papa had insisted that his girls learn the European alphabet. She recited the letters under her breath. *Z* followed by a *W*. Nothing more.

Charbonneau, with Malick putting on his show of subservience standing at his side holding a large packet, faced another white-skinned man wearing similar clothing to Charbonneau. But instead of sun-colored, this man's hair looked the shade of the darkest day of the rainy season. What she could see of the strands protruding from his knit cap looked gray. The man, shorter than the Frenchman by a head, and with a belly that poked over the top of his dirty blue pantaloons, spoke in a tongue strange even to Charbonneau.

The man turned an agitated face to the Frenchman. He passed more than a cursory glance at Malick.

"Well, what's it to be?" The stench of the man gagged in Bibi's throat. She understood not one word of the tongue he bellowed. "I can carry about three hundred of these Black bastards. I've already signed up almost that many." He nodded toward Malick. "If your man's right, you've got a special cargo. I'll dump this lot of dumb bastards overboard if need be." A stream of something brown dribbled from his lips. "You don't understand a bloody word I've said."

Malick began his translation, with a smoothness Bibi was sure Charbonneau couldn't miss.

English. Malick and the sea captain conversed in the tongue of England. Yes, Bibi had seen English words written in one of Papa's books. The Bible, Papa had said. The Holy Book of the Europeans. Bibi knew none of the words nor the sounds. Still, she had to try. Adaeze and Folashade depended upon her.

Bibi took a step closer to Charbonneau, her head down, her eyes reaching upward. "Monsieur"—she kept her voice to a whisper as she uttered her French—"Folashade speak the English." In truth, her sister might well know a few English words. Whatever her sister's level of expertise, Bibi needed an ally.

Charbonneau cocked his head with curiosity in his eyes as he turned to her. "Folashade. You speak of that child?" One hand stroked the fur on his chin. "I think not, but that odious woman guarding them might." With a startled look in his eyes, he turned to Malick. "Let's bring Manuela in on this." He lowered his voice. "I don't trust the English. Tell him I have a specialty cargo of women and jewels. If he wants to know more, he'll have to follow me." He pointed to the prison.

◆ ◆ ◆

The crease running from eye to chin on the Englishman's face looked caked with dirt as the group made the trudge up the hill to the dungeon of a fort. Bibi walked behind Charbonneau, and Malick brought up the rear. Though Charbonneau removed her shackles, on Gorée Island and with no place to run, she remained a prisoner. The Englishman, smelling three times more foul than a four-day-dead wildebeest, moved next to Malick. Bibi turned to unravel the glances between them only to find the Englishman staring at her. The man's eyes climbed over her form, his lips parted just enough to show off his jagged yellowing teeth. Bibi snapped forward and pulled the caftan tighter in the chill that engulfed her although the wind off the ocean was nil. The group trudged through the gates of the old fort. The new-looking guns seemed trained on her. Her head went light. She'd forgotten to take a breath. Charbonneau's orders of this morning had been hurried. *Put on the clothes,* he'd barked. *And be quick about it,* he'd badgered. Wrapping herself in the finest of Cathay silks, for some unknown reason, foretold nothing but more disaster for the sisters.

"Ah, there is the mongrel, now." Malick had lost none of his venom as he spotted Manuela. The woman strode across the courtyard, herding three naked Yoruba women in front of her.

She laid a stout stick into the flank of the slowest of the trio. Malick broke ranks and approached Manuela, still attired in her unusual garb except for the hair ribbon. Today it was red. The Englishman called Welles made his way to Bibi. She grimaced at the smell and stepped closer to Charbonneau.

"You tell me you've got special women in your proposal. Is this one part of your package?" The Englishman's fingers squeezed air as he looked at Bibi's breasts. "Get her to lift that dress."

"Here she is," Charbonneau grunted as Malick approached with Manuela in tow. The Frenchman stepped between Bibi and the ship captain. He turned to Manuela. "If you speak English, tell this Englishman I have both women and jewelry to sell to his investors. For the right price."

Bibi sucked in a breath. She needed her sister. "Monsieur, Folashade speak the English." She repeated the lie.

Manuela's lower jaw jutted forward as she chose Portuguese. "Whore." The woman let the word explode in Bibi's ears, its meaning clear no matter the tongue. "I doubt your sister speaks a word of English. I will be the one to speak to this captain while your conniving brain works overtime to get your way to safety." Manuela's sneer filled her face. "Silly woman. There is no way out of this unless you please me."

"Folashade?" Bibi mixed pleading into her request.

Too late.

Manuela had already made her introductions to the Englishman.

The woman, her back to Malick, looked at Charbonneau. "He calls himself Captain Trilby Welles. His ship is the *Zephyr Wind* out of Liverpool, England. He has investors who want a high return on their money in exchange for a speedy trip with exceptional cargo. He says there are men in Cuba who will pay many pounds sterling for women capable of serving both mistress and master of the house."

Charbonneau nodded. "Tell him I have both rare jewels and rare women. For the right price, he can have both."

A slight breeze kicked up off the ocean. Still, this midafternoon day was warm. Yet, Bibi shivered underneath Folashade's yellow-and-green silk caftan. While the Englishman continued speaking to Manuela in his strange tongue, his eyes swept Bibi's body. They lingered on her woman's place. She shivered anew.

"Captain Trilby wishes to take you up on your offer. He'll see one woman first, then the jewels." A look of disdain flooded Manuela's face as she addressed Charbonneau. "He wants that one undressed, but in someplace private. He wants to sample her to see if she is worth the pounds sterling."

Charbonneau reddened and glared at Manuela. "Tell him I will show the jewelry first. Then the woman, but only if we make a deal on the gems."

The Englishman scowled at Charbonneau as Manuela translated. He grumped and let his eyes roam over Bibi once more. "As you say, but allow me to squeeze one of her tits before we proceed."

"No." Charbonneau turned to Manuela as he thrust Bibi toward her. "Take her upstairs and get all the wenches presentable. I will return before full nightfall." He beckoned Malick toward the gate.

The Wolof pressed a package into Manuela's hand, and walked toward the exit. The Englishman stared Bibi up and down, his purple lips smug, then turned and followed the two.

◆ ◆ ◆

As always, when Bibi entered the second-floor balcony room where her sisters sat imprisoned, she first sought out Adaeze. And as always, she prayed to Allah that, no matter how great the pain, her sister's mind be restored. Many days had passed since she'd last cajoled the barbarian into letting her see her sisters. Over a week, for certain. He'd only consented three other times during this entire month, and she'd performed extra hard to earn that privilege.

Manuela interrupted her reverie as the fiend of a guard hustled her into the room. While Bibi sought out her sisters, Manuela shut and bolted the door behind them. The three bracelets, too snug for the woman's muscular arms, glistened in the sliver of afternoon sun coming through the high window. Manuela laid the Wolof's package on the table next to a basin of water. Bibi spotted both sisters. Folashade sat cross-legged on her cot, her ankle chain secured to a big round ring sunk into the stucco wall. The girl waited. Folashade understood that Bibi had to first assess Adaeze.

Her eldest sister blinked against the bright sunlight that accompanied the door opening. She, too, sat on her cot, but her legs were stretched out in front of her, the roundness of her belly much more prominent than even ten days ago. Bibi calculated. Adaeze was now five months pregnant.

Adaeze lifted a hand to her eyes as though the brief bit of sunlight pained her. "Bibi. It is you, is it not? You've come to Djenné for the hot season. As always, we are delighted to see you."

Bibi felt the knot as it tightened in her own tummy. Adaeze was worse. Ten days ago, there had been an occasional brightness to Adaeze's eyes. Not today. Bibi took a step toward her sister, stopped, and waited for Manuela to issue her customary orders. The woman busied herself untying the packet. She pulled out two pieces of Folashade's trousseau.

"Why in the name of the Holy Mother did that Frenchman send me two outfits?" Manuela spoke to the purple caftan, shot through with golden threads, that she held to the light. "This will do for the young one. As for you"—the treacherous woman turned to Bibi—"you are as presentable as you are going to get. As for that one"—now the hideous woman turned to Adaeze—"there is no need. The crazed one is going nowhere."

Bibi lowered herself to the cot beside Folashade, her eyes on Manuela.

"What are you saying?" Bibi gave her sister's unshackled hands a squeeze of comfort.

Manuela tossed the purple dress at Folashade as she extricated the key from underneath the bodice of her dress. "There is a basin of water on the table. Wash yourself, then look to that packet. Your master has sent perfume to douse over you. A waste!" She grunted.

Folashade rubbed at her ankles as Manuela unlocked the shackles. "The purple is best suited for my sister." Folashade tested her free stride as she walked to the table.

Bibi scanned Manuela's face for signs of fresh disapproval. It would not do for Folashade to annoy this woman. Not now. Bibi walked to Adaeze's cot. "I trust you agree the purple is best for Adaeze." She aimed her words to the empty space between Manuela and Folashade.

"You two do jabber. The pale blue will do for Folashade." Manuela took the perfume from Folashade's hand and sprinkled several drops in the basin of water. "Your Adaeze is going nowhere"—she turned to Bibi—"but you are." Manuela laughed.

Bibi held her breath. She shot a glance at Folashade, who wore the familiar face of a pampered, unmarried girl-child about to speak her unwelcome mind. *Not now, little sister.* Bibi parsed her words. "Monsieur Charbonneau intends to sell all of us. The three of us. As one lot." The words hurt her throat, but she couldn't allow Manuela to hear her distress. "We are all bound for the Americas."

"So tells you, your Monsieur Charbonneau. How ignorant of you both." Manuela chuckled as she walked over to Bibi and Adaeze. "As bereft of knowledge in your head as are you, I will share a thing or two with you. The men in the West Indies are desperate, I am told. They would have to be to take the likes of an uncivil-mouthed woman like you. I suspect the Frenchmen has left precious little of you unused." She nodded toward Folashade. "This one, too, is bound for the Americas. And she is uncircumcised. I am sure to you that appears a calamity."

Bibi's jaw opened, then closed. How crude of the woman.

Manuela watched Bibi's dismay and laughed. "Of course, I check the bodies of all my women prisoners. Of what may seem an oddity to you, your little sister may bring a high price because of her uncut state."

Bibi struggled to control the-woman-has-lost-her-senses expression she felt taking over her face.

Her turmoil brought glee to Manuela. "European men prefer women who have not been cut."

Bibi's head moved side to side without her willing it.

Manuela's smirk broadened. "Oh yes, my dear chief whore. I tell you the truth. And like men everywhere, they prefer their women untouched." She nodded toward Folashade. "And this one also fits that requirement."

Wolof had been one of the first languages Toure's girls had mastered besides their native Bambara, but Manuela's words might as well have been the tongue of the Englishman for all the sense this half blood was making.

"Adaeze has undergone the full circumcision ceremony." Bibi heard her own words in her head, words she'd meant to keep to herself. Manuela's words wracked confusion into her thinking. Adaeze's full procedure should allow her sister a better lot in the new world. If the half-blood woman's words were true, Adaeze would not find herself in the bed of white barbarians.

"I can see she has had the full procedure." Manuela peered at Bibi. "You are a silly one. You do babble your ignorance. You have been taught nothing in your Timbuktu. Your sister is pregnant. Is the father not your Monsieur Charbonneau?"

The scream blasted into Bibi's ears and almost jarred her off the cot. Bibi adjusted herself just as Adaeze's right arm slammed straight into her shoulder. She slipped to the floor. Adaeze grabbed her knees and rocked back and forth, her yells punching the air, her head swinging to and fro. Bibi gathered the girl into her arms. Folashade rushed to the cot, knelt down, and laid soothing strokes over Adaeze's feet.

"Ahh." Manuela sounded jubilant. "I have wondered about the father all this last month. So, thanks to her"—she pointed a finger at Adaeze—"I have stumbled upon the truth." Manuela walked to the cot and separated the three girls. "Are you not the sly one." She bent over Bibi. "You managed to better yourself on the march to the coast by stealing the European from your sister. Too bad your ploy will not work. You failed to get yourself pregnant. How you managed that, I do not know, but you outsmarted yourself, my dear."

Bibi saw Folashade's discarded leg chain lying half on the cot and half on the floor. If she could disentangle it from the wall, she would use the iron to throttle Manuela. How dare this most uncouth woman speak such foul words.

Manuela fumbled with the key at her neck. "How did you stop yourself from becoming pregnant?" Manuela shook her head. "Out of your ignorance, that was quite the foolish move." She held the key in her hand as she made clucking sounds with her tongue. "Had you gotten pregnant by that equally ignorant Frenchman, it would have spelled financial disaster for him."

What was the woman talking about? No, Bibi hadn't gotten pregnant. She had none of the herbs Nago had given her to prevent a second pregnancy she dare not have. Doudou's favorite had made Bibi's choice quite clear. Any second child of Bibi's would be a principal heir to her husband's fortune. Bibi descended from the nobility. With all her husband's wealth, he remained a commoner. A situation her commoner husband could and would not tolerate. The woman made Bibi's choice of getting pregnant or not clear. Any second-born child, even a girl, would meet a mysterious death. Balaboa himself could be in some danger, the wicked woman had hinted. Maybe the potions Nago prepared had long-term effects.

Manuela, wearing the face of someone who delights in inflicting torture, turned full force on Bibi. "Do not look at me as though you do not understand Wolof. My words are clear. Captured women who become pregnant by a European man are not sent to the West Indies. Your sister, even with her mind as simple as a crawling infant, will never become a slave. She carries the Frenchman's child." Manuela's laugh filled the room. "Not you, however. You are going to become a slave."

"What are you saying?" Bibi dismissed all plans at coyness. "Adaeze will not be sent to the Americas? She may be spared?"

"If the Frenchman admits to fathering the child, then yes, she will avoid that fate."

Folashade stood and reached for the blue caftan. "You are telling me my sister is safe in Africa because she"—the girl swallowed—"she may be with child?"

"It will be a glorious day when I am free of the care of you three simpletons."

Manuela walked to the washbasin, dipped a sponge in the water, and tossed it at Bibi. "I have no idea where your Frenchman will send this harlot, but it will not be to the Americas. She has been too badly cut."

Bibi gathered Adaeze in her arms. "Be well, my sister." She stroked the back of the girl's neck. "If you are here in the land of the Wolof, your husband and his father will find you. I promise you Papa will insist," she whispered in Adaeze's ear.

Folashade shrugged her arm into the caftan just as a slanted ray of sun filtered into the room through the opening door. Charbonneau.

Charbonneau squinted against the dimness facing him. "The necklace goes on." His pointing finger located Adaeze. "Damnable woman, she is not yet dressed." He glared at Manuela.

"I don't want her, or any of them, dressed."

The Englishman, Captain Welles, stomped to the cot. "Like all the others, they will be paraded on the ship naked. I'll sell those fine clothes separately." He reached for Bibi.

"You know bloody well she is not one of the two." Charbonneau jerked Bibi from the cot and blocked her from Welles.

Manuela stood between the two men, translating quickly as each one spoke.

"You expect me to pay thirty pounds sterling for that?" He pointed to Adaeze. "I know all about the going rate for a fancy woman. Has she been cut?"

"Welles"—Charbonneau squared his shoulders to the English sea captain—"we've been over this. You know my price."

"And this is the other female you are trying to fob off on me." He took a long look at the form of Folashade. "Pretty enough. The bracelet comes with her."

"Indeed, I am weary of repeating myself."

Charbonneau waited for Manuela. "With the bracelet, I am confident she can bring thirty-five pounds sterling in the West Indies. The half blood tells me she has not been cut."

Captain Welles peeked around Charbonneau's shoulder at Bibi. She slipped farther behind Charbonneau's back. The sight of the Englishman roiled her stomach. "And what if I made you an offer of twenty-five pounds for that one, without any jewelry."

"No."

Bibi blinked. The men were clearly negotiating, but over what? She'd deciphered some of Charbonneau's French but not enough. Perhaps he had just denied the sale of Adaeze to this Englishman. The vise holding her chest loosened. "Monsieur," she whispered as softly as she could. Charbonneau would be angry at her interruption, but she had to be sure.

The Frenchman turned to her. His face showed surprise but not anger. He waited.

"Adaeze no to the Americas?" The smile threatening her lips relaxed her mind and improved her French.

Charbonneau looked puzzled. He slowly shook his head. "Adaeze will be going to the West Indies, but I've arranged a relatively easy life for her."

Most of the French words eluded her, but Bibi had learned to spot a lie even in a foreign tongue. Something was not right. "Adaeze no go," she tried again. "It is of you."

Now, a hint of annoyance crept across the barbarian's face. "Your sisters, Adaeze and Folashade, are going to the Americas."

Bibi pushed her way in front of Charbonneau, brushing past the odious Captain Welles. She faced Manuela. "Tell him! Tell Monsieur Charbonneau about Adaeze!"

Manuela looked as though such trivialities were beyond her consideration. She sighed as she turned to the Frenchman. "You are as confused as your paramour. This one"—she jerked her head toward Adaeze—"is pregnant. Do you know who the father might be?"

Welles turned his leering eyes from Bibi and glared at Charbonneau. "Pregnant. You didn't tell me one of the bitches is pregnant. Point her out."

Neither Charbonneau nor Manuela answered.

"Adaeze," Bibi shouted as she threw herself on the cot next to her sister. She laid a hand over Adaeze's belly.

Adaeze shook as she stared at Charbonneau, her face pinched in grimaces.

"You bloody French bastard. You tried to pass off a pregnant bitch as a fancy." Welles's face turned the color of red henna. "Charging me thirty pounds sterling. I can sell the wench all right. The buyer gets a free slave if the woman's child is Black." Brown spittle from the Englishman's mouth flew around the room in great spurts. "No one is going to pay fifty cowries for a woman who's not a fancy and carrying a white man's bairn." The sea captain rocked back on his feet, stumbling to catch himself. "Well? Who in the bloody hell is the father?"

"Do tell us, Monsieur Frenchman." Manuela folded her arms.

"Mercy from Allah," Bibi screamed. "It is you, Monsieur. You are the father of my sister's child. Tell us so, and she will not be shipped to the Americas."

Charbonneau stared at Bibi, his head making little bobs. "Adaeze is with child? No. Not possible. I barely touched the wench. The cutting disgusts me. No. It is not me. I was there such a short time. No."

"Be the father Black, perhaps I can take her." The balancing question in the Englishman's mind flowed into his words.

Bibi struggled to find the words, words in any language, to plead for the truth when the moan, as low as the deepest note on the drum, first caught her ears. The sound of agony so deep in the soul increased to a keening wail that chilled to the marrow. Adaeze, her mouth agape as that sound spit from deep within her, sat vacant-eyed as her misery clawed at the ceiling.

Chapter 21

"Ow." The cry came out of Bibi's mouth before she could tame the shout. Charbonneau galloped down the staircase as though he were escaping an invading army. He clutched her hand tight. She bumped after him, her foot slipping off a tread, sometimes two, her exposed toes scraping against the rough stucco as he raced toward the bottom step. Halfway down, he navigated the curve of the staircase, throwing her against the uneven surface. Her shoulder scraped against the wall. She pushed aside the pain in favor of the air she was finally able to gulp.

"In the mercy of your Jesus God, help Adaeze."

He stepped off the bottom stair so fast, Bibi slumped halfway to her knees. Without looking behind him, he pulled her around the back of the staircase and jostled her through the nearest arch. In the deepening afternoon shadows, he stopped, grabbed Bibi's shoulders, and pinned her against the speckled pink wall. His expression full of moved anger, Charbonneau, just centimeters from her face, breathed hard, but the sound of his snorting breaths could not keep out the cries and pleas coming from fresh prisoners as they marched into the cells some fifty meters distant.

"Have I not made clear to you that your sisters, both of them, are going to the West Indies." He pushed her shoulders deeper into the wall. "And no lie about your sister's condition can change that."

Bibi winced as the hardened clay dug into her back. "Monsieur, you father. Adaeze's husband in Bamako, not Djenné, many months."

He paused and looked into her eyes, his own disentangling her French and Wolof. "Adaeze's husband. You are telling me the man was not in her bed for months." He relaxed his grip on her shoulders. "Still, this cannot be. Another man."

Bibi managed a shake of her head.

"Malick, then. It must be him. I will do no more business with that traitor."

"Not Malick." Bibi searched Charbonneau's face, praying to Allah for a sign, any sign, the man prepared to accept his responsibility.

He grunted as he pushed back from her. "Your sisters will go to the Americas. I've done the best I can for them. Now, I'll lose money on a pregnant woman."

He searched her face. "You understand, of course, your sister cannot be returned to Djenné. There is no way. She will lead a life of misery if she stays here on the coast with no family and a fatherless child. No, she will go to the Americas, and if I hear another word of protest from you, I will not work to ensure she has an easier life than most slaves. Pay heed to my words. I will hear no more of your nonsense."

A prisoner, a woman on her back, one foot held in the hands of a burly Wolof, her head thumping along the pebbled courtyard, flailed her arms in protest as her tormentor dragged her toward the cells.

Charbonneau paid scant attention to the tumult near him. "Because of Adaeze's carelessness, I've got to come up with something to sweeten the pot for this damnable Englishman."

Bibi tightened her stomach. She had to do the unthinkable. One wrong move, and Adaeze's miseries would only be worsened. "Monsieur make money is good." She tilted her chin upward and clamped her eyes tight. *Please, Allah, guide me.* "Monsieur kind"—the lie hurt—"sell me with Adaeze. We two together."

"You go with Adaeze?" He rested his hands over her wrists as his eyes scanned her face. "If I am to lose a fortune over you, it bloody well will not be to send you to some poor Cuban farmer with no more than a dozen slaves." He breathed in deep, leaned forward, and kissed her on the lips.

Oh, Allah, not this. Not a kiss right here in the courtyard.

Charbonneau released her and took a step backward. "I can sell you for a lot of livres, and by God Most Holy, I will." He nodded his head. "But Mary, Holy Mother of Jesus, help me, just not now. I am not yet ready to part with you."

Livre. His God. Part from her. The words Bibi managed to decipher muddled in her mind. But on one thing she was clear. This man was prepared to deny his own child. Allow his son, his daughter, to become a slave. Only a land of harshness could produce people so detestable. Papa had been right. These Europeans were boorish barbarians.

He paraded her across the courtyard toward the gate.

The man always walked at a fast clip, leaving Bibi short of breath, but her thoughts marshaled themselves. She lifted her voice and stared into those heartless eyes. "No, Monsieur. I go with Adaeze, no stay with you."

"I told you no more talk from you. You will stay with me until I tire of you. I will not let another man have you." Charbonneau sprinkled in Wolof along with his French.

"You make me stay, I will make me dead." Mostly Wolof.

She was not at all sure how she would accomplish the deed. Knife. Poison. Force Charbonneau to use his weapons against her. Whatever method, she was not afraid. Her eyes settled on him. "I will not live without my sisters." All Wolof.

Charbonneau stared at her, his eyes widening. "You would kill yourself rather than stay here in Africa with me. I will not allow it." He raised his voice. "I will have you guarded night and day. Shackled to the wall just as Manuela holds her prisoners."

"Charbonneau. No."

She laid a gentle hand on his arm as she slowly shook her head. "I cannot live a good life here without my sisters. Let all three of us remain, and I promise you great happiness." Her eyes stung with the tears she did not want.

"You wish me to keep the three of you." The French sounded strained. "That I cannot do. I will lose too many livres. No sisters. You, yes.

"Would you really do this thing? Kill yourself." The sounds of a fresh parade of prisoners processing in the courtyard rumbled through the arches. The left side of Charbonneau's jaw twitched. He turned toward the commotion, then back to her. Only a few of the French sounds formed themselves into understandable words. Bibi didn't need words.

"Yes."

Pain flashed from Charbonneau's eyes.

"You are a special woman." Each word carried on its own breath. "So special. I have enjoyed these months with you"—his eyes scanned her face—"but a fool I cannot be." Charbonneau clenched his fingers open and shut but kept his hands from her. "I shall never find another like you, that I know." He sighed as he lowered his head. "Adaeze, Folashade"—he sucked in his lips before he spoke—"and you. All to the Americas."

Chapter 22

"Your sister certainly made a fine mess of things," Manuela chided as she turned the lock on Folashade's ankle chain.

The Folashade of even a month ago would have struggled to fight down the urge to bite back at this most cantankerous of women. But the pain in her heart was growing deeper. Then there was Adaeze.

Her sister, already unshackled, stood beside her cot. She stared down at the cheap, poorly dyed cotton cloth Manuela had wrapped around her.

"Off with that rag." The half blood pushed the three bracelets down over her own wrist, leaving indentations where the too-small ornaments had dug into her forearm. Manuela pulled at the soiled under dress Folashade had worn for months. "Why that Frenchman wants you two dressed, I do not know. All prisoners are stripped naked before they board the ship."

Folashade's head hurt when she had to think. The evil woman had said "ship." A chill ran through Folashade's body. She shivered as she reached for the length of cotton Manuela held out. She faced Adaeze. Her sister lifted her head, her expression as blank this morning as it had been yesterday and the day before. "What ship?" Folashade's knees shook, and her stomach threatened to lose the gruel Manuela had tossed at her this morning.

"Oh, you are a tiresome girl. Hurry yourself. In less time than the sundial can make a half turn, I can wash my hands of the two of you for all time." Manuela pulled open the door. "Thanks to all the saints, be handsomely paid for my considerable troubles."

"Where is Bibi?"

Folashade ran to Adaeze and clamped her arms around the girl. *Oh, Allah, bring back Adaeze's mind, if only for a moment.* Someone, even Adaeze, had to help Folashade sort out the next move.

"Bibi! Bibi!"

Folashade screamed her anguish.

"My, my. I see you have lost all your bravado." Manuela jangled the shackles in her hand. "Follow me, you silly creature, or I will lay these into your sister." She moved to the door.

Folashade squeezed her stomach muscles. She looked to Adaeze. Adaeze turned a face that looked made of Timbuktu brick toward Folashade. Behind those eyes, Adaeze was in Djenné. Manuela snapped the chain in the air.

Folashade grabbed Adaeze's hand and followed her tormentor through the door. Allah would answer Folashade's prayer in time and exact a rightful vengeance against this evil woman. Surely. Folashade stepped onto the second-floor balcony into a blaze of light. Her eyes watering, they shut against the bright assault. The sun blotted out her vision. Outside the deadening walls of her prison room, noises that sounded of an animal killing field battered her ears. She lifted a hand to locate Manuela in the brightness of the sun. A shadowy outline materialized and pressed one end of a chain into Folashade's hand. Manuela yanked and started moving. Folashade grabbed Adaeze. Stumbling and bumping into one another, the two trekked after the half blood and down the makeshift staircase. Manuela marched the duo under an archway. Folashade, her eyes blinking thankfulness for the shaded balcony overhang, plodded along. The din in her ears simmered into words.

"No, no, no!" A woman's Yoruba screams lifted out of the chaos.

Folashade swiped the wetness from her eyes.

"Where do they take me? Let me die!" a man beseeched the Prophet in Mandinka, his voice rising and falling.

Folashade tried to locate the sound.

"A slave I will never be!"

The farther Manuela walked them, the louder the voices. Folashade peered ahead. The half-Portuguese woman was marching them to the jail Folashade spotted on that first day. Up ahead, she spotted a Wolof overseer prodding the last of the line of prisoners through the main archway. A chill streaked across Folashade's back. No. She dropped her end of the chain, let go of Adaeze's hand, and blocked her sister from Manuela. "Why are you taking us to the holding cells?" Folashade's stomach cramped. She needed Bibi. She could not do this alone. "Ship." That was the word Manuela used. Not the holding cells. She had to mount a protest, but one that was more than words. She squared herself in front of the half blood.

Manuela grunted. "If you insist upon being difficult, I will call one of the men to lash you and your sister through that doorway." The monster of a female tilted her head and waited. "Make your choice." She shortened the chain in her hand.

"I—I—" Folashade's jaw wobbled.

"Enough." Manuela clamped one iron hand behind Folashade's neck, forcing her face toward the ground. She sensed rather than saw the woman grab Adaeze's arm.

Folashade, her eyes seeing legs, feet, and crouching women, stumbled into the cell passageway. Manuela halted. The smell of hundreds of unwashed bodies gagged in Folashade's throat.

"Wenches over here." The snarling voice came from the end of the cellblock passageway.

Folashade fought to lift her head against Manuela's viselike grip. She caught fleeting glimpses of a big-boned Wolof standing on a platform near a door secured with ropes and a block of wood. The fellow stood almost two meters high and must have weighed as much as an average man and a half.

"Bucks over there."

Manuela used Folashade as a battering ram to push through the crowd. Pain ran down both sides of Folashade's neck.

"No. No. Wenches over here," the giant man boomed. "Get those clothes off your women. We are about to begin loading. Manuela, you know the rules."

"But these women are to have special treatment."

Manuela spoke up, but not before Folashade saw the arm of a Wolof guard grab Adaeze.

"Do as you are told, and you just might survive the voyage," the big-voiced Wolof who seemed in charge shouted out.

Manuela loosened her grip. Folashade rubbed at her neck as she sought out the man barking orders. There he was. The fellow, his muscular chest outlined by his too-tight tunic, stood on a platform at the end of the passageway. The scowling Wolof, standing next to a rough-hewn door, brandished a firing stick. Folashade clutched the scrap of cloth covering her. Her heart raced, but her lungs ran out of air. Was this the man who would seal her fate? Adaeze's, too.

"When this door is opened, you will follow exactly what I tell you." He leveled the gun.

As quiet as a sleeping night, the holding passageway fell into silence. The pleas to Allah ceased. The groans of the men disappeared. The wail of the women went voiceless. All eyes swept to the big Wolof standing next to the door at the end of the passageway. The guard holding Adaeze pried her from Manuela's grasp, grabbed the girl's ear, and led her to the group of women congregating to the left. Young, old, stout, thin, all trembling, all staring, and all naked. With one yank, the guard unwrapped the cloth covering Adaeze's body. Folashade's sister blinked once, twice, and fell to her knees. The guard headed toward Folashade.

"Now!" The chief Wolof jerked the gun toward the door.

Folashade turned to the Wolof leader. The slighter of the two guards flanking him lifted a heavy-looking plank holding the door closed.

A silence as deep as death engulfed the room. The candle lighting the passageway let out only flickers of light. Folashade stared at the door. The sturdy construction looked made of mahogany. She couldn't be sure, but the door stood just over two meters high and a meter and a half wide. Folashade wrapped both hands around her stomach. If she didn't hold on to herself, she might shatter into pieces. All around her, everyone, prisoner and captor, fixed on that door. The heftier of the two guards pulled on the handle. She could not find breath. The door swung to the right three, four, centimeters. A smell of the sea, and more, wafted inside. The second guard, more muscular by a quarter, grabbed the rope attached to the door and pulled. Ten, twelve, more centimeters. All the way open.

"Aghhh!" Folashade could not hear her own voice among the three to four hundred shouts of terror that must have reached Allah. She couldn't tell if she'd screamed or just swallowed a roomful of air. Before her, before them all, and glimpsed through a small rectangular opening, lay a gangplank leading directly from the slave house holding cells. Folashade struggled to see between the bobbing bodies to discover what lay on the opposite end of that gangplank. Only part of the English alphabet, painted in a fading blue, could be seen between the many Africans. The letters, *Y* and *R* to the left, and *W* and *I* to the right of the gangplank, stood out. *A ship! Allah, oh, Allah, give mercy to us all!*

"Load them up!" the Wolof in charge ordered. "March every damnable one of these wretched souls through that door!"

The cacophony of sounds bounced off the decaying walls. Folashade broke free of Manuela, pushed past the guard heading toward her, and struggled against the moving masses to Adaeze's side. With strength that must have come from Allah, she pulled her sister to her feet just as a clutch of women threatened to trample the girl. Stick and lash rushed the hapless women through the door and up the gangplank.

"Mind me, woman. Clothes off." Her guard caught up with Folashade. "You will not need a thing until your new master sees fit to clothe you." He reached for the tie at her waist. Folashade lifted a knee straight into his man place.

"Get your hands off her!" Charbonneau. His sun hair stood out in the crowd. "That girl is to have special handling." He held a coin in his hand.

Manuela huffed her way to Folashade's side, punching one woman in the back, another on the shoulder, and pushing a third to the ground. "No, you oaf," she barked at Folashade's guard, and jerked Adaeze's cloth garment from his hand, "this is one of the special cargo." She pulled Folashade and then Adaeze from the crowd boarding the ship. "This way, you two."

Charbonneau rushed to Manuela and grabbed Folashade by one hand, Adaeze by the other. Folashade could only see the Frenchman's back as he pushed through the screaming throng. He stopped short, and she smashed into his tunic.

"Here are your wenches." Charbonneau pulled Folashade in front of him. He slapped Adaeze's hand into hers. "Take them and give me my money."

Manuela stared up at the English ship captain while Folashade gathered Adaeze to her.

"And the jewels?" The captain, both his coat and trousers stained, looked even more odious than Folashade last remembered. The stink of the man clogged her nose.

Charbonneau took Adaeze's wrist and slipped on the Doudou bracelet. "This deal is done." He shoved Adaeze against the captain.

"Not quite yet, it isn't." Welles leered at Adaeze's naked breast. "You, Manuela, ask this French thing about the necklace."

The half blood translated. She pulled Adaeze from Captain Welles and wrapped the retrieved cloth back around the girl. "Monsieur

Charbonneau reminds you he has paid for this privilege. She is to be clothed at all times I am to tell you."

Folashade caught the woman's wink at Welles, her body turned sidelong to an unobserving Charbonneau.

The Frenchman laid a hand on Folashade's back and shoved her toward the English seafarer. The door in front of her now loomed as large as half the Sahara. Her knees trembled. Her entire body joined her knees in shaking as she gathered Adaeze into her arms. She turned to Charbonneau, working a plea into her eyes. As awful as the barbarian was, this other, this unknown from England, looked far worse. Folashade sucked in her lower lip. She and Adaeze faced disaster. Still, no sign of Bibi.

Captain Welles reached into a pantaloon pocket smelling of urine and tobacco and withdrew a pouch. He stroked the velvet ties of a money bag.

For some reason, Charbonneau looked stricken. Folashade watched the barbarian as he turned around. Malick appeared and walked to the bottom of the gangplank. He stood beside Charbonneau just inside that ominous-looking door. A figure moved behind the Wolof leader. Bibi!

While Charbonneau and the English ship captain argued to and fro over the necklace, Folashade watched Bibi maneuver Malick out of hearing distance of the two men. Folashade's sister gave a tweak of the head to the girl to keep her distance.

Bits and pieces of Bibi's words drifted into Folashade's ears amid the clamor.

"Malick"—Bibi shifted her eyes to Charbonneau and the captain before she focused on the Wolof—"how do you do this? Send those close to you to a faraway land."

"Now you wish to play the bargaining game, Princess." The Wolof leader shook his head. "You weighed your options at first capture, and you put your future and those of your sisters on the man from France.

A mistake." His laughter cut through the screams, cries, and prayers straight into Folashade's ears.

"I plead with you to arrange our transport back to Djenné. I assure you the reward will be well worth it." Bibi's eyes stared hard into those of Malick.

"As you sail to your fate, do not fret you have made the wrong choice, nor pretend the Wolof owe the Bambara anything." To Folashade's surprise, Malick's face looked softer. "You cannot be so naïve as to believe slaves were not bought and sold in the public square in Timbuktu for centuries."

"Yes." Folashade detected befuddlement on her sister's face. "They were not being shipped to unknown ports."

"Mistake me not, Bambara. Timbuktu's days of glory are long in the past. Mali is of an earlier day. There are many powerful tribes here on the coast, and we have our right to rise. You, your sisters, and all the Bambara are commodities to us. Goods for trade. Weep not. Use your body and you may survive." Malick turned as Charbonneau called out to him.

Folashade's face wrinkled into the tears she felt coming. Even with Bibi, there was no hope.

Charbonneau approached a trembling Bibi. He slipped his arms to her shoulders. "You will be shipped to the Americas. Hard life."

Bibi lifted her eyes, dry of the tears Folashade knew her sister wanted to shed. The girl's eyes scanned Captain Welles, and followed the horror along the gangplank.

"Careful, you sons of whores," Captain Welles bellowed. "Make sure none of the bastards tries to throw his Black ass overboard. Drop more of that blood in the water." The captain's reddened face glowed plum as he took off his cap and ran a sleeve over his forehead. "That'll bring in more sharks, for sure. Show the bastards they will be eaten alive if they try to jump overboard and cheat me out of my purse."

Folashade clung to Adaeze so tight she heard her sister murmur. Out of one eye, Folashade glimpsed the scene on board the ship. Everyone and everything moved in slow motion. White-skinned sailors dug into deep, smelly bags and extracted bits of flesh, dripping blood. They leaned over the rail and tossed the rotting mess into the waters below.

"This door." Charbonneau's voice, speaking to Bibi, crackled in Folashade's ear. Now, time raced as fast as a king's messenger bearing news of victory in battle. The barbarian looked pale, even though the sunlight streaming through the rectangular opening bathed his face. He stood in front of Bibi no more than a meter away from that gangplank. "This door, Bibi, means you leave Africa." He pulled her close. "This door means you will not come back. Ever. This is the door of no return."

Folashade watched the man search her sister's face. "Bibi, do not go. Stay with me. Here, in Dakar."

Adaeze allowed Folashade to cling to her, but neither a tremble nor a shake wracked the girl's body. Perhaps Adaeze's mind would always dwell in Djenné. A blessing from Allah. Now Bibi could escape her sisters' destiny. Folashade would be alone in this new place without Adaeze's mind or Bibi's strength. She looked down at her tapered fingers. She was Toure's daughter. She would do what she must. A tear, dried almost to dust in her eye, struggled to free itself.

"Bibi, remain with me." He pulled her into his arms, stroked her face, and kissed her.

Folashade looked on as Bibi broke the embrace. Her mouth opened, closed, and opened again. "Goodbye, Charbonneau."

Chapter 23

"No, you dunderheads!" Captain Welles swatted the head of one of the white-skinned sailors swarming around him on the washed-down deck of this English ship. "I paid a bloody bit of good English sterling to get these wenches on board. Too damned much to have you push them about. Now take 'em to my cabin. Make sure you keep the clothes on 'em. Nobody gets that pleasure but me."

Bibi heard the man's bellows, but the sounds seem to pass through another pair of ears before they reached hers. What he said, she didn't know. That Folashade's suffering would increase, she was certain. As for Adaeze, Bibi prayed for Allah's continued mercy. And now she asked that Allah allow her the same reprieve. Let her mind dwell forever in that pleasure place where the hot sands of the Sahara gave way to the cooling waters of the Niger.

"Down here." One of the sailors, his face a patchwork of red blotches and old scars, lifted a part of the wood deck revealing nothingness save a black hole. The man gestured to an infidel adolescent younger than Folashade. "Fredericks, show the wenches the way." The child-sailor, wearing a gray sweater dotted with holes, scrambled into the depths. The pockmarked older youth grabbed Bibi, spun her around, and backed her toward the opening.

Bibi dug her fingernails into the sailor's arms. This fool of a boy was about to thrust her to her death. He broke her hold and pushed down on her shoulders. Bibi lost her balance, and her right leg plummeted into the opening.

"Oh." She felt a small hand grab her ankle and guide it to a narrow perch that felt made of wood. A ladder! But one that went straight up and down with no leaning at all.

"Move her down, Fredericks. Hurry her up!" the voice from above called out just as Bibi spotted Folashade's foot dangling into the abyss.

Rung after rung, Bibi lowered herself through the gloom with young Fredericks guiding until she stepped onto a solid expanse of wood. A second deck! Folashade quickly landed beside her.

"Inside." The older seaman bounded down the ladder right after Adaeze alighted. He led the group down a darkened hall and pushed open a door. He shoved Bibi inside first.

"So, you're supposed to have something special under that fancy gown." The lead sailor leered as he stepped through the door. "Think I'll take me a peek. You can't tell the captain whether I did or didn't." Despite his youth, the man's crooked smile showed four front teeth with rot.

Bibi took measure of the young Englishman. As ugly as his spotted face, she saw his want. A man's desire had long ceased to frighten her. She sought out the sailor's gaze. Let him take what he wanted. She would let him know by her inaction that he would never possess the best of her.

The scarred-face sailor looked away. "But if the captain finds out somehow, that old man will have me drawn and quartered." He snorted as he backed out of the door, Fredericks following him.

"Allah." Folashade's voice shook. "Mercy on us."

Bibi turned to her sister and sent up her own silent prayer. *Allow Folashade's thinking to go to sleep, too. Banish all wonder about her fate.* Hope was no more.

"What is this place?" Folashade looked around the room.

This place. What difference the makeup of a death cell? The dungeons on Gorée, Manuela's little room upstairs at the slave house, Charbonneau's bed, a ship's cabin. What difference could the place of one's dying make? The wooden floor, ceiling, and walls of this space, just a little larger than the room Manuela commanded, felt as reasonable a spot as any to fly to Paradise. There were no windows, not even that small slit that let in the light back at the slave house. One lit lantern, sitting on a desk that looked much too fine for these surroundings, pushed away only part of the gloom. Bibi blinked as she strained to see the outline of a bed, one large enough for two people. Shadows covered the farthest wall. A chest with four drawers stood in the near corner. A small stool rising no higher than the second-to-the-bottom drawer pushed against it. There was something next to the chest, something attached to the wall but shadowed by dim light filtering through the still-open door. Bibi moved closer, the pit of her stomach jumping as she stepped around a bucket filled with rolled-up scrolls. She passed the writing desk. One scroll lay open. She moved closer to the chest. There, pushed deep against the back wall, she spotted a trunk with unusual striations. She took another step. Yes, she was certain. Charbonneau's zebra-striped trunk. He had sold it along with her, and both with little remorse.

Bibi stepped away, bumping into a chair with a curved back and armrests stationed askew from the desk. A cylindrical bottle that looked almost like the ones that held Charbonneau's firewater rested, uncapped, beside the large sheet of paper. Bibi leaned over and peered at the scroll. The document contained the letters of the European alphabet scattered alongside a number of lines, some intersecting, some not. A navigation chart. She'd seen many in Papa's books on the adventures of the great explorers like Marco Polo.

"Bibi, are we going to the Americas for certain?" Folashade walked beside Bibi. "There must be something we can do to stop it. Anything. We must think of Adaeze. Make Charbonneau at least save our sister.

She's about to have his baby." Folashade's voice threatened to rise into a loud wail, endangering the sisters even more.

Folashade's words, still tinged with the magic of youthful expectation, played in Bibi's ear, but she had no fresh solutions for her sister. If they lived, and that was doubtful, all three would be slaves in some distant land where neither the king nor Adaeze's husband would ever travel. Bibi turned back toward the chest. Adaeze, as still as a stack of mud bricks, leaned against it. Bibi guided her sister to the stool and stooped to arrange her. Something jutted from the wall behind Adaeze's head, just below waist height. Bibi looked up at an iron ring with an open lock like the ones Manuela used to confine Adaeze and Folashade to their beds. Bibi scrunched her forehead. What an odd place to confine a prisoner.

"Bibi." Folashade squatted beside her, the girl's eyes searching her face. "Tell me what we are to do."

Bibi turned to her sister and remembered. Folashade, despite the horrors of the last five months, was not quite fifteen and uncircumcised. A child, even one who'd gone through so much, would still harbor hope. But the truth had to be said. "Nothing."

The cabin door flung open with a dull thud as it banged against the cabin wall. "Let's get to it." Captain Welles, followed by the blotched-faced sailor carrying an armful of shackles, walked into the room. A third white-skinned man, older and dressed more like the captain, frowned as he stood in the doorway.

"I'm keeping the wenches here in my cabin. All three." The captain pointed to the wall behind Adaeze. "Slap the irons on the bitches. Hook those two up over there." Welles nodded at Adaeze and Folashade.

"Captain Welles"—the man in the doorway, his gray hair poking from the billed cap on his head, sucked in his stubbled cheeks—"female slaves are usually kept in the hold. On the women's side. The captain selects the one he wants each night, and she's brought to him. Safer that way."

"Mr. Lytle"—Captain Welles moved closer to Bibi, his voice dripping put-on authority—"this may be my first trip to Gorée, but I've run ten other slavers to Hispaniola." He turned to face the man. "I think I know how to handle Black bitches."

Sparks of the now poked through Bibi's head, even though she tried to find that darkness that would put her mind to sleep. Lytle. The captain had pronounced his English sounds in a way that made her wonder if "Lytle" was a name.

Folashade stood trembling while Fredericks and his superior rushed over to Adaeze. The ugly-faced sailor grabbed Adaeze's hand and threaded a link from her wrist shackle through the iron ring. He clamped the lock shut with a loud metallic clunk. He grabbed at Adaeze's other wrist and attached it to the ring.

"Oh?" A small sound of curiosity escaped from Adaeze as she tried to stand upright. Caught between the iron ring placed low on the wall and a wrist chain shorter than half a meter, Adaeze, with both hands bound, could not reach her full height. She looked puzzled but settled herself on the cabin floor, her makeshift dress still wrapped around her.

"You cannot do that! Her chains cannot be that tight," Folashade shouted. "My sister is carrying the baby of a white man."

The man called Lytle startled. "That one speaks Wolof." He cocked his head as he stalked toward Folashade. "And she speaks of a sister pregnant by a white man." He spoke his odd language to the captain as his eyes challenged Folashade. "Tell me how a heathen like you from the interior came by knowledge of Wolof."

Folashade pointed a steady finger at Adaeze. "Monsieur, chain me but not my sister. She is not well."

"French, too, I hear you speak." The Lytle man stared at Folashade. "I am addressed as 'Mister' in English."

"And I see you lie. If your sister does, indeed, carry the seed of a white man, she would not be on this boat." The sailor whirled around to his captain. "Sir, these three are up to no good. I beseech you to keep them with the other women where they will be well guarded."

"Lytle, keep your advice to yourself unless I order you to speak." The captain trooped around the room. "Fredericks, hurry up your business with those shackles."

Young Fredericks moved from Adaeze to Folashade, a fresh pair of iron cuffs in his hand. Folashade stepped away, her head shaking a refusal. She flattened both arms behind her back and bumped into Mr. Lytle with a thud. Before Folashade could make a full turn around, the graying man grabbed her arms and held them while Fredericks clicked the shackles over Folashade's wrists. He dragged her to the iron ring and forced her to her knees. Clunk. Clunk. The metal slammed shut over Folashade's wrists. The girl brushed against Adaeze as she faced Bibi, a look of *you must have an answer for this* staring out of her eyes.

Bibi forced her own eyes closed, awaiting the blackness, the one that so nicely cushioned Adaeze. She wanted neither sight nor sound of the English ones, but her mind refused to obey. Mister. The man of England had translated "monsieur" into "mister." Now her mind insisted she uncover whatever else the stinky Englishmen had said. Bibi held her breath to keep out the stench. Even so, the blackness eluded her.

"Hurry it up!" Bibi had never before heard the English tongue spoken by one who hailed from England. Even so, the voice of Captain Trilby Welles, as Charbonneau had called him, carried the sound of roughness and a definite lack of culture as he ordered the young sailor to slap the shackles of iron over Bibi's wrists.

She looked down at the heavy iron restraints. Curious. Only two links of chain dangled from each of the metal bracelets, no longer than two centimeters, even shorter than those on her sisters.

Bibi turned to Captain Welles, who walked next to the bed. The man pointed.

"I like to spread-eagle 'em. Sometimes these whores get to complainin'."

The man's raucous laugh sent a chill through Bibi's body, a body that longed to be free of all feeling. Behind the ship's captain, she spotted something attached to the wall above the bed. A second iron ring.

"Mr. Lytle, if you serve me well as my first mate, I may be inclined to put in a good word for you with my investors." Welles ran his tongue over his stained lips. "Do right by my men, and I might take a notion to put in a good word for you to captain your own ship." Welles's eyes, the color of dark marble that sent a shudder down Bibi's back, shot out at Mr. Lytle. "Do wrong by me, and I will see to it that you will never set foot on another boat"—the English sea captain let silence hang between his words—"that is, after I have you keelhauled for insubordination. I am not a man who wishes to repeat himself." Welles walked over to the desk and leaned over the navigation chart. The venom Bibi detected in his voice softened. "As I said. I have sailed these slavers before, but never from this port. Gorée Island. Lytle, speed is the name of this game. You give me speed, and your future could be bright."

He turned his head toward Mr. Lytle.

"Speed, sir?"

Lytle walked to the captain's desk. "The trip from Gorée to Havana runs eleven to twelve weeks, if the winds are right. But Havana is crowded with other slavers year-round." The man scratched his cheek. "Given the option, I would take the *Wind* to a less-traveled docking." He paused. "Like Port Royal."

"Port Royal?" Spittle from Welles's mouth sprayed the air. "What hellacious thing are you trying to put over on me, Lytle? That place was destroyed by a quake back in ninety-six."

"Ninety-two, but Port Royal has rebuilt. At least, most of it. Too few slaver captains nowadays are aware of that little detail. Planters there are anxious for fresh cargo. Pay top guinea for the few slavers that do make it to their port." The Lytle man turned to Bibi. "And if this cargo is as special as you say, then the fortunes of your investors are assured."

The captain stubbed a forefinger at a place on the map. "You say to me Port Royal is a possibility." He glared at the man called Lytle. "Unless we can make landfall in seven to eight weeks, I don't give a damn if it's Port Royal, Havana, or some other godforsaken place in the Americas, I am not interested. I've got investors back in England who want a fast turnaround with a substantial payday." His face folded into a deep scowl as he pursed his lips. "But if what you say is true . . ." The man's voice trailed off as he grabbed at his chin. And jerked his head toward Bibi. "This one's said to be a good roll in the hay. Claims to be somebody's princess." He walked over to Adaeze.

The ruined Bambara princess sat on the floor looking up at Captain Welles, her eyes hidden in shadows, as the man reached down and jerked hard on her arm. He pulled off the Doudou bracelet.

"Return that immediately." Adaeze snapped into today. "That is a bracelet intended for a queen, not the likes of you."

Bibi held her breath. Yes, her sister had returned to the here and now, but the price might be too great.

Lytle took four quick steps to reach Adaeze. She tried to rise from the floor, only to have the chains hold her stooped. The man's open hand slashed through the air. He slapped Adaeze hard across the face. His ring, glinting of brass and decorating his fourth finger, slashed into her cheek. A trickle of blood flushed down and bathed her upper lip.

"Oh!" Bibi grunted as she watched Adaeze crumple, her head bouncing against the back wall. The girl's chin fell forward on her chest. Her sister did not move. Bibi held her breath and willed her feet not to rush to Adaeze's side. Best not to provoke an even greater beating.

"The next time you dispute your master, you'll receive worse." Lytle loomed over Adaeze. He switched to the language of Welles as he backed away. "I believe all these wenches speak Wolof. Yet they do not look Wolof. Their skin is brown, not black. The noses not as broad." The first mate's face crinkled into a wrinkle as though he wanted to speak more but had a change of mind.

Welles fingered the bracelet. "Lytle, I'll do the disciplining of my bitches, not you. I can't afford to have one of them scarred where it shows." He walked to the table and held the bracelet to the light. "Too damnable much money involved. Oh yes, I do recall the Frenchie saying something about Timbuktu. Caught 'em someplace near Timbuktu."

"Timbuktu. Doubtful. Not many whites allowed deep into the interior."

Lytle reached for the bracelet dangling from the fingers of Captain Welles. "A piece like this will sell well in Port Royal." The man watched as the ship's captain rotated the gem in the light, then returned it to the table. "Captain, I will check the cargo and alert you when it is time to sail."

"Mr. Lytle, I expect to make landfall in no more than nine weeks. See to it!"

"Aye, Captain."

"Now to see what I've paid for." Welles moved to the zebra-topped trunk and lifted the lid. He grinned his gap-toothed smile as he pulled out a handful of gems that cast off faint glints of purples, reds, and blues in the subdued lighting.

"Oh, Bibi"—Folashade spoke in barely a whisper as she stroked the side of Adaeze's face—"I recognize those jewels. Some are part of my trousseau, and some belong to Adaeze."

"Bitch, shut your mouth! Don't speak your bloody savage tongue aboard any damnable ship I command. Ever! Is that understood?"

Welles kneeled in front of the chest. "You want a taste of what your sister got?" He laid Doudou's bracelet inside and slammed the lid.

Bibi longed for the pleasure of an empty mind but not at the cost of harm to either of her sisters. She rubbed at her wrist shackles and their curious too-short two-link chains. Out of the corner of her eye, she spotted the bed as Welles walked toward her wearing that disgusting look men put on their faces when they wanted what a woman had to give. Even if Allah had not granted her total blackness, she would find that little corner of her mind where she would seek a bit of refuge while Welles discharged his man place. He could do whatever he wanted with her body, but her mind would dwell in Papa's library among his precious books. She watched the captain's corpulent belly jiggle as he advanced, fully clothed, upon her. She read his face. This man would be no Charbonneau. There would not be even the occasional foray into care when Captain Trilby Welles came into her.

"Let us see what the hell my investors paid for. I would not dare tamper with their goods if that Frenchie hadn't already tried you out." His voice dropped lower.

Bibi willed the muscles of her face still. Whatever he was saying in his English boded ill for her.

"You'd better damn well be worth the guineas I gave for you." Welles, lice crawling in his hair, grabbed the iron shackle covering Bibi's right wrist and pulled her to him. "Clothes off first. Every damnable thing on you and in you belongs to me."

Bibi stared at the man's mouth. She wanted darkness, but the juices rumbling in her stomach told her she needed to turn this man's sounds into words she could understand if she and her sisters wanted easy deaths. She stiffened as Welles reached around her neck to push the sleeve of her caftan over one arm. This fiend was going to be hurtful. With Charbonneau, she had learned to probe a man's weakness when he was in the throes of his passion to lessen her pain. Now was the time to use that knowledge on this English lout. She reached for Welles's pudgy hand and guided it to the hem of her under dress. Her hand over his, she pulled the garment over her head. To spare herself from gagging at the sight of the man's bulging vein at the center of his forehead, she fixed on the iron ring holding her sisters while Welles's eyes roamed over her naked body. She heard his short, snorting, disgusting breaths. She could not control the little tremor that overtook her.

"No wonder that Frenchie was so taken by you. You'll give a man a rollickin' good time."

The speed with which he threw her on the lumpy mattress snatched away Bibi's breath. Before she could recover, Welles rolled her to her back. The man's oversize tongue lapped at her face, breasts, belly, and woman's place like a goat sucking up water. His hands, as rough as unsmoothed brick, poked and prodded at her. He laid a knee across her belly and pulled her right arm high above her head. She held her breath. His grunts moved into a rhythmical pattern as he reached for something on the wall behind her head. Bibi tried to turn her head. Captain Welles fumbled at the short chain attached to the shackle on her wrist. He jerked hard. She groaned as her right shoulder protested. She looked up as Welles inserted the second link of her wrist shackle into the open iron ring. He slammed the lock shut.

"Oh, Allah," Bibi mouthed. She couldn't move her right wrist. Her arm angled fully out from her body. Welles pushed down on her belly. She groaned as her stomach pressed against her spine, pushing air out of her lungs. The man clamped his teeth around her right nipple.

"Ahhh!" Bibi screamed out her pain.

"We're just startin', my beauty." He turned and reached for her left ankle. Before she could bend her knee, Welles wrapped his meaty hand around her calf and stretched her leg iron toward the edge of the bed. He fumbled for something near the footboard.

Bibi twisted, struggling to see what the monster intended. She heard the clunk of the left ankle chain fasten into an iron. "No! No!" Bibi screeched. What sort of miscreant was this? She pounded the top of Welles's head with her free hand. She lifted her unfettered right knee and punched into Welles's backside as he bent over.

He ignored her blows. "Oh, you'll squall all the more when I get goin' good." The man turned and snatched her right ankle. Bibi tried to shake her leg free. He crammed the ankle into irons on the right side of the bed.

Clunk. The sound of the shackle imprisoning her lower body slapped into Bibi's ears. Demented. The word pounded in her ears. Charbonneau had handed her over to a demented miscreant. With her one free extremity, she grabbed the captain's nose and twisted.

He bit down on her left wrist. Bibi called out. Welles pulled her arm high above her head and slapped on the last iron.

"Now you're lookin' good." Welles's breath came out low, almost guttural, like a man at the top of his passion. He backed off the bed and lumbered to the desk, his back to her, blocking her view.

Bibi struggled against the restraints, but the irons left her little room to move. She felt stretched so tight in four directions, she feared her arms and legs might separate from her torso. Pain wracked her joints. She managed to lift her head as Welles removed his coat. He tossed it on the captain's chair next to the desk. The Englishman swept a hand across a strip of leather holding up his pantaloons. He pulled a short-handled firing stick from his waistband and laid it on the table. He slipped off a scabbard containing something with a bone handle and dropped it to the floor. A knife. He turned to her. His lips, wet with saliva, his eyes wide, Welles climbed back onto the bed. He positioned his clothed body between Bibi's spread knees. The monster slid one hand inside his pantaloons and began moving his arm up and down over his man place. She closed her eyes, her mind sending bits and pieces of prayers to Allah to keep her sisters silent. Soon, in the time it took to drop his pantaloons and remove his shirt, Welles would lower his big-bellied body over hers. She stiffened against the soon-to-come assault.

"No!" Bibi's eyes flew open.

Welles held a candle, the tallow oozing down the side. "I'm going to mark you as mine."

"Captain, is everything all right?" A man sounding like Lytle pushed open the cabin door.

Bibi struggled to turn her head as Welles looked up. She stared at the other Englishman. A cry for help to stop this atrocity might subject her to even worse. And her sisters, too. She opened her mouth just as Welles smashed his other hand smelling of body release over her mouth and nose.

"I told you these bitches complain a little. Don't worry, Mr. Lytle, she'll get used to it." He turned back to Bibi. "Now get out of here."

"Aye, Captain." Lytle stared at the bed without moving.

Bibi's head crushed deeper into the mattress, but she was certain she caught a glimpse of disgust on the face of the other Englishman.

"The cargo is all stowed and the ship is ready to sail." Lytle's voice registered low. The sound of his footfalls backing out of the door sounded in Bibi's ears. "I will alert the bridge to make way. You are obviously busy." The sound of the door closing echoed in the room.

The light in the cabin blazed, danced, and dimmed. Lytle was gone, her sisters chained. Nothing more lay between her and merciful death. Balaboa's sweet baby face materialized out of the throbbing light, pushing away the sight of Welles. The lantern extinguished itself, and darkness dove its comforting arms down to finally bless Bibi. Balaboa blinked a little tear. Balaboa. Her baby. Her boy. Her only child. After tonight, there may never be another.

Chapter 24

The ship rolled to the right. Folashade had long ago learned to move with the vessel as it lurched about in these storms. She no longer toppled onto Adaeze. And no more did she monitor her sisters' every move. These past six weeks as the *Zephyr Wind* rode the waters of the ocean called the Atlantic, Adaeze had spoken barely a word. And then there was Bibi.

On that night, that awful first night aboard, Folashade hoped her own mind would join Adaeze's in oblivion. Folashade's head refused to believe what her eyes and ears reported to her. What that Englishman—even letting his name form in the silence of her own mind pained her—did to Bibi defied everything Folashade ever thought of marriage. Although Nago had forbidden her to ever bring up the subject, Folashade had known since her ninth year that a woman's place and a man place came together somehow in the marriage bed. But she was unclear on the details. The English sea captain had never approached Bibi with his man place. During his torture sessions against Bibi, using every sort of foreign object, even the barrel of his short gun, the man had always been fully dressed. He kept his man place well concealed under his pantaloons, though one hidden hand always massaged furiously at something.

Oh, she'd seen it, all right. His man place. The captain had no shame when he used the chamber pot in front of his female captives. For the first time, she'd seen the private part of a human male. Of course, she'd lowered her eyes so the Englishman would not catch her staring and deliver her a fresh beating. She couldn't help but wonder. A fat blob of skin surely no longer than three centimeters caused such secrecy and fear among Nago and married women. Why would that little thing that looked stuck to the underside of the Englishman's fat belly require a woman to undergo the circumcision procedure? Certainly, women should not suffer the bother if all men possessed such a tiny thing that looked of nothing to Folashade.

The ship moved again as the vessel fought through another storm wave.

"Keel," Folashade said out loud.

"Aft," Bibi murmured.

Folashade turned to her middle sister. Bibi, unlike Adaeze, still held on to remnants of her mind. Sometimes Folashade wondered how or why Allah would allow such a thing, then banished the unworthy thought. Folashade stretched out her legs to lay reassuring strokes against her sister's thighs. During the day, while the monster went to captain the ship, he freed Bibi from her awful stretched-out position, let her sit on the floor, and shackled just her hands to the foot of the bed. Bibi was separated by no more than a meter from Folashade and Adaeze. If all three stretched out, their legs could intertwine.

"Are you certain it's aft?" Folashade gave Bibi her best encouraging smile.

Bibi, though her mind was still operational, rarely spoke. Most days, she sat at the foot of the bed, her eyes staring at something, someone, or somewhere else.

"Folashade," Bibi whispered. These days, her sister's voice came out on thin wisps of air since the monster sometimes choked her to the point of unconsciousness. "You will try to learn the words of the English." Bibi seemed to run out of breath as her head lolled to her shoulder.

"I'm trying, Bibi, but I'll need your help. I thought when the ship pitched backward, that was called 'keel' in English. I know the front of the ship is 'forward.'"

"Aft. The rear is called 'aft.'" Bibi laid a hand over the folds of the cloth covering her. "It's important you learn."

Folashade reached over and straightened Adaeze's draped green-and-brown leaf-print robe that threatened to expose her. The captain usually dropped two lengths of cloth in Folashade's lap each morning when he unchained the sisters, one at a time, to use the chamber pot. He ordered Folashade to dress both herself and Adaeze while he garbed Bibi. The fiend talked aloud in his English as he busied about the cabin. Folashade sorted out that the captain wanted no man other than himself to see the women naked, especially not Mr. Lytle, who came once each day to take the women for their daily walk on the top deck where sun and salt spray could refresh them. The sound of approaching footsteps stopped outside the captain's door.

"The weather's foul this damnable day. And now I'm to take these three topside." Mr. Lytle stepped through the door, Fredericks behind him. "Empty the chamber pots." The anger in the man's voice startled Folashade.

"Mr. Lytle." Fredericks. "She wasn't a fresh wench, was she, sir?" Fredericks bounced on his toes like the uncontrolled thirteen-year-old he looked. "I mean, the older lads told me only the officers are allowed the wenches"—the boy's face reddened—"to play with. Of course, I've seen it myself, none of the crew can get a woman. Just officers like you."

"Fredericks"—the first mate turned a peculiar shade of angry red—"such matters are of no concern to the likes of you. Now keep your mouth shut or I'll have you keelhauled."

"That's what the captain said he would do to you since you was the one responsible for Owens. Captain give him twenty lashes for leavin' his post and puttin' it to one of them old women." Fredericks's voice rode high and low notes as he leaned in closer to First Mate Lytle. "I watched him. With the woman. What he was doin' to her." The boy-sailor bobbed his head in rhythm with his words. "By my count, wasn't gone from his post at the mainmast too long. That sail still caught the wind pretty good without Owens bein' right there. But Captain Welles was furious mad. Laid that lash into him good. Said everybody on any boat sailin' the ocean knew only officers got to play with the women. Not a lowly seaman like Owens. Still, twenty lashes is a lot."

"Shut your mutinous mouth, Fredericks."

Lytle, the words coming out of his mouth choked with anger, turned to Fredericks. "Empty the chamber pots and get to Owens now. Tend to his wounds, or I will keelhaul you myself."

The boy backed out of the room.

Lytle moved to the captain's desk without a look at the prisoners. "Never again." He pounded a fist on the table. "Of all the wrongheaded choices that damnable fool could have made, this was the worst." His last sounds filled the room.

Adaeze and Bibi showed no reaction to the ravings of a man speaking to himself. Folashade held her breath. Something was terribly wrong. If she could sort it out, she might find favor for her sisters. The man called First Mate Lytle complained about his problem in his English. The man was oblivious to her and her sisters. Not only did he believe none of the women understood a word, he showed they were of no consequence in his rantings. Folashade looked at both her sisters. This Englishman may well have been correct. Allah blessed them both by taking their minds to other places, but she had to await her turn. Folashade's mind still bedeviled her. She had connected some of the English sounds into sensible words.

"Of all the damnable things that bastard son of a whore could do, the bloody man did." Lytle jerked his chin toward the low ceiling. "Take my best crewman at the mast and put him out of commission for the rest of the journey because he took a woman." The first mate grabbed at the navigation map on the desk. "Bloody fool of a man. Owens been at sea over ten years. A natural seaman. But by Christ Most Holy, that damnable fool could see none of that. Lay the lash on Owens, then threaten me with ruin if I didn't make Port Royal on time." The man's shout bounced off the walls of the cabin.

Folashade, in the shadows, watched Lytle's every move as he bent over the chart. "If I tack to the south, I can shave off another six days. That should put us in Port Royal in another twenty-two, twenty-three, days."

As though ten or more lanterns had suddenly been lit, Lytle jerked around to her and her sisters.

"And if lashing Owens wasn't the greatest sin under the bloody sky, look at the unholy mess the fool of a man has made of these three." He pushed the map aside and walked over to Bibi. He stooped and lifted her chin to face him. "What that bloody fool has done to you is beyond belief. You, alone, could have made all our fortunes."

Folashade kept her head down, but her eyes lifted upward as Lytle shook his head. She'd made out some of his English sounds.

"You are, indeed, a beauty, but that foul man has ruined you. Damn his soul." He took a step toward Adaeze and laid a hand across her belly. "And these wenches told the truth. You are with child, and now with not much time to spare. Might even be that of a white man. By my reckoning, you are close to seven months." He turned to Folashade. "You are the only hope we've got to make any money at all. Pretty, yes, but you do not possess the beauty of your sister." He strode to the trunk in the rear of the room.

Folashade held still as Lytle rummaged through a drawer in the back. She strained to see the man retrieve a squat blue-flowered jar holding the yellow cream Captain Welles ordered slathered over the women's bodies each morning. The task usually assigned to Fredericks. Lytle pried open the stopper, and Folashade wrinkled her nose. The odious Captain Welles must have obtained the most rancid version of the silk-soft shea butter from a tree that had sickened years before her own birth. The captain's cream smelled of a bush that had died of some dreadful stink-producing disease. She remembered the floaty feel of the almost-white substance Doudou had so proudly presented all the royal women to celebrate Ramadan, and how Nago had purred as she slathered the shea all over Folashade.

First Mate Lytle shoved the jar into Folashade's hand. "Here. You do the deed." The English captain had made it clear the lotion had to be rubbed into the sisters' skin to make them glow the look of health if not the reality. She hadn't bothered to indicate to the captain the stuff he kept in the blue jar smelled worse than the rotting carcass of a hyena.

Lytle stroked the stubble on his chin again, his brow carrying the furrows of planning his next move.

"Argan oil. If I can just get my hands on some before you three are paraded about in Port Royal."

Argan. Folashade was sure that was the word the first mate had just used. That precious oil from the land of the Berbers. A substance so prized that even Adaeze used it only on the most formal royal occasions. But Lytle had just uttered the sound.

Lytle turned back to Bibi. "What a bloody, stupid fool is Trilby Welles. Ruining an exquisite piece of merchandise like you. Now it's up to me to right this catastrophe. Perhaps I can still salvage something from you." Lytle shook his head as he left the cabin.

Chapter 25

Folashade crossed her legs. Where was that stupid little Fredericks? She was too far away to reach the chamber pot, and Captain Welles had been gone long before daybreak. She and Adaeze still rested their backs against the wall as they had when they were chained last evening, meters of fabric fashioned around them. Bibi alone lay naked and spread wide in the captain's bed, her chains cranked tight. At least the monster had not assaulted her last evening. Instead, he had taken frequent gulps from two liquor bottles as he'd scribbled in his journal. Often, he would laugh out loud, push back from his captain's chair, and stagger over to examine the contents of the zebra-striped trunk. Each time he passed her or Adaeze, he looked down at them and laughed even louder. When Fredericks pounded at the cabin door hours before the usual wake-up time, yelling out his English, Folashade understood the sounds coming from his mouth.

"Land ho!" The sailor never even ducked his head inside the cabin as the sound of his feet clattered away.

The captain stumbled through the door, slipping only once, and left it ajar. Folashade heard the jubilant calls of the men as bare, and leather-clad, feet pounded up the ladder and across the top deck. She heard the sound of rope uncoiling and wood slamming against wood. The *Zephyr Wind* was about to make port in this place called the New World.

"Bibi! We Port Royal." Folashade had tuned up her English skills. She'd try them out on a silent Bibi.

Her sister stared at the cabin ceiling.

"Land. Bibi. We land." A wave of bathroom urgency struck Folashade. "Where is that damn Fredericks?" She glared at the door as she switched back to Bambara.

"Promise me, Folashade." Bibi stared upward as she stuttered her English.

"Promise what?" Folashade answered, praising Allah for allowing a response, and reaction, from Bibi.

"No matter what happens to me"—Bibi lifted her head from the mattress and stared between her spread feet to Folashade—"or to Adaeze, promise me you will struggle with all your might to survive. One of Papa's girls must live." Her head dropped back onto the mattress as though speaking her native Bambara drained her of all energy. "His seed must go on even if it is a foreign seed."

Folashade couldn't hide her grimace. Charbonneau's child. A baby who would not be all Bambara. Would Papa accept a mongrel grandchild? "Of course, I'm going to survive." She glanced over at Adaeze, who sat with her usual immobile face. "We're all going to survive. You mustn't forget Adaeze already has a proper son and heir. You have Balaboa. All we have to do is return home."

"Folashade, pay me close attention." Bibi raised her scratchy voice. "You are a child no longer. You just passed your fifteenth birthday. By now, you know the truth that neither Adaeze nor I can save ourselves, but you must, for Papa's sake, live. If you are not able to return to Timbuktu, you must do your best to find a Bambara man to husband you and father your children. Settle for a Yoruba, if you must."

"Husband? I'll never willingly take one of those."

"Why did we make landfall in Port Royal and not Havana?" Fredericks's voice squeaked as he bounded through the door.

An older, unfamiliar sailor followed. "You ninny. You know nothing. Money's supposed to be better here." He retied his bandanna, revealing a series of enflamed red spots dotting his forehead. "That's the word we hear, though none of us have been here before."

"Does that mean all the wenches will sell?"

Fredericks looked disappointed. "I heard if some don't go at auction, sometimes the captain will let the crew have a go at 'em." He stared at Folashade as he grabbed at his boy-place.

The scar-faced sailor pushed Fredericks aside. "You're growing up, boy, but you've got yourself a ways to go." He leaned over. "Some captains give the say-so. Sometimes, but this one"—he lowered his voice—"not likely, considerin' Owens."

"But it's not a fresh one I'm askin' for." He looked at Folashade. "Not like one of these. If I could just get a look. Close up."

"A look is it. You say 'down there.' Well, lad, let me tell you. The 'down there' on these Black wenches is different than a normal white woman back home. These are all cut up something damnable awful."

"Cut up?" Fredericks nodded toward Folashade. "Think I could take a peek at that one?"

"And if the captain catches us, we'll both be lashed and keelhauled. You best unlock the wenches and get to those chamber pots."

Fredericks walked over to Folashade and inserted the key.

"I'll tell you this, lad. Not likely you'll get a woman this trip. Pick another boat next time you go to sea. Not the *Zephyr Wind*. On my second sailing, I had me a captain on another boat that allowed us cabin boys an old woman. Had me a time."

Free of her chains at last, Folashade raced to the chamber pot.

Fredericks moved to Adaeze and her chains. "You tell me Captain says no to any of these, but a quick look can't hurt." A hopeful look plastered itself across the boy-sailor's face.

"A hard head is not what makes a good sailor. A quick gander is all you want, say you." The older man shook his head. "You ought to know by now Captain Welles is hard-arsed. Aboard the *Wind*, you gotta work your way up. Took me three tours to get in line with nine others to share some old hag on this one. Said she was called Nago. Just lays there. Tits in her armpits. Scarred down there like all the rest."

Nago. The older man had called out Nago's name. Folashade rearranged her garment as she eased herself off the chamber pot. She congratulated herself for picking out about five or six of the words the two English louts had exchanged. Nago and that word, "tits," rummaged in her head. Folashade shuddered. Her governess had suffered, but Folashade prayed to Allah Nago had not faced quite the same fate as Bibi.

Fredericks. Nago. What she had to do boomed into her head. There it was before her eyes. Clear as fresh water during the wet season. Folashade saw the end before she saw the beginning. It was the only way. She looked up to catch Fredericks's eye. "You like look Folashade?" She struggled with her English. No matter how hard she tried, she couldn't paste the smile on her face she knew should be there. "No chain Bibi. You look me." She found the beginnings of a fake smile. Her face hurt.

Both sailors stared at her.

"English. How in the name of God Almighty do you speak English?" the older man questioned as he stared at Folashade.

"Look at you?" Fredericks broke into a wide grin. "Any place I want?"

"No chain Bibi."

Folashade nodded toward her sister, set her jaw, and lowered the cloth covering her left breast halfway. Men were such fools, and boys twice as dumb. "Bibi, no lock. Fredericks look." She dropped the fabric a centimeter more.

"I can see you, and you won't tell Captain?" Fredericks rushed to the foot of the bed and pushed the blanket up to Bibi's knees. He clicked open the locks on both feet before Folashade could sort out all his words.

"What in damnation are you doing? How this wench can speak English is more worrisome than you taking a look-see." Confusion splashed all over the face of the older sailor.

"I don't care if she speaks the tongue of the French. All I need is a look." Fredericks cranked apart the third chain holding Bibi.

Folashade watched the exchange between the sailors. Thoughts exploding in her head told her once all three sisters had been released, she would grab Adaeze. Then all three girls would race topside and throw themselves overboard before they could be sold in this place called Port Royal.

Fredericks opened the last lock. Bibi slowly moved her arms toward her body, crossing her hands over her covered breasts. Folashade readied herself.

"No," the older sailor shouted.

"Mr. Lytle," the slurred voice of Captain Welles burst through the slightly open cabin door.

Folashade jumped. The seasoned sailor flattened himself against the wall.

"First Mate Lytle, get your arse topside and then ashore and round up all those damnable buyers in Port Royal you've been blabbing about for nine weeks. I am ready to rake in good old English pounds sterling," Trilby Welles called out to an out-of-sight Lytle.

"Aye, Captain."

Welles tripped as he stumbled inside. Even in the dimness, his eyes bleared red. "What are you two dunderheads doing in here? Looking at my woman." The man weaved as he turned toward the bed and Bibi, her legs bare from the knee.

The bone-handled knife flashed from Welles's waistband to his hand in a blur before Folashade's eyes. She sat stock-still as the captain lunged at the older sailor who stood closest to him. Welles missed.

The bandanna-wearing sailor bolted through the cabin door. The captain whirled toward Fredericks. The boy's pink face drained to parchment white. Folashade watched as Fredericks's pants stained yellow. She scrunched her nose as the scent of bowel release filled the air. The boy jigged up and down on his feet as his eyes made frantic glances toward the door. The captain, balancing against his chair, blocked the child-sailor's exit.

"Son of a whore! I'll feed you to the sharks!" The knife cut a swath through the air. Welles put one booted foot forward and caught on the rung of the chair. He tilted to his right as he wielded the knife in an upward move.

"Mama!" Fredericks shrieked as the knife slashed into his arm.

"That seaman-fuckin' whore of a mother can't save you now." Welles took one more step, teetered, and fell across the chair.

Fredericks, clutching his bleeding arm, thundered upstairs, kicking the cabin door shut behind him. His screams rattled the very boards of the *Zephyr Wind*.

"Motherfuckin' bastard of a boy!" Welles used his elbows to hoist himself to his feet, the knife still in his hand. "I'll be damned if another man takes a look at a bitch of mine." He staggered toward the bed.

Bibi scrambled to her knees, kicking off the blanket. She edged to the far end of the mattress. Welles's thick fingers grabbed her around the throat, twisted her around, and forced her, facedown, to the mattress. He jammed her knees under her.

"I know how to mark you so every man jack of 'em will know you once belonged to Trilby Welles."

Folashade's hands, her fingers spread, scratched at her own cheeks. What this man wanted to do, she had to stop, but her mind refused to give her directions. Her arms and legs jerked, ready for action, awaiting the signal to become unstuck.

"Come on, wench." Welles forced Bibi's knees apart. Her nose, her mouth, jammed into the mattress. Her bottom raised in the air. The captain stretched her toilet place open with one hand while he reached to the desk. "A candle will brand you good." He laid the knife on the table and fumbled the glass off the lantern. He plucked the candle from its base. "Drip a little tallow into your arse and then mark my initials with me knife." The man chuckled as he bore down on Bibi. "Any man going in there will know Captain Trilby Welles got there first!"

Feet! Move! Now! Folashade's brain unrusted itself, but her muscles had not yet translated. Out of the corner of her left eye, she saw a conglomeration of browns, blacks, and dark greens. Cloth. A whirling blur of cheap cotton goods moving on its own faster than a gazelle. How could that be? The cloth lingered less than a half blink of an eye over the desktop before it descended on the back of Captain Welles like an avenging cloud sent by Allah. Folashade sensed the downward tug on her lower jaw leaving it agape, but how to close it escaped her. She struggled to put sense to what her eyes were seeing. The right side of the cloth floated high toward the ceiling, and then, with the strength that reminded her of a marauding herd of angry mother elephants, slammed downward toward the mattress. Once. Twice. Three times. Four. Five. Six.

Oh, Allah, help her understand what was happening.

A cry, low and garbled, stabbed its way into Folashade's ears.

Red spurted from in front of the cloth. To the left. To the right. Finally, the cloth backed away from the bed. It whirled toward Folashade. In its right hand, the knife of Captain Trilby Welles.

"Help me get the bastard off Bibi." Adaeze stood taller than Folashade had ever seen, but now the green-and-brown leaf-print cotton Folashade had laid over her sister yesterday morning was splattered red. "Folashade," the queen voice insisted as the printed cloth lay draped quietly over Adaeze's shoulders, "we have no time for you to stand there with your feet planted on the floor. Help me roll this miscreant to the far side of the bed and off our sister." Blood dripped from the knife and spattered Adaeze's feet.

Folashade's brain still worked only in starts and stops, but it had little to do other than order her to follow her sister's command. Adaeze tucked the knife into the knot of her dress. Folashade's sluggish feet joined Adaeze on the near side of the bed. Together, the two rolled the bloody, dead mess that was Captain Trilby Welles to the far edge. Adaeze grunted as she wrestled the man's hips and legs to the floor. Folashade climbed to her knees and shoved the man's head and trunk out of sight. Only the curve of one arm remained visible when Adaeze moved off the bed. She tugged Folashade with her.

"Folashade, get fresh clothing from Charbonneau's trunk. Pull out our finest. Bibi, do precisely as I say."

The stench of stale alcohol, blood, and death flooded Folashade's nose. She couldn't move.

"Now!" Adaeze pulled Bibi, stone-limbed, off the bed and covered the blood-soaked mattress with the blanket. She grabbed the gun on the table. "I believe I can shoot this thing if need be." Adaeze played with a piece of metal on the underside of the firing piece. "Folashade, clean Bibi first, then change into your own clothes."

"Clothes?" Folashade's body moved faster than her brain could order. She dropped to her knees in front of Charbonneau's trunk and plunged in both hands, scattering the royal jewels. There, sparkling even in the skinny light from the candle, was Doudou's bracelet. She pushed the glittering ornament over her wrist before she snatched out three caftans. Never mind the under dresses she uncovered did not match the caftans. No time. Folashade raced to Bibi, tossing one garment to Adaeze.

Adaeze caught the dress in midair. "When the English come back, you both must listen carefully and follow my lead." Adaeze sighted down the length of the gun.

Folashade doused water over Bibi and herself while Adaeze donned the purple-and-gold caftan. Adaeze snuffed out the candle and placed it back in the lantern.

"Folashade," Adaeze commanded as she tossed the knife to the floor next to the chest, "sit down and hide the knife under your dress. Hang on to the iron ring with both hands as though you are still chained. And, for the sake of Allah, give me that bracelet." She turned to Bibi. "I regret doing this, but you must lie back on the bed with your arms and legs spread open. You must pretend you are still chained." Adaeze positioned Bibi and hurried herself to the floor beside Folashade just as one set of footfalls eased toward the cabin door.

"Captain Welles." Mr. Lytle's voice sounded unsure. "May I be of some assistance, sir?" Lytle knocked softly before he pushed the door open.

Adaeze grabbed onto the iron ring and shoved Folashade even far-ther back into the shadows, Captain Welles's firing stick rested under the folds of her caftan. With the light now filtering behind Lytle's back, Folashade watched the man take a tentative step into the darkened cabin. Two, then three, as he stood fully inside.

"Captain, sir?" Lytle squinted as he approached the desk. "Captain, are you in here?" He stepped toward the bed, looked down, and halted. He stared at Bibi's green caftan. "Unlike Welles to deck you out like this. Where is he?" Mr. Lytle lifted his head as he scanned the darkened bed. He jerked as his eyes settled on a bit of blue stuffed between wall and mattress.

"Sir, you've fallen." He started toward the foot of the bed.

Adaeze jutted out a leg just as the first mate raced around the bed toward the far wall.

"Uhh." Lytle gasped as he tripped over Adaeze's foot. His head banged against the zebra-topped trunk. The right side of his face grazed the metal edging as he slammed flat onto the floor. One hand landed in a puddle of blood and slid out from under him. Lytle's face lay twisted toward the booted foot of the very dead Captain Welles.

"What in the name of God Almighty is this?" The sound burst out of Lytle as he scrambled to his hands and knees, slipping on slick blood.

He backed into Charbonneau's trunk. "Some hellacious thing has happened here." Lytle reached out a shaking right hand and fumbled it under Welles's pant leg. He worked his way up the leg. Mr. Lytle pulled his blood-covered fingers away and held them to his face. "By God in all His glory, the man is dead!"

"Same to you if you no listen me."

Sounds, sights, smells, thoughts no longer sought any reasonable resting place in Folashade's mind. That Adaeze, whose thinking had long since left this world for the soft grasses of the Niger River, was now in deep conversation in the English tongue of a barbarian jumbled into the mass of confusion now in her head. Only the face of one other in the room matched that of Folashade's. First Mate Lytle.

Despite her pregnancy, Adaeze moved to her feet with the agility of a schoolgirl. She aimed the firing stick straight at Mr. Lytle, the Doudou bracelet dangling from her right arm.

Even in the darkness, Folashade saw the Englishman's mouth open and close. Sputtering sounds that bore little resemblance to words flecked out of his mouth. He lifted his hands, palms open to his shoulder, his eyes wide.

"Hear you careful. Plan work for all." Adaeze aimed the gun between his eyes.

"Plan. English. You. Welles." Mr. Lytle fought to regain his lost voice. "Damnable. Wench. You. Who did this?" Heavy breaths from First Mate Lytle as he worked to focus on Adaeze. "A pistol. The captain's gun." Mr. Lytle shook his head as his chest heaved. "You can't possibly know how to use that thing."

"Evil man dead. You, Lytle, you want be next?"

Lytle slumped further against the trunk gasping in more air, settling his breathing. "Are you daft, wench? You dare not fire that pistol. Every man jack of the crew will thunder down here. What will you gain?" The man's face glowed white in the dimness. "If you speak English, you must know neither you nor your sisters can escape the *Zephyr Wind*.

Or Port Royal. You are to become slaves, for God's sake. Blackamoors. All of Jamaica will be looking for you." With speed that resembled a sand turtle, the man eased his right hand, palm upward, toward Adaeze. "Hand me the firing pistol, and I will see that things go easy for you. For all of you."

"I squeeze here."

Adaeze pressed her index finger against a metal projection. "I squeeze here, pistol boom. At you, Lytle."

Both hands shot upward as Lytle called out. "No, no. Don't pull the pin. Adaeze, it is Adaeze, is it not? I understand you may be a queen. Perhaps I can find a way to help you and your sisters. Just do not squeeze any harder."

"Mr. Lytle. Good you listen me."

Adaeze placed both hands around the handle of the firing pistol.

"All crew know you hate Captain Welles. You want be captain *Zephyr Wind*." Adaeze straightened her elbows as she circled the firing pistol around First Mate Lytle's face. "I cry. Tell crew you kill Captain. Blame me. All crew believe me. I savage."

Lytle batted his palms at Adaeze. "May my soul be damned. You are a clever one. Give me that pistol, then we can speak together."

Adaeze held her place. "You take us Djenné. King pay many sterling for me and sisters. I marry his son."

Lytle cocked his head as though heavy thoughts weighed down one side. "A queen you may well be. You behave like a royal. But your plan may not work. You may kill a few, but we will overpower you."

"What good for you if you overpower?" Adaeze's voice was as smooth as the silk brocade caftan she wore. "You kill us. We dead now. Sell for slave. I tell Port Royal buyer I kill Welles. Sisters help. Who buy us then?" Adaeze took a step back as a small smile flitted across her face. "Who next captain of *Zephyr Wind* you no care. You dead if you no agree."

First Mate Lytle kept his hands in the air. "I always had a feeling, here, in my gut. There was something different about you three, but I never believed you all are really from Timbuktu."

"First Mate Lytle. Listen with care. You sell jewels. You keep sterling for just you. Then you take me and sisters to safe place. You pay some sterling for boat ride to Mali. You come with us. King see us safe, give you many jewels, cowries. You rich man forever."

Lytle's breathing slowed as his brows clenched together. "My arms are tired. May I lower them?"

"No."

"As you wish. Your Majesty. I understand your plan, but it is one with many flaws. Pray tell, how am I to explain the death of the ship's captain to the officials in Port Royal?"

Adaeze shook her head. "Timbuktu people say barbarians of Europe uncivil. Live like animal. No smart."

Folashade, her ears following the back and forth between the sailor and her sister, laid a hand over the knife she concealed. For all Adaeze's words in the English tongue, Folashade understood her sister depended upon her if help were needed. Folashade shifted her glance to Bibi. The girl had eased herself toward the desk. With one quick lunge, Bibi could have the lantern within her grasp. With the knife in Folashade's hands, and a broken bit of glass from the lantern in Bibi's, the two sisters could kill Mr. Lytle if he attacked Adaeze. But by the way her sister held the firing stick with such a steady hand, Adaeze presented the look of invincible power.

First Mate Lytle sighed. "You think we English are barbarians. Tell me, Majesty, what story you would use to explain the murder of an English sea captain."

"You speak murder." Adaeze's voice purred authority. "No murder, Mr. Lytle. Accident."

"Accident!" Lytle's voice boomed throughout the cabin. "Just when I thought you were so clever."

"Bad accident. Captain order me to clear desk. I pick up knife to move. Welles drunk. He walk not good. Body turn. He fall backway onto knife in my hand."

"You are a damnable liar. But you're good at it."

Lytle slowly lowered his hands.

"Me lie, or you. Welles dead. You new captain. Port Royal boss put fault on you. What you do then?"

Lytle grunted as he stared at Adaeze as though he were measuring her for a new dress.

"Thinking hard for barbarian. No try hard. Hurt the head of you." Adaeze looked down at Lytle. "Use wrong hand. Slide pistol of you across floor. One you hide at top of pants." She inclined her head toward Folashade. "No trick. Folashade have knife."

"Knife," spoken in the English tongue, registered with Folashade. She brandished the weapon now covered with the congealed blood of Trilby Welles. "I do," she managed.

Lytle raised his right hand in the air while he pulled at the handle of his firing pistol with his left. He laid the weapon on the floor and kicked it with his foot. "I will speak to the crew. Every man jack of them wants a share of the bounty, that's for damn sure. This has been a damnable voyage under Welles. Thanks to you, I now must make a silk purse out of this sow's ear to save any of us." He moved to his feet.

Adaeze stepped against the wall but kept the gun aimed at her captive.

"I will say this about the hellacious mess you've made." Lytle tugged at his jacket. "It will serve us best if the buyers are unaware there has been an insurrection on this ship." Lytle jerked his head toward the body of Captain Welles. "Wrap the fool of a man in a clean blanket."

Lytle moved past Folashade. Adaeze followed his moves with the gun. Folashade held the knife with both hands, handle tight against her belly. If the English seaman made one unwelcome move, she would thrust her entire body into his.

The first mate nodded. "For all our sakes, I will stick to the lie you just made up. The men deserve their booty, and they know the sort of bounder was Captain Trilby Welles." He looked over at Bibi as he approached the cabin door. "You and the young one, go back to pretending you are still in chains." He turned to face Adaeze. "You go back to pretending you're crazed."

Chapter 26

Adaeze slid her right hand over the hard metal handle of Welles's firing stick. Her left dangled from the iron ring, looking for all the world as though the key had been turned in the lock. She'd ordered Mr. Lytle to pretend-lock Folashade and Bibi in the same fashion. As she awaited the first mate's return with the Port Royal authorities in tow, she nodded over to Bibi, who sat at the foot of the bed.

"Folashade, hold your knife at the ready. Bibi, be sure you have powder enough for two shots." Adaeze looked at Bibi's face. The girl's glazed eyes stared back the merest trace of understanding. Adaeze had to put her trust in her sister if the need arose.

"Here are the captain's quarters." Lytle raised his voice in secret warning. "As I've explained, our captain met his unfortunate accident yesterday. He has been properly laid out, I assure you. If you must view the body, Captain Welles lies in here."

"And you say you are the first mate." The cadence of the voice matched Lytle's. "That would now make you acting captain. Of course, we must see the body, and where your captain sustained his most unfortunate accident."

Adaeze stored the new information in her head. Port Royal was ruled by the English.

The door squeaked open slowly. Lytle stepped inside, followed by three men wearing similar blue-coated outfits. In Lytle's absence, Adaeze had trimmed the wick of the candle so she could take the measure of visitors entering the cabin before they got a good look at the occupants. Clearly, these three white-skinned men with their bizarre three-cornered hats and uniforms were meant to be officials of some sort, but the too-short sleeves on one, the patched tear in the jacket of another, and the missing brass button on the third told her these officials were neither particularly important nor well paid.

Lytle stood in the doorway, making entry and view into the darkened cabin difficult. "There are captives inside, but they are snugly chained."

"Wenches." A voice sounding full of the grit of sand spoke out. "Women captives, Africans, are chained in your captain's cabin."

Lytle eased aside, allowing a man with an overly round belly and a missing button on his jacket to step into view. The fellow squinted into the darkness.

"First Mate Lytle, here, did say the man was in his cups."

Adaeze watched as another official entered, this one taller than the other two, and wearing a jacket with more than one patch.

"Did not your captain understand keeping African prisoners in his cabin was highly irregular? Women meant to become slaves are kept in the hold. If the captain requires housekeeping, the wench is brought to him." The man looked around the room as though he were finally gaining a clear view of the occupants.

"As I explained, there are three of them." Lytle clasped his hands behind his back. "Captain Welles wished all three women be kept in his cabin because of their value."

The third man, wearing a uniform with sleeves that looked a good two centimeters too short, spoke up. "Yes, yes, Mr. Lytle, we have heard your story. It is, indeed, a very odd circumstance you present. An accidental death just as your ship arrives in our waters."

"Enough of this twaddle." The portly one spoke up. "Which of the wenches actually held the knife?"

Adaeze watched the exchange among the four men. She'd picked out enough of their English words to know their attention would soon turn to her.

First Mate Lytle pointed. "That one. Of course, she speaks no English, but she does have a bare-bones familiarity with Wolof. It is the misfortune of this crew that no crewman speaks sufficient Wolof."

The too-short-sleeved one waved a hand. "I speak a smattering of Wolof. Necessary in this job."

Adaeze chanced a glance at Bibi. Her sister kept her head down, her focus on a knot in the cabin's floorboard. Folashade's soft sighs drifted into Adaeze's ears. Out of the corner of her eye, Adaeze watched her sister's fingers flex and open exactly over the spot where the knife handle lay concealed.

Too Short Sleeved walked closer to Adaeze, peering down at her. "What name you give yourself?" His Wolof was barely passable.

She kept her hands still, but her left side, where she'd hidden Lytle's gun beneath her under dress, throbbed with the imprint of the weapon.

"Name." She drew out the Wolof word, pitching in an accent to further convince. "Adaeze." She opened her eyes as wide as she could as she tried on that innocent face Folashade used so often to successfully implore Papa.

"I believe I heard her say Adaeze." Mr. Patched Jacket scowled.

Adaeze pasted on her most quizzical look as Too Short Sleeved posed his question about what happened. "Me here. Sisters here." She looked at the floor, her mind calm. She'd rehearsed her speech as many times as she had fingers and toes. "Captain say I clean room, or he beat."

The official with the missing button caught the English translation from Too Short. "Whore. That's what she's saying. She was Captain Welles's whore. But look at the belly on her. She's about to drop a bairn." The man shook his head in denial. "I sense something amiss here." He glared at Lytle.

The man with many patches spoke up. "Let us see the body."

"The body?" Lytle sounded uncertain.

Adaeze sent up a curse against the first mate for Allah to consider.

"Yes," Patched Jacket said. "That thing lying on the bed wrapped in a blanket." Without another word, the man leaned over and pulled back the blanket. He stared at the corpse. "Light one of the lanterns. I swear to Christ Almighty, I see not one knife wound."

"Uh." Lytle sounded as guilty as he looked.

Adaeze ran the man's possible plots and counterpoints in her mind. She had to speak to salvage anything.

"Captain drink fiery water. No walk good. Captain tell me to pick up knife to clean. I obey. Captain stumble, fall backward on knife." She allowed pretend fear and shame to color her words.

Too Short Sleeved rolled the dead body of Trilby Welles onto his side as Patched Jacket held the lantern. "Damnation. The man's been stabbed more than once." He straightened up, and his eyes swept past Adaeze and landed on First Mate Lytle. "Get on with it, man. Explain this." He tilted his head toward the dead captain.

Lytle pointed to Adaeze. Too Short shot a volley of Wolof at her.

She took her time to respond as though she were sorting out the official's Wolof. "Knife hurt captain little. Captain mad. He take knife from me." Adaeze dropped her voice and lowered her eyes in mock shame. "Captain throw Adaeze on bed. Get on top of me. Lesson, he say."

She swallowed. "Captain drop knife. Knife stick in blanket." She made her lip quiver as her hands drew the air outline of the weapon, blade side up in the blanket. "Captain roll off Adaeze on knife." She stopped and forced her chest to gulp in three big breaths.

"Yes, yes, woman." Mr. Too Short Sleeved. "You claim the captain suffered two accidents with his very own knife. But the man has three wounds."

Adaeze cupped her mouth with her free hand as she let her head wobble back and forth. "Knife slice captain back. He say damnation.

Knife fall floor. Cut part stick up. Captain try reach. Fall off bed onto knife." She willed her lower lip to tremble.

"The captain fell on his own knife three times?" Mr. Missing Button shook head his no at the translation.

The furrow in Mr. Patched Jacket's forehead almost reached the bridge of the man's nose. "And you, Mr. Lytle, this is what you claim you observed when you walked into the cabin."

"It must have been. Captain Welles lay on the floor. The wench"—he turned to Adaeze and slowed his words—"she stood there, looking at the body."

Adaeze took in the look of all three officials. In the quiet of the room, the long intake of breath from the other two slammed into her ears. Patched Jacket shouted first.

"Lytle, what sort of fools do you take us for?"

Missing Button shouldered Too Short aside as he stepped next to Lytle. "Something occurred in this cabin. That we all can see. But the accident you claim did not come at the hand of that wench." He nodded toward Adaeze. "Even blind Tom can see the wench is about to drop a bairn. No woman in her condition could overpower a man the size of the captain."

Patched Jacket laid a hand on Too Short's shoulder. "The wench is a Black savage. She could not possibly possess the wherewithal to hatch such a plot. That"—the man's face set in anger—"is something you planted in her head."

"You take us as the king's fool." Too Short shook free. "The investors ensured us we would receive a high-value cargo." He glared at Adaeze. "And this is what you present us. I will tell you now, Mr. Lytle, you will never off-load these women in Port Royal. That one"—he pointed a finger at Adaeze—"will speak her Wolof about the murder of a sea captain in the waters of Port Royal. We will be ruined."

"Ruined," Missing Button added. "We are just making our way back into competition. Word of a mutiny aboard a ship will damn us forever. We want you, and your entire damnable cargo, to get out of these waters. If the truth be told, sail this stinking boat out of the Caribbean altogether."

"What?" Lytle's head shook as though he were in the teeth of a great gale. "You are mistaken. Your investors are correct. These women are valuable. They are the valuable cargo you were promised. They are royalty. From a royal family."

Adaeze slipped glances at both her sisters. She suspected both Folashade and Bibi followed a bit of the Wolof, but little English. Yet, the small twitches in their cheeks and the lifting of the eyebrows alerted her that at least Folashade understood something drastic was amiss.

"You claim a royal family. Uncivilized savages cannot have a king." Mr. Patched Jacket croaked out a dry laugh. "Mr. Lytle, each lie you speak further condemns you."

Mr. Lytle opened his hands in a plea. "I can only share with you what Captain Welles confided in me. These women, all three, are direct descendants of a king."

Adaeze felt his eyes directed at her.

"King Solomon, to be precise."

"King Solomon."

This time, Mr. Patched Jacket's forehead furrowed his hairline almost down to his eyebrows as he kept his voice low. "King Solomon, you claim is ancestor to these women. Preposterous."

Lytle put urgency in his voice. "You know of the wealth of King Solomon's mines. Mountains full of emeralds, rivers filled with gold. Underground caves sparkling with diamonds. King Solomon's mines and the wealth within are all known to these women." The first mate sounded breathless.

"You are pompous enough to take us for fools. The mines of King Solomon live in the land of make believe." Patched Jacket sounded certain. "If they ever existed, which I doubt, they have long been lost to time." He wagged a finger in the face of Mr. Lytle. "Hear what we have to say. You should face trial for the mutinous murder of your captain. I can assure you a conviction will follow, and you will be hanged by nightfall. If you wish to spare your life, leave Port Royal and all the Caribbean now."

"The jewels. Emeralds, gold. Diamonds. I have it all as part of the treasure that goes with the sale of these women."

"You jest with us, do you, Lytle?" Too Short showed his authority. "We've not seen you in these waters before, so perhaps your ignorance of the ways of these islands can be forgiven. We produce the finest and best sugar in all the world. Yes, it has made us wealthy but at great expense. Our workforce costs us many pounds sterling. These African buggers your lot brings us for work last no longer than two years."

Missing Button interjected. "Do you carry strong slaves who can survive under the hot sun of our sugarcane fields? It is quite a monetary loss for you to bring us weaklings who give us so little for our money. These Black savages are forever dying on us."

Patched Jacket nodded his agreement. "Of course, our wealthiest planters will enjoy a fancy woman, but she must be extraordinary. These wenches do not look that special, and now we discover one is an aid to murder. No. No. Mr. Lytle, you and they must leave these waters now."

"Taxes." The new captain, Lytle, put certainty into his voice. "I will pay you whatever extra taxes you may require. We do have strong bucks in the hold. They will, indeed, give you at least three years of good service even in the conditions you describe as difficult."

"And, Lytle, you will offer that guarantee. We trust you will sail back into Port Royal waters after three years to assure your cargo still lives." Patched Jacket's words landed questioning in Folashade's ears.

"Better yet, gentlemen. I will execute a document so stating. A paper that I will take back to England."

Mr. Too Short smirked. "Give us the name of your man in England." He waited while a soft grunt erupted from the former first mate. "With each statement, the depth of your ignorance and treachery shows itself,

Lytle. We have made it our business to develop and maintain contact with people of importance in England. The most important people. Especially in the House of Commons where the laws are made. You are a common seaman with limited intelligence to grasp how the wealth of the Caribbean came about."

"My abilities may not extend to control of the House of Commons, but I far exceed any of you on the operation of a ship and its expensive cargo," Captain Lytle shot back.

Missing Button acted as though his ears heard not one word of Lytle's explanation. "You see by now your departure from these waters must be imminent. You, and this foul-smelling vessel, contaminate Port Royal and all the waters around it."

Adaeze prayed her quasi-partner's narrowing eyes hadn't alerted the Port Royal officials of his desperation.

"You take me wrong, gentlemen." Lytle came close to a stutter. "The taxes I mentioned. I will hand them directly to each of you for you to distribute as you see fit. I can assure you I am prepared to pay quite a handsome bounty in taxes."

"Your 'taxes' are of no consequence to us. You will use them to sustain yourself and your crew. You have one hour to leave these waters forever." Missing Button headed toward the door. Too Short and Patched Jacket followed.

Chapter 27

In these almost nine months of horror, Folashade had kept track of the days and nights. She made certain she ordered them within her head every night. The two-month march from Djenné to Gorée; another four in the clutches of that affront to Allah, Manuela; and now the ten weeks aboard the *Zephyr Wind*. Day to night and back again. The three-to-four-hour daily outings on the top deck of the ship helped her battle the constant mind-confusing gloom of the cramped, smelly, windowless cabin.

Last night, when the *Zephyr Wind* signaled her body alert, night still presided. After a ten-week stomach-churning sail to Port Royal and these last fourteen days riding Lytle's frantic search to find harbor, Folashade's prison ship had finally found a willing port.

Clunk. "Lad, can you not open the damnable door? Step aside, Fredericks." The older sailor laying anger into the cabin boy startled Folashade away from her recount of day from night.

"I don't fancy going in here. This boat is cursed." Today Fredericks's voice rode more lows than highs. "You know as well as me, all the crew believes the same."

"Lookin' at these three locks and bolts on this cabin door, doubtless even a simpleton like you could be right about a curse."

Even in the unlit blackness of the cabin, Folashade sensed both her sisters awake and listening to the commotion outside their door. At

Adaeze's insistence, Mr. Lytle gave orders to the crew to keep the women unchained but inside a securely locked cabin.

A weak patch of sunlight filtered in as the older sailor let his lantern circle around the darkness of the now-opened cabin.

"Inside with you, Fredericks."

"Me?" the voice squealed. "You hold the lantern, but you want me to face her in the darkness."

Folashade watched the trembling child wave his hand in Adaeze's direction. The older sailor stepped inside and lifted the light aloft.

"The lads say he put her up to the deed." Fredericks stood just inside the cabin door, his body looking ready to escape if need be.

"Who did what is not of import. This has been a hellacious journey. First with a captain who didn't know his arse from the hull. Then the first mate killing the captain." The sailor walked to Folashade and held the light close to her face. "And these wenches have brought every man jack of us nothing but troubles and woes."

Folashade clamped her lips shut to keep out anything sounding of glee. That these foolish Englishmen believed they could speak their tongue without a concern their captives might pick up a word or two brought her a rare flicker of amusement. She followed the sailor's light as it lit up Adaeze's face. With each morning's inspection-and-grease-the-body ordeal, she took careful inventory of her eldest sister to make sure Adaeze's mind still dwelled in the world of today. Sometimes when she gazed at the ruined queen, Folashade caught the inner struggle that was Adaeze. Strength had poured into the girl from somewhere, but Adaeze's battle to maintain reality played out in the girl's eyes. On the sisters' forced daily promenade on the deck, Folashade maneuvered herself close enough to look deep into the eyes of her eldest sister. She saw the girl's fight to hold on, to resist the mighty pull of her thinking to return to Timbuktu, to home, to Papa and safety.

With feet that looked held to the floor by pitch, an unmoving Fredericks remained at his post while the other seaman played light on Bibi's face.

Poor Bibi. Folashade's middle sister, so unlike Adaeze's battle with what was then and what was now, knew her truth. Allah had not blessed Doudou's wife with the gift of a mind able to dwell in the land of Paradise. Bibi remained fully in the today. A today that must have raveled her mind and body to the core of herself. The center of Bibi—her Glory—had been stolen. Killed by Trilby Welles. For certain, she remained the prettiest of Papa's daughters on the outside, but the shine that radiated from within was no more. Her wit, which knew no bounds, lay in shreds. The quick thinking even under the most perilous circumstances, shriveled to nothingness. Bibi undoubtedly rivaled Adaeze in understanding the English tongue. Yes, the girl breathed, but in each breath her sister took, Folashade heard the plea to Allah for a quick and merciful death.

"What in damnation is taking you two this interminable amount of time to get these women topside?" Lytle's voice broke Folashade's reverie.

"Fredericks here is just about to grease them up. That is if you are certain this port will allow us to dock. We will be docking, won't we, Lytle?"

Folashade watched the first mate stiffen.

"I've already told the crew I've sent an advance boat ashore. Last night. As soon as we arrived in French waters."

"But that boat has yet to return with either a yea or nay, has it, Lytle?"

Lytle's face reddened. "See here, must I remind you I am your captain." The last words sounded strangled in the man's throat. "Your acting captain." The first mate filled the slight pause. "Your acting captain until the position can be properly filled, of course."

"The crew wants to be paid now. Nigh three months, and none of us have seen even a ha'penny."

Lytle grabbed Fredericks by the arm.

"Mr. Lytle, sir. That's my hurt arm." The boy sounded close to tears as he pushed up a sleeve on his soiled jacket. "See." He patted around a forearm-length scar. "It's still a-pustering."

The old sailor shook his head as he widened his stance and faced Lytle. "Wouldn't be a-pusterin' if we'd gotten what every other ship makin' this crossin' gives its crew. Rum. Good for the belly. Good for treatin' wounds. We was promised a boatload of the stuff. Part of our pay. Instead, we got nary a jigger nor a drop."

"You whine like a woman. Quit your complaining and get these women topside. I want them ready to parade before the locals by midafternoon."

"Do you now?" The older sailor folded his arms across his chest. "No more promises about money that's comin' as soon as we make port. We are all aware now no port will have us." He nodded toward the back of the cabin. "What's in that zebra trunk? Word in the crew is all about the fabulous jewels these wenches were supposed to have brought with them. Well, Lytle, I say to you, sell them now, or every man jack on this hellacious craft walks away from you and the *Zephyr Wind*."

"And England. You would be walking away from England, too. The only ship you'll find carrying you back to the motherland will be one that clamps you in irons for the mutineer you are. You'll travel in the hold. Headed for the gallows." Lytle pushed confidence into his words.

"England or no England, I speak for all the men. Even young Fredericks here. You load up them rowboats with those jewels, meet up with them French Catholic heathens, and make a bargain. Bring the money back here and pay the crew. And pay us good, or we don't move this damnable wreck of a ship one foot closer to the dock."

"Can I come with you?" Fredericks looked more hopeful than confused.

"You behave yourself, and I might take you with me when this entire crew takes its leave of this wreck." He headed to the door. "Lytle, me and the crew, if we must make our lives here in this Louisiana, nothin' will stop us from tellin' these Frenchies how you killed the old captain so's you could be captain yourself. By God's grace, that'll get you a swing from the gallows for certain." The old sailor swaggered through the door, Fredericks after him.

Mr. Lytle stepped on Folashade's thigh as he rushed to the zebra-skin-topped trunk. He flung it open as he spewed objects at its base. He grabbed at the pouch holding Adaeze's necklace.

"What do you?" Adaeze revealed the concealed pistol. "What say man about ship no dock."

"You have it correct, Princess. If I do not pay these men, then"—he stopped his frantic search through the trunk—"the future bodes poorly for all of us."

"You sell jewels for pay to take me, sisters, home to Timbuktu."

Lytle turned and stared at Adaeze, who'd leveled the pistol at the man. "Yes, of course. I just pray to Christ Almighty we have sufficient funds." He stood and pointed to the table where the jar of grease stood. "Folashade, grease up your sisters, but wait for my return before you're taken topside."

Folashade heard the locks and bolts placed on the cabin door. She also heard the uptick in Adaeze's breathing. Something was amiss.

Chapter 28

Oh, Allah, were these pains worse than those with Amadou? They came often and seemed to last an eternity. No need to wish for her absent husband. This was not the time to think about what used to be. Adaeze sprawled in the captain's chair, praying the change of position would ease her misery. She tugged at her caftan. Too tight. The edges barely met over her breasts. As for the under dress, stretched to tearing despite the slits Folashade had cut on both sides, she had few words. Adaeze looked over at Bibi sitting on her pallet. Her sister needed her. All the Bambara needed her direction.

The sail from Port Royal to this new port had been smooth if both frantic and speedy. The *Zephyr Wind* had been aptly named. Adaeze's reluctant partner, Mr. Lytle, had tried to make dock in nearly every port in these sugar waters. To no avail. A place called Santo Domingo had fired weapons at them. Even belowdecks, Adaeze had heard the pop, pop, pop of long firing sticks and felt the abrupt left turn of the ship. With her insistence, and his gun in her hand, Lytle had put the *Zephyr Wind* under full sail to the next port, and the one after that, and to a third, all with the same result. Advance word had traveled faster than Lytle could maneuver the fully ladened ship. The *Zephyr Wind* was unwelcome across the blue-green waters of this place she'd heard more than one sailor call the Caribbean.

Lytle, in his desperation, muttered something about heading north, but was he to be believed? He was an infidel, a man who knew no moral truth. But last night, Adaeze felt it. At last, the ship had found safe haven. And now this. Pains that came and went across her belly.

Bibi, her voice as thin as a silk sewing thread, sat with her back to the bed. "We've been moored here since before daybreak. I heard Folashade awaken." As she often did, Bibi allowed time to pass between her words. "Wherever we are, I do not trust First Mate Lytle."

"Nor do I." Adaeze grunted as a fresh wave of pain assaulted her. She leaned to the right. "But we mustn't let him know. Keep your weapons ready. I am required to make the best deal possible for all of us."

Folashade, no hint of sleepiness in her voice, sounded into the room. "But you've done that. We're to be transported back to Mali."

Folashade's innocence, despite everything, would always please Adaeze.

"I will do my duty by my people. Ugh." A strong wave squeezed Adaeze's insides. *Not now, oh, Allah. There is much to do before the birth.* "Uh."

Adaeze heard her sister roll to her knees as she pushed up from her pallet.

Bibi made her way to the table, where she lit the lantern. Folashade followed, grasped the water gourd left by Lytle last night, and began heating tea water over the lantern. "Folashade," Bibi ventured, "we must be prepared for all things."

"I am prepared. Prepared to return home." Folashade turned to Adaeze. "That is the plan you worked out with Mr. Lytle. He gets the money from our jewels, and we sail back to Africa. Back to Timbuktu and Papa."

Adaeze struggled to sit upright in the chair. "Yes. Back to Papa and Timbuktu. Ugh. I will keep some of the jewels away from Lytle's bargaining for our return. I will keep use of them to buy favors on our way back home."

Footsteps at the barricaded door signaled the probable arrival of First Mate Lytle.

Adaeze eased herself around as the man undid the locks and bolts and stepped through the door. He turned to her, his face wreathed in a puzzled look. A shiver ran down her body just as another pain doubled her over. She laid a securing hand over the gun now lying on the captain's table.

Lytle walked over to her. He stared into her face. "I can assure if you use that gun on me, it will not change your fate. You are about to deliver."

Adaeze lifted the weapon and aimed it at the first mate. He sat on the side of the captain's table.

"Here 'tis the truth of it, Your Majesty." Lytle did little to hide the mockery that assaulted Adaeze's ears. "All the vessels leaving these waters return to their home ports. Barcelona. Flushing. Liverpool. Lisbon." He bent closer to her, and the gun. "They are all carrying goods they've taken from this part of the New World. Mostly fur pelts that will be well received in Europe."

The gun wobbled in her hand. Adaeze stretched her mind. First Mate Lytle was telling her something. A thing of great import that she prayed to Allah she would understand before the words left the lips of this infidel.

"I could take that weapon from you." His hand brushed the handle. "With ease." He turned to face Bibi. "Yes, I have no doubt you would shoot me. Your young sister, stab me. Though I would be no more in this world, none of that would save any of you."

Adaeze straightened in the chair as the pain stepped back from its zenith. "This port. This New Orleans. Tell me story."

"Tell you about New Orleans? The story contains no complications, Your Majesty, as far as you and your sisters are concerned." His fingers played at a scratch on the desk.

The shiver erupting over her body brought on a tremble plain to see even in the dark cabin.

Lytle continued to play with a scratch mark on the captain's desk. "This port is held by France. Its ships will report to Marseille." His fingers stopped their dawdling. "I did try, Adaeze"—whether his voice carried a hint of sincerity, Adaeze could not tell—"but none will have you."

Adaeze's left hand shook as she squeezed the pistol handle with both hands. A quickening in her low belly caused her fingers to twitch.

"Lytle." Her voice shook. "You have failed to show jewels. Worse, you have plan to keep them for yourself."

"I repeat, I have done the best I could for you, but I am no fool." Lytle straightened his back. "I did as you asked. I offered possible buyers the jewels. Just not all." His voice grew stronger.

"I have a crew to pay. A crew to keep silent."

Folashade held the knife handle against her stomach. "What talk you. Pay crew."

Lytle turned to her. "Young one, if you dare use that knife on me, your fate will be much worse than what I have arranged."

"You've held back most of our jewels? My husband's jewels?" Bibi shouted as she advanced, the pistol aimed at Lytle's back. "You keep jewels? Jewels of my husband. Jewels need for ship home. Timbuktu. For crew of filth? No!"

A little smile played across the first mate's lips as he turned to Bibi. "You are fulsome. I would have loved to have a go with you, myself. And I swear, I would never abuse you in the way of Welles." He pursed his lips as he glanced at the floor. "Damnable bastard. Ruined a beautiful woman. I regret not that he is dead." He worked his lips as he stared at Bibi. "Still, your fate is settled, and no amount of gems can unsettle it." He turned back to Adaeze. "You are a woman of strength, that I now believe. Though I am in no way bound to do so, I will tell you of the day's dealings."

"Oh, Allah."

The pain brought both hands to her middle as Adaeze rolled to her side in the chair. The gun clattered to the floor.

Lytle swooped it up before Folashade could rush him. Adaeze heard Bibi's gasp as the first mate pressed the weapon against her sister's head.

"I am not going to shoot Bibi. Put down your weapons." He used his free arm to right Adaeze in the chair. "This one is about to give birth any minute."

"You," Adaeze grunted. "You betray."

"The deed is done. The *Zephyr Wind* is not in Caribbean waters. Because of you, we can only make port in a swamp filled with men who can barely write their names. I am forced to deal with rough, unlettered louts."

She tilted her head away from the gun as the infidel berated her.

"Fortunate for all of you, I have been able to round up men looking for women who can do more than work the cane fields. Some are in need of servants for their households."

"Servants?" Adaeze fixed her gaze on Lytle.

"Yes. Servants. All of you are royal. You must know something about the duties of servants." Lytle waved one of the guns in the air. He moved to his feet as he stashed the guns in his waistband. "Ready yourselves. The auction will take place within the hour."

"Auction?"

Folashade repeated the unfamiliar sound first.

"Auction. What is word?" Bibi challenged the acting captain.

"The place where captives are sold into slavery."

Adaeze was the first to unfurl the man's words. "Slavery. Say you, we be slaves?"

Folashade screamed the loudest while Bibi stamped both feet.

"Lytle, me, sisters, no can be slaves. No lessons in how." Bibi looked as though she considered advancing on the new captain, Lytle.

"No, Bibi, I agree. You were not meant to be a slave. You were slated to be a wealthy man's mistress. That body of yours decorating the finest silk sheets from Cathay." Lytle's eyes took on a faraway look. "No doubt capable of making him incredibly happy. Thanks to Welles, that has all been changed." He turned to Adaeze. "Do your best not to deliver that baby until after the sale."

Sale. Another pain threatened, but Adaeze pushed hard against her stomach. It was so. They, all three of Toure's daughters, were about to be put on the auction block. Agony snaked around her midsection twice. She gasped in a breath. No. Folashade, at the least, must be returned home.

Mr. Lytle laid a hand on the cabin door. He looked at Bibi. "If you are able, care for your sister. If God's fortune smiles on you, one buyer may have enough livres to buy all three. Train you as housekeepers." He walked from the cabin, not bolting the door.

"Adaeze, what are we to do?" Folashade screamed.

"I refuse to be a slave." Bibi grabbed a cup as she made a slow walk to Adaeze's side. "We have weapons. We should"—her head took small wobbles—"we should turn them on ourselves." Her eyes stared into those of Adaeze. "We would be welcomed into Paradise."

Adaeze grabbed Bibi's wrists and squeezed. "My dear sister. Yes and no. Allah would welcome me. And you. But not Folashade. She must survive." Her words came slowly as though she were talking to Amadou. Another pain wracked her. "Not now. Not now," she whispered. "Now is not the time. Please, Allah. Keep these pains at bay. There must be more time to plot Folashade's salvation. Perhaps there is still hope."

Chapter 29

"Who will give me two hundred livres for this strapping buck? An Ibo. Skilled in the growing of rice." The accent was Charbonneau's French, Folashade was certain. Though behind the heavy canvas curtain where she and her sisters were confined, she could see nothing of the calamity occurring outside.

"Fifteen guineas for the buck." An English voice rose out of the cacophony of noise spewing beyond the brown curtain, filthy with stains and dirt.

"Six escudos." An odd, unfamiliar sound.

"How about a doubloon?" the English one again called out among shouts from shrill and loud voices, none of them accented with African.

Folashade first heard the commotion a good twenty minutes earlier, but she had just now sorted out the meaning, and without asking either of her sisters. Bibi was busy comforting Adaeze, who had donned the best caftan. Even so, the girl looked stricken, haunted.

"All right. It is time." Mr. Lytle stepped through the canvas flap separating the women from the atrocity happening just beyond that hanging cloth.

Adaeze looked up at the first mate but said nothing.

"I will be taking her out first. Before she delivers and I have a babe on my hands." He reached for Adaeze's arm.

She snatched it away. "I ask but one thing of you." Adaeze spoke through gritted teeth.

"And what might that be?"

"Allow us, my sisters and me, ten minutes alone after this most foul of treachery has been done."

"Treachery, this is not, Princess. A favor to you and your sisters. That is what I have done for you. I did what I must. I paid my crew to save us all." Lytle tightened his grip around Adaeze's arm.

Folashade's sister winced. "All I ask is for a small amount of time. Alone."

"Time alone? The three of you. I think not. Princess, this is an auction. The buyers, not the merchandise, set the time."

Lytle scanned Adaeze. "Besides, I suspect you are up to some devilment." His lips set in a straight line. "You've threatened death often enough. That may suit you just fine, but that will not do for me."

Folashade's mouth hung open. Understanding flooded her. Adaeze had decreed Toure's girls would all die rather than be slaves.

Adaeze glanced at the floor before she met Lytle's eyes. "We have given up our weapons. Are we not trustworthy now of ten minutes?"

"No."

Adaeze rubbed circles over her stomach as she pushed away a fresh grunt. "Then remain in the room while we speak in our native tongue for our last time together."

Lytle pursed his lips. "I can give no such agreement."

Adaeze struggled to her feet. "If you do not agree, I will cry out my delivery pains on the auction stage."

Lytle frowned, his eyes glowing dark.

Adaeze turned to Bibi, whose lips made little twitching movements. She sought out Folashade. Sound caught in Folashade's throat. She could only nod her yes.

"Wench, you are in no position to argue."

Anger punched the first mate's words as he yanked Adaeze toward him. She jerked back. "But I am, Mr. Lytle. We are all in a position to argue. And truth of it, we all prefer death to slavery." Adaeze kept her back to Folashade. "You may prevent that from happening tonight, but we, each of us, will end our lives as soon as possible after the sale if you do not allow us our ten last minutes together as sisters." She called over her shoulder, "Is that not right, Folashade?" She turned to Mr. Lytle, both hands gripping her underbelly. "I give you my word, the word of a princess of Mali. Each of us will welcome Paradise."

Lytle's eyes swept over each of the girls but lingered longest on Folashade.

Did he doubt her determination? Adaeze wanted her to die. She was a noble of the house of Toure. Her mother, sister to a Malian king. No family member had ever been a slave. Unthinkable. The thumps of her heart skipped around her chest. Adaeze had been remarkable these last few weeks. Her mind clung to the today. Folashade should die along with her sisters. But other thoughts pummeled Folashade's mind. The need to live. She could not imagine life as a slave, but if Allah so willed such a fate, He would provide her the tools to accomplish something filled with miracles.

A chill made its way out of the stickiness of this New Orleans. Lytle stood there, unmoving, his brow creased in a frown. Waiting. Waiting for her confirmation. Waiting for Adaeze. For Bibi. None of Folashade's turmoil could she allow to show on her face. She pressed her lips together. She balled up her fists and, with a pretend knife, jammed both hands into her stomach.

"Foolish girl. Wrong choice." Lytle turned toward the curtain with the precision of one of the Malian generals of old. "If you three give me no trouble, then you may have your ten minutes." He swept the cloth to one side as he clamped down on Adaeze's wrist. "After the sale."

Folashade's belly did somersaults with her head and flip-flopped in time with her stuttering heart. Air, not as hot as Timbuktu, but that felt as wet as a cleaning cloth soaked in camphor oil, smothered her face. She scrambled behind Bibi, her hand placed over her nose and mouth. Live or die. The choice was not to be hers. Allah, where was she going to catch her breath in this fetid place called New Orleans?

"I have three women here." The first French voice carried through the opening. "A very special cargo."

Folashade could not see the speaker as she shrunk behind Bibi.

"Here is the first one." Lytle dropped the curtain just as he pulled Adaeze through, leaving Bibi and Folashade to hear and smell but see nothing of this new world.

Bibi, her eyes hollow, gathered Folashade in a sudden hug. "Little sister, despite all that has been said, you must survive."

Folashade's mind reeled. Live, not die. Adaeze said death, Bibi life.

Bibi pushed Folashade's face into her left shoulder and covered her ears with her hands.

Folashade placed her own hands over Bibi's, but to no avail. The sounds from rough voices carried through the canvas curtain.

"What is so special about this Black wench other than she is about to drop a babe?" A French voice, and Folashade deciphered almost every other word. "That dress, it does look of fine goods. And why does she wear clothing? No slave standing on that block is ever clothed. Always they are naked so we can see what we purchase."

"A special cargo was promised, and here is the first of the lot." Lytle's English was translated into French. "The finest silk from Cathay and patterned in Persia. As for the babe, two for one. The child is not due for another two weeks. Plenty of time to get the wench to your homeplace. And, gentlemen, she is special."

"Man of England"—the French voice pounded in Folashade's still-hearing ears—"if you wish your goods sold here in New Orleans, I will be the one to do the talking."

An English voice called out of the crowd. "I got no need for a woman with a babe suckling at the tit for a good year. I have a mercantile to run. I need a bitch who can stitch cloth together. Can your 'special cargo' do that?"

"The Englishman tells me this wench"—the voice was that of the French speaker Folashade first heard—"all three of the wenches he is offering, are some kind of princesses. Very trainable for inside service."

Guffaws and cries that sounded of taunts bounced from the crowd.

"Can the wench cook?"

An English voice. "We see she can give a man a good time."

Sniggers, shouts, and peals of laughter.

"Can she be taught to skin my trappings?" A different French voice.

"She is already skilled in the arts of a lady." Lytle dared utter his English. "Look to her garments.

"Allow me to speak of this," Lytle announced.

"What is this?" Folashade mouthed to Bibi as she pushed her sister's hands away.

"Worth forty-eight pounds English sterling." Lytle. "Without the woman or the babe."

Folashade's right hand circled her left wrist. The Doudou bracelet. The man had not bartered the jewel to save himself.

"Yes, yes," the first French voice hissed. "The Union Jack man, here, tells me these wenches are royal." He raised his voice. "And this is the proof."

Folashade heard the shuffle of feet and a quick cry from Adaeze. She pushed at Bibi to get to Adaeze's side. Her sister blocked her path.

Ahh. Sounds from the crowd in more than one language. "That thing real? Yes. Looks it. Damnable fake. But no. Fool's gold. No. Look at the gems. Polished rock. Sparkling like emeralds."

"Gold from the mines of King Solomon." Lytle.

"I have tested the jewels myself." First French Voice. "I cannot give my assurance the gems come from the mines of King Solomon, but by the name of the Sainted Mother of Jesus, these jewels are of gold, rubies, and emeralds."

Folashade lifted her head and sought Bibi's face. King Solomon's mines. More barbarian lies. She puffed out her cheeks as she sorted out her first lesson. Whatever became of her, to survive, she knew an infidel could never be trusted.

"Opening bid for the woman and the bracelet. Three hundred livres."

"A fancy woman that hasn't been touched goes for twenty-four pounds sterling."

An English voice, but accented differently from Mr. Lytle's, spoke up. "That's two hundred livres. If that wench can help me clear my land up the canal, I'll give three hundred for the pair. Her and that doodad."

"Her dress alone is worth twenty-five livres."

Lytle forgot his whisper.

"Take that damnable dress off her and let me see the wench." The same rough English voice.

"She is a noble. To see a royal naked will cost you twenty livres."

"Twenty for a look-see. You are a buffoon." The English voice sounded disbelief.

"You claim she is of the nobility. Trainable as a servant." A sound, neither French nor English, floated behind the canvas curtain into Folashade's ears.

"Sir"—First French Voice, and from the sound of it, standing on the platform with Lytle—"is that Spanish I hear?"

"I am Señor Miguel Herrera of Santa Fe, Nueva Mexico." More meaningless sounds. "Tell me, if you will, if this woman is of the nobility, may I assume she is educated? Prove to me she can speak more than one language."

Folashade locked eyes with Bibi, and the noise from the crowd quieted. First French Voice mumbled something and was answered in an even lower rumble by Lytle.

"My Spanish is not of the best, Señor. Speak your words in either French or English." First French Voice again.

Folashade dug her fingers into Bibi's shoulders as quiet shrouded the air.

"Speak this woman in words more than own of her?" The badly accented French escaped from the cultured voice.

"Ahh." First French Voice. "Señor Herrera wishes you, Union Jack, to ask the wench a question in a language of Europe other than his own Spanish."

"Bibi, what does 'Herrera' mean?" Folashade watched Bibi shake her head in confusion. Her sister knew as little as she.

"Wench, where did you get that bracelet?" A new English voice climbed out of the crowd.

Bibi squeezed Folashade's hands as time sifted down. She could feel the air in this New Orleans multiply itself as she, Bibi, Lytle, and all those unseen men waited for Adaeze.

Adaeze's reed-thin voice puffed out its English with pauses between every other word. "Father of my husband give to me."

Folashade detected her sister fighting through a fresh onslaught of pain. "Father of husband, king of Mali." A soft grunt made its way inside the tent. "Me next queen. King pay many pounds sterling, diamonds, emerald, see me again. Mine of King Solomon."

Noise from the crowd pounded into Folashade's ears.

"That wench is telling us she is a Black princess." Another French voice colored in disbelief. "One that knows how to locate the mines of King Solomon."

"Monsieur, know you the wealth of Timbuktu?" Adaeze's French challenged the man. "Father-in-law King of Timbuktu."

"Five hundred livres."

The unrecognized sounds from the cultured voice boomed out of the crowd.

"Sold to Señor Herrera of Santa Fe."

Chapter 30

"Bibi, give me your hand," First Mate Lytle commanded as he parted the curtain and reached inside.

She recoiled and took a step back, Folashade still wrapped in her arms.

"The two of you, then." Lytle moved inside, disgorged Folashade from her sister, and shoved both girls through the canvas opening.

As Bibi stepped onto the squeaking wood-plank floor, wrestling Folashade beside her, she sought out Adaeze. There she was, her sister, standing next to a mustachioed man. Bibi maneuvered Folashade's body to shield them both from seeing what lay in front and below them. For down there, almost two meters below the platform where she stood, congregated ill-bred men who would buy nobles and turn them into slaves. She could hear their grunts, their cries, their curses, all accompanied by the stink of alcohol and seldom-washed bodies.

"Bibi, you are squeezing me too tight." Folashade tried to break Bibi's hold.

Bibi buried her sister's head deeper into her shoulder. Not yet. Protect Folashade from the horror until she, herself, caught the first glimpse of what awaited them. Now was the time. Bibi closed her eyes and lifted her chin over Folashade's head. Her sister's plaits tickled. With her feet gripping the planked floor, Bibi eased her eyes open. And there, spread before her, a crowd of twenty to thirty men, all with great leering eyes. Brown ones, black ones, a sprinkling of Charbonneau-blue ones, all boring into her and Folashade. Their faces, most white, some ruddy like Captain Welles's, some tan like a Tuareg, and a few reddish brown. All men, and all looking at her as though she were a bolt of fabric being assessed for its value.

"This one first." Lytle had been speaking all along before his hands separated her from Folashade.

"Bibi." Folashade swallowed as she looked into the face of the crowd. She clenched her fists at her side as she stepped to the rear of the platform.

Bibi nodded. Here was her baby sister, a child no longer.

"Union Jack tells me this is the most prized. Well trained in the arts of entertaining a man." Vulgarity colored First Voice's words as he shouted out to the group of unsavory-looking men standing wide-legged, sitting on barrels, or lounging against stuffed crates.

Bibi glowered under lowered lashes at the crowd, some dressed in the style of Charbonneau and Lytle, others wearing wide-brimmed hats and tight britches, while a few donned baggy pantaloons with bright-colored scarves tied around their heads. Whoever they were, and whatever their intentions, she would let them know she would never go easily to any man's bed, no matter how hard the sell from First Voice.

"Twenty-five livres to see this one naked." Another French voice.

Bibi looked out at the crowd, seeking the man who'd purchased Adaeze. "Mr. Lytle"—she spoke without moving her lips the way she and her sisters had done to torment Nago so many years ago—"where is the man who placed the bid on Adaeze?"

First Voice stomped across the makeshift stage, grabbed Bibi by the upper arm, and marched her to the front of the platform. "Our Englishman here tells me the dress this one wears, and her jewels, are worth two hundred livres by themselves. Then there is the woman, herself. Very talented." He turned to Bibi. "You understand me, wench. Speak French for the gentlemen."

Oh, Allah, help her. She felt her body turn toward the lout who acted as auctioneer in this affront to all things holy. The trembling started in her shoulders. Nago had often warned her that her impulsivity would be her downfall, just as her decision to forgo the full circumcision procedure had condemned her to marriage to Doudou. The trembling spread through her chest. Bibi's head told her to ignore the anger building in her body. *Just stand meekly at the front of the stage. Cast modest eyes to the floor and eke out a simple "yes" in French.* But before she could command her body to obey her head, the trembling's tentacles squeezed her belly. Not even Nago's most damning threat could save her now.

Bibi whirled to First Voice and scanned him from head to foot as though he were a rotting jackal. Her nose twitched, and she felt the corner of her mouth turn itself into a sneer. If she spent whatever was left of her life in a cane field, so be it. This insect would never shame a daughter of the house of Toure. She turned back to the crowd, lifted her chin, and uttered not a word.

"French, you say?" An English voice, and joined by laughter. "Perhaps Portuguese is her game."

"How much do you ask for this one?"

That voice. Bibi tilted her head toward the sound. She scanned the crowd, the tall ones, the short, the fair-haired, the bearded, and there, at last, stood the man. A fellow no taller than Papa but clothed in a wide-brimmed black hat decorated with something that glistened like silver in the hazy air of New Orleans held one finger aloft. This had to be the foreign-tongued Herrera.

"Señor, would you pay another five hundred livres for this one?" The odious First Voice pounded optimism.

"And the jewels on her." Señor Herrera, in his indecipherable tongue, sounded noncommittal.

Bibi's heart thumped as First Voice clamped down on her wrist. Adaeze had instructed her to put three bracelets on each arm—all gold, four of them studded with a few diamonds and emeralds. But none matched her husband's bracelet in elegance. Pain shot through her right shoulder as First Voice yanked her arm high in the air, the bracelets sliding halfway down her forearm.

"Worth two hundred livres." Lytle spoke up as he kept his tight grip on Folashade.

"They sparkle the little." Señor Herrera, his forehead creased in a scowl. "Jewels not much value. I bid you two hundred livres."

The auctioneer spoke. "Señor Herrera, let us not be absurd. Look at the wench. You can see she is worth more than two hundred livres."

"For sure." An English voice. "But right after a man has had his jollies, this one will make a hellacious amount of trouble. She looks like she could slit a man's throat."

More grunts and murmurs from the crowd. Bibi lifted her chin even higher. If no other bidder spoke up, then maybe Herrera's offer would send her on her way with Adaeze, who looked ashen with pain.

"Señor Herrera." First Mate Lytle strode across the platform dragging Folashade with him. He stationed the girl just behind Bibi as he moved next to Adaeze. "I will be taking your first purchase inside to ready her." Lytle slipped both arms around Adaeze and led her through the canvas opening. He kept the sight away from Herrera, but Bibi watched Adaeze's knees wobble.

"Take a good look at this wench." A grumpy First Voice grabbed at Bibi's under dress as he pulled her close.

She sniffed in the rot of unclean teeth as the man's fingers clutched at the top of her garment. With a sound that resembled the last scream of a dying gazelle, the under dress ripped from neck to waist. Heavy New Orleans air caught in Bibi's throat and clogged it shut. A different shaking wracked her body as heat from the man swamped her face and upper body. She felt her jaw and knees go slack as her eyes tried to stare sense into what was happening. The man's rough hands spread open the jagged edges of her under dress. She stood there, in front of a dozen or more men, half naked, as First Voice maneuvered behind her. Calloused fingers reached around her and fingered her left breast. "Ah" escaped on a wave of pain and shock.

First Voice held her tight against his body. A veil of darkness clouded Bibi's eyes. The fiend gathered her breast and pointed her bare nipple at the crowd of hooting, whistling men.

Allah's voice flickered in Bibi's head but disappeared before she could make out His words. Charbonneau's face flashed in her mind's eye for a fraction of a second. Captain Welles. A bloody body rolled out of the secret place in her mind. But none offered her a full thought, an order to let First Voice do with her what he willed. Instead, her right elbow jabbed hard into his middle. He released her with a low grunt as his arms flailed in the air. She turned to face the miscreant. Her forearm, driven by a force stronger than the best of the Malian warrior spearmen, smashed into the sleeve of First Voice. The blow slammed his own hand hard into the underside of his nose. The man's cries of pain collided with the sounds of surprise rising from that miserable crowd of men. Bibi backed away, closing her caftan over her torn under dress. She stared down the crowd and glared her defiance.

"Oh no," a French voice screamed.

"Never a wench like that." A new combination of angry sounds.

"She will slay us in our beds." English.

"Not for me." More strange sounds.

Señor Herrera was her last hope. Where was the man now? She searched between the moving bodies. No, not the black-haired man with the multicolored shirt. Nor was it the one with hair the color of a Sahara sunset. There. A man as tan as a Tuareg underneath that broad-brimmed hat, but with eyes as dark as a Yoruba, looked as stricken as the rest of the crowd. Señor Herrera. What had she done? Nago was right. She, Bibi, had just destroyed herself and Adaeze.

"Someone, any of you, take this bitch off my hands," First Voice rasped as he wiped blood from his face. He turned toward the canvas curtain. "Union Jack, get your ass out here and get this wench. I cannot sell a crazed bitch like this one."

"One hundred fifty livres."

The deep-throated French floated out of the angry sounds of the crowd.

"You are a man of courage, Frenchie."

An English voice. "I will be at your funeral within the fortnight."

More new sounds.

"Sold!" First Voice.

"What name are you called so I can write it in my record?"

"Claude-Phillipe Babineaux."

Brown-haired and blue-shirted, the man kept his seat on a crate where bits of fur protruded through the slats.

"This wench is yours, Claude-Phillipe Babineaux."

First Voice made the sign of the cross against his chest. "Now in the name of the Saints Most Holy, take this wench off my hands." He turned to Folashade.

The girl looked at Bibi without turning her head as First Voice jerked her to the front of the platform. Bibi stepped back before the man could lay hands on her again.

"I will pay the same. One hundred fifty livres."

Bibi turned toward the sound. Her eyes caught sight of a man who stood taller than most of the surrounding crowd. His straight black hair hung below his shoulders, kept off his face by a red bandanna tied like Fredericks's cohort back on the *Zephyr Wind*. But most remarkable was the color of the man's skin. It glistened a light brown, for sure, but a glow from underneath lit it a burnished red.

"She is yours, Chief." First Voice jig-danced across the platform. "She will make a good Cherokee squaw. In fact, I will sweeten the booty by giving you safe passage back to your land of the Overhill."

Chapter 31

"Just when I thought you three could not fall more afoul of your own good than you already have, you exceed my worst nightmares." Lytle squatted beside Adaeze, who lay on her back on the bare floor, covered by a thin blanket. Her face turned away from the squalling babe who lay squirming beside her. "I cannot decipher which of you wenches lacks the ability to use common sense the most." He stood up and glared at Bibi as though the fault belonged to her. "Your sister refuses to take the babe to the tit." He shook his head as he adjusted his pantaloons. "Thanks be to Jesus, I have done what was necessary. Tended many a swab, but I have never pulled a child out of a woman before."

Folashade brushed past Lytle as she rushed to Adaeze. Her sister's eyes lay closed. Folashade stared at the bawling, writhing thing thrusting its white arms and legs in all directions. Though she'd seen very few, she recognized a newborn, but something was dreadfully amiss with this child. A face far too fair, this babe showed a color that sung out all wrong. "Bibi." Folashade tried to keep her voice as soft as possible to avoid awakening her sister, if Adaeze actually slept. Folashade would have rejected surprise if her sister had fainted at the shock of seeing a child who looked nothing like a Bambara. "Bibi, what is this?"

"What is this? So that is what you ask, you fool of a girl," Lytle boomed as he walked over to Bibi. "A girl-child. Tell your sister that is the what of it. As for you and the downfall that has befallen all of us because of your uncalled-for actions, see to it you make your sister feed the thing. As it is, I must explain this 'early' birth to Señor Herrera."

"Your disappointment in me will be even greater if you expect me to do your bidding." Bibi stood clutching the edges of her caftan tight. "You have sold me to a man of France." She turned to Lytle, her eyes glaring that defiance that had so exasperated Papa and annoyed Nago. "Your words are lies. With better jewels to offer, we could all have been sold as one lot."

"I am well rid of you and your sisters. Though you call my words lies, I have arranged you ungrateful wenches the best possible futures."

Lytle glared. "You are off to a fur trapper. Learn to skin a fox and a beaver, and you will be in your owner's good graces."

"And what of Folashade? Tell me what you know of her buyer." Bibi squared herself in front of Lytle. "I wager it is nothing befitting a noble."

With the commotion going on around her, Folashade took her eyes off the newborn as she knelt beside Adaeze. She grabbed a corner of the coverlet and wiped perspiration from her sister's face. Perhaps Adaeze had willed herself dead along with Bibi. Her middle sister seemed determined to do everything in her power to anger the acting captain of the *Zephyr Wind*.

"I know precious little of your sister's buyer. But she should get along well with him. He is a savage, just as are the three of you."

Bibi held an open palm toward Mr. Lytle. "Your words are true. My sisters and I have faced nothing but savages these past nine months."

Lytle looked away. "Wake your sister."

The first mate walked to the pallet, stooped, scooped up the baby, pulled back the coverlet from a closed-eyed Adaeze, and laid the baby against her breast. "Princess, this is not the time for your crazed behavior. I have given you a great opportunity with Herrera. I am told he lives in Nueva Mexico. No sugarcane fields there. The labor should not be hard." He leaned closer, his tunic brushing the baby. "Listen to me close, Adaeze. I can assure you if you or this child dies before you are both safely in Mexico with Señor Herrera, your sisters will suffer far worse than what I have arranged for them." He moved to his feet.

Adaeze lay still. Folashade picked up her sister's right hand. It was warm. Adaeze lived.

"The choice is yours, Princess, but the ten minutes for which you asked begin now." He walked through the canvas flap, pushing it closed after him.

Bibi rushed to Adaeze, pushed Folashade aside, and knelt next to the new mother. "Adaeze, open your eyes. We have such a short time before the worst may happen. Tell us your plan." She looked down at the baby. "Here." She placed the open mouth of the baby over Adaeze's breast.

"No!" Adaeze jerked as she pushed the baby to the pallet. "This cannot be a child of mine. Look at this aberration."

A fireball formed in Folashade's belly. *Not now, please, Allah.* Their time together, possibly even on this earth, was simmering down to nothing. Adaeze could not allow her mind to slip away perhaps for all eternity this time.

"If this is the child you birthed, she must be Allah's will," Bibi soothed as she picked up the baby. She leaned closer to Adaeze, who scooted her back against the wall of the makeshift shelter.

Adaeze rubbed a hand over her eyes, turned her hands palm side up and back again. Her voice wavered between the here and now and the long ago. "I know the truth of it." She kept her face away from the infant. "My husband's second son has died."

Folashade watched Bibi's back twitch as she straightened herself, the baby still in her arms. "You have been through so much, my sister. And you are so brave. But now we must, the three of us, decide on our next plan."

The muscles in Folashade's left cheek twitched. If Adaeze could just return to herself, she would share the next steps with her sisters. Slavery or no. Life or death. "We have but fewer than ten minutes, Adaeze. We have all been sold into slavery." The tears gushed from her eyes unbidden. "We will not see one another again, I fear."

Bibi took Adaeze's hand while she juggled the newborn. "Adaeze, this is not a child you wish to suckle, that I understand, but you have been gifted this babe. Look at me, sister." Bibi waited while Adaeze stared at the opening in the tent flap. "This is Charbonneau's child, and no, his seed cannot make a royal baby." Bibi shot a supportive glance toward Folashade. "This is, indeed, a foreign child, but the people of Mali are kind people. In the name of Allah, will you please care for this unfortunate child until we can find a wet nurse?"

Folashade sucked in her lips so hard the muscles hurt.

Adaeze's arms lay still at her side while the baby girl trembled in her fury. "You wish me to suckle the child. A child you tell me is not the son of my husband but the daughter of a barbarian." Adaeze's head lolled to her right shoulder. She switched her stare to the top of the canvas flap. Her arms remained still. "The child of a man who demeaned me. A barbarian from Europe. A man of cruelty. A man called Charbonneau." Adaeze's arms embraced her knees before she turned her head with a slowness akin to bricks baking in the sun toward the baby whose shrieks filled the shelter.

"It is the truth. This babe is not from your husband, who had been away from your side for more than four months. This is the child of a man from France." Bibi raised her voice. "Look."

Adaeze blinked once, twice, before her hands inched toward the tiny girl. She laid eyes on her daughter. Adaeze's look was long, though Folashade could not detect the meaning. "A name," eked from a throat that sounded of dryness. Adaeze took in the look of her sisters for precious seconds.

Folashade fought to keep the questioning frown from her face. "A name?" Fear swept over her. Even the sound of her own breathing might tip Adaeze back into that land from which she might never return.

Adaeze blinked, and the film that threatened to envelop her eyes and senses disappeared. "A name that cannot be forgotten." The words came out as though each one carried the wisdom of one of Papa's most precious books. She laid one hand under the baby's bottom as she turned to Folashade. "I admit, I am not clear on the why of it, but I know we must all remember who we are. Daughters of Toure. Though this is Charbonneau's child, she must have a name to remember us by. All of us." She grasped the girl under the head and took her to her breast.

Bibi nodded her question. "You feel an urging to bestow a name on this girl? You wish to give this child a name right now. But, sister, dear, in moments, we will be separated and sent to who knows where for what may be the rest of our lives. Papa's seed will be scattered forever." The sound in Bibi's throat tightened.

Folashade lowered her head. She did not need to see her middle sister weep. Hearing the strangled breath threatening her ears would bring enough pain.

"Bibi, Folashade, I feel a new truth of our lives. One that is not fully clear." Adaeze focused first on Bibi, then Folashade, as the baby's cheeks puffed in and out in her first suckling. "I sense our desire to return home, to Timbuktu, is not to be. For all our threats to die rather than become slaves, I believe the opposite truth is before us."

Bibi leaned into Adaeze, her face and body turned slightly as though she wanted her best ear to catch Adaeze's words.

"For whatever reason, we three have been given a responsibility. No. Rather, an opportunity. A chance to do a necessary, important thing. An opportunity to bring honor. Not just to Papa but for the whole Mali Empire. And I sense more. We are now in a foreign land, one where my husband, in the light of truth, is incapable of reaching. He commands neither the ships, the courage, nor the intelligence to conduct such a campaign." She adjusted the baby.

Folashade dared kneel closer to Adaeze. "When we first reached Gorée, I knew your father-in-law would never find us. But I always held hope we, the three of us, would find a way to return home."

"Of course, you did, sister. We all did." The timbre of Adaeze's voice sounded infused with certainty blended with strength that had never before entered Folashade's ears. "At various times, each of us clung to hope to see home, Timbuktu, again." She raised her voice. "Folashade, Bibi, when I say to you that hope in that fashion was never meant to be, I do not want either of you to fall into the well of despair."

Bibi shook her head. "I will never give up hope."

"Though I cannot tell you the why of it, I want you to hear my words and keep them in your hearts. I know to the core of my being that we have undergone all our sufferings because of an opportunity offered by Allah."

"Allah would never permit this atrocity on faithful followers," Bibi blurted out.

"That is just it, Bibi. Allah has not permitted an atrocity upon us. Not from the kidnap on the beach in Djenné to the march to Gorée. Not even when we underwent the torment of Manuela." She set soothing eyes on Bibi. "Not even with Trilby Welles on the *Zephyr Wind*. All these things have befallen us because we are precisely where we belong at this very moment."

Folashade shifted her position with a sudden shake. "No. Allah would not allow such a thing." Her mind flashed back to Papa's library and her unauthorized reading of *The Body of the Virtuous Woman*. That this was her punishment for her indiscretion lingered in her mind.

"I do not know the hows or whys, but we are meant to be in this place and in this moment. I sense we stand at the pinnacle of a thing momentous that straddles the old world and this new one. I know not what, but this much is clear. No matter how difficult the days ahead may lay on our minds and bodies in the future, we are here for a purpose. I believe that reason has something to do not only with Papa but also with our homeland."

Folashade shook her head. "You may be clear about your feelings, but I do not understand your words. Are you saying I must go off with this chief person, and never try to escape?"

Adaeze reached out a hand to her young sister. "Legacy, Folashade. I speak to you about our opportunity to pass on the stories of all those who have gone before. The tale of their and our lives to those who will come after us. We must live, and we must forever push onward."

Bibi leaned forward, the signs of understanding flickering in her eyes. "And you sense we can preserve these legacies best here in the new world, rather than the old. Why?"

"Oh, Bibi, if only I had enough of my thoughts together to reassure you that the days ahead of us will not be dark. I wish I could tell you I could return to Djenné, and you to Timbuktu. But if that is to be our story, our legacy, then we have chosen wrong. Taking that path will forever bury our story and what we have endured in these nine months will not be told in all its ugly truth."

Bibi pressed her lips together, her eyes waiting for Adaeze.

"That is the why. Here is the how. Again, I say to you, legacy. We preserve and revere our past by never forgetting who we are and where we came from." She patted Folashade's hand while she turned to Bibi. "To do that, we must never forget one another." She looked down at the child whose suckling had slowed. "No matter how, this child has been fathered by a barbarian. For a reason. She has a purpose. I sense the purpose is to guide us all home."

"Home?" Folashade stared at Adaeze. "You have just said we cannot go home again." She watched Adaeze for signs of a wandering mind. There were none. "How can a new baby guide us home?"

"By the name we will bestow upon her. I feel it. Here." Adaeze rubbed at her swollen belly. "A name that will convey the history of Papa, the wealth of Mansa Musa, the memory of Buktu, and a well she found in the middle of the Sahara and the spot she turned into an oasis. All the glory of old Timbuktu. As long as these tales are remembered, our lives and the lives of all those on that ship of horror, the *Zephyr Wind*, will never be forgotten. We are not alone in this new world. Perhaps thousands, hundreds of thousands, of others will suffer our same fate of kidnap and torture. We can all make choices. Bibi, Folashade, we may choose to sap all our strength in protesting our fates. We can allow our minds to drift away to some faraway place disconnected from reality and from where it will shrivel and die, taking the essence of us with it. Our story lost forever to both the old and the new worlds. Or we can choose a different path. One where we live forever." Adaeze searched their faces. "Our lives may be separated forever by time and distance, but never by connection. It is my prayer we sisters will grab and hold this opportunity in our hearts forever."

"And this is all in a name?" Folashade managed.

"All in a name." A smile played across Adaeze's lips. "Folashade, our names carry the essence of us. Your name calls you out as more than a Mali girl of fifteen years. Your name connects you to your past and to your future. Can you see that?"

The idea rummaged in Folashade's mind and came out on slowed words. "My name means honor to the crown. A name chosen especially for me by Papa and our mother." Images ran through her head. "I am special in Timbuktu. In all of Mali."

Adaeze nodded. "You are beginning to understand, little sister, your part in carrying out our legacy. Not just of us, the three daughters of Toure, but for all of the other men, women, and children who have been snatched from all they have ever known and thrust into the New World. We will not see Timbuktu again." Adaeze stroked the baby's head as the infant fell asleep. "But she will. If she knows our truth, our story, she will, with Allah's help, find her way back home. If not her, then if need be, her daughter's daughter. Even her daughter's daughter's daughter. Perhaps even to a hundred years. No matter, one day, our history, our truth, will be revealed in our own voices, be it Bambara, Wolof, French, or English. We will be heard."

Bibi nodded. "I understand, Adaeze. It is the story of the lost warrior who left clues to those who came looking for him. Follow his trail, and one day, he will be returned to Mali."

Adaeze wrapped the coverlet around the child and cradled her in her arms. "Even better. We are of the nobility. We do not leave crumbs or tiny trinkets hoping we will be found. We make our own path." She stroked Folashade's wrist. "I have chosen a first name that will guide those who follow us into the future in the years and generations to come. And every time this babe hears her story, I, her mother, will tell her to pass on every precious detail to her own daughter. I want this babe to tell both the happy, the sad, and the funny. All the little details of her family back in Timbuktu. Tiny bits of information that will ring so true in the future. I want her to tell the story of my very brave, courageous, and headstrong sister. A sister who considered me too shallow, too pretentious. A sister who brought nothing but pride to her family and honor to all of Timbuktu. A sister I love very much."

Adaeze's smile dazzled as she patted the baby's back. "Meet the new Folashade."

She buried her head in Adaeze's chest as she pulled Bibi next to them. Underneath her, she could hear the whimper of little Folashade. The sobs wracked her body.

Adaeze dried away Folashade's tears with the coverlet. "What I want from each of you is a promise." She looked at Bibi.

"You needn't ask. In my heart, both you and Folashade must always hold the truth that I will pray to Allah for you both to continue our legacy. As for me"—Bibi laid a hand over her empty belly—"there will never be another child."

Folashade heard the tears straining her sister's voice.

Adaeze reached out a hand. "No, Bibi, you understand no such thing. A child of your body will come your way."

"No. And Balaboa will not remember me." Words stuck in her throat.

"Papa will keep our memories alive in our children. He understands the importance of legacy. The three of us will live forever in Timbuktu, just as the names and times of those we leave behind will always remember us."

Folashade's lessons on the ways to motherhood had been harsh, but she could not deny Adaeze's belief in the possibility. But what of herself? She tried to put the impossible into her head. "And if a child comes my way, I do promise to give her a name to carry on our history." She leaned in close to Adaeze. "But how do I do that?"

"Folashade, you possess the tools already. Papa has given us a great gift. We, each of us, possess an ability to absorb foreign tongues. You, Folashade, have already sorted out the sounds associated with the man who will take you to the land of the Overhill."

"The sounds?" Folashade pondered. "I know only 'chief.' I do not yet know what that sound means."

"But you will by night's end," Adaeze reassured just as the tent flap flew open, allowing in more moisture-soaked air. Lytle blasted out his strident voice. "You, Folashade, are going first. Your Cherokee chief is anxious to get you on your way. He has a writ of some sort to move through enemy territory."

The first mate's voice slammed his English into her head and brought in a new wave of fear. She kept her face buried in Adaeze's chest.

"Come on, girl." Lytle pulled her to her feet.

Folashade felt the scream forming, but the look on Adaeze's face trapped the sound in her throat.

"You are a daughter of Toure. You will bring him nothing but honor." Adaeze's eyes bored into her.

Lytle frowned as Adaeze spoke in Bambara, but said nothing. Folashade turned toward the seaman as he waited just inside the open flap. Behind him stood the tall man with the reddish skin and nose that jutted at an awkward angle from his face. He wore a medallion of some sort across his chest.

"Here is your purchase, Chief."

Lytle reached her in two strides, grabbed her wrists in a tight grip, and marched her in front of the tall man. "She will serve your wife well."

The man, who believed he now owned Folashade, held a thick, knotted rope in his hands.

She tried to step away, but Lytle held her fast. The man called Chief slipped the noose over her head and down her body. He pulled out her arms before he cinched the apparatus at her waist.

"She is your squaw now." Lytle nodded his head for emphasis.

As the man yanked her through the canvas curtain, Folashade turned to her sisters. "Squaw." She would learn that word and many more. She would use the tools gifted her. Adaeze was right. Folashade would not only survive, she would gain strength little by little through every obstacle put in her way. She pulled back against the rope as she caught one last glimpse of her family. She would remember them always. The last picture in her mind's eye would be the hope that would sustain her until she flew to Allah in Paradise. Her eyes settled on her niece—Folashade.

ABOUT THE AUTHOR

Francine Thomas Howard is the author of *The Daughter of Union County*, *Page from a Tennessee Journal*, and *Paris Noire*. A descendant of an enslaved African, Howard writes stories that explore the multicultural legacy of African-descended people throughout the diaspora and reflect her own African, European, and Native American heritage. Raised in San Francisco, Howard earned a BA in occupational therapy from San José State and an MPA from the University of San Francisco. She left a rewarding career in pediatric occupational therapy to pursue another love: writing. Desiring to preserve the remarkable oral histories of her family tree, she began writing down those stories with little thought of publication. That all changed when she turned a family secret about her grandparents into *Page from a Tennessee Journal*. Francine Thomas Howard resides with her family in the San Francisco Bay Area. For more information, visit www.francinethomashoward.wordpress.com.